No Country
for Love

No Country for Love

YAROSLAV TROFIMOV

abacus
books

ABACUS

First published in Great Britain in 2024 by Abacus

3 5 7 9 10 8 6 4

Copyright © Yaroslav Trofimov 2024

The moral right of the author has been asserted.

A CIP catalogue record for this book
is available from the British Library.

Hardback ISBN 978-0-349-14531-0
Trade Paperback ISBN 978-0-349-14532-7

Typeset in Garamond by M Rules
Printed and bound in Great Britain by Clays Ltd, Elcograf S.p.A.

Papers used by Abacus are from well-managed forests
and other responsible sources.

Abacus An imprint of Little, Brown Book Group Carmelite House 50 Victoria Embankment London EC4Y 0DZ	The authorised representative in the EEA is Hachette Ireland 8 Castlecourt Centre Dublin 15, D15 XTP3, Ireland (email: info@hbgi.ie)

An Hachette UK Company
www.hachette.co.uk

www.littlebrown.co.uk

To my mother Alevtina and all the mothers of Ukraine

Author's Note

This novel is a work of fiction, but it is based on true stories of my family in Ukraine. I have taken care to portray historical events as accurately as possible. All similarities to living persons are purely coincidental.

Prologue

Kyiv, March 1953

Stirring a slice of lemon into a cup of weak tea, Darya peered through the window at the snowfall. It was well past midnight, but she couldn't sleep. Her husband, a colonel in the Ministry of State Security, was late once again. Although not so late as for it to be unusual.

In the bedroom, Darya had tried to read, a tattered old novel with the superfluous letters of pre-revolutionary Russian spelling portraying a quaint world of leisure. But she kept raising her eyes from the page, tormented by the same poisonous thoughts that had kept her awake for months. Cradling the warm cup in her hands, she pressed her forehead against the window's icy, comforting pane, hoping that her headache would go away. The night was moonless, the lights in other apartments long ago turned down. Darya strained, trying to see through the gauze of snowflakes swirling in the wind.

That was when she noticed a portly, familiar shape trudging uphill, struggling to keep his balance on the slippery cobblestones of St Andrew's Descent. The colonel was navigating the obstacles with surprising success considering the degree of his inebriation. Then another familiar figure stepped out of the shadows. Darya felt light-headed. She had imagined this moment, in vivid detail, night after night, but never allowed herself to believe that it would happen.

The colonel seemed surprised, opening his arms in giddy recognition. Then, pressing his hands to his chest, he crumpled to the ground. Soaking his grey uniform, blood spread like an ink blot through a pile of fresh snow.

Darya couldn't hear the gunshot or see the muzzle flash because the pistol had been equipped with a silencer. But she made out the weapon in the killer's hand as he extended it to dispatch a final shot into the colonel's skull, calmly following proper procedure. He kneeled for a couple of seconds, frisking the colonel's pockets, then strolled away, down the street and into Podil, the downtown area that had been the city's riverside Jewish quarter before the Germans came in and murdered the Jews.

On the way, he couldn't resist raising his eyes to glance at Darya's window, on the third floor. He didn't see how she recoiled and stepped behind the heavy red velvet curtain.

The tea, boiled when Darya wasn't yet a widow, was still hot in her cup. She closed the curtains, trying not to look at her husband's sprawled corpse being coated by a layer of fresh snow. She tiptoed into the children's bedroom, kissing her daughter and son on their foreheads, envious of their untroubled sleep. Then she slid under her sheets, sheets still smelling of the colonel's sweat, a sweat revolting to her, and tried to force her mind into numbness.

It didn't last long. The bulky black phone, a treasured perk of the State Security job that also gave access to uncommon delicacies like fresh citrus fruit and smoked sturgeon, started to ring, an ear-splitting, urgent rattle. The colonel's aide was on the line.

'May I speak to your husband?' he said in a formal, bland voice. 'It is urgent business.'

'I'm afraid he isn't home yet. Wasn't he supposed to be with you at the party?'

'The party ended a while ago.'

'Oh. Did something happen?' The pitch of her voice edged up a bit, just the way a slightly worried spouse would be expected to speak so late at night. The phone probably wasn't monitored, but you could never know for sure.

'Have a good night. I'm sure there's nothing to worry about,' the aide said evenly. 'Nothing at all.'

PART ONE

PART ONE

1

Kharkiv, December 1930

Debora strode into the hairdresser's salon filled with impatient determination and pulled a precious American magazine from her tattered cloth bag. 'I want my hair cut the way she has it, short, just like that,' she said, opening the magazine at the picture of actress Louise Brooks. 'Can you do it?'

The hairdresser, a stout woman in her forties with heavy make-up, held up the foreign publication, sliding her thick finger over the unusually glossy paper. Taking her time, she leafed through the photos of unimaginable American plenty, advertisements of pink-cheeked housewives serving oversize steaks to their solemn, sober husbands.

'Can I keep it afterwards?' she asked, knowing that the answer would likely be no.

'Of course you can keep it.' Debora surprised her. 'But you'll cut my hair for free, now and next year.'

'Until the summer,' the hairdresser bargained. She pointed to the chair by the sink. 'Now, sit down.'

'Until the *end* of the summer,' Debora shot back, and sank into the chair, proud of her negotiating skills.

'Fine, fine. But why you would want your hair so short, like a boy, I don't know.' The woman sighed as she reluctantly levelled her scissors. 'Such a shame.'

A small ventilation window was open and the cacophony of industrial Kharkiv, the new capital of the Ukrainian Soviet Socialist Republic, wafted through it. Hammers beating at construction sites, trains, car horns, sirens, piped radio music, the yelling and shouting of the busy streets.

Debora had been living in Kharkiv for more than two months, and yet she still found pleasure in the perpetual energy of the big city. She felt a knot of excitement in her stomach every time the tram rolled past the cabbage fields and whitewashed village homes into the capital's humming heart. Kharkiv was nothing like Uman, Debora's sleepy hometown, set on gentle green hills that wrapped around an overgrown park full of ponds, waterfalls and statues of Greek gods and goddesses. This was the metropolis of the future, a place where everything changed before your eyes, where every day brought something unexpected.

In Kharkiv, new buses plied the broad avenues, competing for space with horse-drawn carriages and an occasional American- or German-made car. The pavements swelled with crowds of elegant old-timers who looked with disdain at the rural new-comers, so bewildered by the hustle around them, so hesitant to even cross the street. Pedlars hawked their goods on the corners, anything from miracle potions against venereal disease to partially mended shoes. Cinemas advertised the latest releases in big, glittering letters. New buildings were mushrooming everywhere, surrounded by construction cranes lifting blocks of concrete. Soaring above it all were the nearly finished futuristic skyscrapers of Derzhprom that would house the Ukrainian government, their bold straight lines defying the pastel-coloured embellishments of pre-revolutionary architecture.

And bookshops! Unlike Uman, the bookshops in Kharkiv's glass-topped Old Passage sold the latest novels, Russian and Ukrainian, and recent translations from Germany, France and America. Unconstrained by capitalist copyright laws that the Soviet Union did not recognise, publishing houses shipped a new batch of these translated bestsellers every few weeks.

Just an hour earlier, Debora had jumped out of the tram and walked past the towering Dormition Cathedral, which, shorn of its crosses and bells, now housed Ukraine's national broadcaster, a symbol of obsolete religion displaced by scientific progress. Entering the art nouveau walkway of the passage, she had headed through the arcade to her favourite bookshop. She was a regular, buying two or three novels every month, and the assistant, as usual, had put aside the latest arrival for her. It had a promising title, *Twenty-Four Hours in the Life of a Woman*, with a drawing of Monte Carlo's casino on the cover.

As she paid for the slim volume, she inhaled the smell of fresh newsprint that filled the shop, a smell she had grown to love. She wished she had time to linger and browse. Not today. Only twelve hours remained until the end of the year. It would take her at least an hour to return to her dorm at the construction site of the Kharkiv Tractor Plant, one of the great ventures of the First Five-Year Plan. And after getting her hair done, she needed to prepare for the evening's big party, a party to which she had managed to score a coveted invitation because of her recent promotion into the comforts of the Political Section. A promotion that carried perks for those ready to take initiative.

One of the American engineers helping to build the tractor plant – mysterious creatures whom Debora occasionally sighted but never had the occasion or permission to speak with – had left behind a slightly creased copy of *Vanity Fair*. One of the cleaning women, afraid of being tainted by this ideological impurity, had brought the magazine to the Political Section, where Debora had effortlessly managed to intercept it and examine every detail. The American actress's bob, framing her taunting smile, seemed so liberating. It was the look of the future. Debora wanted to be part of the future. Life, after all, was bound to get better and better. The future, as signboards all over the city predicted, was bright.

'It won't make me look like a boy,' she replied to the hairdresser. 'And if it does, so what?'

'Up to you, up to you, though I am sure your mother wouldn't approve,' the woman said. 'But I am not your mother.'

'No, you're not,' Debora replied, perhaps too rudely given their age difference.

As the hairdresser washed Debora's hair and brushed it for lice, Debora's mind wandered to her mother and father, to her last day in Uman, the day she'd hauled her cardboard suitcase onto a Kharkiv-bound train.

Uman. She used to feel trapped among all that stuffy leather furniture in their family home. Cupboards displaying crystal vases and trinkets that had survived the pogroms and the violence of the civil war a decade earlier. The heavy curtains that kept the living room permanently darkened. Everything in the Rosenbaums' home recalled the lost past, a life that was swept away by the Great October Revolution of 1917. A life for which, unlike her parents, Debora did not feel in the least nostalgic.

When she'd first mentioned that she planned to join the volunteers building the Kharkiv Tractor Plant, responding to a recruiter's presentation at her school, her father, Gersh, had frowned. Pulling together his bushy eyebrows, he breathed out a sad, resigned sigh. 'But why? What have we done that you want to leave us here? Now that your brother is gone, we thought that at least you would stay with us. Why are you in such a rush?'

'Didn't you tell me yourself, all these years, that I need to have broad horizons, to open my mind?' Debora's voice climbed. 'That we shouldn't be like *those* people?'

Those people, in Gersh Rosenbaum's world, were the other, different Jews, of whom he was ashamed. Despite all the recent advances and opportunities of Soviet life, many of Uman's Jews clung to the old ways. They insisted on speaking Yiddish, wearing anachronistic black coats and hats. The women still shaved their heads and wore wigs. 'How could they do this, now, in the twentieth century?' Gersh often muttered over dinner. 'They make all of us look bad, uncivilised.'

Though Gersh Rosenbaum himself was descended from a famous Uman rabbi whose grave was still venerated by some of the shtetl's townsfolk, he grew up in the big city of Kyiv and preferred to go by a Slavic variant of his name, Grigori. He and Debora's mother, Rebecca, one of the few Jewish graduates of the now-defunct Kyiv Institute for Noble Maidens, never spoke Yiddish at home, and certainly didn't teach the bastard tongue to their children.

'Forget all this nonsense. We are not narrow-minded provincial Jews, we are educated Russian intellectuals,' Gersh, who never read anything other than a newspaper or an illustrated weekly magazine, would often tell them. 'We're equal now. No more Pale of Settlement, no more anti-Semitism. The revolution has swept away all these distinctions for ever, one good thing it did.'

The 1917 revolution and the ensuing civil war also swept away much of the Rosenbaums' wealth. The dairy processing plant near Odessa that Gersh had developed under the tsar, with an investment from Rebecca's family, had once funded a French governess for their children and, before the world war made overland travel impossible, annual holidays in Capri or the Swiss Alps. The dairy plant had been nationalised by the Bolsheviks and the governess had fled back to France long ago. None of this was mentionable in Gersh's new life. On official forms requiring him to disclose his class origin, he put down 'industrial worker' in confident letters. With this, and a few other less innocent ruses, Gersh Rosenbaum, now of impeccable proletarian origin, managed to do rather well in the new Soviet order. Unlike Rebecca, he never complained about the life they had lost, the life that by now he sometimes doubted ever existed.

Not that he believed in the rosy communist future, or in the virtues of the Soviet system. What Gersh believed in was not complaining. A glass that is quarter full is still better than an empty glass, and an empty glass is still better than no glass, he would tell his children.

'Why do you need to go there? You think it's going to be easy, building that plant in Kharkiv? Do you even know what you are getting into?' He had tried to talk sense into Debora. 'There is so much more opportunity for you here, with your family. I know people, we can arrange things, I can open all kinds of doors for you in Uman.'

Debora didn't know for sure, but she suspected that her father would open these doors by using his position in the People's Commissariat of Trade to make sure that some grain, butter or sugar would be distributed in a slightly different way, to somewhat unintended recipients. This increasingly bothered her sense of justice, though not enough to confront her father.

'Papa, you just don't understand,' she replied, exasperated. 'I don't want you to *arrange* anything. I want to open my own doors! By myself! And this thing in Kharkiv – all the best of the best young people of the whole country are going there, to make this miracle happen, to show that we can become the world's leading industrial power, second to none. How can you ask me not to go, to give it all up and stay here, in Uman, when I can make history with my own hands! We're so lucky to be living at this moment, this moment that people will be writing about centuries later.'

Gersh was about to counter this point, inhaling loudly as he gathered the appropriate words, when Rebecca interrupted him.

'My sweetheart, you're such an idealist, and that's not a bad thing. All I will tell you is that you can come back here any time. The door of this home will always be open to you. If it's too hard in Kharkiv, there is no shame in returning to the family. Nobody will think less of you.'

'It won't be too hard.' Debora was impatient. 'I can handle it.'

At the Uman train station, Gersh managed to suppress his emotions, cheerfully waving as the train pulled away. Rebecca, however, broke down in tears and ran the entire length of the platform after the carriage. Debora cried too, for a few minutes, but forgot all about it a half-hour later, once she encountered a couple of university students returning to Kharkiv and listened, enthralled, to their tales of big-city life.

Olena Tkach, a representative of the Kharkiv Tractor Plant trade union, met Debora and a handful of other new recruits at the city's train station. Clutching their belongings, they all jumped into the back of a tarpaulin-covered truck and headed south-east on a bumpy dirt road. Broad-shouldered, Olena was taller than most of the new arrivals, moving with the self-confidence that came from physical strength. She examined with scorn Debora's shoes, which, she knew, wouldn't survive the encounter with the construction site's mud for long. Her front teeth were crooked just a bit, an imperfection she revealed whenever she spoke. With ruddy cheeks, blonde hair parted in the middle and a straight nose, she reminded Debora of the statue of Venus under the waterfall in Uman, one of her favourite childhood hideaways.

'Have you ever done this kind of work before?' Olena asked.

'No, but I'm sure I can manage,' Debora replied.

'Good. How old are you, anyway?'

'Seventeen. You?'

'Twenty-one.'

'She will manage, she will manage. And if she doesn't, she won't eat,' interjected another recruit, and everyone laughed. Except for Olena.

'Mind your own business, will you.' She scowled at them. 'You,' she looked at Debora again. 'There is space for you in my room if you want to join.'

'I would love to,' Debora responded, intimidated.

The room was shared with twelve other women, and Debora used the lower mattress of Olena's bunk bed. A makeshift cotton screen gave them some privacy from the others. 'Welcome home, I guess.' Olena grinned. 'You can put your things in this cup-board.' She watched as Debora began to unpack, first her clothes and then a stack of books she intended to read and maybe share with her new friends.

'Wow, that's a regular library you've brought out here.' Olena whistled incredulously. 'You're going to read them all?'

Debora just smiled shyly.

Once she had unpacked, Olena escorted her to pick up ration cards at the canteen. It was already time for dinner. Most of the women and men in the unheated dining hall were much older, their faces creased and sullen as they chewed with open mouths, wiping the grease from their lips with their sleeves. Food was served on scratched tin plates, with wooden forks and spoons. 'You're lucky, today is meat day. We only have it once a week,' Olena said as they lined up to get their plates filled.

The meat's stringy fibres stuck between Debora's teeth and she felt too embarrassed to try to pick them out. Unlike the university students on the train to Kharkiv, the volunteers at the tractor plant site didn't offer the intellectual conversation she had been expecting. Many, it turned out, didn't know how to read and write, let alone wish to discuss movies and books. They were in Kharkiv for a simple reason: the construction site's canteen provided enough reliable calories to survive the coming winter.

After dinner, the lights went off in Debora's room and it was impossible to read, something she had always done before falling asleep. The women collapsed into bed after a day of hard work, snoring and coughing loudly. With the communal bath fired up once a week and the windows sealed shut for the winter, a cocktail of stale sweat and flatulence permeated everything.

In the morning, after waiting for her turn at the latrine, Debora drank lukewarm tea accompanied by a piece of dry bread and joined her work detail. Though the Kharkiv Tractor Plant, the pride of Soviet industrial might, would manufacture the machines of the future, the sprawling construction site didn't quite match the enthusiastic descriptions proffered by the recruiter who'd visited Debora's school in Uman. In fact, it wasn't much more technologically advanced than the building of the Egyptian pyramids, Debora thought. Men, assembled in details of three and armed with giant hammers, crushed the rock, digging deeper and deeper into the hard earth of the frozen wasteland. Women removed the debris in rusty wheelbarrows and then shovelled it onto horse carts.

When Debora returned from her first shift, her hands were swollen and bleeding. Her back also hurt. Still fully dressed and splattered with dirt, she fell onto the bed and curled up in pain. Olena gave her a withering look.

'You're not really cut out for this, are you?' she concluded. 'Such delicate fingers. I can see that you've never held a shovel before.'

'Not really,' Debora admitted. 'But don't worry, I will manage.'

'How can it be? Didn't your parents ask you to help in the garden or around the house? To plant vegetables, maybe?'

'My mother made me play the piano and take drawing classes.'

'Piano?' Olena snickered. 'Piano? I didn't know that people like you really existed.'

'I don't play that well.' Debora blushed. 'I draw much better.'

'Draw? Show me,' Olena demanded, handing her a newspaper and a pencil.

Debora took off her coat and straightened up. Making quick, confident lines on the newspaper's margin, she sketched Olena's face.

'Not bad!' Olena assessed the drawing.

'I used to paint posters and banners for the high school,' Debora said proudly.

Olena pulled out a jar of honey-based ointment. 'Rub this into your hands, and you'll feel better tomorrow,' she said.

Debora didn't feel better. She coughed and sneezed all night, and ran a fever in the morning, shivering under the threadbare blanket. For almost a week, Olena made her tea and brought her food from the canteen. When Debora had recovered enough to be able to walk, they plodded across the road to the two-storey brick building that housed the construction site's Political Section and knocked on the door of the director, Comrade Lev Katz.

Short, skinny and slightly cross-eyed, Comrade Katz wore a pinstriped suit two sizes too large. 'Olenochka, my dear, so nice to see you again,' he said, hugging Olena. Debora had to try not to stare at the copious black hair that sprouted from his ears and nose.

'This is the girl I've talked to you about, the artist,' Olena said. 'She is really good. I can vouch for it.'

'I reckon we will have to test that proposition, my dear,' Katz grunted in response, motioning at Debora to sit down. 'We do need help in that department, we most certainly do. Everything changes so fast, and we need to keep up to date with the demands of the time. Every day, new slogans, new campaigns, new goals. Wonderful times we're living in. Let's start with the basics.'

He put in front of her a strip of red cloth, a can of white paint and a jar of brushes, and observed carefully as Debora, biting her lip in concentration, focused on making the straightest lines possible in the capital letters that, fifteen minutes later, grew into a full sentence: *Death to the Clique of Traitors and Bourgeois Counter-Revolutionaries!*

'Very quick and steady,' he muttered, examining the brush-work. 'Most impressive, my dear. You can leave the shovel to others for now. The revolution needs you here more.'

They walked into a nearby room with a desk in the middle, a bright naked light bulb hanging from the ceiling. Rolls of red cloth and vats of paint occupied half the space. A tattered couch was squeezed in the corner.

'Welcome to your new office,' Katz said. 'I don't care about the hours, day or night, as long as what needs to be done gets done on time.'

Debora couldn't look away from the couch. She imagined how she could curl up there to read once all the work was complete. She composed her first letter home that night, without mentioning her bout of sickness. *This has been so much better than I expected. I love it here, everyone is so interesting and I am learning so much*, she wrote. *Coming to Kharkiv was the best decision I've made.*

2

Kharkiv, December 1930

Clad in a revealing blue-and-white-striped dress completely unsuitable for the cold weather, Debora walked arm-in-arm with Olena into the New Year party at the Culture Hall of the Kharkiv Tractor Plant. Her bare back turned into a field of goosebumps and then, briefly, went completely numb. At least it was warm indoors. The space was already crowded, the air filled with loud music and drunken laughter.

All around them, hanging from the ceiling, was Debora's handiwork, neat block-letter slogans on wide strips of red cloth. *WE COMMIT TO COMRADE STALIN: WE WILL COMPLETE THE FIVE-YEAR PLAN IN FOUR YEARS*, pledged one. *DOWN WITH ANGLO-AMERICAN IMPERIALISTS, LONG LIVE THE PROLETARIAT REVOLUTION*, screamed another. The freshly painted banners floated above the decorated tree linking the portraits of Stalin, Lenin, Engels and Marx – an evolution of facial hair, from the German philosopher's endless beard to the trimmed Georgian moustache of the Beloved Leader of Progressive Mankind.

Hardly anyone could read the banners tonight, however.

The lights were off, except for a fine ray shining onto the dance floor.

'Oh wow, I can't believe it, they're playing the two-step!' An excited Olena tried to pull Debora into the scrum. 'Come on in, let's show them what we've got!'

Debora wasn't much of a dancer and had never even heard of the two-step before. On the unfortunate occasions when she had ventured onto a dance floor in the past, she'd flailed her limbs randomly for a few minutes before realising that she had made a fool of herself and retreating to a quiet dark corner. She yanked her hand from Olena's. 'You'd better start by yourself. I'll join you later.'

Picking up a glass of the fizzy sweet wine from Crimea that everyone called Soviet champagne, she sat down on a couch at the back of the hall. The clock just in front of her showed that more than an hour remained until midnight. When she had finished her wine and moved to get a refill, she spotted Katz dancing with Olena, his chin nestled between her breasts. He was whispering something, and Olena chortled, turning red. Inch by inch, his bony fingers moved lower, finally pausing as they firmly grasped her buttocks. Olena laughed again, and as she gyrated, she locked her eyes with Debora's. Blushing, Debora turned away.

She had lived a life of innocence in Uman, except for a few furtive kisses with classmates in the last year of school. She definitely wasn't used to drinking. With her intense green eyes that seemed to promise much more than she intended to offer, and a long, delicate neck, she had attracted her share of male attention in Kharkiv. Until now, she had been too timid to respond to anyone's advances. Tonight, she resolved as she finished her second glass of wine, would be different.

Debora was pondering whether to get herself another drink when a man dropped onto the couch next to her. Sweat dripped from his forehead and his breath stank of garlic and moonshine. He wiped his face with his sleeve and then, unsteadily, turned towards her, his eyes running up and down her body. She pretended not to notice as he leaned closer, clicking his tongue. 'Fancy,' he blurted. Then he opened his palm and, slowly and deliberately, grabbed her thigh, at the hem of her dress. She recoiled, but he pressed harder, so hard that it started to hurt. I will have a bruise, she thought.

'You're new here, aren't you,' he slurred. 'Come dance with me.'

She tried to move away, but he kept pressing, pinning her to the couch.

Her breathing accelerating, she attempted to push his hand off her thigh, but he just grinned, enjoying his strength and her powerlessness. The hall was dark, and amid the noise of the party, nobody else seemed to be paying attention.

'Please let go of me,' she implored. 'You're drunk. You should go home.'

'Drunk?' he protested. 'Me? Drunk? It will take a lot more than this for me to get drunk, sweetie.'

'Please!'

She didn't notice at first how his eyes narrowed in pain.

Another man, tall, in a military uniform, had seized her tormentor's forearm. The force of his grip was clear from the officer's white knuckles, and from the instant relief that her thigh felt on its release. The man in the uniform murmured something into the drunkard's ear. Within a few seconds, Debora's offender stood up, smiling apologetically, and wove his way across the hall, trying to keep his balance.

'Thank you.' Debora exhaled.

'Oh, anyone would do the same. Can't let boors get away with that kind of behaviour. What happened to good manners, eh?' After a brief pause, he introduced himself. 'Samuel.'

'Debora.' She extended her palm, expecting a handshake. Instead, Samuel kneeled for an old-fashioned kiss on the hand. This had never happened to her before.

'I must admit, with an officer's honesty, that I am star-struck by your ravishing beauty, my dear Debora,' he said.

She took in his pomaded black hair and thin, curled moustache. The man had clearly spent an hour or two in front of the mirror. His eyes were keen and cocky at the same time.

'A seducer, are you? Do you say this to all the girls?' she laughed.

'Not at all. Only you.' He clasped her hand. 'Would you honour me with a dance?'

Debora let Samuel lead her during the dance and tried her best not to stumble and embarrass herself. He knew what he was doing, however, and it all suddenly seemed so much easier. 'You are a beautiful dancer,' he whispered into her ear. 'Beautiful.' Her mouth remained frozen in a terrified smile as she focused on not stabbing his foot with her heel. His neck was doused in cologne, and the cloud of its spicy-sweet smell finally overshadowed the faint odour of industrial disinfectant and heating coal that saturated the hall.

Once they returned to the couch, Debora learned that Samuel Groysman was a military cadet, just like her brother, Yakov, except that he was learning to fly aeroplanes instead of sailing ships. She didn't need him to tell her that he was also a fellow Jew. Back in Berdychiv, close to Soviet Ukraine's western border, Yiddish had been his language at home, and Ukrainian alongside Polish was spoken on the streets. This left his Russian with an overlying patchwork of accents, a soft Yiddish 'r' betraying his Jewish origins.

When the dances were over and the party broke up, he accompanied her home. He insisted that she wear his grey coat and hold on to his elbow as they navigated the icy path to her dorm.

As they parted, he gave her a kiss – a chaste one, on the cheek, to her faint regret. His moustache tickled her as it brushed against her cold skin.

On the first Sunday of the new year, Samuel appeared at the dorm and invited Debora to a performance by the visiting Moscow Circus. She was embarrassed by the surprise visit, and angry with herself for having unusually messy hair that morning. She spent more than an hour in her new office at the Political Section, away from prying eyes, perfecting her make-up as she prepared for the date.

She had never been to a proper circus before – Uman was just too small for visiting troupes. Arm-in-arm they walked through the entrance hall of the Kharkiv Opera, which had been copied from the Tuileries Palace in Paris, past neoclassical columns topped with winged female sculptures that supported the balconies. Once they'd settled into their red velvet seats, the orchestra played 'The Internationale' and a seal undulated onto the stage, nudging forward a huge leather globe with the map of the Soviet Union highlighted in bright red and imprinted with the Cyrillic *CCCP*. A dozen dogs in sequinned outfits scampered out after it, each with their own, smaller ball that they kicked into the audience.

One of these mini globes came their way. Samuel jumped to intercept it and handed it to Debora. 'All yours,' he laughed. 'Throw it back out.'

She was afraid she wouldn't be strong enough, or would miss, but the ball landed in the middle of the stage. She blushed as the entire audience applauded her, and sat down again.

Once the seal and the dogs were ushered out, bigger animals filled the stage – an elephant, a dromedary, a bear, all wearing pink glittery skirts and swaying to a waltz. Magicians followed,

18

and Samuel kept explaining the secrets of their tricks in a loud whisper that annoyed their neighbours.

Then a huge cannon was rolled out, and a woman in a silver suit, her haircut identical to Debora's, began to sing atop the barrel. With the orchestra playing a dramatic drumroll and the lights dimmed, she was lowered into the cannon and, with a loud boom and an explosion of multicoloured smoke, fired into the ceiling studded with shimmering lights.

Debora shrieked, grabbing Samuel's hand, then exhaled with relief as she saw the performer catch hold of a crescent-shaped contraption that lowered her slowly, upside down, still singing as she hung by her knees. 'Bravo, bravo!' Samuel shouted. Debora disengaged her hand so that he could stand up and clap with abandon. 'What a talent!' he exclaimed, excited.

Minutes later, a shaggy lion ran onto the stage, halting to roar at a moustachioed tamer. The man, dressed in a striped sleeveless shirt, roared back, cracking his whip and flexing his oiled biceps. Seemingly cowed, the lion sat down and opened its mouth. The violins in the orchestra hit a crescendo. As the tamer slowly inserted his head into the animal's jaws, Debora grasped Samuel's hand once again. He squeezed her palm, just a little, in acknowledgement. She watched the rest of the show with her hand firmly nestled in his. It seemed to be the most natural thing.

They finally kissed a week later. Samuel tasted of bitter tobacco and held her tight to his chest, in a way she had never been held before.

On their next date, she let him slide his broad hand into her blouse, and then under her skirt. She tightened her muscles in anticipation and terror, and was embarrassed by the wetness spreading between her legs. Samuel grunted appreciatively. He knew what he was doing, moving gently and slowly at first, then

19

picking up pace. She closed her eyes, breathing heavily, her pulse quickening. 'You are crazy, crazy,' she whispered into his ear, hoping he wouldn't stop. 'Crazy.'

'Definitely,' he grinned, satisfied as he pressed her hand onto his crotch.

Back at the dorm, she told Olena what had happened.

'What, you haven't done any of that before? Not even with the hand?' Olena enquired with disbelief.

Debora shook her head, ashamed.

'You don't know what you're missing,' Olena laughed. 'I need to teach you some tricks. Anyway, that Samuel of yours seems like a solid man,' she went on. 'And it is rule number one in this world: a woman always needs a man. Without a man, we are nothing.'

'No,' Debora protested. 'That used to be true in the old days. But now, women have equality, we have rights, we are important just by ourselves.'

'Is that what they write in the textbooks now?' Olena mocked her. 'Without a man, nothing. Trust me.'

Debora itched to ask her about Comrade Katz, but didn't dare.

Neither Samuel nor Debora had private quarters, and so their romance – for lack of accommodation – developed mostly in the dark recesses of public spaces. Since a movie theatre was the cheapest and most accessible venue, they had a weekly Sunday date at the Karl Marx Cinema, a cavernous hall in need of fresh paint that most locals still called after its pre-revolutionary owners, the Bommer Brothers. There, they would usually get sunflower seeds, cracking and spitting the shells under their feet as the curtain rose, the lights went out and the half-hour pre-movie newsreel began.

The newsreels were all alike. The old, inefficient farming of

20

yesterday was about to end, as the new tractors would revolutionise the Soviet countryside, a narrator intoned over military music. Peasants all over the country were already realising the benefits of this revolution, and were spontaneously coming together to create collective farms, where dozens of small, inefficient individual plots would unite to allow modern, mass-scale agriculture. The Soviet Union – and especially Soviet Ukraine – would soon feed the entire world. Only a few rare enemies among the rich farmers who didn't want their neighbours to escape poverty opposed this unstoppable progress. The newsreel showed a fat, bearded farmer being led away from his estate by trim young women and men. Weapons had been found in his haystack. 'These class enemies won't be able to stand in our way, the way of progress, and will all be destroyed soon,' the newsreel went on. The audience, as if on cue, clapped thunderously.

Most movies, to be sure, weren't all that different from the propaganda newsreels that preceded them. But Debora and Samuel didn't care. They usually sat in the back row, their laps strategically covered by Samuel's coat and their hands busy exploring each other underneath.

One day in February, Samuel managed to sneak her onto his military airfield to watch training flights. Debora looked on with childish admiration as, wearing his flight goggles and bomber jacket, he strode purposefully towards the small Tupolev I-4 biplane. It took off with a whining noise, like a mosquito, and then circled overhead, becoming smaller and smaller. This was the first time she had seen an aircraft up close, and she was anxious until the tiny dot in the sky returned to land on the icy airstrip.

'I'm so proud of you,' she repeated after he came out to salute her, and covered his face with kisses.

'Hey, I'm just flying a little plane,' he said with false modesty.

In the late afternoon, once he was allowed to leave the airfield, he pulled out two keys on a string from his pocket and waved them in front of her.

'I've got a surprise.'

'What is it?'

'Follow me and you'll see. No questions allowed.'

He led her two blocks around the corner from the base and up the stairs of a drab, unheated building. On the second-floor landing, he opened a door and headed down the corridor to another door at the end. The key turned with a creak. Inside, the single bed was covered by a grey woollen blanket, with just enough room for a stool and a small desk. Embers glowed in the fireplace. It was warm, and smelled of onion, pickles and coarse tobacco.

Closing the door behind them, he wrapped his arms around her, his hands firmly resting on her breasts.

'Whose room is this?' Debora asked. She knew that Samuel, like her, slept on a bunk bed in a room shared with many.

'Let's say my friend has lent it to us. So right now, it's ours.'

He threw a couple of logs into the fireplace, and a few minutes later, the fire lit up the space, flickering shadows on the walls.

For the first time, they were alone.

Debora stood in the middle of the room and closed her eyes, letting Samuel slowly undress her. 'How many girls have you done this to before?' she asked. He just hummed in reply and gently led her to the bed, continuing to take off her clothes. She tensed with anticipation.

She had heard it would hurt once he entered her, but it wasn't as painful – or pleasant – as she had imagined. With her eyes shut tight, she bit her lip and thought: this is it?

Samuel had prepared a piece of cloth to clean up. The room had become so warm that they no longer needed the blanket.

They fell asleep on top of the sheets in each other's embrace, the hair on Samuel's chest brushing against her pale back. It was such a luxury, this gift of privacy.

They had to leave the room after an hour, before the owner was back.

'I love you,' Samuel whispered into her ear as they walked onto the cold, dark street outside. He thought it was polite to say such things after having sex for the first time with a woman. Debora responded with a dreamy smile.

In the evening, she finally wrote home about Samuel. *Mama, Papa, I think I've found someone with whom I am truly in love. I think you will like him*, read her round schoolgirl's cursive. *He is very handsome and he flies aeroplanes.*

It was the first time that Sasha Grinenko, Samuel's friend, had let someone use his bed. At night, he couldn't sleep, distracted by the faint traces of Debora's perfume. He kept imagining where a woman's buttocks and breasts had touched his sheets, and was surprised to find himself aroused.

'So tell me, who is she?' he pressed Samuel as he received his payment for using the room, a half-bottle of vodka.

'Someone special,' was the only reply.

This was unusual. Samuel was renowned for boasting about his conquests, imaginary or real. He usually went for older women with their own quarters (and, preferably, kitchens). His clinical descriptions of the most pertinent parts of the female anatomy had earned him admiration from fellow cadets, many of whom were still virgins, even though few would admit it. But this time, he didn't want to spill the beans, not even to Sasha. Debora was not like the others. To him, a kosher butcher's son and a ward of the Workers' and Peasants' Red Army since his teenage years, she radiated the possibility of a different world

23

to which he didn't belong, at least not yet. Naturally, without a conscious attempt to impress, she could quote poetry, and in conversation brought up characters from long Russian novels of which he only knew the titles, or from foreign ones of whose existence he had been unaware.

'Oh, come on,' Sasha pressed him. Sasha, two years older than Samuel, was no longer in the dating game. He had a fiancée, the round-faced Larysa, and was engaged to be married shortly. 'You can't just keep drinking and stay silent. Is she a local girl? From Kharkiv? How did you two meet?'

'Actually, no, from Uman,' Samuel replied. 'Same town as you.'

'Incredible! Uman! What is her name?'

'I can't tell you,' Samuel replied. And for now, despite all Sasha's attempts to winkle it out of him, he didn't.

Unlike Debora and Samuel, Olena and Comrade Katz were never seen in public together. But once a week or so, Olena would disappear into Katz's apartment, coming back to the dorm only in the early morning, before breakfast.

'What do you find in him? Isn't he too old for you?' Debora finally confronted her.

'He's not that old at all, he just looks it.' Olena didn't like this line of questioning. 'And he is very sweet, not like the young boys. He is a real man, a serious man. I think we may get married one day.'

'Really? When?'

'I don't know. But he has mentioned it, so maybe soon,' Olena replied with a giddy smile. 'What are you going to do without me here, silly little girl?' She pinched Debora's cheek, the way one did to a small child.

Debora received a letter from her mother that day. Enclosed in the envelope was a black-and-white photograph of her parents, an image retouched by the renowned Uman photographer Altman to make them look a decade younger and several kilograms slimmer. She placed it by the bed.

'They look very handsome,' Olena said enviously, studying the snake-shaped necklace and the bow tie in the picture. 'I only have my mama left. My papa passed away.'

'I am so sorry to hear that,' Debora replied.

'Oh, never mind,' Olena said. 'It was a long time ago. But I still miss him. I would love to have a father.'

Debora unfolded the letter and started to read. *My dear daughter, I am so happy for you, and so happy that you are in love,* Rebecca wrote. *But do only what you want to do, and do not fall under any bad influence. Make sure you are always the one calling the shots.*

Oh Mama, Debora winced. She was so exasperated by the lecture that she almost didn't read the rest of the letter.

We would love to come and visit you, but unfortunately that won't be possible for a while: your father is not feeling well. He fell down and broke his leg. It will take at least a couple of months to heal. For now, the doctor says there is no question of taking trains.

3

Kharkiv, April 1931

Once the year's first strawberries matured, Olena's mother, Zinaida, arrived in Kharkiv bearing gifts from the countryside. Carefully packed in a reed basket and covered by a white linen cloth were cheese and poppy seed rolls, pickled cabbage, a slab of *salo*, or salted lard, a jar of thick sour cream, and – Olena's favourite – *varenyky* dumplings filled with sour cherries. The train ride from the village had lasted seven hours, but Zinaida didn't seem to be tired. 'Come, daughter, eat with us,' she said to Debora as soon as she had settled in the dorm's waiting room and laid out an improvised table.

Unlike Debora, who made sure to speak proper Russian with all the right accents, Olena and Zinaida mixed up their Russian and Ukrainian words. Several years ago, the authorities had begun to promote the use of literary Ukrainian, now the official language for most government business. But few in the mostly illiterate villages that dotted the steppes of the eastern Ukrainian countryside had mastered that standard. Instead, they spoke the Surzhyk dialect, in which the grammar and vocabulary of the two languages bled into one another, a dialect that everyone understood even though it jarred the sensibilities of educated Ukrainians and Russians alike. A similar Surzhyk was spoken across the border in nearby parts of Russia.

Zinaida pulled out a piece of rye bread, cut off a slice of *salo* and topped it with half a pickled garlic. 'Eat, daughter, eat,' she urged, proffering it to Debora.

Debora's parents, despite all their emancipation, had drawn the line at eating pork. *Salo* never entered the Rosenbaums' home. But Debora did not hesitate, taking the sandwich and biting into the silky fat. She was done with antiquated superstitions. She discovered she liked the forbidden taste.

As Zinaida was illiterate, Olena's letters to her had to be read by a neighbour, who usually also wrote down her brief replies. He couldn't be trusted with everything, however. Nobody could. In rapid volleys, Zinaida began telling her daughter about the village news that she hadn't dared put in the letters.

'Looks like the crops will be really good this year. Thank Lord Jesus, the snows were abundant, and the spring is not too cold,' she began. 'But I don't know how much of it we will be allowed to keep. They keep increasing the quota. Soon the quota will be more than the entire crop, the way this is going.' She sighed. 'What will we eat then?'

'I am sure there will be enough,' Debora said cheerfully. 'We are growing more and more every year. Especially with the tractors that we will soon be making here in Kharkiv. I expect your collective farm will get some.'

Zinaida looked at her the way one looked at a toddler, and took her soft hand, stroking her uncalloused fingers, her manicured fingernails. 'Daughter, have you ever worked at a farm?' she asked gently.

'Not really.'

'Let me tell you what's happening in our village. All the

farmers who know how to grow crops, and who have the good houses and the healthy cattle, they are now called enemies of the revolution. *Kurkuls.* And all those who were always too lazy to do anything, they now run the collective farm committee. How is a tractor going to change anything about that? You people in the cities, you have the good life. Always have. You never go hungry. But we in the villages, we struggle. That's our fate, I suppose. Under the Polish lords, we were slaves, under the Russian tsars, we were slaves, and now we've become slaves again, under the collective farm. Poor Ukraine. Nobody under the sun loves our country. Nobody.'

This was heretical speech, and both Olena and Debora instantly knew it. Olena winced nervously. Sensing the tension, Debora reached out to touch her arm. 'Your daughter is my best friend here,' she told Zinaida. 'My best.'

'So she tells me. Have some more strawberries.' Zinaida's wrinkled hands pushed more treats Debora's way. 'God protect you, sweetheart.'

4

Kharkiv, May 1931

The party had been going on for an hour when Samuel and Debora finally found the right apartment and pushed open the unlocked door. The building still smelled of fresh paint, and the newly planted pine saplings outside were no higher than reed stalks. They heard jazz from a gramophone and the din of tipsy voices punctuated by giggling.

They'd been exhausted by their separate mandatory participation in the May Day parade, managing to meet up only in the late afternoon. Debora barely had time to change into a new summer dress she had left behind the counter of her hairdresser's, and to swap walking shoes for high heels. Samuel remained in his airman's leather jacket and polished boots.

They had never been to Slovo before, though they'd heard of the building. Slovo – meaning 'word' – had been specially built for the Ukrainian capital's new literary and theatre elite, and housed the city's most fashionable minds. Modern and minimalist, it was shaped like the letter C – the Cyrillic initial of Slovo – with a playground in the middle and a solarium on the roof. It didn't even seem to belong to the same universe as Debora's tractor plant dorm.

Neither Debora nor Samuel knew any writers or actors, and she was anxious, afraid of making a fool of herself, as she stepped into the apartment. Holding a glass of wine in the doorway was Samuel's friend Sasha. He slapped them both on the back.

'So glad you could make it,' he said. 'And you must be Debora,' he continued, staring into her eyes. 'Samuel – we call him Syoma – has been talking so much about you. So much.'

'Not too much, I hope,' she chortled.

'Only telling everyone how unbelievably amazing you are,' Sasha said.

None of them acknowledged the fact that Debora and Samuel spent an hour or two every Sunday afternoon between Sasha's sheets, a favour that was unusually generous. Sasha no longer even demanded payment in vodka. After those sessions, they would usually go to the cinema – where, in the cosy afterglow of sex, they actually watched the movies.

Sasha had been asking to meet Debora for months. Samuel had finally revealed her name back in March, but it didn't sound familiar to him. Uman, of course, was a small town. But it wasn't small enough for everyone to know each other. And with Jews making up at least half of the population, Rosenbaum was one of the most common surnames.

Debora felt awkward about meeting the owner of the bed where she had lost her virginity, and weeks earlier had flat-out refused Samuel's proposal to join Sasha for lunch. But an invitation to the May Day party at Slovo was another matter. It was on neutral ground, and – with all those fascinating people in attendance – it was something hard to pass up. She wondered if she would encounter someone whose books she had read.

With his hazel eyes, muscular frame and square jaw, Sasha looked faintly familiar, but she couldn't place him. For his part, his stare burrowed into her as he tried to remember where he might have seen her before. She was much prettier than he'd thought. He couldn't help imagining her lithe body in his bed, her cheeks flushed, breathing uneven. He shook his head to chase away the image, but couldn't look away from the tiny droplets of sweat above her nose, or the wet tip of her tongue as she ran it over her lower lip.

'Syoma says you're also from Uman. Which part?' he asked her.

'On the hill, near the river.'

It took them only two minutes to discover a dozen shared acquaintances. Another minute later, Debora clapped loudly.

'So your father is a maths teacher, isn't he?'

'Affirmative,' Sasha replied. 'Not an easy man to deal with, let me tell you.'

'I know.' She laughed. 'Gave me such a hard time!'

A blue-eyed woman in a silk dress that was clearly too tight sidled up to Sasha, holding two wine glasses in her hands, a worried frown creasing her forehead.

'Syoma, Debora – let me introduce you to my fiancée, Larysa.' Sasha turned, switching from Russian to proper Ukrainian.

Larysa's stare was icy as she ran her eyes up and down Debora's body, pausing to glare at her clothing with visible contempt. Her lips curled into a forced smile. 'Welcome, welcome, enjoy the party,' she said. 'Sasha's friends are my friends.'

Another man, with a full head of frizzy hair and wearing different-coloured shoes, pulled Larysa by the elbow. 'Come, come, you have to meet Mykola,' he shouted. Pushing the two glasses into Samuel and Debora's hands, she shrugged a wordless excuse and vanished into the living room.

'Come on in, let's move inside too.' Sasha shepherded them into the depths of the apartment. Debora had never been to such a spacious home.

'Thank you so much for the invitation,' she said as she walked behind him. 'How do you know all these people?'

'Oh, it's thanks to Larysa. She's got so many friends in these circles, so many,' he added. 'She's a student at Kharkiv University. Literature. And many of the people here are her professors.'

'I'd like to study too,' Debora said dreamily. 'Maybe once the tractor plant is finished.'

'As a volunteer at the plant, you will have no problem getting accepted,' Sasha replied. 'They really need people with that kind of background. Especially if you come recommended by the Political Section.'

Earlier that day, Samuel had briefed Debora about why Kharkiv's intellectual set wanted to be so friendly to Sasha's fiancée. Her father, Bohdan Skrypka, a large man with a thick drooping moustache modelled on Austrian Emperor Franz Joseph's, headed the culture department of the Ukrainian Communist Party. The famous writers, some of them teaching at Kharkiv University, needed his good graces to publish their books, receive their allowances – and get their Slovo apartments. That helped them appreciate just how special their new student, Larysa, was.

The party's host, Mykola, a short man with scorching eyes and thick curly hair, held a cigarette in one hand and a glass of wine in the other, gesticulating wildly with both. He spoke loudly in melodic Ukrainian, well-rehearsed phrases rolling off his tongue.

'We must get away as far as possible from Moscow, Moscow that has enslaved us for centuries, Moscow that used to crush our culture, that used to outlaw our language. The Little Russian dialect, they would say. Enough. We're Ukraine, not Little Russia. Kyiv was a great European capital, with cathedrals and libraries, for centuries and centuries when Moscow was nothing but a swamp. It is to Europe that we must look for inspiration, for lessons, for modernity,' he intoned. 'Anything else would be counter-revolutionary. What is our ultimate goal? It is the world proletarian revolution, right? Everyone joining the Union of Soviet Socialist Republics. A German Soviet Socialist Republic, a French Soviet Socialist Republic, a Danish Soviet Socialist Republic, just like the Ukrainian SSR. It's only temporary that the centre of gravity lies in Moscow, a fluke of circumstances. One day it will be in Berlin, or New York. But we must get ready for the day it will change. That's why we have to speed up Ukrainisation, to stamp out the tsarist, reactionary legacy.'

Several admirers – Larysa among them – had gathered around him, hanging on his every word. 'That is so well said,' she sighed. 'Away from Moscow!' He squeezed her elbow appreciatively. Everyone here knew that Larysa's father was the man in charge of implementing Ukrainisation, a government plan to replace the use of Russian. Stalin pursued a similar policy in every one of the USSR's non-Russian republics.

Debora was fluent in Ukrainian – after all, many people in Uman and everyone in the surrounding villages spoke Ukrainian or Surzhyk at home. And of course, in line with Ukrainisation, she'd learned the proper literary language at school. But her parents had taught her that Ukrainian was the tongue of uneducated peasants, just as Yiddish was the vernacular of backward shtetl Jews. Only the great Russian language, with its enlightened legacy of Pushkin, Dostoevsky and Tolstoy, was a gateway to the future, according to Debora's father, who had memorised a few poems by Pushkin in high school but had read neither Dostoevsky nor Tolstoy.

'I understand what you're saying, but what do you do with the fact that here in Kharkiv, most people still speak Russian? What do you do with them?' she asked the host. 'It's reality, isn't it? People can't just switch to a different mother tongue, start thinking and dreaming in another language, can they?'

Mykola was prepared. 'That's a great question. Guess what, when I was a child, I was also speaking Russian at home. Just a decade ago, most people in Prague or in Riga spoke German. But once those cities were overrun by the energies of the indigenous countryside, the language changed – to Czech or to Latvian. The same will happen here in Ukraine if we are determined about reclaiming our land. If we properly turn our backs on Moscow.'

'Mykola, Mykola!' A lanky woman in a shiny black dress and bright-red lipstick interrupted the writer as she puffed a thin clove cigarette. 'You should stop saying these things in such a harsh way. You never know how they can be perverted. Times are changing.'

'But it is all true,' he insisted. 'That is what we have been fighting for. I myself joined the Cheka in 1919, killing enemies of the revolution with these very hands. Nobody can doubt that I'm faithful to the cause.'

'I read your novel, in school!' Debora exclaimed. 'The one about you killing your mother!'

She realised that she was inappropriately enthusiastic, given the subject. Mykola raised his hand, about to explain. 'No, no, this is much more complicated,' he began, but the woman in the black dress wrapped her hand around his waist and pulled him away.

'Come dance with me, darling,' she purred. 'It will make everyone happier.'

A pianist in a concert tuxedo started playing a foxtrot. Clouds of cigarette smoke floated across the room. Debora looked around but couldn't see Samuel. He had found a couple of fellow military men and was drinking with them on the balcony.

Another guest topped up her glass with more wine. 'Happy May Day,' he said. 'I don't think I've seen you here before.' He was about thirty, in a well-cut suit with a white shirt and black tie, his hair carefully combed to the side.

'I am a friend of Larysa's,' Debora replied. 'My first time here – I just recently moved to Kharkiv, from Uman.'

'Valerian,' he introduced himself. 'I write books. Do you like to read?'

'Yes, of course. I read a novel or two every month, sometimes more. Though to be honest, I have read very few of the new Ukrainian ones.'

'The bane of Ukrainian writers.' His lips parted as if in pain. 'Everybody thinks we only write about shepherds and milk-maids by the cherry tree in the village. It's so ingrained that all that is new about civilisation and culture comes through Russia and Russian.'

'So what *are* you writing about?' Debora asked.

'A novel about the city. It's actually called that, *The City*. Our cities, like Kharkiv, like Kyiv, used to be Russian ships floating on a Ukrainian sea, but that is changing now. The water is seeping in, so to speak. Not a lot of people have read it, though,' Valerian smiled. 'So now I am translating books by others. Diderot, Anatole France, Balzac. Did you know that Balzac got married here in Ukraine? Not very far from Uman, actually.'

'Ah, I read a lot of translations. But more modern ones. Stefan Zweig. Romain Rolland.'

'I see, going for the more fashionable ones. So do you think you want to be a writer too?'

'Oh goodness, no.' Debora dismissed the idea with an eye roll.

'Why not? Everyone else does.'

'You're joking, right? What can I write about? Nothing has happened to me.'

'Well,' Valerian said, squinting as he marvelled at her inno-cence, 'you are very lucky then. Very lucky.'

She was unsure how to respond.

Breaking the awkward pause, Sasha stepped in between her

and the novelist. He was already drunk, and direct. 'Come, compatriot, let's dance.' He yanked her by the hand. Debora flashed an embarrassed smile, but Valerian wasn't about to be offended. 'By all means, go enjoy.' He bowed. 'It has been such a pleasure to meet you.'

Sasha led Debora into the centre of the dance floor. He inhaled her perfume, the same smell that permeated his room and his sheets, and felt entitled to hold her closer and closer. It was starting to hurt.

Nearby, Larysa was dancing with a long-haired poet who kept murmuring into her ear. She didn't notice Sasha and Debora until he almost brushed against her. Once she did, her eyes narrowed, her eyebrows arched. Sasha didn't seem to pay attention.

Debora pushed herself away from his chest. She spotted Samuel in the corner of the room, talking to a long-legged woman, likely a theatre student. He looked up momentarily, and Debora signalled at him with her eyes to come over, right away. He reluctantly abandoned the conversation.

'May I?' He inserted himself into the dance. Debora gratefully switched from Sasha's to Samuel's embrace.

Sweaty and tired, Sasha didn't mind. He ambled to the kitchen to pour everyone a round of shots.

'They sure drink a lot, these intellectuals,' Samuel smirked.

Debora felt a nail-studded headache spread from her temples to the rest of her head, and pulled his sleeve. 'I want to go home,' she said. 'Now. Please.'

They left before Sasha reappeared with the vodka.

5

Kharkiv, July 1931

Larysa's father had spared no expense for his daughter's wedding. Crystal chandeliers sparkled in the hall, reflected in the long line of Crimean and Georgian wine bottles. Spread with a crisp linen cloth, the long serving table was laden with smoked salmon and sturgeon, fine hunters' sausages and pickled forest mushrooms, all arranged around a giant roasted pig, red strawberries placed in its eye sockets.

Sasha and Larysa sat at the centre of the room, clasping hands, their faces frozen into masks of tired smiles.

Debora was assigned a table with Samuel halfway to the back. Sasha had sent them an invitation at the last minute, and they were grateful to accept. From a distance, Debora nodded to Sasha's father, her former maths teacher. He recognised her and walked to their table. 'So glad to see my students making it in the capital,' he said. 'I hope your parents will dance at your own wedding soon!'

She suppressed an embarrassed giggle. Samuel pretended not to hear.

'This is a real feast,' he muttered as he inspected the displayed delicacies. 'I didn't think this kind of extravagance was possible nowadays.'

Debora and Samuel's table stood behind the one occupied by Bohdan Skrypka's guests of honour – a new member of the Ukrainian Communist Party Politburo dispatched to Kharkiv from Moscow, and several lesser government functionaries. Debora was struck by how well fed most of these men were, their girth straining the jackets of their suits. The Politburo member was skinny, however, with close-cropped hair and a thin, wide mouth that, whenever he spoke, reminded Debora of a scowling dog.

The wedding guests also included the city's leading intellectuals, who could not refuse Comrade Skrypka's invitation no matter how much they disdained him privately. Debora could see some of the writers she'd met at the May Day party, a singer or two, and a handful of old-fashioned Galician academics from Lviv, wearing ancient tuxedos that seemed to come out of a caricature in a satire magazine.

Bohdan opened the wedding's festivities with a mandatory toast to Comrade Stalin and the party that was leading progressive mankind into the bright future. Then, without pausing, he burst into a patriotic Ukrainian song. 'The wide Dnipro roars and moans,' he thundered in his deep baritone. 'An angry wind aloft is howling.' The guests instantly picked up the familiar stanzas, the song booming throughout the cavernous hall.

Debora, who sang along, noticed the newly arrived Politburo member's frown. He whispered loudly in Russian to one of his underlings, asking him to explain the lyrics. 'Those Ukrainians, why do they always sing so much?' Then he extracted a small notebook from his breast pocket and, using a finely sharpened pencil, wrote down the names of several guests, looking carefully at the writers and artists.

*

'That's a brilliant idea, my dear, absolutely marvellous,' Katz exclaimed once Debora told him she was considering applying to Kharkiv University. 'You are, of course, the right person for this. Of proletarian background – your father was an industrial worker, correct? – and I can see your ideological purity. I am making no promises, but I don't see why you shouldn't be able to start the course come September.'

'I am so thankful.' Debora blushed. 'This would mean so much to me.'

'You said you're interested in literature,' he went on. 'I have noticed that you read a lot. What would you do with that degree?'

'Teaching,' Debora replied. 'I like to share what I love. To make others enjoy what I can see. To explain.'

She had tried that with Samuel, but he wasn't interested in discussing books. The only ones he read were aviation manuals. It would be different with children, of course. She could mould them, she could open their eyes to that huge, wonderful world beyond their dreary everyday lives. Take them along on her journey.

'You are making a very timely choice, and may I suggest you apply to the Russian literature department instead of the Ukrainian one,' Katz replied. 'The quota for Russian literature and language students is going up. We've been neglecting things on that front for far too long. Now there are new instructions, from Moscow. Makes it much easier.'

She was sweating in her linen dress, and wondered how Katz hadn't melted in his dark suit. The summer heat wave had hit Kharkiv with fury, and there was no escape from the buzzing flies and mosquitoes that proliferated at the construction site. The tractor plant, however, was nearing completion, with engineers already installing equipment imported from Europe inside the orderly pattern of new brick-and-concrete halls.

The sleeping quarters and the dining halls were beginning to empty out.

'You still have plenty to do here first,' Katz said, his hand touching her bare shoulder. 'We will have a huge opening ceremony in a few months, once the first tractor rolls off the assembly line. Everyone will be here, people from Moscow, people from Kharkiv. A trainload. There will have to be banners at every step, so you'd better get to work.' He rummaged in his drawer and pulled out a sheet with the slogans on. 'You can start with these, they are evergreen.'

'Of course, Comrade Katz.'

Her step bounced as she closed Katz's door. University! She painted banners all afternoon, making mistakes as her mind wandered into the future, a future in which she would learn new things every day. A future in which she would walk into a classroom, rows of attentive children hanging on her every word.

The red banners became so etched into her brain that she dreamed about them at night. In her nightmares, they came alive, walking on stick-like feet, knocking down the furniture, chasing after people on the street with an evil grin, white letters jumping off the red fabric like lassos.

In the afternoon, she heard muffled sounds of arguing in Katz's office, but didn't pay attention. Who cared? Soon she would have a new life. At dusk, she almost ran to the dorm, impatient to share the good news with Olena.

Olena was sitting on Debora's bed, all dressed up. A packed suitcase stood by her feet.

She got up and gave Debora a tight, silent hug.

'Are you all right? What's happening? Why the suitcase?' Debora fired off her questions. 'I thought you were staying here until the plant's opening?' She noticed Olena's bloodshot eyes. 'What's wrong? Have you been crying?'

Olena had been getting up in the morning to throw up in the latrine all week. Probably food poisoning.

'Are you sick?'

'I must leave right away. I'm going to have a baby and I can't stay here any more,' Olena replied in a distant voice, as if she was speaking about someone else. 'You're not allowed to stay here if you're pregnant. Against the rules.'

'Pregnant? How? From Katz?'

She nodded. 'Who else? You don't think I'm fucking everyone too, do you?'

'But wasn't he going to marry you? Doesn't he want to have this child?'

'I found out today that I was pregnant, and I told him a few hours ago. I thought he would be happy, stupid cow that I am. I thought, of course, that we would get married . . . I was already picking out the wedding dress in my mind. But he just crossed his arms and told me that I'm deluded. That marriage is a bourgeois superstition, and that after the proletarian revolution he believes in free love, relationships of equals between women and men. He brought up this whole glass of water nonsense.'

'Glass of water?'

'Haven't you read that book? Kollontai, I think . . . I haven't read it myself, but I've heard enough. In the Soviet Union, a liberated woman should open her legs like drinking a glass of water – whenever she feels thirst, or whenever he feels thirst, or whatever, with no inhibitions and bourgeois moralising. Convenient, no?'

Debora remembered reading articles on the subject a few years earlier. Such attitudes were no longer promoted, however.

'Bastard piece of shit. I was just a cheap fuck to him,' Olena went on. 'Said that it was my responsibility not to get pregnant, that I failed in my duty, and that thankfully the plant's clinic can provide a free and safe abortion.'

'Abortion? Will you?'

'No way! But he was angry when I told him I wouldn't. He started saying it's probably not his child anyway, that I'm a slut, and that I must leave the city immediately or I'll regret it. Then I started to cry, and he just threw me out. So here I am. Leaving.'

'What a horrible little man. Where will you go?'

'For now, back to the village, to my mama. We have a big house, a garden with cherry and peach trees, not a bad place to raise a child. Maybe it's better this way. My mama will help me, you know her. I should never have come to the city anyway. Silly me for thinking I can fit in, thinking I can escape what's written for me.'

'But can we complain? To the party committee? He can't just get away with this, can he? In this day and age?'

'Sure he can, my dear Debora.'

'You must complain,' Debora insisted. 'This is unacceptable.'

Olena sighed loudly. 'My father,' she said finally, 'he fought for the other side during the civil war, as an officer with the Ukrainian Riflemen, until the very end. He fought against their revolution. I was stupid enough to confess this to Katz. I trusted him. Who's going to take the side of the daughter of a class enemy against the political secretary?'

Debora hugged her again.

'You know better, Olenochka, you know better what to do now. I will miss you, all the time, and I will write often and I will come and visit,' she promised. 'And you will have a beautiful child. You will be happy. I know. For sure.'

'Of course.' Olena smiled. 'Hope the baby looks like me!'

Debora went with Olena to the Kharkiv train station that night. She stayed on the platform, tears streaming from her eyes, until the locomotive pulled away with a loud whistle.

6

Kharkiv, September 1931

Debora sat on the porch of her new university dorm, checking her watch every few minutes as she waited for Samuel. He had been away for several weeks, training manoeuvres somewhere secret, and she imagined how he would pull her to his chest, running his hands along her cheeks and kissing the nape of her neck. She already felt her skin tingling. Any minute now.

He arrived on time, moving with his usual determined stride, but stood stiff, looking away, as Debora ran to hug him.

'What is it, what's the matter?' She recoiled, alarmed, when he didn't respond to her kisses. 'Is something wrong?'

His eyes didn't meet hers. 'Bad news, I'm afraid. They're opening a new air academy, in Kyiv, and I'm being transferred there. In two weeks.'

'Two weeks? That's all we've got?' Her eyes welled up. 'My love, I don't want you to go. I don't want us to be apart.' She spoke softly but quickly. 'What if I come with you, what if we both go to Kyiv? I would do that. For you, I would.'

'That's nonsense, Debora,' he replied. 'You've just started studying here. You can't abandon everything like this, you can't destroy your future. Maybe you can finish the year at the university and move then. Definitely not now.'

He tried to wipe away the tears that rolled down her cheeks. She hadn't expected this. First Olena. Now Samuel. Gone. She would be all alone.

'Why, but why?' she asked. 'Why are they doing this? Why do they have to move you?'

'I don't know, my love. This is how it is – they tell us we must go, and we go. We are military men, you know that, we are not masters of our own fate. Anyway, we are kind of lucky. Kyiv is not very far. They could have sent me all the way to Siberia. With Kyiv, you can come and visit often.'

'I will come to you,' she promised. 'As soon as I can.'

The day before his departure, Samuel threw a small going-away party in Sasha and Larysa's large new apartment in the Slovo building. The newly-weds had their own gramophone, and Sasha made sure to procure enough of a spread for the guests. There were no literary and theatrical luminaries this time around. Only Samuel's military academy classmates, and their women.

Samuel was smoking on the balcony when Sasha walked into the kitchen and put his hand on Debora's waist. She was slicing a smoked pork sausage and was startled by the touch. Sasha was breathing heavily, and she could see dark sweat stains on his blue shirt, under the armpits. He gently took the knife from her hand and put it down, then ran his hand over her cheek. 'You are so sweet, Debora, you have always been so sweet,' he said. 'And your smell, it's such a sweet smell.'

She tried to move away, but he held her. 'Now that Samuel is gone, maybe we can see each other more often.' A dreamy smile spread over his lips.

'I don't understand what you mean,' she protested,

understanding exactly what he meant, and wriggled free just as he pulled her face towards his own.

'Sasha, I think you've had too much to drink. Stop it.'

She picked up the tray of sliced sausage and held it out in front of her. 'Take this and carry it to the guests.'

Sasha nodded obediently, like a scolded child. He took the tray and, after an almost imperceptible pause, pushed the half-closed kitchen door open with his knee.

Larysa was just outside. How long she had been standing there, Debora didn't know. She stepped aside as the door opened, letting her husband pass, and then slowly approached the counter, getting so close that Debora could smell the pickles on her breath. 'Don't you dare try anything funny with my husband.' She enunciated every word, staring into Debora's eyes. Her cheeks were red, blood vessels bursting.

'Why would I?' Debora retorted. 'What are you implying?'

'I know your kind,' Larysa hissed. Her voice was low, almost a whisper, but the threat was unmistakable. 'I know everything about your kind. So. Don't.'

Debora grabbed a tray of sandwiches with both hands and bolted out of the kitchen. Larysa stayed put.

Samuel came towards her, a cigarette dangling from his mouth, his collar unbuttoned. He'd been enjoying himself.

'Oh, my love, I've been looking for you. Everything all right?' he asked, taking a sandwich with one hand and pulling Debora towards him with the other.

'Yes, of course.' She softly kissed his shoulder. 'Everything is fine, everything is fine.'

Debora had convinced her roommate to spend the night elsewhere, and they had the university dorm to themselves until the morning of Samuel's departure. They made love hastily, almost sadly, and Samuel quickly dozed off, naked, sprawled on the sheets, his limbs pointing in different directions. Debora propped herself on her elbow and looked at him in the flickering light of a candle. She gently ran her fingers over his body, from his chin down the crevices of his neck, through his curly chest hair to the mole on his stomach, and all the way along his inner thigh and the inside of his knee to his toes. She catalogued his topography in her mind so that in the weeks and months ahead, the weeks and months without him, she could remember him, she could will his presence into being. Then she kissed his forehead and tried to sleep.

Samuel's orders were to present himself at the Kharkiv train station for 8 a.m. departure. She refused to accompany him there, knowing that the longer the farewells lasted, the more the moment of separation would hurt. He noticed how hard she tried not to cry and held her face to his chest, the polished brass buttons of his uniform leaving an imprint on her skin. 'Don't worry, my love, don't worry,' he whispered into her ear. 'We'll see each other very soon.'

She pulled away and pushed him towards the door.

'Go,' she almost shouted. 'You are the one who has to worry. Enough now, go.'

7

Kharkiv, November 1931

Debora thought about Samuel all the time. But the nights were the worst. When she closed her eyes, she saw his face – blurry, up close, eyes half shut, the way she remembered him kissing her. He spoke to her in her dreams, whispering naughty words in her ear, laughing as he recounted jokes that she couldn't remember in the morning. She would wake up disappointed, realising again that he was gone, that she wouldn't be able to see or touch him – not today, not tomorrow, not next week, not even next month. She made plans to visit him in Kyiv during the January break, the earliest she could travel. In the meantime, the high point of her day was checking for mail. He wrote often in the beginning, in his bad handwriting peppered with spelling mistakes to which she'd long stopped paying attention. She replied with carefully written reports about her life, usually after multiple drafts. For every letter she wrote home to Uman, she posted ten to Kyiv.

It had been two weeks since Samuel's latest letter, far too long. As Debora scanned the stack of mail in the dorm after returning from classes, she spotted an envelope with the familiar handwriting and eagerly sliced it open with a pencil. The letter, one page on ruled paper torn from a notebook, was unusually short.

My dear Debora, Samuel informed her. *I hold you very dear in my heart, and I think of you every day. But we live too far apart and that isn't going to change for a while. You must study for your degree; I am likely to be assigned somewhere far away once I graduate here. So I am telling you that you shouldn't wait for me any more. It would be unfair of me to ask you to do so. You are young, and beautiful, and intelligent, and should not spend your best days in loneliness. I am sure that we shall meet again one day. Your Samuel.*

She read the letter twice before she understood the meaning. Then she added it to the pack of Samuel's other letters in her suitcase. She felt more numb than angry, and tried to write a reply, first a furious one, then a distant and sarcastic one, but nothing that she'd put together seemed satisfactory.

Almost obsessively, she replayed her conversations with him in her mind, remembering his words, his gestures, the tone of his voice. What was it, what was it that she had done wrong? When was the moment he decided to abandon her? Was this already in motion before his departure for Kyiv, was he already planning to discard her then, months ago? She couldn't find answers alone and was too proud to talk to anyone.

But she did compose a long letter to Olena, filling two pages and not caring about the turns of the phrase or the calligraphy: *'Not spend your best days in loneliness'! I am sure he has already found someone else to fuck in Kyiv. Maybe more than one. What an asshole! Men are such pigs. But you already know that, my dear.*

Two weeks later, Debora ran into Sasha on her way to the library.

'Hello, compatriot,' he yelled at her. 'Don't turn up your nose at a fellow Umanite.'

She hadn't seen him since the attempted kiss at Samuel's going-away party. She paused, hesitant and unsure how to react, then walked up to him with what she intended to be a smile of genuine, innocent friendship. 'Are you here to pick up your wife? What a good husband you are!'

Debora had occasionally crossed paths with Larysa in the university halls. Every time, Larysa tried her best to ignore her – and limited herself to a cold hello when that proved unfeasible.

'Oh no, she can find her way home by herself, she's a big girl,' Sasha said. 'I am actually assigned to a new job here. Which means that I will see you a lot more often. Quite happy about that.'

'Oh! Doing what?'

'Well, vigilance about ideological purity is very important. Maybe you want to work with us? I've heard good things about you from Comrade Katz, back at the tractor plant.'

'Ah yes, dear Comrade Katz.' Debora paused. 'Well, good luck here. Great to see you around. But I don't think I have time now for anything other than my studies. Exams are difficult, you know.'

'Yeah.' He put his hand on her shoulder. 'I just wanted to say: too bad about you and Syoma,' he said. 'I'm sorry.'

'You know? He told you already?' Debora shuddered.

'Word travels fast. I hear he's dating some hot blonde or two. Kyiv ladies are something else, apparently.' He grinned. 'Well, you know our Syoma. That's what he is. He likes the ladies.'

Debora moved away and his hand fell from her shoulder. 'I'd better run,' she said quietly. 'I'm late for my meeting.'

'Of course, you don't want to miss anything.' He patted her on the back, his hand lingering just a moment longer than was appropriate. 'See you soon, I'm sure.'

8

Kharkiv, December 1931

The mood at the university turned chilly with the arrival of the snow. In her first few weeks, Debora had often encountered the professors and writers she had met at the May Day party in Slovo. Then, one by one, they started to vanish. At first their books were no longer displayed in the university shop, and no longer available in the library. Then the academics themselves stopped showing up for classes, and substitute instructors arrived to teach their courses. Many students didn't mind, and nobody dared ask where the professors had gone. Unlike the cranky older academics, the younger substitutes were generous with grades. They also steered clear of incomprehensible expressions in Latin and Greek.

In the university – and even more so on Kharkiv's streets – the ever-present banners with revolutionary slogans were no longer only in Ukrainian. The fresh ones were mostly in Russian, with a new emphasis on celebrating the eternal brotherhood of the Russian and Ukrainian peoples. Even the fonts changed, returning to more traditional Slavic motifs. In the bookshops of the Old Passage, the shelves had been purged, the stream of translated novels dried up. No more fellow travellers, the shop assistant told Debora. Only bona fide proletarian writers focusing on the class struggle in the decadent West. Shortly before New Year, dozens of students and teaching staff arrived from Russia, joining the department of Russian literature and language. The once half-empty classes became cramped.

On the morning of 31 December, the entire university had to attend an annual meeting with the rector. Usually Larysa's father was the guest of honour at such events. But this year, another official presided over the proceedings: the Politburo member with the angry dog scowl whom Debora had seen at the wedding. As Debora took her seat in the hall, she noticed that Sasha was perched among the notables on stage, wearing a fancy new suit with a red tie.

The Politburo member started to speak into the microphone, Sasha dutifully nodding at the man's every word.

'Comrades, it's time to admit that some mistakes have been made, some exaggerations that didn't take into account the true interests of the working classes of our great socialist Motherland. What I am talking about is the policy of Ukrainisation. There have been excesses, I will be honest with you. Some enemy elements have tried to abuse this policy, to put a wedge between the brotherly Russian and Ukrainian peoples. But the Party has been vigilant, and the Party is making sure that the course is being corrected.'

'Long live our Party, long live Comrade Stalin,' Sasha shouted at the top of his lungs. Everyone, including Debora, instantly stood up and clapped until their hands hurt. No one wanted to be noticed as the first to stop.

'Today we must focus our attention on the great Russian language, which is the window through which all the peoples of the Soviet Union gain access to the best of world culture, the language of the revolution, the language of Lenin, the language of Stalin,' the Politburo member went on. 'And this means we need you, the future teachers of Russian to the children of Soviet schools, to redouble your efforts at mastering your skills.'

As the crowd dispersed after the speech, Debora found herself next to Larysa. 'Happy New Year,' she said. 'I hope you have fun celebrating 1932. It should be a great year.'

Larysa seemed hollow, her eyes red from crying. 'Thank you,' she replied quietly. 'Though I'm not sure there is much to celebrate.'

'What do you mean? Is everything well?' Debora asked.

'Of course. Everything is very well.' Larysa turned away and squeezed through the crowd and out of the hall. Sasha left separately, sharing a car with the dignitaries in the VIP convoy.

9

Kharkiv, February 1932

'Comrade Rosenbaum, so nice of you to come by. We truly appreciate it,' a young man in uniform said in a soft, almost whispering voice, showing Debora an OGPU secret police identity card. He had a shock of jet-black hair and thin, delicate features, with clear blue eyes squinting behind rimmed glasses.

Her muscles tensed as she glanced at the card. The investigator was used to such reactions. 'No need to fear.' He patted her arm. 'Relax, Comrade Rosenbaum. It will only take a few minutes. Your Soviet Motherland needs your help.'

Debora hadn't realised she was meeting the OGPU. She had been asked to come to the university's Political Section and assumed it was for some routine duty. She thought they might need her help in refreshing the arsenal of propaganda banners, a prospect she dreaded.

The morning was sunny, after days of heavy, dark skies, and she had arrived for the meeting in a good mood. She had just secured a week of leave and train tickets for next month, when she would go home to Uman, visiting Olena in Pisky on the way.

'Comrade Rosenbaum, as I am sure you know, we are surrounded by enemies, foreign and domestic,' the investigator went on. 'Political and economic counter-revolution is just waiting for the right moment to strike back. Have you heard about the trial?'

The trial had been all over the news: various Kharkiv Ukrainian intellectuals confessing to plotting against the Soviet system and spying on behalf of imperialist powers. Poland. Germany. Or was it Japan? Debora had read about it in the newspapers, and recognised some men from Larysa and Sasha's wedding in the grainy photos of the accused.

'Yes, it is wonderful that the competent organs have been able to discover and stop it, to keep us all safe,' she said, as she knew she was supposed to. She still didn't understand what all this was about.

'Well, that is true,' the agent said, taking off his glasses to wipe each lens carefully with a handkerchief. 'But this is just the beginning. Confidentially, Comrade Rosenbaum, things are much, much worse. That rot, the rot of bourgeois nationalism, it goes much deeper. We have allowed it to penetrate deep inside the Party. Some officials have used Ukrainisation as an excuse to smuggle in something totally different, something pernicious and hostile. Someone like you, Comrade *Rosenbaum*, surely understands what I am talking about.'

Debora winced.

'Of all people, I am sure, comrade, people of your kind, who have suffered so much from Ukrainian bourgeois nationalism and its pogroms, understand what I am talking about,' the OGPU man continued.

She remained silent.

'What can you tell me about Bohdan Skrypka?' he asked. He pulled out a large folder and prepared to write down her answers.

'I don't really know Comrade Skrypka that well,' Debora said meekly.

'Well enough to attend his daughter's wedding.'

She realised she was about to bite her fingernails and pulled her hand away from her mouth.

'Tell me what you do know about Citizen Skrypka. Even something that does not seem important to you may turn out to be crucial,' the investigator encouraged her.

Debora froze. Using 'Citizen' instead of 'Comrade' before Skrypka's name could mean only one thing – he had been or was just about to be arrested. Fear made her dizzy.

'I don't think we have ever spoken, to be honest. I only know his daughter, Larysa, and Sasha.'

'Let's leave Comrade Grinenko aside for now.' The investigator grew stern. 'Tell me all you know about the daughter of Citizen Skrypka, Larysa Bohdanovna.'

Debora knew that she should remain quiet, that anything she said would turn into poison. But she was frightened and wanted to please the officer. She began to talk. Words that should have been carefully measured escaped before she had time to consider the consequences. Once uttered, they became more than words, turning into real, material things, weapons as palpable as a bullet or a dagger.

'Nothing, really. It's only that she always spoke to me in Ukrainian, even if I spoke Russian to her,' she blurted out. 'But that's not a crime, is it?'

The agent emitted a satisfied grunt and made a note in his file.

'And did she ever disparage brotherly Russia?' he pressed.

Debora recalled the May Day party in Slovo, but remained quiet.

'In particular, I am referring to a party you attended on the first of May 1931.' The investigator consulted his notes. 'You did well to uphold the Party's position against nationalist deviations there, I am told. We are proud of your loyalty.'

'She wasn't really saying anything that others weren't,' Debora said.

'Indeed, indeed, but she *was* saying the deviant, nationalist things that others were expressing at the time, wasn't she? "Away from Moscow", all that stuff?'

Debora nodded almost imperceptibly. She was afraid to lie, and why lie if the OGPU already knew everything? Nothing she said or did could really change the outcome, could it?

The investigator made another note in his file, then went on: 'So did you ever hear Larysa speak ill of the Party, of Comrade Stalin, of our Soviet system?'

'No, of course not,' Debora rushed to reply. 'Never. I would have reported that right away.'

'Of course, of course you would,' he comforted her. 'As a cunning enemy, she'd be too clever to be so open in front of a loyal Soviet citizen like you, Comrade Rosenbaum. But like I said, even something you may not think is significant is really important to us.'

He handed her a sheet of paper with his notes of her testimony. 'Please sign here. I am glad to note that you are worthy of the honour of being a student of this university. I will refer you accordingly.'

It didn't even occur to Debora at that moment that she could refuse. She took the agent's pen and scribbled her name at the bottom of the sheet, without reading the text.

She lay sleepless that night, wondering what she had done, trying to lull herself into thinking that nothing serious had occurred. It was just a friendly chat, after all. She hadn't said anything that would really endanger Larysa or anyone else. Had she? And why would they go after Larysa anyway? The thought was ridiculous. She wished she could discuss this with someone, but there was nobody she could talk to in Kharkiv. Olena was gone. Samuel was gone. Everybody else, she couldn't trust.

10

Pisky, March 1932

'I didn't really believe you would come,' Olena said as she hugged Debora on the deserted platform of her village's train station. 'We truly are in the middle of nowhere. Come, come, we must get home before the sun goes down. It's not like they have street lights out here! Or trams. Or cinemas. Or anything, really.'

An old horse pulled their cart slowly through the fields, some still covered with patches of snow, past thatched houses, a church decapitated by the Atheism Department, and a flood plain dissected by a new power line that would soon bring electricity to the village. Pisky meant 'sands', and the village had a sandy strip by the pond where local boys swam in the summer and hopeful villagers fished for pike and perch.

With the snows melting, the road was an oozing river of mud in places, and their cart got repeatedly stuck. Olena, in her felt boots, got out to push. Debora, in her elegant city shoes, also wanted to help, but gave up after Olena and the driver, a bearded man in a black cap, yelled at her to remain inside. 'You'll never fish out your shoes if you come down.'

Olena's family house was big, a mark of past prosperity, but it had bowed under an accumulation of disrepair. The roof leaked. In the garden, the cattle shed looked like it was about to collapse, its beams tilting in opposite directions. There were a few chickens huddling together, but no cows or pigs. Water dripped steadily from the icicles above the door. Debora had to balance herself, walking on a log, from the cart to the door to avoid getting stuck in the mud.

Zinaida had heard the cart arrive and stood waiting. In her right arm she held Olena's newborn son, who cried inconsolably, waving his hands.

'Little Taras has been hungry while you were away,' she said, and then tickled the baby's belly. 'Mummy's back now, Mummy's back to feed you.'

Indoors, Olena quickly unbuttoned her blouse and firmly pushed her nipple into the boy's demanding mouth. He began sucking loudly.

'There's not much milk in there any more, I'm afraid,' she complained. 'But that'll keep him busy for a while.'

'He's so handsome,' Debora said, stroking the boy's fine, translucent hair.

'Luckily he doesn't look anything like his father.'

'Don't even mention that old Yid to me!' Zinaida cursed. 'Let him burn in hell, that Judah. I would spit in his face if I could, I would claw out his eyes.'

Debora had not heard such language in a long time.

'Mama, this has nothing to do with the fact that he is a Jew. Debora is also of a Hebraic nationality,' Olena said gently.

'Oh, I am so sorry, sweetie, I didn't realise.' Zinaida clasped Debora's hand. 'I didn't mean it that way. I have nothing against you Jews. Just that bastard.'

'That's fine, I understand,' Debora replied.

Jews, a persecuted minority in the bad old days, were in the highest positions of power and government now. A former Kyiv cobbler named Lazar Kaganovich had led the Communist Party of the Ukrainian SSR until a few months ago, before becoming the third most senior official in Moscow. Debora was not going to be upset by an old peasant woman and her outdated prejudices. She glanced around the room, noticing icons of Jesus and the saints over the fireplace, glazed ceramic pots, a portrait of Shevchenko – the moustachioed Ukrainian national poet – and a few books. Olena must have brought the books from Kharkiv, she thought.

'Daughter, come eat with us,' Zinaida said. 'You must be hungry after the trip. Forgive us, but times aren't easy these days. The commissars have come by to take most of our wheat, so we live on potatoes for now – they've let us keep those. Potatoes and what we've managed to find in the woods and dry for the winter – mushrooms, berries, nuts. And apples.'

She took a large earthenware plate from the oven and placed it on the table. Lifting an embroidered white cloth, she revealed a mound of baked potatoes and onions topped by chunks of roast chicken. 'We've slaughtered a chicken in your honour. One of the few we still have left – but what can we do, there isn't much to feed them with anyway.'

Olena's nostrils widened as she smelled the roasted flesh. 'Haven't had meat in a while, you know,' she said. 'So thanks for giving us a reason to have this feast.'

While the Kharkiv University canteen wasn't as good as the tractor plant's dining hall, Debora's ration cards allowed her to eat meat at least once a week, in addition to the parcels with tinned veal and sardines that she received from her father. Here in the village, she suddenly felt guilty for not having always finished her portions.

In recent months, she had noticed a growing number of

villagers in patched, ragged clothes begging for something to eat on the streets of Kharkiv. Yet she hadn't realised how widespread the food shortages had become in Ukraine, Europe's granary. In cinema newsreels, the villagers appeared more prosperous by the day, aided by the collective farms' superior management and new technologies. On screen, these tractor-riding farmers always reported record crops.

'Please, go ahead, I am not that hungry,' she lied.

'You know what we say here, never say no to food.' Zinaida picked up a chicken thigh, fat glistening on its skin, and put it on Debora's plate. 'Eat, daughter, eat, while we still can.'

'It's been hard to adjust to the village,' Olena complained. 'I didn't think it would be that hard. I've changed, and the village changed too.'

'Changed how?' Debora asked.

'Our home is no longer our home. The commissars and the soldiers come and go as they please and take what they want. We used to have our own wheat – it is all gone now. We used to have our own pigs and cows – all gone. Thank God they've left us our chickens, for now. The men from the village – they take them as well. Dozens have been branded as *kurkuls* and sent away. We no longer talk to our neighbours. Everyone is just scared. And I don't know what we will use to sow the fields when the snows melt. They've even taken away the grain that we'd put aside for seeds. The collective farm says they will send a new supply to the village soon, but who knows.'

'Children are supposed to live better than their parents,' Zinaida sighed. 'That's how the world is supposed to work. And now, look at this . . . What have we done to bring this curse upon our children? Upon our country? God have mercy on us.'

Debora noticed a faded photograph of a smiling couple on the window ledge, and walked over for a closer look. It was a young

Zinaida, with a thick black braid, standing next to a man with a moustache that curled up at the ends. He wore tall black boots and a uniform, but not the kind worn by the Red Army. Debora made out the banned Ukrainian trident coat-of-arms on his fur hat.

'Is that your father?' she asked Olena, picking up the frame.

'He commanded a Riflemen platoon in the Ukrainian Army, fought against the Reds in the civil war and got killed in 1919. He hadn't even turned thirty. They didn't have much of a chance or much of an army against the Reds, to be honest.'

'Yes, the Red Army is strong and invincible,' Debora said, mechanically repeating the words inculcated since childhood.

'We've had the Reds come through here, and they killed the priest and raped the nuns. Then we had the Whites, and they strung up the Jews. And we had the Greens, how do you call them, the anarchists, and they looted everyone and raped too. And then the Reds again. Only the Germans, when they came here, did not loot anything or kill anyone. The Germans were good people,' Zinaida said. 'Everyone else just killed, killed, killed. It's like they loved the smell of blood. And in those wars, the best go to their graves. Only the cowards survive.'

She kissed her husband's picture, paused to look at it again and put it back.

'He wasn't a coward,' she said. 'Though sometimes I wish he had been.'

'Mama.' Olena touched Zinaida's hand.

'There won't be any more wars here.' Debora tried to cheer everyone up. 'We can all sleep peacefully now.'

'Amen.' Zinaida made the sign of the cross.

Olena smiled and offered Debora her son to hold. Carefully she took the little boy. It felt so natural, the baby unquestioningly accepting her embrace and falling asleep in her arms. Until now, she had never thought of having her own.

'He likes you,' Olena laughed. 'He doesn't usually like strangers, but he likes you. Means that you are a good person.'

Debora felt so comfortable, so welcome in Olena's home that she had forgotten all about the OGPU and Larysa. This remark, however, stung her like a bee.

'A good person?' she repeated. 'You really think that?'

'You're the purest person I know,' Olena replied instantly. 'I wouldn't trust anyone else the way I trust you.'

'If you say so.' Debora bit her lip.

Trying out the chores of motherhood, she gave Taras a bath, learned how to change his nappy, and listened as Olena sang him a folk lullaby that put millions of frightened children to sleep every night: 'Baby, baby, do not sleep on the edge of the bed, or the grey wolf will come and bite off your side.'

Once Zinaida fell asleep alongside Taras, her loud snores carrying over the partition, Olena and Debora lay down under a heavy wool blanket near the fireplace. The dying embers projected flickering shadows on the whitewashed walls.

'It's too bad that it's over between you and Samuel,' Olena said. 'You seemed so good together. And you would have made such a beautiful baby. Are you still thinking of him?'

'I am,' Debora confessed. 'I know I shouldn't, I know I should see other men, but nobody else interests me. I'll get used to it, I know.'

'You will. You'll find someone to love, someone to have a child with, and you will be happy.' Olena stroked her hair. 'The heart needs time to heal. Have you even replied to his letter?'

'No. What can I say? I won't grovel, I won't beg, I won't ask him to change his mind. I've got my pride.'

'Pride,' Olena repeated, pondering the sound of the word. 'Pride is such a luxury.'

The house was getting cold. Olena edged closer to Debora

under the blanket. She smelled of milk and lavender, her warmth pulling Debora in. 'I'm so happy you're here,' she whispered, and put her hand on Debora's breast. The tip of her index finger made a circle around Debora's nipple, which turned hard from the touch, and then ran down her ribcage. 'I haven't hugged anyone for a long time, you know,' she whispered. 'It's nice. So nice.'

Startled, Debora turned to look into Olena's eyes, half shut and dreamy.

'Yeah, it's nice,' she whispered back.

'You're so pretty, and you're so not from here,' Olena went on. 'Like a creature from another planet. An alien.'

She leaned in and kissed Debora's mouth, with a forceful, probing push of the tongue. After a few seconds, she pulled back, embarrassed.

'I'm sorry, but I'd forgotten what it feels like,' she said. 'I hope you're not upset.'

'No, I'm not. But let's sleep now. I've got to get up early to make the train,' Debora said gently, and turned away.

'Yes, of course, let's sleep,' Olena agreed reluctantly. She spooned around Debora's back, holding her in a tight embrace until the morning, breathing steadily into the nape of her neck.

Everyone was up before dawn, with little time to spare until the train. Olena took Debora to the station and hugged her tight just before she stepped down from the cart. Neither of them mentioned their kiss.

The two policemen manning the platform checked Debora's identity documents, noting her all-important registration in the capital city of Kharkiv and asking her what she had been doing in the village. She told them the truth and, after writing down Olena's name in his notepad, the senior policeman let her board the train.

Some others, she noticed, had been turned away.

11

Uman, March 1932

It took most of the day for the train to chug through the birch and pine woods and the unsown plains of central Ukraine into Uman. Debora passed the time by drinking hot water supplied by the conductor and reading a newspaper left behind by a previous passenger.

The front-page story, as was often the case, outlined the uncovering of yet another dastardly imperialist plot against the Soviet Motherland. She was about to skip it and turn to the fashion and cinema section, but the large photograph caught her eye.

Among the convicted traitors were the unmistakable features of Larysa, the daughter of Bohdan Skrypka. Skrypka himself, the article noted, had committed the cowardly act of suicide, blowing out his brains in his office in the Derzhprom skyscraper rather than face the righteous wrath of the Soviet people. Debora felt sick. She put down the newspaper. Then she looked at the photograph again. Some of the other faces seemed familiar, possibly writers she had met at Slovo. But Sasha wasn't in the photo, and wasn't mentioned in the article. Larysa, she also noticed, was listed under her maiden name.

Blood drained from her face as she read the details, so much so that an old woman sitting opposite reached out to touch her knee. 'Is everything good with you, daughter?' she asked. 'You look like you are in pain.' A sharp, ripping pain did indeed pulsate through Debora's stomach, subsiding after a few minutes.

'I am fine,' she responded drily. She had learned how to hide her feelings, most of the time.

She tucked the newspaper in her bag and walked off to the toilet at the end of the car. Locking herself inside, she splashed ice-cold water on her face and stared into the chipped mirror, swaying. 'Is this the face of a murderer?' she said to herself, quietly, and slapped her right cheek. 'What have you done with your big mouth? What have you fucking done, you idiot?' She closed her eyes for a minute and reopened them to look at the newspaper once again. 'I am sorry, Larysa,' she whispered. 'I didn't mean it. I really didn't. It just happened.'

Someone banged on the door. 'Hey you, princess, you're not the only one who needs to piss. Uman is coming up in half an hour,' the conductor shouted.

Debora's parents were already on the station platform, scanning the windows of the carriages as the train pulled in to Uman. So, to her surprise, was her brother, Yakov. She inhaled deeply and tried her best to put Larysa out of her mind.

'Hah, look at you, so fashionable!' Yakov exclaimed as he squeezed her in a bear hug.

She pinched his cheek. 'You too, you've grown up to be a big man,' she said.

'You have both grown up,' added their father.

Yakov was back home on leave, all the Rosenbaums together for the first time in a year and a half. As they sat around the table for a festive dinner, Gersh surveyed his two children with pride.

Yakov, broad-shouldered in his spotless navy uniform, soon to be an officer. Debora, an adult who had opened her own doors in the big city.

Rebecca, like many women who had lived through lean years, best expressed her feelings of love through an overabundance of food. She had spent days cooking in preparation for tonight. She'd mixed ground herring, chopped onion and boiled eggs into salty *farshmak*. Mayonnaise, potatoes, sausage and peas went into the Olivier, a dish that most people in Ukraine believed to be a French delicacy but that was actually known as Russian salad elsewhere. Blood-red beetroot salad with walnuts stood at the centre of the table. There was jellied carp, and pickles, and a steaming cabbage-and-egg pie she had baked overnight. And there was also a lot of vodka, the spicy Ukrainian kind with honey and chilli pepper.

Gersh was senior enough in the Uman branch of the People's Commissariat of Trade that he didn't have to worry about what to put on the table in his own home. But he knew that last year's crops had been bad, and that so much of what had been harvested in the area had been immediately shipped abroad, to earn the hard currency with which the Soviet Union could purchase industrial equipment needed to build new tanks, ships, planes and tractors. The harvest plans for the coming year, sent down from Moscow, were even more ambitious than those of the previous year.

'I worry, I worry about what is going to happen,' he said as they finished the first course. 'The big cities are going to be fine, but in the villages, it will be very hard this year. And maybe here in Uman too.'

Gersh's acquaintance had just offered him a transfer to Kyiv, the city where he and Rebecca had spent the happy days of their youth, before the revolution and wars. 'It's a rare chance, a rare opportunity,' he said.

Yakov enthusiastically endorsed the idea. 'We could all be together again,' he said. 'And you too.' He pointed at Debora. 'You could come live with us!'

It was only now, sitting in the overdecorated living room of the home she had yearned so much to escape, that Debora realised how much she missed being together as a family. She would have died of boredom in Uman, of course. But Kyiv, Kyiv was even more of a big city than Kharkiv. Kyiv was the mother of all cities, her schoolteachers had taught her.

'I'm sure you could transfer to Kyiv University, with your good grades and everything,' Rebecca pressed her. 'It's even better than Kharkiv's. And you will be close to that boyfriend of yours, what's his name?'

'Samuel, Mama,' Debora said. 'His name is Samuel.'

She still hadn't admitted to her parents that it was over. Now was not the right time for baring her wounds, however.

Gersh poured another round of shots for everyone, including his wife, who didn't usually drink. '*L'chaim!*' He raised his glass. 'To family. Family is everything, especially during these times. You can't trust anyone nowadays, but one thing you know – you can always trust your family. I would do anything for you all, anything.'

'Anything?' Debora asked. 'Even if it was illegal?'

It came out harsher than she meant, but Gersh didn't hesitate with the answer.

'Illegal? Things that were legal became illegal, and things that were illegal became legal, and back and forth like this time after time since my youth. But the family, that stays. Family is permanent. It's the only thing that matters to me.'

Later that night, Debora asked her father whether he had heard anything about Sasha Grinenko, the son of her former maths teacher.

'Ah, Sasha,' he replied, furrowing his brow. 'Yes, I saw his parents walking down the street a while ago. I said hello, they said hello, they were not very friendly really. But I asked them how Sasha was doing and they said he was doing well. He's got a big job now, working in the Organs.'

'He's working for the OGPU?' she almost shouted.

Gersh was surprised by the intensity of her reaction. 'Why wouldn't he be?'

She showed him the newspaper. 'This one, she was his wife, I used to know her,' she said, pointing at the photograph of Larysa, gaunt and sullen in the courtroom. 'Though I suppose he has now divorced her.'

'"The sentence is the highest measure of social defence."' Gersh's eyes narrowed as he read the article. 'Means she's been shot.'

Debora nodded, tensing.

'What kind of a man is that, working for the people who shot his own wife?' Rebecca exclaimed.

'Shh.' Gersh raised his voice. 'Don't judge people until you are in their shoes.'

'Don't shush me.' Rebecca turned assertive. 'There are things you just do not do. We are not cattle, after all, we are humans, we always have a choice.'

'Easy for you to say.'

Gersh noticed the painful wince on Rebecca's face. He didn't see how Debora hid her face in her palms, struggling not to cry.

'Out there, it is not the same world it used to be, and you know it,' he continued. 'The past, the past as it was when we were young, it doesn't exist any more. Out there, people will do anything to survive. And if you treat people like cattle, they will forget they are people and behave like cattle, they will moo, they will chew grass, they will do anything just to live another day, and they will march quietly to slaughter, just because they are used to doing what they're told to do.'

'You are so wrong.' Rebecca shook her head slowly. 'So wrong.'

Yakov would not have any of this. 'Papa, why are you being so negative? You just sit here in little Uman, which hasn't really changed, and you don't notice all the great, good things that are happening. All the industries, the education, the sports, the progress. The aviation! It's in the past that people lived like cattle, but now we are free. Yes, there are problems, and some things are not the way they should be. Blemishes. But these are just growing pains, that's all.'

'Son, let me tell you one thing,' Gersh said slowly. 'Have you ever been to a barn at one of the collective farms around here?'

'No, not really.'

'I know you haven't. It was, how do you say, a rhetorical question. Well, I go there often when we pick up cows to take to the abattoir. And you know what – when I look at them, grazing, the cows all think they are free. They even think they are free when we put them in the truck. They think they are free until the second they are dead.'

'How do you know what the cows think?' Debora asked, and Yakov burst out laughing.

In her childhood bed at night, Debora was unable to suppress her thoughts about Sasha, and Larysa, and her ten-minute conversation with the OGPU agent. Maybe that conversation was inconsequential after all. Maybe Sasha was already reporting on his wife by then, and her testimony was just an irrelevant last-minute bureaucratic addition. Maybe she didn't have to feel guilty. Maybe. Please, she prayed to no one in particular before falling asleep, please let it not be my sin.

*

70

In the morning, the Rosenbaums walked down the hill to the Sofiivka Park, built in 1796 by Count Stanisław Potocki to humour his young wife, Sofia. The immensely wealthy Polish magnate once owned much of Uman and the surrounding countryside. 'Who do you think you are, Count Potocki?' was how Rebecca usually scolded her children whenever they asked for something she judged to be extravagant.

Count Potocki, of course, was long gone, and the park was now called the Garden of the Third International. 'I like the new name,' Rebecca said. 'It's a shame that all these years we kept calling it after that snake of a woman.' Debora, like all Uman natives, knew the story well. Sofia, a Greek courtesan from Constantinople, had married her way into Europe's noble society, eventually ending up as the spouse of the elderly Count Potocki. That didn't prevent her from breaking his heart as she carried out a shameless affair, in full view of the servants, with the count's twenty-two-year-old son.

'Betrayal, betrayal, nothing new about betrayal,' Gersh said. 'But let's thank fate that we now have this beautiful park. Too bad it's still too cold for a boat ride. Anyone want to warm up?' he asked, and pulled out his silver flask, engraved with an outline of the snow-capped Alps. It was a treasured memento of his honeymoon with Rebecca in Switzerland, in their old, pre-Soviet life.

'Sure,' Debora said, putting the flask to her lips and feeling the warmth spread from her throat.

'I didn't know you had started drinking,' Rebecca noted with undisguised disapproval. 'It's unbecoming.'

The next morning, when Gersh went to work, Debora accompanied her mother to Uman's market. The offerings were scant, and every time Rebecca asked about the prices, she reacted with a horrified *tsk tsk*. 'How can anyone afford this any more?' she wondered.

As Debora walked the familiar streets, past the two-storey brick buildings slowly fraying after years of neglect, she sensed how alien to Uman she had become. In Kharkiv, she was no longer accustomed to the sight of Orthodox Jews, still so plentiful here, with their ridiculous frocks and wide-brimmed hats. With her blonde hair, green eyes and proper accent, she herself was usually taken for a Russian or Ukrainian Gentile.

On the way, a shopkeeper's wife, a bulky woman with a hairy mole on her nose, saluted Rebecca in Yiddish, words that Debora didn't really understand. 'You are so grown up, I barely recognise you,' she added in Russian. She was a distant relative, seen only at weddings and funerals.

'These people, they are so different,' Debora couldn't help saying when they were alone. 'Thank God we aren't like them.'

'To some people,' Rebecca said, 'you will always be like them.'

Debora didn't want to argue and let silence hang in the air.

That night, she hugged her father. 'Let me know how the Kyiv thing goes,' she said. 'Maybe I'll join you there.'

'Is it because of us, or because of that lad of yours, Samuel?' he asked, delighted.

'Because of you, silly.' She kissed him on the cheek. 'And Mama. I love you both.'

As she went to bed, she wondered why she no longer jealously guarded her freedom and was suddenly considering living with her parents again. Could it be that, despite the break-up, it was Samuel's presence in Kyiv that drew her, subconsciously, like a magnet? Kyiv ... Kyiv ...

That night, she dreamed about Samuel again. They were walking by a waterfront, holding hands and watching fireworks. Then the dream became confused and suddenly a bloodied

Larysa appeared, her dress shredded, her bare feet streaked with mud. She repeated a phrase in a giggly, bewildered voice, and at first Debora couldn't make out the words. Then she finally understood. 'The highest measure of social defence,' Larysa kept saying, pausing for a short laugh. 'The highest.'

Sasha was standing behind a tree nearby, dressed in a black leather jacket, his trousers unbuttoned. He was smiling and making indecent gestures, as if Larysa weren't there. And when Debora switched her gaze to Larysa, she was indeed gone, just some droplets of blood left on the floor. 'What have you done to her, Debora?' Samuel asked, his voice steely and threatening all of a sudden.

12

Kharkiv, January 1933

Life in Pisky went on as usual, Olena wrote cryptically in one of her frequent letters to Debora. *You remember how it was when you came by? Remember what Mama told you? That's what we are all thinking about all the time.* There was a lot more to say, but – Debora understood – it could not be put down in a letter that a censor somewhere along the way would read.

Why don't you come visit me in Kharkiv over the New Year? Maybe you could leave Taras with your mother? We can go to the movies? Or the theatre? Debora wrote back in September. She enclosed the latest picture of herself, wearing a wide-brimmed hat and a flower-print dress.

How I would love to come, Olena replied. *I have been looking at your picture all day, and imagining myself in Kharkiv again. But it isn't that easy any more. There are new rules, and those of us in the village now need a passport to travel to the big cities. I am trying to get one, but it will take time.*

Debora wrote once again in December. *It may be easier for me to come visit you then. I will try closer to the spring. Can't wait to see how big Taras has become. What do you want me to bring?*

Olena replied: *Maybe it will be very difficult for you to get here. Things are getting out of hand, I don't even know how to describe it. People are eating apricot pits, dead dogs, corn husks. I hope things are better in the city. If you have any food, come with food, but be careful. It is probably best that you don't risk it. I am thinking about you all the time. Your friend for ever, with love, Olena.*

That letter, steamed open by the censor at the Kharkiv post office, never reached Debora. In the last one that did, Olena enclosed a picture of her son, sitting sternly and gazing into the camera, wide-eyed and without a smile. He looked very thin. Debora examined it for a long time, trying to spot a similarity with Katz. At times, she felt Katz's features were obvious. At others, she couldn't see any resemblance at all.

Letters from her parents continued to arrive every week, full of questions about her life, and about Samuel. Tired of lies, she finally wrote back: *I have decided to sever the relationship. He is too far away, and too busy with his service. It wasn't going to work, anyway. No big deal. There will be another man, a better man.*

I hope you know what you are doing, Rebecca responded disapprovingly. *You know I don't like it when you make rash decisions.*

Debora didn't reply.

As the winter grew colder ahead of February – a month known as Liuty, or 'ferocious', in Ukrainian – Debora started noticing unusual things on her morning walk from the dorm to the classroom. Groups of municipal workers scoured the ditches and the bridge underpasses in the pre-dawn darkness. Occasionally they dragged out thin, rigid bodies in snow-encrusted clothes.

'What happened? Who are these people?' she had the courage to ask one morning.

The municipal worker, himself a few sizes too small for his

overalls, looked at the well-dressed young lady and decided to tell the truth.

'Peasants,' he said, lighting a cigarette. 'They come here to Kharkiv and think they can get food, but they can't, and so they die and freeze. Every morning we have to haul them away. The army and the police are patrolling the roads, stopping the trains, and still they keep coming and coming. I don't even know how.'

'I don't understand. Why do they die? It can't be that there is nothing to eat here, now, in this day and age.'

'What are you? A student at the university?' The worker sized her up.

Debora nodded.

'For people like you, life is not the same as for people like them,' he said. 'You are the ones who survive. Enjoy.'

She wanted to ask more questions, but the worker extinguished his cigarette and headed to rejoin the rest of the crew. As they threw the frozen corpse into the back of the truck, another, tiny body fell out of the folds of the dead woman's coat. It landed on the snow and rolled towards the gutter. 'Not another baby,' the man cursed, and scooped it up. Then he got into the cabin and drove off.

Shaken, Debora continued walking to the university, past the morning bustle of a city waking up for a new day, a city whose residents might not have been eating well but were eating enough to live.

Several days later, Debora and a few other students were called into the dean's office.

'You have been chosen for a very responsible mission,' he said. 'A delegation of workers representing the proletariat of the capitalist nations is visiting the capital of Soviet Ukraine, and they will be coming here. We will throw a party for them, with dancing and a show, and you have been picked to attend. But you must be careful. We don't know if all of them are indeed who they say they are. Some may be wolves in sheep's clothes, if you know what I mean.'

The students laughed, as if on cue.

'They may try to give you gifts, or food, or even money, hard currency. You must refuse, of course,' the dean went on. 'We are the hope of the proletariat worldwide; we offer an example to which they aspire. We don't need gifts, and we won't be humiliated by accepting them. Is that understood?'

The foreigners showed up three days later, about a dozen of them. Like everyone else in the group, Debora wore her best clothes. The university laid out a buffet dinner of the kind she had not seen since Larysa and Sasha's wedding, but the students were strictly instructed not to touch the food until the foreigners had filled their plates – and under no circumstances were they to attempt going for seconds.

The guests were a diverse bunch. There were a couple of ageing Labour Party ladies from England, who kept oohing and aahing as they watched the boys vault up and down dancing the Ukrainian *hopak*. 'There are so many lies being spread by reactionaries in Britain about your wonderful country,' one of them said. 'If only people really knew the truth.'

An Italian communist organiser was less easily fooled. It reminded him too much of the regime back at home. But precisely because he knew how such states operated, he kept his mouth shut and just drank shot after shot of the abundant alcohol.

A lanky American with thin, sensuous lips, puffy eyes and a balding head had arrived with the group. He walked on crutches and spoke passable Russian, in a soft, almost saccharine way.

'My name is Walter,' he introduced himself. 'I work for the

New York Times.' He sat down next to Debora and just across the table from the dean. His plate was filled with sausages, buckwheat kasha and pickles. 'This is absolutely delicious.' He licked his lips.

'We always eat this well. This is normal here in Ukraine,' the dean quickly replied.

'Yes, yes, I know, Europe's granary.' Walter smiled. 'You may have heard that some of your adversaries are spreading rumours about bad crops and food shortages in Ukraine. Just recently, a very malicious British journalist published an article about alleged starvation in the villages around Kharkiv. Absolutely not what I am witnessing so far, truth be told. There is no famine, obviously, but maybe some food shortages?' He turned to Debora, who felt obliged to respond.

'Food shortages?' she repeated. Shrugging, she smiled and pointed at the buffet. 'You must be joking. The proletariat of the capitalist countries can only envy the way we eat here in Soviet Ukraine.'

'Yes. Clearly all these rumours of a famine are terribly exaggerated, actually outright wrong,' Walter said. 'Malignant.'

'You should try the suckling pig, it's really good,' the dean said. He was exempt from the no-second-helpings rule.

'Yes, I guess I should,' Walter said, and got up.

Debora offered to help, but he waved her off. 'I can manage by myself, thank you very much.'

'Good answer, good answer. A high level of political literacy,' the dean commended her when the American was out of earshot.

Later that night, once the lights had dimmed and the visitors were dancing with the students, Walter sprawled in his chair with a drink in his hand. Feeling obliged to entertain him, Debora sat next to him.

'I've always heard so much about Ukrainian women and their

good looks,' he whispered, his eyes glowing with contentment. 'What a blessed place,' he went on, putting his hand on her knee and then slowly sliding it up her thigh.

Without breaking her smile, she got up. 'It's been a privilege getting to know you,' she said as she left. Walter did not utter a word in response. She never saw him again.

Once the foreigners were gone, the students wolfed down whatever remained of the buffet. Then the cleaning staff picked out and took home all the uneaten leftovers that remained on the guests' plates. Orange peel. Bones. Smudges of whipped cream where the cake used to be.

13

Pisky, February 1933

In their pointed hats bearing red stars, soldiers patrolled the Kharkiv train station, the bayonets on their rifles gleaming in the sun. They looked amused when Debora walked in with a suitcase in one hand and a pink stuffed dog with droopy ears in the other. The dog was for Taras, and she had spent an entire afternoon choosing the oversize toy in the city's Central Department Store.

Her just-issued transfer papers for Kyiv were in her coat's inside pocket. Olena's village was more or less on the way, and Debora had arranged the railway tickets so that she could spend a night in Pisky. It had been a while since she'd last received a letter from her friend, and she was worried.

She sat down on the bench next to a table occupied by the station clerk. A train rolled by quickly, without stopping. It was made of rough cattle cars. Inside she could see people, far too many to fit comfortably. One man, without any inhibition, urinated through the side. Another, behind, emitted a mad laugh.

'Who are those people?' she asked.

'*Kurkuls.* Saboteurs. Hoarders,' the clerk answered without looking up. 'Going east. Every day these trains go east and mess up our schedules. Your train will be half an hour late – apologies, comrade.'

'That's fine, I can wait.'

Once on board, Debora settled by the window to watch the countryside. It was odd. In the past, peasant women would come to the tracks at every rural station, offering pickles, lard, boiled eggs and cheese pies for sale. But nobody approached the train this time. Every platform crawled with troops, and hardly anyone got on or off. The few villagers she saw had sunken, spent eyes. And there was a stench, an unfamiliar stench that she couldn't quite recognise.

She reached Pisky in the late afternoon. Though she had received no reply to her telegram, she still half expected Olena to be there to greet her.

The platform was empty, except for a dozen uninterested soldiers. Their job was to prevent people from leaving, not arriving. Debora left her suitcase at the station and, clutching the toy, walked into the snow-covered road outside. She scanned it for horse carts, looking for a villager who could give her a ride to Olena's home. She hoped she still remembered the way.

But there were no villagers or carts. The streets were deserted. Only the former church appeared inhabited, its chimney spewing out thin smoke. It should be warm inside, she figured as she headed to the building, trying not to slip on ice.

As she pushed open the front door, the reek of diarrhoea and rot punched her in the face. A short, bald man sat by the entrance, behind a scratched wooden desk. 'Good morning, I've just arrived on the train from Kharkiv,' Debora said by way of introduction.

'From the inspection commission?' the man asked. He stared at the pink dog, bewildered.

'From the university,' she replied confidently.

'Ah.' The man clicked his tongue. City women didn't come often to Pisky. He had been told that important guests from Kharkiv would arrive this week. He didn't quite know whether this was one of them, but decided to be helpful just in case.

'What can I do for you, comrade?'

'I'm here for the Tkach family.'

A shrill sound from the depths of the building eclipsed their conversation. Then there was banging and more wailing, this time in a different pitch.

'What is that?' Debora asked, her eyes wide.

'That's what you came for. Tkach.'

'I don't understand.'

'Tkach?'

'Yes . . .'

'Come with me.' The man got up.

Debora followed him into what used to be the priest's quarters behind the altar. A bored soldier sat on a stool. Behind him, she spotted four women chained to a bench. The youngest had her hair covered with a shawl. She seemed bloated, with round cheeks and a cracked lip. Her eyes were closed.

Debora gasped.

'This one is Tkach.' The man pointed.

Olena sensed Debora's presence and opened her eyes. They were glazed over, the eyes of a different person. Her mouth slowly widened in a grin, the same slightly crooked teeth, but now unfamiliar and frightening. She sized up Debora, examined the toy dog, and then cackled in a long, hoarse bout of laughter.

'You, you!' she bawled. 'You've come to me after all. You did. With a gift, a real big-city gift! From the Central Department Store?'

She tried to get up and come closer, to offer a hug, but the soldier sprang to his feet and hit her in the stomach with his rifle butt. 'Get back, you murderous cow.' He spat on the ground.

Olena stumbled, fell and curled up in pain, whimpering. The other women broke out in loud, satisfied laughter. 'And who is this tasty bird?' one of them shouted, staring at Debora. Another yanked Olena's chain.

'Why are you beating her?' was the only thing Debora could say to the guard. The words came out so softly it was as if she hadn't said them at all.

'Who is she?' the soldier asked the bald attendant, glaring at Debora. 'She's not supposed to be here. Get her out, now.'

'She said she is from the committee sent by Kharkiv,' the attendant replied.

'I *am* from Kharkiv,' she insisted.

Taking advantage of the distraction, Olena bounced up with unexpected energy and spat into the soldier's face. He hit her again, harder, and she fell down once more. 'You can keep hitting me, I don't care,' she muttered. 'I am no longer a person. I am unbreakable. I don't feel pain. Nobody can hurt me.'

The attendant squeezed Debora's elbow. 'We'd better go back, comrade,' he whispered. 'We don't want any trouble.'

Debora followed him obediently back to the entrance.

'What is this?' she asked, the toy still in her hands, the only hint of colour in the dark church. 'What is happening?'

'You mean Tkach? You don't know? She made soup. Soup. From her own son,' the man said.

Debora didn't understand. 'What soup?'

'Soup. First she hacked her mother to pieces to feed herself and her son. There wasn't much flesh left to eat by then. Only the organs remained juicy – the heart, the liver. Then, when the mother ran out, she smothered her child and made soup out of him. Taras, that was his name. Nice little boy.'

Debora leaned against the wall.

'Fourth such case in recent weeks. Nobody lets their kids

outside any more. I certainly don't,' the man continued. Unlike ordinary villagers, he could count on official rations because of his job. They were meagre but – if supplemented by snails and bony fish from the pond – would be sufficient to get him through the winter. 'Funny thing, now that they've been arrested and are awaiting their trains to the prison, they will actually be fed. They'll get more bread than the rest of them. Where's justice?'

'How long ago did this happen?'

'Oh, a week or so. They're holding them here until the commission arrives,' the man went on. He paused. 'You're not from the commission, are you?'

'Not really,' Debora admitted.

'You'd better not stay. Get the first train out,' he said, suddenly alarmed. 'Yes, better not linger here much longer. Problems for both of us.' His eyes narrowed with fear as he thought about being stripped of his rations.

Debora nodded. Another animal shriek pierced the air.

As she trudged back to the train station, the sky was clear and the village was bathed in a warm sunset light that coloured the snow orange and pink. Everything seemed so placid, so pleasant. Her mind wandered to her last time with Olena, to that kiss, to the taste of her lips. She remembered helping to wash Taras, his soft skin, his baby hair. Zinaida, always with her delicious treats. The reality was so absurd, so outlandish, that she refused to believe it. That half-animal half-person in chains, that couldn't really be Olena, *her* Olena, could it?

The toy dog in her hands was so ridiculous, so *useless*. How had she not come here earlier, much earlier, with bundles of food that she knew how to get, the parcels that her father sent? The signs were everywhere, she had known for weeks about the famine, she had seen the gaunt, frozen corpses on Kharkiv's streets. How could she not have realised, not rushed to save Olena, to save

Taras, to save the old woman? Why didn't she pay more attention, so caught up in her own egoistical routines? Why did she not become alarmed by Olena's missing letters? Why?

A man in a leather jacket, a pistol attached to his belt, interrupted her thoughts. He barred the entrance to the station. 'You're not from here, are you?' he said, pronouncing a verdict rather than asking a question. The city toy in her hands was a clear giveaway.

'No, I think I got off at the wrong station by mistake,' she replied. 'I need to get to Kyiv.' She showed him her assignment letter to Kyiv University, and her permission to change residence.

He examined the papers carefully. City people. Documents in order. He was too busy to bother anyway.

'Yes, you are at completely the wrong station. The next train in your direction is in two hours. You can wait in the cafeteria, though I doubt they will have anything other than hot water,' he said politely. 'I wouldn't recommend leaving the station. You never know what might happen here at night. For your own safety.'

Debora followed his advice. She sent a telegram to her parents, and two hours later, she was lying on an upper bunk bed on the Kyiv-bound train.

The train approached the shimmering Dnipro river in the early morning. The sun was already up. The sparkling expanse of ice and snow, set against the blue sky, almost blinded Debora as she looked through the fogged-up window. Straight ahead, on the other side of the river, the gold-domed Kyiv Lavra monastery towered atop the wooded ridge that contained a labyrinth of caves filled with the mummies of Orthodox saints.

Once the train crossed the Dnipro and came to a stop with a loud whistle, Debora tried to leave the pink dog behind. But

85

the carriage attendant ran after her, waving it: 'Young lady, you forgot something that's yours.'

'That's not mine,' Debora replied rudely.

'Of course it's yours,' the woman said with clear suspicion, squeezing the toy to probe whether anything illicit had been hidden inside.

'Take it. I don't want it,' Debora insisted.

Shaking her head, the woman walked away. Who would throw out a perfectly nice toy?

Gersh and Rebecca, who were waiting for Debora on the platform, were puzzled by the scene but didn't say anything. They all hugged, and Gersh picked up her suitcase. Debora tried to act normal, fielding questions that seemed to be about matters so trifling, so irrelevant that she could hardly focus on her replies. She soon gave up, after walking into her parents' apartment and seeing the spread that awaited her.

'I can't eat, I'm sorry,' she said, feeling light-headed. She headed to the bedroom, tucking herself under the blanket, still fully clothed. 'I'm sorry, I'm just not feeling well.'

Rebecca followed her into the room. 'What's wrong, sweetheart? What's going on? You're not yourself.'

Debora, who had resisted crying until now, broke down in her mother's arms.

'What's going on with us? What *is* happening? What have we become?' she sobbed. 'Do you know that people out there, good people, are turning into cannibals? They *eat* people. And nobody says anything, nobody is even talking about it. How is that possible?'

Rebecca had already heard the rumours of horrible things going on in the villages but had chosen not to pay attention. There was nothing to be gained from knowing too much. Now she listened silently as Debora spoke about Olena, about

86

the dead child, about the stench of death that still burned her nostrils.

'These are hard times,' she said as she stroked her daughter's hair. 'Hard times. And in hard times we must survive and be strong. Thank God you are now here with us, that your father got us moved to Kyiv. Together we will pull through all of this, God willing.'

'I should have known. I should have gone to Olena earlier with food, not that useless toy. I could have saved them,' Debora wept. 'I could have.'

'No, nobody could have saved them. Nobody. We are up against history. History is a wild and bloodthirsty animal. It is on a rampage through this country again, breaking and remaking it anew. You can't stand in its way, and you can't stop it. All you can hope is that it misses you as it lashes out and claws its way forward. That it doesn't notice you. That it crushes someone else. All you can do is try to be invisible. Invisible to survive.'

'It's a terrible world,' Debora said. 'How did it become this way?'

'I don't know,' Rebecca replied. 'But among animals, it has always been like that. Maybe we were mistaken to think we humans were different.'

PART TWO

14

Kyiv, April 1933

Springtime in Kyiv came abruptly, and the city rushed to embrace it like a lost child. As icicles started falling from roofs, sometimes causing grievous harm to the inattentive passers-by, streets turned muddy and dirty water trickled down from the hilltops. Housewives unsealed the windows that had remained closed throughout the winter, and fresh air poured into the stuffy apartments. Municipal workers carted off piles of grey snow and ice in wheelbarrows, to slowly melt and die out of sight. One by one, buds appeared on the chestnut trees that overlooked the city's boulevards, in preparation for the flush of blooms that would carpet Kyiv with pink and white petals come summer.

The end of the winter also meant the end of the famine. Late in April, the land started producing new food, with cabbages, onions and strawberries ripening in the fields. Debora no longer saw dead villagers collected by municipal crews in the mornings. The routine of returning to her studies was a distraction from her dark thoughts. Slowly but inevitably, she began to forget about Olena and Larysa, and her Kharkiv life. Whenever she noticed a plane in the sky, however, a thought about Samuel – no matter how fleeting – still crossed her mind. Sometimes it seemed to her that she had spotted him in a crowd, among men streaming to a soccer match, at the exit from the cinema, in the tram. But it was always someone else. She knew his address – if it was still his address – but was far too proud to go looking for him.

On this Sunday afternoon, she rode a tram to the city's main avenue, Khreshchatyk. Sunshine caressed her cheek through the window. She didn't have any particular plans: it was the first really warm day of the spring, perfect for an aimless stroll and window-shopping. The tram was nearly empty. A man in mud-stained boots climbed aboard with a curse and, ignoring all the available seats, headed towards her with an unsteady gait. He grabbed her by the shoulder as he fell into the seat next to hers. 'Morning, beautiful,' he beamed. 'What's your name?'

'Morning's long gone.' Debora stared at him icily.

He tried to touch her leg, but she intercepted him by the wrist and returned his sweaty hand to his lap.

'You, my friend, it looks like you've had too much to drink again. What's your wife going to say, huh?'

The man's eyes signalled confusion.

'How do you know about Masha?' he asked. 'Are you that girl who works with her?'

Debora got up and yielded her seat. 'Here, just make yourself comfortable. I won't tell Masha anything.' She winked.

'Is there a problem?' She heard a loud, commanding voice behind her. 'Is someone bothering you, comrade?'

It was a familiar voice.

'No, comrade, everything is under control,' she replied as she turned her head.

Samuel was even more handsome than she had remembered. He had matured – his face looked chiselled now, his gaze more confident, his moustache fuller and immaculately trimmed. The red square of an air force lieutenant graced his collar straps.

'You?' She exhaled. 'You?'

'Dear comrade, I am star-struck by your ravishing beauty,' he said, as if he had been rehearsing this conversation for years.

Debora was lost for a moment, swinging between anger and joy. Then she smiled back.

'Do you say that to all the girls, comrade?'

'Not at all, just you,' he grinned. 'Comrade.'

He hugged her and kissed her on the cheek. He smelled of aftershave, and of the comforting, uncomplicated past. They sat down together at the other end of the tram.

'I hadn't realised you were in Kyiv these days. Why haven't you written? I was actually looking for you in Kharkiv, you know. Are you visiting? How long for?'

She wanted to be cold and hurtful, but found herself unable to do so.

'Can I buy you an ice cream? Offer you a movie ticket?' he went on. '*Circus*? Have you seen *Circus* yet?'

Posters for the comedy film were all over town, its protagonists dressed in shiny white overalls and winged helmets, with the famous actress Lyubov Orlova turned into a Marlene Dietrich lookalike.

'No, not yet,' she replied. 'I've heard it's pretty good.'

'Shall we go, then?'

'Right now?'

'Of course right now.' He opened his arms. 'This is the moment. I'm dropping all my very important business to be at your service, comrade.'

The important business was a date with a giggly secretary who would wait for him in vain all afternoon.

Debora pretended to be undecided, even though she was

already imagining the two of them in the back of the movie hall. Samuel pulled her off her seat and they jumped out of the tram at the stop by the Spartak Cinema on Khreshchatyk. With half an hour left until the next screening, he purchased two scoops of expensive ice cream. He listened as she recounted, briefly, her move to Kyiv. He didn't mention their break-up, and neither did she. But he made sure to slip in that he wasn't seeing anyone else.

'Single as a monk these days. What about you?' he asked.

'Well, it's hard to find interesting men.'

'I can be very interesting.'

She didn't want to seem to encourage him, but couldn't control her smile. 'Maybe too interesting for me.'

'Time to go in.' He got up, checking his watch.

Once inside Spartak's cool, welcoming darkness, Samuel headed straight to the back row. It seemed natural for Debora to be following him there, the movie routine honed so many times before. In the opening scene, Orlova's character, an acrobat hounded by a lynch mob in an imaginary Sunnyville, USA, ran for her life clutching a black child. Minutes later, Samuel clicked his tongue appreciatively at the feats of the Moscow Circus's animals and athletes. Debora, who had never met a black person, couldn't help crying as the exiled American found love and acceptance in the Soviet Union. Once the boy was passed around to hear lullabies in several languages, including Yiddish, the circus director held him aloft: 'In our country, we love all children, black or white, red or blue, even pink with stripes or grey with polka dots!'

By then Debora's hand was already nestled in Samuel's. She didn't know how it had happened.

For days after that, she kept humming the movie's catchy theme song. *'My country's wide and full of forests, fields and rivers,'* it went. *'I don't know of any other country where a man would breathe as freely as he breathes here.'*

94

They went to the movies again the following Sunday. Samuel kissed her as soon as the opening credits started to roll. She had vowed not to let him, but lost her resolve a second after his eager, probing tongue touched her lips. She was angry with herself, but then let it happen again, and again.

After the movie, they went for a walk in the park. Debora finally felt able to speak about her trip to Pisky. Ukraine's famine was a prohibited topic, she knew. Yet she decided after the kiss that she should trust Samuel. You couldn't hide your thoughts from everyone.

He listened quietly as she recounted the smallest details, something she hadn't done with her parents. He wasn't surprised. 'I've heard of these things. We've been sent to the villages too, to confiscate grain. We found only dead bodies, spent all our time digging graves,' he said. 'Best to forget about this now. The famine is finished. It's in the past, and there is nothing we can do about it.'

'How can I forget Olena?' Debora disagreed. 'How?'

'You must,' Samuel replied. 'To keep going ahead, we must know how to leave things behind. Like I left Sasha behind after what he did to Larysa. We used to be friends, but not any more.'

'Sasha? What did he do?' Her voice trembled. How much did he know?

'You haven't heard? He testified against Larysa, disowned her, so that he could thrive in the Organs. Bought his new job with her blood.' He spat on the ground with disgust. 'A worm.'

'How terrible.' Debora squeezed his elbow. I can never tell him what I have done, she thought. Never.

She leaned towards him and gave him a deep, guilty kiss. 'I am thankful to fate,' she said as she pulled back. 'Fate has brought us back together.'

'Yes,' he replied. 'So lucky.'

*

A few days later, Rebecca asked Debora point-blank over breakfast: 'Sweetheart, anything you want to tell me?'

'What do you mean?'

'You're like a cat in springtime, all bouncy, and spending hours in front of the mirror, with that dumb happy smile that I haven't seen on your lips in a while. What is that? Are you seeing a man?'

'You're a regular Sherlock Holmes, Mama,' Debora laughed. 'Yes. Samuel. Again. We bumped into each other by accident.'

'He forgave you after you dumped him last year?'

She had forgotten that she'd never told her parents the truth.

'Yes, Mama, he's open-minded like that.'

'He must really like you then,' Rebecca concluded. 'Is it serious?'

'I don't know.' Debora shrugged. 'Maybe.'

'Maybe . . . Well, maybe you should invite the gentleman over to meet us.'

The apartment building on Shevchenko Boulevard where they lived had been built before the revolution, and was meant for a different era, a time when the city's moneyed professionals vacationed in Montreux, benefactors established libraries and museums, and women at the opera tried to impress each other with the newest French fashions. Each apartment had five or six bedrooms, plus a small room or two for the servants. In the big cities of Soviet Ukraine, nobody – except for the few men at the very pinnacle of power – had the luxury of having an entire such apartment for themselves.

Debora's father, a man of relative importance but nowhere near that pinnacle, was allocated a generous three bedrooms, one of which he transformed into a living room where Yakov occasionally slept on the couch. Another was now for Debora's exclusive use, the first time she had enjoyed such privacy since childhood. The kitchen and the toilet, however, were shared with the apartment's other residents, which meant that Gersh and Rebecca kept the family's considerable food stocks in a locked cupboard in the living room. Since every family paid for electricity separately, the toilet had three light bulbs, with a switch for each.

The apartment's original owner, known as Pani Helga, was a shrivelled grey-haired woman of noble German lineage who had been foolish enough to remain in Kyiv when she could still get out and rejoin her sons and grandsons, currently living in Königsberg. She rarely left her room, which lay at the end of the corridor, and seemed to subsist on biscuits and tea. The other family consisted of a mid-ranking editor at the *Visti* newspaper, Ostap Boyko, his two perpetually bickering boys, and his pregnant wife, Halyna, who had become accustomed to having the kitchen pretty much to herself. The previous resident of the rooms assigned to the Rosenbaums, a noted Kyiv sculptor, had been arrested and sent to the camps as a 'bourgeois nationalist', in part because of a long letter the Boykos had dispatched to the OGPU detailing his deviant conversations maligning the brotherly Russian people, and his even more deviant seduction of young and innocent models, male and female, from vulnerable proletarian backgrounds.

The Boykos, who occupied one room and considered that fact to be painfully and self-evidently unfair, had expected that at least one of the sculptor's rooms – if not all three – would be reassigned to them. But they had obtained no immediate reward for their efforts, and were galled to see the Rosenbaums move in instead. Rebecca claiming her share of the kitchen was a particularly painful affront. Any hopes for further reallocation were dashed with Debora's arrival. Still, they remained welcoming and polite. One never knew.

*

Samuel showed up two weeks later at the Shevchenko Boulevard apartment in his neatly pressed uniform, bringing flowers and a bottle of brandy. He showered compliments on everyone, even Pani Helga and Halyna – who looked at the young officer with a mix of faint suspicion and lust. He was visibly impressed by the Rosenbaums' living arrangements, inspecting the elaborate plaster decorations on the ceiling, the arched windows, and the Bukhara carpet they had brought from Uman. He sat down carefully on the edge of the leather couch, as if trying it out. This was the kind of apartment the young lieutenant could only aspire to once he had risen through the ranks to become a colonel, if then.

Rebecca had cooked all afternoon, and the dinner of roast lamb, cheese dumplings and assorted appetisers went well beyond what Samuel had been accustomed to in the air force canteen. He repeatedly complimented Rebecca on her haircut, and discussed world affairs with Gersh, endorsing every one of his opinions. That man Hitler who'd just come to power in Germany was a temporary aberration, Gersh explained. Gersh had been to Germany back in the day and was certain that he knew the country well. They were very civilised people. 'Yes,' Samuel nodded. 'No way will the German proletariat stand for that idiot.'

Only Yakov disagreed. 'I think you two are fooling yourselves. A war is coming, and it won't be easy.'

'Come on,' Samuel shot back. 'Haven't you seen the new tanks, the new planes that we're building these days? Nobody can beat us. The Red Army is invincible. We will crush anyone.'

He settled back contentedly and, after a few more shots of vodka, talked about how much he enjoyed flying. 'You are there in the air, free from everything. You are stronger than nature, nothing is beyond reach.'

'I just can't imagine it,' Rebecca said with admiration. 'Aren't you afraid you will fall down?'

'Mama!' Debora interrupted. 'Of course he won't fall down.'

After dinner, as Rebecca washed dishes, Gersh told her that he approved of the young man. 'He seems solid. A bright fellow.'

'I don't know. He's just a bit too eager to please,' she replied. 'A slick boy.'

'Nobody will ever be good enough for you,' he laughed.

'True,' she agreed.

Magnolias and lilac trees were in full bloom, petals already falling on the succulent grass and perfuming the air, when Samuel met up with Debora in the Kyiv Botanical Garden, just behind the red-painted university building. The exotic plants all around had burst into exuberant growth, making up for lost time during their winter slumber. He stopped by an ancient oak tree in a remote corner of the park, bowed theatrically and kneeled.

'Is this what I'm thinking?' she asked, her eyes widening. She hadn't expected it, at least not this fast.

'You're so smart. I can never surprise you.'

'So?'

'Debora Rosenbaum, will you be my wife and live with me happily ever after?'

'This is so quick . . .'

'Why wait? Why put it off?' Samuel opened his arms. 'If it's meant to be, it's meant to be.'

'But how do I know that you won't abandon me again?'

'I won't.' He turned solemn. 'No matter what, I will always be there for you. If we are ever separated, I will always come back for you. You would have to chase me away with a pitchfork. You won't get rid of me. It's a promise.'

'With a pitchfork?' She laughed and kissed him.

She wanted to play hard to get, to delay her reply, but couldn't control the grin of unbridled delight that spread across her face. 'Let's do it,' she said. 'For ever and ever.'

15

Kyiv, September 1933

They hired a small river steamboat for their wedding and invited only a few dozen people, mostly Debora's university friends and Samuel's air force buddies. They didn't even think of inviting Sasha, or anyone else they used to know in Kharkiv. Their past life was best left behind and forgotten.

The ceremony was strictly secular, of course – officiated by the municipal clerk rather than a rabbi. Before they began, Rebecca handed Debora a necklace made of snake-shaped pieces of gold studded with rubies, sapphires and emeralds.

'My mother gave me this the day I got married, and I am giving it to you on the day you are getting married. She had it made in Venice, on her own honeymoon. Pass it on to your child, God willing,' she said.

Samuel clicked his tongue. 'You look like a true princess in this, my love. A Venetian princess.'

Debora beamed, hugging them both.

A band started playing and the party kicked off. Once everyone was sufficiently drunk, Samuel's friends hoisted up the chairs with the groom and the bride and danced with them on their shoulders. It was not easy on a moving boat, but being soldiers, they all had strong legs and backs. The musicians they'd hired didn't need any encouragement and broke into one merry Yiddish song after another.

Samuel moved into Debora's room in the morning, carting a box of his possessions up the staircase. The neighbours didn't appreciate his arrival. 'Soon they will have children and there will be no room for anyone any more,' Halyna whispered into her husband's ear.

'There's already a queue to get into the toilet every morning,' he grunted. 'Terrible. So unfair.' He suffered from constipation and didn't like having to rush.

But Debora and Samuel didn't have children at first. She wanted to finish her studies so that she could teach. He was often away, flying on training missions – some all the way on the Chinese border in Siberia. Debora often felt a tingling of guilt when the doorbell rang and he walked in after these assignments, sometimes bearing small gifts from faraway cities. What had she done to deserve this happiness?

Like everyone else, she was aware of the tragedies occurring every day, of the black cars rolling up in the dead of night to arrest the latest batch of enemies of the state. Newspapers were filled with reports about unmasked saboteurs and foreign agents, and about their executions. Distant acquaintances kept vanishing without warning, disappearances that were not to be mentioned or discussed in public. Yet Debora's immediate circle seemed to be sheltered inside some magic cocoon. In fact, their lives were getting better. There had been bountiful harvests, and the food rationing system had gone. Delicacies reappeared on restaurant menus. Kyiv, which had regained its status as Ukraine's national capital, buzzed with new life as theatres, libraries and museums were transferred from Kharkiv.

Private lives could be out of synch with history, at least for a while. One could relish private happiness in the middle of a national tragedy. But it wasn't easy to extinguish the fear.

'I worry sometimes,' Debora told Samuel after they'd made love. 'There is so much misery out there. How long can we remain shielded? How long can we stay so blissful? I fear every day that it may end, just like that, puff and it's gone.'

'Silly, all will be perfect now. You will be bored with our happiness,' he replied, spooning with her and kissing the nape of her neck, his moustache brushing against her skin.

'Yes, happiness is boring,' she laughed. 'All the happy families, they look the same, while every unhappy one is unhappy in its own manner,' she added, quoting *Anna Karenina*'s opening line to him.

He hadn't read the book. But as he lay in bed, sprawled on his back like a well-fed cat, he thought that he was, in fact, happy. Was he in love? Yes, he thought, this is what love feels like.

'You bring me joy,' he said.

Samuel had other reasons to be satisfied with life. He had advanced in rank, with the two squares of a full lieutenant on his uniform, and moved on to flying the new I-15 fighter planes. It was a great time to be a pilot – one of Stalin's Falcons, as they were usually called in newsreels. Everyone admired the pilots who rescued the stranded crew of the SS *Chelyuskin*, landing on drifting Arctic ice. Movie-goers gasped in disbelief as they watched Chkalov the ace fly his plane upside-down. At times, Debora feared that Samuel had become too cocky, too careless.

Her brother wasn't doing as well, and was envious of Samuel's luck. Because of his deteriorating eyesight, Yakov was likely to be assigned to office work in the Kyiv military district, rather than to the new battleship of his dreams. That was a depressing thought, especially once it was suggested to him that he might have to work in the military district's food supply department – following in his father's footsteps. Gersh, however, was secretly relieved.

Samuel tried to cheer him up. 'Don't worry, if there is war, everyone will be on the front lines with a rifle,' he said. 'We'll all have plenty of glory then.'

Debora's teaching career didn't begin as expected. All those years at university, she had imagined the day she would step into the classroom for the first time. The day she would read aloud Gogol's tales, tales that would make children giggle about the hidden devils, the adventures of drowned maidens and the counters of dead souls. The day she would see them recite the poems of Lermontov, the romantic young officer who had achieved so much before dying at the age of twenty-six, and whose thin moustache reminded her of Samuel's. If she gained enough confidence, she might one day even share some extracurricular verse about tragic love by Anna Akhmatova, or maybe Marina Tsvetaeva, verse from old books that had been published before the new edicts on socialist realism and that she knew by heart.

But there was no room for extracurricular literature at the school where she started as a middle-grade teacher in September 1936. The library had just been purged of ideologically tainted volumes. The deputy director who greeted her, a tall, wiry man named Roman, offered some carefully worded advice. 'Before you do or say anything in the classroom, dear Debora, please think about how you might be misunderstood. Misinterpreted. There is no need for improvisation, let's just stick to instructions, word by word.'

The first literary work she was required to teach was about Pavlik Morozov, the country's new hero, whose statue had just been unveiled near Moscow's Red Square. The twelve-year-old boy, a role model to be emulated by all Soviet children, had

104

courageously denounced his own father to the authorities for hoarding grain and conspiring with anti-revolutionary elements. For this, according to the official version, he had been brutally murdered in the woods by his grandfather.

'After losing such a fighter in our ranks, our children will burn with hatred for his killers,' she led the class in recital. 'No example is better for all children than Pavlik the courageous pioneer.'

She wasn't surprised that all her twelve-year-old students wrote in their essays that they too would report on their relatives should they turn out to be part of a counter-revolutionary conspiracy. She marked the essays with disgust, but inevitably gave the highest grades to those who showed the most zeal. Those were the rules, and who was she to ignore them?

In December, she woke up dizzy-headed and ran straight to the bathroom to throw up. After it happened again the next day, Rebecca looked at her knowingly and with unusual warmth. 'You should probably see a doctor,' she said. It was an accident – Debora and Samuel had used precautions – but one they were both happy about. In any case, they had little choice. Abortions, free and widespread in the past, were now banned: Stalin desired to replenish his state's decimated population.

A few days later, Samuel's new orders arrived. He was being transferred to the airfield in Zhytomyr, near the western border. It was a promotion, and it was close enough to visit on weekends. The housing there would be basic at first, he told her. Until the baby was born, it was best for her to stay in Kyiv with her parents. She would finish the academic year – her first year of teaching – and then join him in Zhytomyr. Now that he was going to become a senior lieutenant, it would be easier to arrange a transfer. There appeared to be plenty of vacancies in the Zhytomyr school district.

*

A few weeks later, as Rebecca shopped for sauerkraut and pickled cucumbers in the Bessarabka market, haggling with stocky farmer women who displayed their wares on slabs of black granite, she noticed two familiar faces at a nearby stall. Sasha's father, the maths teacher from Uman, walked slowly with a cane. His wife's hair was tinted a near-purple hue and she was wrapped in a pricey fur coat. The father seemed irritated, but the mother was pleased to see Rebecca. 'Ha, just like in Uman,' she laughed. 'Remember how many times we bumped into each other in the vegetable market there? So, how are the children?' she went on.

Rebecca briefly mentioned the wedding, and Debora's academic successes. But she was afraid of bringing bad luck and didn't talk about her daughter's pregnancy. She also tried to say as little as possible about Yakov. 'And Sasha, how is he getting on? Settled in here?' she asked breezily.

Sasha's father frowned. The mother, seeming not to notice his disapproval, was eager to reply. 'Actually, things have turned out really well for him. He's becoming very senior. Very. We live in a large apartment, in Pechersk. He even has a car now. We're so happy for him,' she beamed. 'Engels Street 15. Apartment 6. You should come visit for tea one of these days. I'll bake a cherry cake. Tell Gersh and Debora and Samuel and Yakov to come too. I am sure Sasha would love to see them all.'

Sasha's father was getting impatient. 'We have to go,' he interrupted his wife.

'It was so pleasant to see you. Yes, we will definitely come by soon,' Rebecca replied. She didn't really mean it.

16

Kyiv, February 1937

'I'm going to Spain,' Samuel whispered into Debora's ear when he returned to Kyiv on one of his frequent weekend trips.

'Spain? To war?' She was alarmed.

Soviet pilots were already fighting, technically as volunteers, in the Spanish Civil War. His unit would likely sail from Odessa before April, hidden with its planes in the bowels of a Soviet cargo ship heading to Valencia.

'It's only for six months. I will be back before the baby is born. And they will pay us in hard currency, so we will be set up for life. It's good money. This won't be dangerous at all,' he lied as she remained silent. 'All we're going to do is to teach the Spanish comrades how to fly and how to maintain the aircraft. I won't be anywhere near the front lines. We're not that involved.'

'I don't know, I have a bad feeling about it,' Debora said. 'Do you really have to go?'

'Don't worry, it will be fine, and I will be back in no time.' He hugged her and patted her belly. 'You'll see.'

'I'd rather you didn't go,' she replied tersely. 'We don't need the money.'

'It's not just about the money.'

'I know,' she sighed. 'I know.'

'Don't tell anyone. It's a secret.'

After dinner with Debora's family in the apartment's living room, Samuel couldn't resist talking about the civil war. The struggles of the beleaguered Spanish Republic, after all, were all over the news. He sprawled on the sofa, a drink in his hand, and argued with Gersh and Yakov. Debora and Rebecca were cleaning up and ferrying the dirty dishes and leftovers to the kitchen. The door to the living room remained open.

There was no way the republic would be defeated, Samuel said. Now that international volunteers from around the world had started arriving, preventing the fall of Madrid, the war was bound to turn against Franco and his fascist allies. 'I know what I'm talking about,' he added for effect. 'Trust me.'

Gersh had been reading reports from Spain in the Soviet newspapers, and was less optimistic. 'I don't know,' he said. 'Looks like the Trotskyites are still very strong there, especially in Catalonia. Nothing good can come out of that. They are bound to become another fifth column.'

Gersh profoundly disliked Trotsky. At least Stalin respected some basic institutions of life, like family and marriage. Gersh didn't forget how Trotsky used to rail against the family hearth. How did he label it again? 'An archaic, stagnant and stuffy institution in which the working woman is enslaved from childhood to death.'

Yakov backed his father. 'With their stupidity, Trotsky and his people in Spain will hand over the republic to the fascists,' he said.

Samuel topped up his glass and responded loudly. 'I'll agree that Trotsky is a bastard, but he's a damn smart bastard. Let's be honest – he, not Stalin, led the Red Army to all its victories after the revolution. Damn, he *created* the Red Army. We all know that. He even designed the hats we still wear. So yes, a bastard maybe, but he's not a dummy.'

'You should be careful saying those things.' Yakov cut him off.

'Ah, come on, I have nothing to hide here.' Samuel waved him away. 'Everyone knows that Trotsky's a genius.'

He didn't notice that Boyko, the journalist neighbour, had returned home minutes earlier. Hearing Trotsky's name mentioned, he took an unusually long and quiet time taking off his boots in the corridor, just by the living room's open door. He listened to the entire conversation and was eager to share it with his wife.

After quietly shuffling past the living room door into his own quarters, he whispered into Halyna's ear what he had just witnessed. She listened carefully, then got up, opened a drawer and handed him a sheet of ruled paper.

'Write,' she said. 'What are you waiting for? You're a writer, right? Then write.'

17

Kyiv, May 1937

At first, the only sign of something amiss was that Samuel didn't make it into the initial batch of pilots sailing to Spain. 'Don't pay any attention, you'll go in the next one,' the base commander told him breezily.

But then spring arrived, and strange things started happening.

On 1 May, the leadership of the Ukrainian Soviet Socialist Republic gathered on a newly erected podium, under banners in all major European languages that flapped in the wind, to observe the military parade in honour of International Workers' Solidarity Day. The commander of the Kyiv military district, General Yakir, the Swiss-educated son of a Jewish pharmacist, towered above the other notables, flashing an unsuspecting smile as row after row of troops marched by, their freshly polished bayonets glinting under the sun.

Debora watched the parade from her window, looking on as light armoured vehicles and cars topped with machine-gun turrets drove up the boulevard, followed by columns of soldiers and then navy cadets in white uniforms. It took an entire squad to hold a building-sized poster that proclaimed: *Envy me – I am a citizen of the USSR!* Flying above it all were several dozen biplanes. Piloting one of them, as far as Debora knew, was Samuel.

The plan was for Samuel to join them in the early afternoon once the parade was finished and the planes had landed for the day at the Kyiv military airport. He had told Debora he could stay the night, and Rebecca had spent the previous three days cooking an elabourate May Day dinner.

Samuel didn't come in the afternoon.

He didn't come in the evening, either.

There could be many innocuous reasons for this – a military pilot, after all, was never the master of his own time – but Debora couldn't stop worrying. They pushed dinner from seven to eight, and then from eight to nine. As they finally sat down to eat, in silence, she glanced at her watch every few minutes, willing the doorbell to ring.

The bell only rang at four in the morning, and when Gersh opened the door, standing behind it were three uniformed troops wearing the insignia of the NKVD, or the People's Commissariat of Internal Affairs, the newest acronym of the dreaded security Organs. Two of them held rifles with bayonets attached to the barrel. The senior officer, eyes bloodshot from too many sleepless nights, shoved Gersh aside and strode into the apartment. 'Here's the warrant we need to search the room of Citizen Groysman,' he said. 'Which one is it?'

Gersh was slow to respond. Woken by the noise, Boyko, wearing a sleeveless T-shirt, peered out of his room. Seeing the NKVD men, he ducked back inside. 'Finally,' he whispered in his wife's ear. 'But we'd better not get involved.'

'So where is that room?' the NKVD officer asked impatiently. 'We don't have all night.'

By then, Debora was also awake. She stepped out into the corridor, holding her belly.

111

'What's going on? Why are you here?' she asked.

'First of all, I am the one asking questions here. Second, please step aside and let us do our job.' He motioned the two troopers into the room, and they got to work rifling through books and pulling out drawers. Debora watched motionless as they sifted through her underwear and nightgowns and poked the floorboards looking for secret compartments.

'My husband doesn't really keep a lot of things here,' she said. 'It is all with him in Zhytomyr. Is he in trouble?'

'In trouble?' The officer whistled. He was really tired of doing this. This was his third wife tonight, and they all asked the same stupid questions. Though this one was by far the prettiest. 'In trouble? We wouldn't be here otherwise, would we?'

The troopers found some of Samuel's letters, all perfectly innocuous even in the unforgiving glare of hindsight, and put them along with some old books in a cardboard box. 'There is nothing else here,' one of them said.

'This is all a terrible mistake, Samuel couldn't have done anything wrong,' Gersh tried to interject. 'Don't worry, sweetie, this will be cleared up very soon.'

The officer lit his pipe. His lips curved into a wry smile.

'There is no such thing as a mistake. The Party doesn't make mistakes.'

He signed a receipt for the confiscated letters and books, and told Debora that she would be contacted in the coming days. She ran after him as he turned to leave. 'You can't just go like this, you have to tell me what he is being accused of. Where is he?'

'I can't?' He stared at her. 'You really think you can tell me what I can and cannot do?'

Once the NKVD men had left, slamming the door, Debora crumpled onto a chair in the corridor. Gersh, in his pyjamas, sat on the floor just across from her as Rebecca, not knowing what else to do, went into the kitchen to boil some sweet tea.

Halyna stepped out of her bedroom and looked at the scene with great disappointment. She had hoped that all the Rosenbaums, or at the very least Debora, would be gone. But the NKVD hadn't even searched Gersh's room, where she knew he was hoarding tin cans of stewed beef and who knew what else.

Pani Helga was also awake. She shuffled towards Debora and embraced her with her bony arms. 'Don't cry, my child,' she said in her crisp German accent. 'All will pass. This too shall pass.'

No one got in touch with Debora. At Samuel's military unit, nobody replied to her telegrams, or gave more than gruff and vague responses when she phoned from the post office. Three days after the NKVD raid, she packed a big bundle of food and clothes and headed to Zhytomyr with Rebecca. The train seemed to stop in every village. Upon arrival, they hired a horse carriage, sitting precariously as it swayed on the broken road.

Samuel's airfield was outside the city, in the overgrown countryside where sunflower plants were just beginning to lift their heads, their buds preparing to bloom. New fighter jets and bombers were visible on the runway behind the barbed wire. But the sentry – a Kyrgyz conscript – wouldn't even consider letting them in, or contacting his superiors.

'Forbidden,' he kept repeating. 'Need written permit. No permit, forbidden.'

'Look at me, I am a pregnant woman, I am just looking for my husband,' Debora argued, pushing up her belly. But the Kyrgyz was unmoved, and she wondered to what extent he actually understood what she was saying.

Dejected, they returned to the carriage. 'You too, huh?'

the driver sighed loudly. 'They've taken your husband away, haven't they?'

'How do you know?' Debora asked.

'You're not the first one I've driven here this week, and they didn't let any of you in,' he replied, scratching his shaggy beard. 'Though you're the first pregnant one. That's just too bad. Too bad.'

The driver was old enough to be her father. He took off his cap, brushed off the dust, and put it back on. Birds were chirping. A bee buzzed above the carriage. The horse peed in front of them and then stood immobile, as if asleep.

'What shall we do?' Debora wondered.

'I know where they take them. Want me to drive you there?'

'Please. Please, that would be so kind of you.'

He whipped the horse, which, with little enthusiasm, started trudging back to the city. The driver turned right at the train station and headed to a tsarist-era compound of faded brick buildings surrounded by walls topped with razor wire. 'That's where it is.' He pointed at the jail. 'Every cell packed with prisoners nowadays.'

A throng of women had massed outside, many of them holding bags and bundles. A bored-looking clerk sat behind a grille at the entrance. As Debora and Rebecca tried to approach the window, one of the women closest to it, in a peasant headscarf, hissed loudly, 'Where do you think you are going, madams?' – using a word that had become an insult after the revolution. 'We've been here since before dawn, and you think you can just march to the front? You think you are the only ones with a sorrow? Shame on you.'

Debora started to apologise, but Rebecca just led her to the back of the queue. 'Is this where the line begins?' she asked an older woman, whose bundle, she noticed, also contained several books.

'It's too late. You should probably come tomorrow – they make the list of names in the morning and won't see you today,' the woman explained helpfully. 'Then, when you come to the window, you can pass the food, the clothes and other items through. If your relative is inside, they will take them. If he's not, they will give them back to you. That's really all we can know.'

'Who do you have inside?' Rebecca asked. 'Your son? Your husband?'

The woman, warm and friendly until now, suddenly turned hostile. 'What is that to you? Why do you want to know?'

Another woman pulled them aside by their sleeves. She wore an embroidered shirt and a black headscarf, and spoke quietly but forcefully in a lilting village accent. 'Don't ever ask that kind of question. Everyone here thinks it's a mistake and that their men are innocent. The only innocent ones.'

'Well, my husband actually is innocent,' Debora said.

The woman chortled. 'You see! Innocent. Of course. Come tomorrow morning, sweetie, and God protect you.'

'Thank you,' Rebecca replied. 'And God help you too.'

'God, God, still going on about God,' Debora muttered once they were out of earshot. 'God doesn't help people like us.'

'Too late for today?' the driver asked them. 'Need a place to stay? I've got a spare room, won't cost you much.'

Debora and Rebecca dined on the bread and cheese they had brought from Kyiv and fell asleep early. Getting up before dawn, they headed back to the jail, staking out their spot in the line of women, each cocooned in a private tragedy that they all feared to share. It was only in the late afternoon that their turn finally arrived. Rebecca silently mouthed Hebrew prayers as they approached the window. Debora handed over her documents and a piece of paper with Samuel's full name and date of birth.

She held her breath as the clerk thumbed through his ledger.

Finally he looked up and, without a word, opened the side window through which Debora could pass her parcel. She was relieved – this was the first certainty since he had been detained. Now she knew where he was, and she knew that he was alive.

As she fussed with the parcel, an orderly knocked at a door at the back of the clerk's room. He brought in several typewritten sheets of paper. The clerk put them on his desk, scratched his head and sat down again. Waving the pen in his hand, he yelled at Debora: 'Hey, woman, you'll have to take your things back. Your husband is no longer here.'

She leaned on the window, feeling dizzy. 'What do you mean, not here? Where is he? What happened to him?'

'All I know is that he was here, and now he is gone. So don't waste anyone's time. Move along now. Next!'

The next woman in line, a visitor who had just arrived from far away, judging by the smell of her unwashed body, the kind of aroma that usually permeated long-distance trains, pushed Debora aside. Her eyes puffy from too much crying, she dropped her bundle by her feet and, with shaking hands, thrust her paperwork into the window.

'We should go now.' Rebecca took her daughter by the arm and gently guided her to the horse carriage.

They travelled in silence back to Kyiv. The baby in Debora's womb was restless, and she winced as the little feet kicked her from the inside.

18

Kyiv, August 1937

Pasha took the first gasp of air into his lungs and erupted in a desperate cry just before midnight in the maternity ward of a new Kyiv hospital. Debora, fighting off pain, put the baby, so small, so vulnerable, on her chest. He moved his tiny fingers slowly, purring, his brain still adjusting to the sensory overload. Did he look like Samuel? She stared at his face, searching for familiar features. Wrinkled and hairless, her son looked more like an extraterrestrial creature, she concluded.

She still had no news about Samuel. Nurses at the hospital had mistaken Yakov, who brought her flowers, for Pasha's father. Nobody bothered to correct them.

Word of Samuel's arrest had filtered down to Debora's school, and when Roman stopped by the Shevchenko Boulevard apartment to congratulate her on the birth, he also delivered an unpleasant message. It just wouldn't be possible for her to come back as a teacher when term began on 1 September. 'I am sure you understand, but this is just the way things are,' he said, rubbing his nose nervously. 'Out of our hands. Anyway, it will give you more time with your son, so that's a good thing.'

This wasn't something Debora had expected. After a summer of waiting for news about Samuel, she was looking forward to going back to work, to momentarily forgetting her worries with something to do.

There were good reasons for worry. Just days after the May Day parade, General Yakir had been arrested, along with other senior military commanders across the USSR. Accused of plotting with Hitler and Trotsky to undermine the socialist Motherland, they were all executed to universal acclaim by mid June. Most of these 'traitors' had Jewish or Polish surnames. The wildest rumours were floating around, and after a while Debora decided not to think about what might have happened to Samuel until she encountered at least a shred of reliable information. Gersh's attempts to find out through his acquaintances led nowhere. Yakov, everyone agreed, shouldn't even try asking, so as not to draw attention to his family connection with a political detainee.

None of them suspected Boyko. Whenever the matter of Samuel's arrest came up in the apartment, he assured his neighbours that it was most certainly an absurd, regrettable mistake that would be rectified very soon.

Three weeks after Pasha's birth, Debora was just about able to fit into her best dress, a black-and-white number that now barely contained her breasts. She examined her curves in front of a mirror, pulled up her hair, and took the tram to Engels Street. It was a sunny Sunday afternoon, the time for a nap after an abundant weekend lunch, at least for those in the Kyiv elite.

It was Rebecca who had come up with the idea of contacting Sasha. 'They used to be friends, and who knows, it never hurts to ask. What do we have to lose?' she had said.

Gersh was dead set against the plan. 'That weasel didn't help his own wife, why would he help our Samuel? This can only make matters worse. He wasn't even invited to your wedding, remember?'

'I remember. But I will try,' Debora interrupted him. 'At least I will know I have done all I can.' She squashed all further discussion by raising her hand. 'I am the wife. I am the mother. I am the one who decides what to do.'

Despite Debora's expectations, Sasha wasn't home. Instead, a young woman opened the door. She looked up and down at Debora's figure and then stared her right in the eyes. 'Who are you?' she said in a coarse voice. 'What do you want from us?' Debora could hear a crying child inside the apartment. The woman's eyes were red, either from tears or lack of sleep.

'Good afternoon, my name is Debora. I am looking for Sasha Grinenko. I'm the wife of his good friend. Can I come in?'

'Wife,' the woman repeated, enunciating the word in a mocking way. She didn't budge, but in the dark corridor behind her, Debora spotted her old maths teacher shuffling towards the door. He smiled in recognition. 'Ah, look who's here. Come inside. Annochka, please welcome our guest. Sasha's old friend from Uman. What brings you to our parts?'

The woman stepped aside, letting Debora through the door. 'My husband isn't here,' she said coldly. 'And I don't know when he will be back. I never do.'

'Debora, come in, have some tea with us,' Sasha's father insisted. 'How are your parents? How is the family? Sasha would love to hear your news.'

Annochka locked the door and, without speaking, headed to one of the bedrooms. The child's crying got louder. Then there was the sound of a slap, followed by a moment of silence and a new bout of squealing, animal-like in its intensity. 'I can't, I just can't!' Annochka screamed.

Sasha's mother emerged from another bedroom, still half

asleep, and headed towards the unseen child. 'Annochka, calm down, let me handle this,' she implored, without even noticing Debora.

With an apologetic smile, Sasha's father motioned Debora to follow him into the living room. 'Children. Not so easy. Sorry for all this chaos. Annochka is finding it hard to manage, and Sasha is rarely here,' he sighed. 'So much work, so much work for him these days.'

They settled on stuffed chairs embroidered with gold lace. Debora admired the white piano, a Japanese painted chest and soft Persian rugs, all left behind by the apartment's original owners.

'Annochka's child is not very healthy. Some birth defects. A burden that we must carry,' Sasha's father said. 'I guess everyone has some weight on their shoulders.'

'Oh, I'm sorry.'

'Do you have any?' he asked.

'Any what?'

'Children, of course.'

'Yes, as a matter of fact. A newborn boy, Pasha.'

'Your parents and your husband must be very proud. Is he in good health?'

'Thank you, yes. Though regarding my husband ... This is what I wanted to talk to Sasha about.' Debora raised her eyes. 'He's been gone since May. We went to look at the airbase in Zhytomyr, but he is no longer there. I was hoping that Sasha could help ...'

'What do you mean, gone?' The teacher's face hardened. The smile disappeared as he perked up, alert. His eyebrows arching and his eyes narrowing, he locked his stare on Debora's face. 'Do you mean taken?'

'Yes.'

'Taken, as in taken by the Organs?'

'Yes,' Debora repeated with a tentative smile. 'I don't know where and why, and I was hoping—'

'How dare you!' Sasha's father cut her off, standing up abruptly. She was surprised by the violent energy of his move, not something she'd thought him capable of. 'How dare you come here and bring this *poison* with you! How dare you!' He lunged towards her and grabbed her by the elbow, tugging her to her feet. 'Leave now and don't ever try to come back. There have been enough problems without you. Can't you see the pain we are living in?'

'No need to scream or push me.' Debora pulled her arm away. 'I am going to leave. But you must tell Sasha that I've come here to ask for help. It is not your decision to say no. He must know.'

'Out!' He kept shoving her. 'Out.'

'You must tell him! You must!' she shouted as the door slammed behind her.

She walked down the staircase breathing heavily, with a child's animal cries still ringing in her ears. Outside in the bright sunlight, she felt dizzy and leaned on the wall, fighting back tears. But she didn't cry.

'I am strong, I am strong, I am strong,' she kept muttering as she boarded the tram for the ride home. Her breasts hurt. It was time to feed Pasha.

Three days later, late at night, a sleek black M-1 sedan, the new Soviet car modelled on Ford's Model 40, came to a stop under the windows of the Rosenbaums' apartment. Cars were rare in Kyiv these days, and this particular model was the vehicle of choice for the Organs. Halyna, hearing the engine's roar, peered through the window. 'Wake up,' she hissed at her husband. 'The Black Crow is here. Maybe the NKVD is coming after them, finally.'

But to her disappointment, only the driver stepped out and went up the stairs. If it were an arrest or a raid, it wouldn't be just one man. That much she knew.

The driver, a uniformed young soldier, rang the Rosenbaums' doorbell. Debora was also awake – Pasha had just had a feed – and opened the door.

'Comrade Debora?' the soldier asked.

'Yes?'

'Please come with me.'

Rebecca and Gersh stepped into the corridor, still in their pyjamas.

'What is this, is this an arrest?' Gersh asked loudly. 'What is going on?'

'No need to panic,' the soldier replied. 'Look, I am not even carrying a weapon. You just have to come down for a few minutes.'

Debora put a coat atop her nightgown and walked down the stairs. The driver opened the back door of the car for her to slide in, then closed it, remaining outside. He leaned against the building's front gate and lit a cigarette.

The Rosenbaums from their window and the Boykos from theirs stared at the street below. All this was very unusual.

Sasha was sprawled on the back seat, smelling of alcohol. It was hard to make out his face in the dark, but Debora could see just how much he had aged since she'd last seen him, how much his good looks had frayed. His hairline receded to the point that he had shaved his head. There were bags under his eyes, and he had the persistent cough of a frequent smoker.

'It's been a long time,' she said finally. 'I guess your father has told you. I am sorry I invaded your home.'

'My home,' he cackled. 'My home? My home is a fucking inferno, my home.'

He pulled her close, inhaling the air in her hair. 'You smell rather nice,' he said. 'Ah, that sweet smell. I remember.' She tried to move away, but his grip was firm. He sniffed again.

'Sasha,' she said softly. 'Can you help me? Do you know what is going on with Samuel?'

'Did you ever like me?' he asked dreamily. 'Back in Kharkiv, did you ever like me?'

'Of course I liked you.'

'It's my job to know when people are lying, do you know that? I know you are lying,' he went on. 'You know what job I do now, don't you? That's why you came to look for me, the only reason you did.'

'You are good friends with Samuel. I know you don't want anything bad to happen to him.' She deliberately used the present tense.

He burst out laughing. 'Ha ha, anything bad. Of course. Friends. Now that he's in trouble, we are such friends . . .'

He reached out to her and pulled her head close to his, staring into her eyes. 'Debora, my dear good friend, do you know what happened to Larysa, my wife, who was going to be the mother of my child? Normal child, not some freak?'

'Yes, I have read in the newspapers,' Debora said.

'Newspapers, huh . . . Read . . . read in the newspapers. Did the newspaper say that she was pregnant?'

'No.' She recoiled.

'And you know what else, my dear friend Debora? In this job, I read a lot. A lot of files. Interrogation files. Arrest files. Evidence files.' He paused. 'I didn't expect your signature to be there. When they came to me with your testimony and showed me the file, I had no choice. Would you contradict an ideologically verified impartial witness like Comrade Debora Rosenbaum? they asked me. And what could I respond? Of course I said that what you had testified was the truth. That I hadn't noticed the venomous snake in my own home. And that I would be the first to eliminate it.'

'It's not my fault,' Debora said quietly, willing herself to believe it. 'None of this is my fault.'

'I had to shoot Larysa with my own hand, this hand here.' Sasha raised his index finger, imitating pulling a trigger. 'In the back of her head. It was a very small hole. Between the braids. Puff, and gone. She was blindfolded, but I am sure she knew it was me. She could smell it.'

Debora pulled back and crossed her arms. 'Is this why you've had my Samuel detained?' she asked. Her voice was defiant. 'Is that what happened? You want me to lose him because you've lost Larysa? But with your job, you must know it wasn't down to me. They were going to get her father one way or another, because they were dismantling the Ukrainisation, and they were going to get her too. Especially after he escaped them by shooting himself, there was no way they were going to leave her alone.'

She remembered that she had to be soothing, and a moment later, she took Sasha's hand. 'None of this was because of me, and it wasn't because of you, Sasha. There was nothing either of us could have done to save Larysa.'

'Maybe you're right.' He nodded. 'I tell myself this every morning. But it's nice to have someone else say it too. My father was very upset that you came to look for me,' he went on. 'I am sorry he treated you badly. He's very afraid that I too won't come home one day. Don't risk anything to help Samuel, he warned me.'

'And yet you are here,' Debora said softly.

'Yes, I am here. But there isn't much I can do. Things just happen and people are in the way. That's how it is. That's how it was with Larysa, and that's how it is with Samuel now.'

The driver outside stubbed out his cigarette and started pacing up and down. Sasha lowered the window. 'Have another smoke, we're not done just yet.' He pushed it back up.

'Do you at least know what happened to him?' Debora asked. 'Where is he? Is he alive?'

'Wouldn't you want to know?' He reached out and touched her again. Her coat slid from her shoulder, and he noticed the lacework of her pink nightgown. It was cold, and her nipples pushed up through the transparent fabric. Closing his eyes, he ran the back of his hand over her breast.

Debora felt her muscles tighten at the intrusion but willed herself to relax. She put her hand on Sasha's, turning it so he would cup her breast. The hand was cold. 'Yes, I would want to know,' she said.

'Show me how much you want it.'

He unbuttoned his uniform trousers, unbuckled the belt, then forced Debora's mouth onto his crotch. Closing her eyes, she obediently opened her lips, sucking him as he grunted. She tried not to feel anything, to focus her mind on something far away, on an imaginary landscape of cloudless skies and fruit trees and ripening fields and circling dragonflies.

Sasha came quickly. He wiped his sperm with the hem of her nightgown, then drew a flask of vodka from his inside pocket and, after a swill, offered it to Debora. She took a gulp, and then another, to wash off his taste.

'You suck like a whore,' he said. 'Just the way I always imagined.'

'Tell me about my husband now.' She sat up straight.

'I've made some discreet enquiries. He is alive and he is very close, right here in Kyiv. Still under investigation,' he replied as he buttoned up his trousers. 'They've been busy with Yakir and the top commanders, so they didn't have time to deal with junior officers like him until now. Very soon they will be moving him to Moscow, along with others.'

'Can you help?'

'Nobody can help him.'

'When? When exactly will he go?'

'What does it even matter?'

'He has never set eyes on his son. Just tell me the day and the time. Pasha deserves to see his father at least once. This you cannot deny us.'

Sasha thought. 'I will see what I can do.' He pulled down the car's window and whistled at the soldier. Curtly the man stepped up to open Debora's door, paying no attention to her newly dishevelled appearance.

'Thank you,' she said softly.

Back upstairs, she took a long shower, then locked herself in her room.

It started to rain, flashes of lightning illuminating the clouds. Samuel, where are you? she thought as she scanned Kyiv's night-time skyline. So close, breathing the same air, hearing the same thunderstorm.

She tried not to think about what she had done with Sasha. It felt as though it had no emotional meaning, like dressing a wound. Like something a nurse would do.

Thoughts about Larysa, however, haunted her through the night. Had Sasha told her the truth: had her moment of weakness with the investigator really unleashed the chain of events that led to Larysa's death? Or was he doing what people in the Organs always did: lie, manipulate, prey on other people's emotions to weaken them? Did he feel so guilty that he needed to share his burden by making her his accomplice? She didn't have the answers, but she decided that she would not feel guilty about Larysa any more. Sasha had pulled the trigger. She could never imagine herself killing her husband, no matter the circumstances.

Sasha's aide returned ten days later, without the car. On the doorstep, he handed Debora an unmarked envelope. Inside was a sheet torn from a ruled notebook. It contained only one line: *Thursday, 6.15 a.m. Track 13.*

Debora took Rebecca with her on Thursday morning, in case something happened to her at the station. She'd washed her hair, applied make-up and polished her black leather shoes. Pasha was dressed like a doll, in a sailor's coat, with a starched white shirt and a bow tie. He was fretful and uncomfortable.

They arrived at Kyiv's main train station at 4 a.m. Track 13 was already cordoned off by police. Debora and Rebecca managed to position themselves between the cordon and the pathway that led out to the street. They sat on the floor, leaning against the wall, and waited. Debora was used to waiting by now, to dulling her senses and letting time flow around her, hour after interminable hour. In the Soviet Union, one needed to know how to wait.

The train on Track 13 was not composed of the kind of over-crowded cattle cars that she had seen packed with prisoners in the past. This one seemed to have normal carriages, apart from the windows boarded up with fresh, unpainted planks.

Just after 5.30, they heard a commotion. Two trucks pulled up outside and several soldiers, their rifles slung over their shoulders, rushed into the station building. 'One step right, one step left, I shoot,' one of them shouted, and then the prisoners began walking in, one after another in single file.

Debora jumped to her feet, picking up Pasha. The child was confused, and started to cry and wriggle in her arms. She scanned the hall for the familiar outline, for the gait that she knew she would instantly recognise.

'Do you see him?' Rebecca asked. 'You're sure he's here?'

Debora didn't answer, straining her eyes as she stood up on her toes. 'There he is,' she finally exclaimed a minute later. 'Samuel!' she cried across the hall.

Most inmates, with their hunched shoulders and swollen faces, moved with the resigned shuffle of men who had lost hope. Not Samuel. He held his head high and seemed just as handsome as before, except that his moustache had been shaved off, in line with regulations. His eyes were alive and curious, and he was looking around, enjoying the brief glimpse of life after months in windowless cells and interrogation rooms.

'Samuel!'

His eyes widened as he spotted Debora, the boy in her arms. She felt a coil unwinding inside her. Holding up the child, she rushed forward.

'Pasha, say hello to your father. This is your daddy, look.'

Pasha blinked, uncomprehending.

'Samuel, your son's name is Pasha. We all love you. You must come back home. Come back, you hear me,' she screamed. 'Come back. We'll be waiting for you.'

The guards raised their guns.

'Stand down, stand down,' Samuel bellowed at them in his officer's commanding voice. 'Nothing is happening here.'

He stopped briefly, his head twisted towards Debora, his eyes absorbing the scene, cataloguing every detail. Pasha crying in her arms. Her ruffled hair, her straight back, her new strength. The boy's ridiculous, laughable bow tie in this cavernous, hot train station that stank of sweaty bodies and fear. His son's sobs piercing the clinking of rifles and the heavy, resigned steps of the prisoners.

'Pasha, that's a great name. Pasha, Debora ... do not forget me. Think about me. I will be back, I will return, I promise,' he yelled through the din.

One of the guards cocked his gun, ready to shoot. Another stepped forward and hit Samuel's back with his rifle butt. Samuel swayed but remained on his feet. 'Keep walking,' the guard hissed. 'Keep walking if you want to live.'

'Do not forget!' Samuel shouted again as he picked up pace. 'Make sure Pasha doesn't forget.' These were the last words Debora heard as her husband disappeared round the corner.

'I promise, my love,' she called back. 'I promise.'

A railway policeman approached her, furious. 'You, woman, you are crazy. Go home now, before we put you on this train too.'

'I am sorry, Comrade Officer, we are leaving. Let's go, daughter, let's go.' Rebecca prodded her gently towards the exit. She took Pasha, who calmed down in his grandmother's arms.

A month went by without any news. Then the postman brought an official envelope. Debora was so anxious to open it that she tore the sheet of paper inside. It bore the stamp of the NKVD and had one precious bit of information.

This is to inform you that Citizen Samuel Groysman has been found guilty of counter-revolutionary activity, the two-paragraph letter said. *He has been sentenced to ten years' incarceration in a colony of special regime, without the right of correspondence or of receiving parcels.*

Debora, who had feared a death sentence, breathed out a sigh of relief. She held up Pasha and showed him the letter. 'By the time you're eleven, you will see your daddy again,' she told him. 'Time will fly by quickly, you'll see.'

Her father, however, was puzzled. He read and reread the letter after dinner, shaking his head. 'This is some new kind of sentence. I have never heard of it before,' he muttered to Rebecca once Debora was out of sight. 'Why would they not accept parcels? Why would they want to feed these prisoners with their own food instead of taking from the families? It makes no sense.'

Debora wrote letters to appeal Samuel's conviction, and a year later received a reply reaffirming his sentence. Initially she also wrote letters to him, chronicling her life and her petty problems, in case he might somehow read them one day. But after a few months, there was no more room for the letters in the drawer, and she stopped. Samuel was far away, and there was nothing she could do.

At night, in pitch-black darkness behind closed curtains, she would squeeze her eyes shut and try to conjure up his face. 'I will not forget, I promise,' she whispered. 'I promise.' But when another year passed, she could no longer summon the sense of his presence, even after spending hours staring at his photographs. The real Samuel faded away. Now, when she closed her eyes, she only saw the cardboard monochrome and felt gnawed by guilt.

PART THREE

19

Kyiv, June 1941

Debora woke on Sunday morning thinking about all the mundane matters that belonged to peacetime. Her squabble with the manager of a trust in charge of distributing matches, the latest of several employers where she had to work long, boring hours after being ousted from her teaching job. The play date she was arranging for Pasha, now a talkative three-year-old. The birthday party she planned to throw for her father the following month.

Yakov was supposed to join them for breakfast. It was going to be an exciting day – Kyiv's beloved soccer team, the Dynamo, was going to play against its main rival from Moscow at the city's brand-new stadium. Gersh had wrangled two tickets, for himself and his son.

They waited at the table, drinking tea, not touching their food. An hour passed. Yakov didn't come.

Debora peered outside the window, hoping to spot him walking down the Shevchenko Boulevard. The city, she noted, was unusually busy for the hour, with military cars zipping up and down the street. At around 10 a.m., they gave up and started to eat. As Rebecca began slicing up the poppy-seed cake she had baked, they heard a whining noise of planes in the skies. The frames looked unfamiliar. The wingspan was wide, and there were dozens of them.

The possibility of war didn't enter her mind even after the *ack-ack-ack* of anti-aircraft guns greeted the planes. If it were real war, the guns would have shot the intruders out of the sky by now. But none of the planes seemed troubled. It must be yet another annoying exercise, she figured.

It had been almost two years since the Soviet Union had secured – and greatly expanded – its borders by signing a non-aggression pact with Nazi Germany. After invading Poland from the east just as the outgunned Polish army was trying to stop the German advance from the west, the Soviet Union had incorporated Ukrainian and Belarussian-majority lands in eastern Poland. It later annexed a swath of Romania, and gobbled up the independent Baltic states too, alongside a large chunk of Finland. Not so long ago, Soviet and Nazi troops had even marched together in a victory parade in Brest, the formerly Polish city that now marked the new border between the two worlds.

That new border was now far, far to the west of Kyiv, which was why the idea that these planes could be enemy bombers seemed so outlandish. In recent days, Soviet newspapers had been full of reports about the flourishing trade and cooperation with Berlin, and had reprinted Hitler's statements verbatim. The world war was only mentioned on interior pages, with wire items that Debora didn't bother to read briefly describing the advance of British and Australian troops towards exotic Beirut and Damascus.

For almost two years now, Soviet propaganda had focused its bile on the warmongering capitalists in London and Paris. Hitler's views on the Jews, while not endorsed, were politely not mentioned. It helped that few Jews were left in positions of power in the Soviet Union after the latest purges. Just before signing the pact with Germany, Stalin had removed his multilingual Jewish foreign minister, the veteran Litvinov, and replaced him with Vyacheslav Molotov, the moustachioed Russian bureaucrat who didn't mind shaking the Führer's hand.

Debora held her morning tea as she watched the planes fly overhead. The large glass was encased in a carved holder made from nickel alloy, an invention of the Russian railways. A handle allowed her to drink it piping hot without scalding her fingers.

But she scalded herself anyway. With a loud thud, their building shook and books tumbled from the shelves. There was another bomb, and another, and she saw flames rising over the train station down the hill. Then the sound of ambulance sirens added to the cacophony of explosions and anti-aircraft guns, a sound that remained even after all the others faded away once the pilots finally ran out of bombs and turned back west.

'What was that?' A worried Pani Helga knocked on the door of the Rosenbaums' living room. Two decades earlier, she had witnessed street battles as Kyiv changed hands between the Reds, the Whites, the Germans and three different Ukrainian governments. She was familiar with the sound of explosions. 'This definitely sounds like war.'

'I don't really know,' Gersh said. He still clung to hope. 'Maybe some kind of exercise? An accident?'

Pasha, oblivious to the gravity of the situation but giddy because of all the unusual excitement in the apartment, started running from room to room, his arms outstretched like the wings of an aeroplane. 'Boom!' he shouted. 'Zzzzzzzzzz. Boom! This is my daddy flying.'

A framed photograph of Samuel just after his promotion to lieutenant, in a bomber jacket and goggles in front of his plane, was always propped on Debora's desk. The boy was still too young to be told about prisons and camps. As far as he knew, his father was on an important mission far away, a true Stalin's Falcon. Used to Samuel's absence, he rarely asked questions.

The youngest of the Boyko sons followed suit, imitating a bomber run, but limited his patrols to the common areas. 'Knock it off, cretin,' his elder brother finally yelled, and gave him a slap.

'Where is Yakov?' Rebecca was suddenly worried. 'Why isn't he here?'

The adult Boykos were already in the kitchen and also wanted to talk. 'This must be some accident, some provocation,' Ostap said. 'There is no way the Germans would be foolish enough to attack us. They would be annihilated in no time. That would be the end of the imperialist system. They must know it.'

They all had watched the blockbuster movie *If War Comes Tomorrow*, released just before Stalin's surprise alliance with Hitler and featuring real footage of awe-inspiring manoeuvres by Soviet armour, warplanes and cavalry. In the movie, after an ill-advised invasion by Germans wearing a three-pronged version of the swastika on their uniforms, it took the Red Army just a few days to destroy the hapless intruders. Gas-mask-wearing Soviet units bravely marched through the clouds of nerve agent to overrun German positions, and soon the communist revolution was spreading all over Europe.

Gersh had seen how the German army had operated in Ukraine two decades earlier, with its superior supplies and disciplined officers. If the current Nazi Wehrmacht was anything like that, he thought, victory would not be easy. But he didn't want to argue with the Boykos, not about such a sensitive topic. His thoughts turned to practical matters instead.

'Soon there will be no food left. That's how it usually works,' he told Rebecca quietly, and started tying his shoelaces.

His wife remained home with Pasha while Gersh and his

daughter, taking big shopping bags, went to the Bessarabka market. The state-run food shops were already closed. They were surprised to see rows of police chasing village women, with their bags of produce, away from the market. A public bus drove by quickly, and Debora saw bloodied men and women inside, a nurse trying to bandage someone's wound.

Just after noon, loudspeakers stationed at major street intersections crackled and came alive. Groups of people started gathering around, and Debora and Gersh joined them. 'Stalin, Stalin is about to speak,' someone said, full of excitement. But instead of Stalin's guttural Georgian voice, it was the flat, uninspiring drawl of foreign minister Molotov that emerged from the speakers.

Germany, he informed the millions gathered all over the country, had violated the non-aggression pact and, at 4 a.m., had started bombing Zhytomyr, Kyiv, Kaunas, Sevastopol and other Soviet cities, killing or wounding a hundred people. For the next few minutes, he spoke about how thoroughly Moscow had observed its obligations under the pact, how the aggression was unwarranted, and how the Soviet Union had no quarrel with the German people. It was only in the final part of the speech that he mentioned that Soviet troops had been ordered to strike back, forecasting that Hitler would meet the same defeat that Emperor Napoleon had suffered in Russia in the previous century.

'Napoleon?' Gersh mumbled, with only Debora able to hear him. 'They're talking of Napoleon? But Napoleon managed to come all the way to Moscow and burn it down.'

'Don't ever repeat that, please,' she shushed him.

They didn't have time to linger, because an air raid siren unleashed its whining shriek, and the anti-aircraft guns opened up again. People didn't yet know they should be afraid, and weren't running. But Gersh took Debora by the elbow and pushed her inside the nearest building, away from the street.

Boom after boom showed the bombs were getting closer and closer. 'They must be targeting the power station,' Gersh said. And indeed, the single naked light bulb that illuminated the staircase flickered a few times, then gave out.

Yakov arrived in the apartment around 3 p.m. The day was unusually hot, and his military shirt was already stained with sweat. His eyes were inflamed behind his fishbowl spectacles and he had no time to spare. He had been busy organising the unit since the first bombs had fallen that morning.

'We're being deployed to the front line this afternoon. The train leaves at five,' he said. 'I just have a few minutes to say goodbye.'

'The front? With your astigmatism and myopia?' Rebecca stood straight, uncomprehending. 'This must be some mistake, there is no way they could be sending you to the front. Didn't they tell you two years ago that you can't even shoot straight?'

'Don't worry, Mama, I will shoot straight,' he assured her. 'You will see. It will all be over in a week or two, and I will be back. They stand no chance against us.'

Rebecca stuffed his bag with canned meat, jam and bread. 'This will be enough for a few days. Once they give you leave, come home straight away,' she instructed him.

Gersh handed him his Swiss silver flask, filled with vodka. 'Don't you dare lose it or scratch it,' he said, hugging his son awkwardly. 'I want it back, full. With German schnapps.'

Yakov was eager to step out of the door, checking his watch, but Rebecca wouldn't let go of a long embrace. 'Are you sure it will all be over soon?' she asked him.

'Of course. Take care of them all.' Yakov quickly kissed his sister, adjusted his glasses and ran down the stairs. 'I will write soon, promise,' he shouted once he was on the street outside.

'It's all so quick, so sudden,' Rebecca sighed as she sat down on the sofa. 'My head is turning.'

'Mama, please stop worrying, everything will work out,' Debora tried to reassure her, the artificially chirpy tone of her voice contrasting with the turmoil in her mind.

As darkness fell and the Rosenbaums lit candles, the doorman rang the bell. He brought a copy of the mobilisation decree printed that afternoon: every man younger than fifty was ordered to present himself to the military commissariat. Gersh was already too old. Ostap Boyko was the only man in the apartment covered by the order.

'Are you going to leave for the front tonight too?' Gersh asked him in the kitchen.

Boyko mumbled something indeterminate. 'I'm going to see what orders I receive from the newspaper tomorrow. We may also have a role to play here, you know. Essential workers!' he replied.

Halyna was frightened. She put on a headscarf and headed to the door. 'I am going to the church, to pray,' she said.

This was not something she would have admitted in public previously, but now, nobody cared.

Rebecca too prayed quietly in her room.

20

Kyiv, July 1941

Children in Debora's courtyard got used to playing with bits of shrapnel that fell from the sky. Even Pasha had a jagged piece of metal, gifted to him by Boyko's eldest son. German air raids continued daily, undeterred by what remained of Kyiv's impotent anti-aircraft batteries.

Workers at the city's weapons factories had not been allowed to abandon the assembly line and seek shelter, and so hundreds were killed in the renewed air strikes, until production ceased at one facility after another.

Women, shovels in hand, began turning every bit of unpaved space in central Kyiv into improvised bomb shelters, piling up bags of excavated dirt on the side. Debora and Halyna joined a work detail near their own apartment building, digging up the tree-shaded median of Shevchenko Boulevard.

The sky was a painful blue, the sun burned the skin and – unexpectedly – swarms of tiny flies engulfed the city, seeking their way up noses and into eyes. Halyna's prayers were answered: Ostap Boyko remained in Kyiv instead of being enrolled in the army. 'The pen is mightier than the sword, as they say. The newspaper must continue publishing, and I am indispensable,' he said, feigning regret.

It wasn't until ten days after the invasion began that Stalin reappeared. He addressed the nation in a radio appeal that frightened with its intimacy. 'Brothers and sisters,' he began. The Germans continued advancing east, he admitted, and the war was now 'a matter of life and death' for the entire Soviet nation. Those spreading rumours and panic, he added, had to be destroyed with particular severity.

By then, panic had spread, with injured soldiers, dull-eyed in their dirt-crusted trucks as they arrived in Kyiv's hospitals, bringing the news of defeat after defeat. It didn't even help that the authorities forced residents to surrender their radio receivers so they couldn't listen to enemy broadcasts: Gersh had to haul their expensive set to the nearest military committee, standing hours in line for the receipt.

On a Sunday two weeks after the war's outbreak, Debora and Rebecca took a stroll through the city, taking care not to trip and fall into the new ditches. It smelled of smoke – NKVD and other government ministries were burning their archives, and charred bits of paper were blasted up chimneys by roaring fires and scattered by the wind all over Kyiv. The basement of the former Institute for Noble Maidens, long turned into a jail, was filling up with the bodies of prisoners executed by the NKVD around the clock. The chaos of wartime logistics meant that the disposal of dead enemies of the state in secret burial grounds couldn't keep pace, and so the sweet stench of decay began wafting from the building onto the streets outside. Everyone knew that smell, everyone knew what it meant.

St Sophia's Cathedral and its gold-domed baroque bell tower were surrounded by fresh scaffolding. Men with brushes and buckets of paint balanced precariously. 'Are they going to repaint churches now, of all times?' Debora asked incredulously as they walked past.

'Just the cupolas, comrade,' one of the workmen replied. 'We're painting all the cupolas red, the colour of the roofs, so that the Germans can't use them as landmarks on their runs.'

There was a long line of trucks near the NKVD headquarters, and Rebecca spotted a familiar white piano and Japanese chest in the back of one. Sure enough, Sasha's parents sat on suitcases under the truck's canopy, together with Annochka and the sick child. The child seemed to be asleep. Sasha himself, in an NKVD uniform and wearing dusty black boots, was leafing through a stack of documents outside the truck. Seeing Debora, he stopped, surprised, and put the papers into his shoulder bag.

'What is this?' she asked. 'Are you leaving the city? Are you *all* leaving?'

He leaned towards her, speaking quietly. 'Listen to me carefully, Debora. Get out while you can. Now. Your kind, you can't really wait any more.'

'My kind?'

'You know what I mean. Take your child, your mother, your father, and run.'

He jumped into the cabin and told the driver to go, banging his hand on the dashboard. The truck roared away, the piano rocking in the back, bumping against the chest. Its strings tinkled at every pothole.

'If these people are leaving town, they know something we don't,' Rebecca told Debora. 'We should go too.'

Gersh huffed dismissively when Debora recounted this conversation that night. He was dead set against the idea of abandoning the city. The Germans, he argued, were far away. They would never come to Kyiv. Who would allow them to seize the capital of Soviet Ukraine? And if they did, how bad could it get?

'The Germans are civilised people, I know them,' he kept repeating. 'And it's not as if we are NKVD. They have nothing against us.' He remembered visiting Berlin and Munich before the revolution, and he remembered when German soldiers arrived in Ukraine in 1918. 'They were the ones who stopped the pogroms and brought order. There were many Jews among them too,' he said. 'And they all respected the Jews because they could speak with us. German, you know, is almost the same as Yiddish.'

'I can't speak any Yiddish,' Debora replied. 'And in any case, the Germans of back then are not the same as the Germans today, just as the Russians of back then are not the same as the Russians we know.'

'That's what we are being told in newspapers, but how do we know it is true?' Gersh replied quietly. 'You've seen, everything they are telling us about the war in the papers has been a lie so far. This whole place is built on lies.'

He had a point. Debora didn't argue.

The next morning, at the match distribution department, the director didn't show up for work. It turned out that the petty cash fund was also missing. There were three new air raids on the city, but now, together with the bombs, the Germans started dropping batches of leaflets. They fell like snowflakes on the Botanical Garden, and Debora, pretending that she had to fix her stocking, kneeled and picked one up. Keeping enemy propaganda was illegal and dangerous, but she wanted to know what the Germans had to say.

The leaflet was crude, a drawing on cheap paper with a two-colour image in red and black. It showed Red Army soldiers killing a long-nosed officer and then surrendering to the Germans. *His mug is asking for a brick. Destroy the Yid and the commissar*, the text said. *Your situation is hopeless.*

Debora hid it in her purse, and once she got home, she showed it to Gersh, behind closed doors. 'See how civilised they are, your Germans,' she whispered. '"Destroy the Yid." Sasha was right. We must leave Kyiv as soon as possible, tomorrow if we can.'

'We could go to my cousin in Moscow,' said Rebecca. 'I am sure she would have us.'

Gersh examined the leaflet, looking it up and down, reading the German-language small print, and then lit a match and burned it.

'Tomorrow you three will leave. I am taking you to the train station. Pack your suitcases,' he decided.

'What about you?' Rebecca asked.

'I will close down our affairs and will join you shortly after that. Don't worry,' he said. 'I will buy the train tickets first thing in the morning.'

Next morning, there was pandemonium at the station. Part of it had been damaged in the bombing raids, and the acrid smell of the extinguished fire still hung over the area, mixing with the aroma of sweat from thousands of panicked women and men trying to get aboard the eastbound trains before the bridges over the Dnipro river were blown up.

Gersh couldn't even get close to the building as fist fights broke out a block away. Big, able-bodied men pushed through the crowds, trampling on women and children, throwing money at security guards, just to reach the ticket window. The guards took the money and let some of them through, but it was all in vain. The ticket window was shut, and wasn't going to open again.

Just two days earlier, on Sunday, railway tickets had been plentiful and had sold at the normal price. On Monday, scalpers were touting them at ten times the official rate. But today, on Tuesday morning, even the scalpers had nothing to sell. All commercial tickets had been voided, an exasperated railway official announced through the loudspeaker at noon, making the crowds sway in disbelief. An official evacuation was being organised by the government, he said. This was now the only way to leave the city. People in the crowd refused to disperse, clinging to hopes of being able to bribe their way onto a train. But eventually even the most optimistic ones gave up and went home.

Grim-faced, Gersh brought the news to his family. 'An official evacuation?' Rebecca asked. 'Things must be really bad then.'

'We'll get ourselves on the list. I know enough people to do it,' he assured her. In normal times, he had plenty of influence. But now was not a normal time.

The postman still delivered the letters that morning. Rebecca had hoped for a postcard from Yakov. 'Why doesn't he write? He promised to write as soon as he arrived,' she complained after seeing that the mailbox was empty.

The match distribution department was closed, and so Debora volunteered at the improvised medical facility in the nearby school. It wasn't really a field hospital – just a place where moderately injured soldiers could recover before being shipped to get proper care further east, with volunteer nurses offering only the most basic of help. The classrooms stank of rotting flesh, diarrhoea and urine, and the bathrooms were clogged and overflowing. Flies swarmed to the open wounds, and the shell-shocked, feverish soldiers were too exhausted to wave them away.

Debora's mission was to serve food, which she brought in big trays to the classrooms where the soldiers lay on newspapers and piles of hay on the floor. Few wanted to talk about the war. No matter how injured, most managed to arrange a supply of the local moonshine, and reeked of it from the

145

early afternoon. On her third day in the school, she saw one of the soldiers, a young man from eastern Ukraine with a sprouting moustache and a bandaged, bloodied eye, pull out a flask and take a big gulp after his meal. The silver flask was familiar – she saw the Swiss mountaintop, and the writing: *Grüezi aus Luzern.*

She hungrily prised it from the man's hands. It was badly scratched, with dirt caked into the indentations, but still recognisable. 'Where did you get this?' she demanded. Her heart was racing.

The soldier looked barely nineteen, and he was intimidated. 'I found it,' he stammered. 'It's a trophy, I took it from a dead German.'

'Where? What dead German?' she almost shouted.

'Actually, Nurse, I don't know if he was a German,' he admitted. 'I'm sorry. We were sent into battle with just rifles and bottles of incendiary liquid against German tanks. What could we do against them? Once the tanks started shooting, it was a meat-grinder. Earth, people, weapons, all blown to pieces and then meshed together, flying up into the sky, and then the bigger bits coming down first and the dust just rising and rising. My ears are still ringing.

'The whole unit was wiped out. I wanted to run away, but the NKVD at the back were shooting at anyone trying to escape with a machine gun, until they too were shelled and killed. The tanks passed the bridge and turned left. Then, after nightfall, I crawled towards our remaining lines, to the right. I fell into a hole, a crater from an explosion, and like everywhere it was full of bodies, of body parts. There was just this one hand, severed at the elbow, clutching the flask. I was thirsty and hungry, so I took it. There was vodka inside. And in the morning, I found our lines, and here I am.'

'Why did you tell me that you took it from a dead German?'

'I don't know, Nurse, maybe it *was* a German. All I saw was a hand, and the writing is not ours. It's in German, isn't it?'

'Yes, it is,' she said. 'It's in German.'

She handed back the flask. Holding on to it meant she would have to acknowledge something that she desperately didn't want to be true.

'Yes, sounds like you've taken it from a German soldier. Definitely from a German. Keep it.'

At home the next morning, Rebecca once again checked the mailbox, and once again it was empty. 'Why is he being so lazy, what does it cost him to write a few lines to keep his mother happy?' she complained.

'I am sure Yakov is busy, Mama,' Debora said. 'He has a war to fight. He doesn't have time to be writing letters.'

Through an open window, she heard Pasha wail. It was too hot indoors and he was playing in the courtyard with the Boyko boys and other kids from the building, a number that was rapidly shrinking. She hurried downstairs to pick him up. Snot ran from his nose, and as he cried, he smeared it all over his face. 'What's wrong, my bunny?' she asked.

'What is a Yid, Mama?' Pasha asked.

She was taken aback. 'Yid? Why are you asking? It isn't a good word.'

'The boys here, they don't want to play with me. They keep saying that I am a Yid and that soon the Germans will come and kill all the Yids.'

'Oh.'

Pasha resumed crying. 'I don't want to be a Yid, Mama. No. I don't want to be a Yid.'

'Calm down,' she said sternly. 'Calm down and stop this

147

nonsense. You are not a Yid. You are a Soviet man. Tell that to anyone.' She took his hand and led him upstairs.

'I am not a Yid,' he repeated, newly confident. 'I am not a Yid. I am a Soviet man.'

Everyone talked about evacuation now, and one after another, the staff of Kyiv's institutions boarded trucks and barges, crossed the Dnipro, and then travelled in long railway convoys far away to the east. The Kyiv movie studios went to Ashgabat, in the Turkmen desert near the Iranian border. The Ukrainian Academy, the Opera Theatre, and the painters and writers closest to power were shipped to Ufa in the remote Bashkir republic, in the foothills of the Ural Mountains. Factories, especially those useful for the military, were also packed up and taken to the east.

Gersh managed to move his family up in the evacuation list, something that cost him most of the food stocks he had kept in the apartment, with some silver cutlery thrown in. By now it was a staggered process. Women and children could leave first. But men had to stay behind and wait their turn.

The Germans were getting closer: at night, the echo of artillery fire on the city's western outskirts already reached the centre, a hum that was occasionally subsumed by the buzz of enemy aircraft and the volleys of anti-aircraft fire.

The Boykos did not seem eager to leave. Ostap, who kept writing front-page – but unsigned – editorials about Kyiv being an impregnable fortress, a hard nut that would break the Nazis' rotten teeth, grew unusually kind to Pani Helga, who now refused to leave the apartment altogether. He kept knocking on her door and bringing her warm tea and sweet treats, gifts that she received with the barest nod of acknowledgement.

She wasn't going anywhere, she said. 'I am too old to flee. If

God says it is my time to die, I want to die with dignity, in my own home.'

At the end of July, Gersh arrived home after lunch waving a wad of permits. 'Pack everything, you are leaving tonight,' he told Rebecca and Debora. Their suitcases of clothes hadn't really been unpacked. But they filled their smaller handbags with carefully wrapped documents, Rebecca's most precious jewellery sewn inside a soft teddy bear.

'The evacuation centre will let me know where you end up, but just in case we are separated, as soon as you arrive send your location to your cousin in Moscow,' Gersh told Rebecca.

'How will Yakov know where to find us?' she wondered. 'And what about Samuel? I know he's been sentenced to ten years without the right of correspondence, but it's a war now, a totally different situation. They must make exceptions.'

'You should write to Yakov's unit with the new address too,' Gersh replied. He tried to sound cheerful. 'It is just a precaution, of course, and you may all be back very soon. It's hard to imagine we'd ever let Kyiv fall.'

'Of course.' Rebecca looked around the living room. 'When you finally come to join us, make sure you double-lock all the rooms, and that the windows are properly closed. When the rains start, we don't want any leaks. And put the dust covers on the furniture, don't forget. And leave naphthalene in the closets, we don't want the moths to eat everything.'

Debora stood up and surveyed the stuffy furniture that she'd yearned to escape when she was living in Uman, the knock-off oil paintings on the walls, the heavy red curtains. Her heart ached. She did not want to go.

At 5 p.m., they sat around the table for one last moment of contemplation together. Gersh drummed his fingers on the pristine linen tablecloth, looking into the distance. Then he helped carry the suitcases down the stairs and they all walked to the evacuation centre in the Botanical Garden. Trams no longer ran, and horses had been requisitioned for the front.

The evacuation centre accepted only women and children, and men were not allowed inside the barbed-wire fence put up at the entrance. Gersh gave his wife, daughter and grandson an awkward hug, and then watched silently as they were ushered beyond the wire, to tents put up in a field blanketed by wilted magnolia petals. 'Your turn will be in a day or two, but you must always be ready if we call you up,' a middle-aged woman running the admissions told Debora, and gave her a booklet of chits for bread. 'Boiling water is over there. You can have as much as you want if you bring your own cup.' The only cup they had brought was the silver cup for Sabbath wine that Rebecca had inherited from her grandmother. They would have to share that.

There were no beds, so everyone slept on their bundles or bags, or on the grass. At night it was chilly, but Rebecca's main preoccupation was not to catch fleas – and the typhus they transmitted – from the other evacuees. Many of them weren't from Kyiv and had already trekked for days or weeks to escape the advancing German armies.

Pasha quickly found a friend his own age, and as they played at war, the only game anyone played these days, Debora chatted to the boy's mother. She was still young, but her hair had begun to turn grey, and wrinkles ringed the corners of her mouth. She hadn't had a chance to take a bath or change her clothes for a week, and though Debora was by now immune to her own smell, she reflexively pinched her nose because of the stench. The woman was originally from Kharkiv, but lived in recently annexed western Ukraine.

'My husband is an officer in the army, and he is fighting the war somewhere there,' she said, making a gesture in a western direction. 'All the officers' wives were told to leave town early on, because the Germans were getting close and they wouldn't spare us or our children. But they only arranged a train for us to go as far as Zhytomyr, which they thought was safe enough. Then the Germans got close to Zhytomyr too, and so we had to escape again. But this time there were no trains, no horses, no cars. We walked for four days. After one day, I was just too exhausted to carry my suitcase, and I dropped it on the roadside. We tried to barter with the peasants for food along the way, but they weren't friendly at all, especially when I told them I was an officer's wife. They definitely didn't want our roubles – one laughed and told me I could use them to wipe my arse. They are waiting for the Germans to come, and they aren't even hiding it.'

She paused. 'We all know what happened in those villages nine years ago. My own husband comes from a village like that – his cousins died in the famine while he was at military school. No wonder they hate us.'

Debora listened quietly. 'My husband is an officer too,' she said. 'A pilot.'

The night was uncomfortable, and Rebecca was too embarrassed to use the open latrine – a transformed trench in the park. Debora had lost her inhibitions at the tractor plant construction camp in Kharkiv, and found the situation amusing. 'No reason to be shy, Mama, nobody is looking at you,' she told Rebecca. 'There won't be any bidets where we are going. Better get used to it.'

In the morning, the officer's wife and other women and children were called up to the gate and put on a tented truck. But Debora, Rebecca and Pasha had to stay behind. As they wandered idly around the camp, Pasha shrieked and ran towards the fence. Debora wanted to yell at him to stop, but then she saw her father waving at the child. He had managed to finagle a couple of lollipops, and pushed them through the wire.

'I've been waiting here for an hour, but they wouldn't call you, so I just hoped you might see me anyway,' he said. 'And you did.' Gersh didn't like being alone, and now that he saw his family again, he grinned like a child.

He pushed his hand through the fence, pinching Pasha's cheek. 'I'm going to bring you something when we catch up,' he said. 'I've got a new European fishing rod, with a spinner. We'll catch a fish like this.' He opened his arms. 'So big you won't be able to hold it.'

Pasha had been asking for a fishing rod since the spring. His eyes lit up. 'What colour?' he asked.

'You'll see,' Gersh replied. 'Soon enough.'

'Did any mail arrive from Yakov?' Rebecca asked hopefully.

'No. I think there is no longer any mail delivery. Everything is being shut down.'

They chatted in the summer heat for a while, until the camp's administrator rang her bell and began reading the latest roster of names into a loudhailer.

Debora flinched when she heard theirs. 'That's us!'

'Go, don't miss your turn,' Gersh urged them.

'We'll see you soon.' Rebecca touched his face through the fence, running her fingers over his bushy eyebrows.

'Of course, I'll catch up with you in a few days,' he replied. 'Just a few more days. You won't have time to miss me.'

As they picked up their bags and hurried to take their place in the line, he wiped away a tear they hadn't noticed.

'I hope he doesn't forget to lock up the rooms. And to cover the sofa and the chairs,' Rebecca told Debora. 'He's so distracted these days.'

'He won't forget. Stop worrying, Mama.'

But they both worried, and not about the furniture. In an unspoken agreement, they didn't mention their true fears. The war, everyone knew by now, would be bloody and long.

They left the Botanical Garden in a tented truck that zigzagged through the city, driving downhill and around tank traps until it reached the Dnipro riverbank. Car-sized craters smouldered near the bridge, but the Germans hadn't been able to destroy it yet. It was, however, clogged with military traffic – tanks, horses pulling artillery pieces, trucks camouflaged with branches and mud.

Civilians had the lowest priority and were ferried to the far bank by river craft. Once Debora boarded the vessel, she realised that it was the same kind of pleasure boat on which she had celebrated her wedding. Maybe even the very same boat. Now it was filled with the detritus of the refugees who had packed it in recent days. One side, perilously close to the waterline, had been sprayed by shrapnel and was full of holes.

'Mama, do you remember?' Debora asked as the boat glided across the slow-moving water. 'Remember how we danced?'

Rebecca's eyes welled up. She pulled Debora towards her. 'We will be happy again, sweetheart. To spite them all, we will be happy again.'

There was hours of additional waiting on the other side of the river, as documents and lists were checked again and again. In the evening, Debora, Rebecca and Pasha finally arrived at Darnytsia station and were herded onto a train. 'Where are we going?' Debora asked the railway attendant on the platform.

'Stalingrad, all the way to Stalingrad,' he said.

'We're going to the Volga,' Rebecca told Pasha. 'The Germans will never get that far.'

'What is Volga?' he asked.

'It is a very big river. Even bigger than the Dnipro.'

'Will we take another boat?'

'No,' Rebecca laughed. 'There is no need for any more boats.'

They were travelling in a modified version of the same cattle car that Debora had seen used by the NKVD to transport prisoners when she travelled to visit Olena in Pisky. A hole in the floor served as the latrine. Three levels of bunk beds were attached to the sides. The window had a metal grille. But unlike the NKVD convoys, the doors were not padlocked from the outside.

As the train started to move, Pasha fell asleep on Rebecca's lap. Debora pulled open the door, letting the fresh air waft in, and sat watching the moonlit country rush by. Just a couple of months earlier, the carriage had been used to deport 'class enemy' families from western Ukraine into exile. She noticed that someone had scratched in Ukrainian, with a spoon or a nail, on the wood by the door: *We will be back. Glory to Ukraine!*

Far on the horizon, flashes lit up the sky. She wondered whether these were explosions or a distant thunderstorm. She didn't know that the Second Panzer Group's tanks were completing their pincer movement and would soon link up with the First Panzer Group east of Kyiv, cutting it off and trapping its residents, along with the giant Red Army force that was meant to defend the city, but that would be annihilated instead.

21

Stalingrad, August 1941

The first thing Debora saw on arriving at Stalingrad's train station was a long line of T-34 tanks, fresh off the assembly line. The paint on their armour was barely dry, without a scratch, and the deadly machines looked to her like shiny oversized toys. The tanks had been assembled at Stalingrad's massive American-designed tractor plant, the predecessor of the one she had helped build in Kharkiv. In wartime, tractors were no longer a priority.

It had taken three days for Debora's train to travel from Kyiv. They had to halt often, to make way for convoys full of artillery pieces, ammunition, fuel, and grim, nervous men who were all heading in the opposite direction, towards the front.

At the station, police shepherded the passengers into a cramped hall where they awaited screening by local officials amid a cacophony of wailing children, sneezes and coughs, and the clanking of trains. Two hours later, it was finally Debora's turn to speak to a tired middle-aged man in a greasy kepi.

He leafed through her papers until he saw her university diploma. 'Russian literature, huh,' he said. 'I see you can read. Can you type, too?'

'Of course. I'm top-notch,' she lied without skipping a beat.

The man looked at Rebecca and Pasha.

'My mama and my son,' she said.

'Where is the husband?'

'My husband is an officer, fighting for the Soviet Motherland,' she replied. She wasn't going to volunteer that she was the wife of an enemy of the people. Especially because now, in the middle of the war, nobody was likely to find out the truth.

'Good. Then I know exactly where to send you.' He wrote a few lines on a piece of paper, breathed on his ink stamp, pounded the note and scribbled a quick unintelligible signature. 'Welcome to the Red Army, Comrade Rosenbaum. Show this outside, where the trucks are, and they will take you where you need to go.'

The truck took them to the camp of the newly created 13th Sapper Brigade, where Debora had been assigned to serve as a typist in the administration department. The job came with a room, where all three of them could live, and a food ration book.

'Mama, not a word to anyone here about where Samuel really is,' she whispered into Rebecca's ear once they were alone. 'Understand?'

They cleaned the room, removing dust and cobwebs and trying to crush the numerous cockroaches. There was no way to get rid of the mouldy smell that tickled her nostrils.

'It's small but cosy,' she told Pasha when they were done. 'Not bad, huh?'

Pasha was unimpressed. 'When are we going to go home?' he whined. 'I don't like it here. I want to go home. Tomorrow, can we go home tomorrow?'

Though Stalingrad was much smaller – and much newer – than Kyiv, its riverside setting reminded Debora of home. The city, barely a few blocks deep, snaked for dozens of kilometres along a bend of the Volga, with a succession of industrial areas marked by rising smokestacks. Functional white housing blocks towered from hilltops on the west bank of the wide, slow-moving river, overlooking the deep-green islands in the middle – islands beyond which the endless Asian steppes began. The German bombers hadn't reached here yet.

It was the first time that Debora had been in Russia proper, and she sensed the difference from Ukraine – in accents that stressed the long 'a', in clothes, in the rhythm of life. Locals, too, immediately put her down as a stranger. There weren't many Jews in Stalingrad, but its citizens, she found out quickly, were a lot less shy than the Kyivites about throwing a casual 'Yid' into their speech. It was especially so because, fooled by Debora's looks and accent, everyone assumed she wasn't Jewish.

'These Yids, it's because of them that this war broke out, and now they are all rushing east, to the safety of Tashkent, while our sons have to die fighting,' she overheard a woman at the market tell another matter-of-factly.

Debora was going to talk back, to mention her brother, but erupted with a simple 'How dare you!'

'What, you are one of them?' The woman squinted. 'Come here to eat off our backs?'

'Shame on you,' was the only reply Debora could muster before turning around and walking away.

She stewed at home. 'What is this talk? I have never heard talk like this. How can Soviet people speak like this?' she asked Rebecca.

'I hear it every day,' her mother replied.

For now, the 13th Sapper Brigade was just an office where Debora typed up requests for food, uniforms and ammunition, and updated the lists of draftees every morning. The recruits were only beginning to arrive. Military commissariats scoured Stalingrad and its nearby provinces for men who hadn't yet been drafted, cancelling medical exceptions and countermanding essential-worker designations. Limping, poor eyesight, consumption – nothing mattered any more. Some were Russian, others were broad-faced Kalmyk and Kazakh nomads from the flatland steppes south of the city. Barely pubescent teenagers straight out of high school and construction workers in their sixties with gnarled hands and bad backs were all herded together, their heads shaved on arrival to eliminate lice.

The brigade HQ engaged in a lot of correspondence, in quadruple copy with carbon paper, but not in much action so far. The commander, Colonel Razin, looked at Debora suspiciously as she typed with two fingers on her first day. 'You sure you've done this before?' he asked.

'I'm a little rusty, but give me a chance, I won't let you down. Everything will be ready on time.'

She hadn't finished by sunset and remained in front of the typewriter through the night, tapping the keyboard as the pile of completed documents on her left grew slowly but steadily. When she could do no more and her hands hurt too much, she just leaned on her desk and fell asleep for a couple of hours. Before dawn, she was done. She got up to stretch and boil some water.

'Did you stay here all night?' Colonel Razin eyed her suspiciously as he walked into the office.

'Of course not,' Debora replied cheerily. 'Everything you've asked for is ready and arranged on your desk, Comrade Colonel.'

He didn't believe her, but nodded and mumbled a reply that she couldn't make out.

In the following days, still using only two fingers, Debora

picked up speed, with documents flying off the typewriter. Colonel Razin no longer had to worry.

Rebecca sent their new address to her cousin in Moscow, but received no reply and no letters from Gersh. She also wrote to Yakov's military unit every week. There was no response to those letters either.

'Every morning I wake up hoping for some news from them,' she told her daughter. 'Knowing nothing, absolutely nothing about where they are, how they are, who they're with ... that's such a terrible feeling.'

'Mama, no news is good news. If something had happened to them, the authorities would have found a way to inform us,' Debora replied. Another typist in the brigade headquarters, she knew, was spending her days filling out the death notices that the military delivered to families of killed soldiers in the city. There were hundreds of such slips, with a round blue seal on coarse paper, every day.

On 21 September, following a raft of optimistic communiqués, and three days after the fact, the Soviet military headquarters admitted that Kyiv had fallen. Rebecca and Debora listened to the broadcast on the radio and said not a word about the fear that filled them. Instead, Rebecca gently called her grandson and sat him on her lap. 'Let's read a book, Pasha. Show me all the letters you already know.'

After that, every Friday at dusk, Rebecca lit a Sabbath candle, something she hadn't done since she was a teenager in Uman. It was all new to Debora, and even more so to Pasha. They watched quietly as Rebecca closed her eyes and recited the prayers in an unfamiliar language, prayers for her husband and her son, for her son-in-law, and for the health of her daughter and her grandson.

'Do you want to pray with me?' she asked.

'No,' Debora replied, irritated. 'If God existed, I don't believe he would have allowed what's being done to us, and to this country.'

22

Stalingrad, February 1942

Rebecca's cousin finally replied in February. She had been evacuated from Moscow to the Volga in November, when the Germans were within a few kilometres of the Soviet capital. But now the Germans had been beaten back – the first real victory of the Red Army since the war began – and the Muscovites could return to their homes.

Dear Rebecca, I hope you too will be back in Kyiv in a few months, she wrote. *Though I must say, we are hearing some really terrible things from people who survived the Germans, and who are on our side of the front lines now. Much of Kyiv's city centre has been destroyed, apparently. And, everyone tells us, the Germans killed all the Jews they could find. I hope Gersh managed to get out in time – I will let you know as soon as he writes to us.*

Debora heard similar rumours, but tried to cheer Rebecca up. 'Mama, you know Papa, he has always been able to find a way. When it rained, he could walk in between the drops, you yourself used to say that.'

'I know, I know.' Rebecca smiled warily.

In the first weeks after leaving Kyiv, Pasha asked Rebecca

every day when Gersh would rejoin them. 'Soon, very soon,' she replied at first. Later, she just patted the boy's head and said nothing in response. Now, he no longer asked. One day, after seeing men with fishing rods walk past their home, he squeezed her hand.

'You think Grandpa is bringing me one like that?'

'Better. Much better,' she assured him. 'With a spinner.'

Every day at breakfast, she said a prayer under her breath, hoping for letters. But no mail came from her husband or son.

Debora wondered if she should tell her mother about the Swiss flask in the hands of the wounded soldier in Kyiv. But what would be the point? The flask proved nothing. It was probably mass-produced at the time, and the model could have been common among German soldiers. And even if it had been Yakov's, it could be that he'd simply lost it during the fighting. Maybe he was hiding among the partisans behind the German lines. It was not a conclusive piece of evidence. And so, she concluded, why give Rebecca an additional torment, more fuel for her nightmares? Better to keep quiet. She was good at keeping quiet.

The Stalingrad winter was harsh. The family weren't used to the kind of skin-blistering cold that enveloped the city, with icy winds ripping through the broad open streets. At night, Debora sometimes tried to imagine how Samuel was coping in his prison camp, in an expanse of infinite snow somewhere much further to the east. Was he among the heavy pine trees of Siberia? Working as a lumberjack to help the war effort, or maybe constructing a railway line? She tried to recall his eyes, burning with life, when she'd seen him being escorted onto the prison train. His proud posture, his self-assured voice. How he'd shouted: 'I will be back.' But he no longer came to her in dreams. Sometimes, while typing up endless travel assignments and provision requests at work, she wondered if he'd disappeared from her dreams because he really was dead. She tried to chase away these thoughts, but they could never be fully extinguished.

Food was getting scarce in Stalingrad. The barley soup Debora received every day in the military canteen was so transparent and devoid of fat that everyone dubbed it 'the Blue Danube'. Still, her job meant that, for now, they had just enough supplies to survive. Rebecca helped with some extra income, knitting gloves and caps. Neither of them liked to talk to outsiders, and so once Pasha fell asleep, they spent the long, dark evenings reminiscing about the past, about their life that had appeared so difficult at the time but seemed so easy in hindsight.

Few of the brigade's new recruits had any military skills. In training, they learned to shoot, to place and defuse mines, and to set up tripwires and defensive fortifications. This resulted in frequent, and sometimes deadly, mishaps on the ranges. When that happened, Debora typed up long after-action reports to the higher command, with one of the carbon copies sent to the NKVD.

Though there were other women in the brigade headquarters, most were nurses and doctors, and many of them were locals. Debora never tried to appear superior, but coming from Kyiv, she effortlessly carried the big-city aura that male officers in the staff headquarters found attractive and many of the women quietly resented. She made sure to do her hair every morning, no matter how tired she felt. She was also successful in transforming her uniform into something of a fashion statement: the strip of smooth white skin between her army skirt and the top of her carefully polished boots inevitably drew attention.

As she walked through the camp, ordinary recruits would often catcall, but nobody tried to flirt with her in the office.

Colonel Razin didn't seem interested in women, and nobody else dared harass the commander's secretary.

Those rules, however, didn't apply to NKVD Captain Dmitri Maslov, a young man with an easy laugh and a habit of cracking jokes about farting and boobs. Snub-nosed, with freckles that ran across his broad cheeks, he was so jolly and sociable that he appeared outright harmless – until the gregarious demeanour vanished in an instant and it was too late.

Maslov came from a village in the Stalingrad region, a once prosperous Cossack settlement that, like so many places in Ukraine, had been devastated by famine a decade earlier. For someone like him, the only alternative to back-breaking labour on the village collective farm was to join the military, or, if one was lucky, the NKVD. He was lucky. As a teenager, he did what he had to, to secure the assignment, assisting the officer in charge, Comrade Raimonds, in compiling the lists of villagers slated for execution or deportation as counter-revolutionary elements. He didn't think of himself as a bad man for doing so, even as he helped dispatch to their deaths the neighbours who used to pat him on the head when he was a child or at whose weddings he ate and drank in happier times. It was going to happen anyway, he reasoned. All he was doing was catching a ride on the train that was moving ahead, driven by forces beyond his control. If not him, someone else would be more than willing to do the same, so why let an opportunity slip?

Then, in 1937, orders came down from Moscow that Comrade Raimonds, whose Latvian origin was now suspect, had himself become a counter-revolutionary element. Maslov was there to help arrest his boss, who seemed a lot less frightening when handcuffed at 4 a.m., still in his pyjamas. The purges of Latvians, Poles and Jews in the NKVD ranks opened up prospects of rapid advancement for a genuinely Russian village boy like Maslov, especially after the pact with Hitler in 1939.

Before the war, Maslov knew full well, the perfidious spy rings and saboteur networks uncovered by the NKVD and highlighted in show trials were usually innocents caught in the unpredictable bone-crushing machinery of the state. But now, with faith in the durability of the Soviet system – a faith that had once seemed eternal – corroded by German battlefield successes, there was real treason aplenty. Hundreds of thousands of Soviet citizens, in Ukraine and in occupied parts of Russia, had in fact volunteered to serve the land's new German masters, as civilians and, increasingly, as uniformed troops.

Maslov's mission in the Special Section of the 13th Brigade was to ferret out the officers and recruits whose faith in a Soviet victory had started to waver and who could infect fellow men with defeatism. Few of these recruits had relatives on the other side of the front lines. Still, as Maslov knew from his own village youth, many had been wronged by the Soviet system, and some would likely switch sides if they had half a chance. The Special Section paid particular attention to the letters the recruits were writing home. Surprisingly, quite a few were dumb enough to put punishable thoughts on paper, thoughts that sometimes had to be interrupted with a quick bullet to the back of the head.

It was to discuss such cases with Colonel Razin that Captain Maslov often visited the brigade's cramped headquarters, a path that took him past Debora's desk. The other officers looked away whenever Maslov arrived, wearing his NKVD blue visor cap and holding carefully tied file folders under his arm: they knew his visits meant trouble.

Maslov had never been very successful with women. His chin was small and weak, and even though he was only in his late twenties, he was already going bald, a fact that he tried to conceal with an uncooperative comb-over. That didn't stop him, however, from pausing by Debora's desk for a friendly conversation that at first she found terrifying. It was just simple chit-chat – *Where are you from? How are you liking it here?* – but all she could think of was whether he would ask her about her husband.

He didn't probe too hard, however.

'I've seen that you have a child, a very nice boy,' he said one day. 'How is he finding it here?'

'Very well, Comrade Captain, thank you for asking.'

'Oh, you can just call me Dmitri, no need for titles, we are among friends!' he laughed.

'Yes . . . Dmitri,' Debora said hesitantly.

'How old is he now?'

'Four. It's hard for him here, to be honest. He misses Kyiv, he misses home. I really don't know how I can cheer him up.'

'I think I've got just the right thing to make him happy. The Moscow Circus is coming through Stalingrad next Sunday, the real stars. We've got some tickets allocated – I may be able to get you a pair. Interested?'

'You are so kind,' Debora said. 'I am sure Pasha would love that.'

'Deal,' Maslov promised, and went on his way.

He left an envelope with two tickets on her desk the following day.

On Sunday morning, Debora and Pasha plodded through the snow to the circus performance in a neoclassical concert hall in downtown Stalingrad, several kilometres from their home. They were running late. Debora didn't expect to see Maslov, but there he was, a cigarette in his mouth, patiently waiting for them in the cold under the imitation Corinthian columns.

'You also like the circus?' she asked him.

'Of course. Who doesn't?' He grinned and extended his hand

to Pasha, speaking to him with the mock seriousness of an adult conversation. 'Good morning, comrade.'

Pasha hesitated for a second, but then grabbed the hand.

'We'd better go inside quickly, before they begin.' Maslov nudged the child.

This was a wartime circus, and so the performance was limited – none of the glitz that Debora had seen with Samuel in Kharkiv, and few of the stunts that had been advertised on the billboard outside. But that was more than made up for by the entrance of eight bears, dressed in glittery little-girl dresses and riding bicycles onto the stage. Pasha had never seen bears before, and was transfixed as the giant animals obediently followed the trainer. Then came the clowns. One, in rags, with a fake moustache and a bandaged hand, was meant to represent Hitler, nursing his wounds after the German defeat near Moscow. The audience erupted in jeers, but Pasha giggled as the other clowns kicked Hitler's padded behind.

'I haven't heard him laugh so much since we left Kyiv,' Debora whispered into Maslov's ear. 'Thank you for this. It means a lot to me.'

'My father died when I was young,' he replied. 'It must be hard to raise a child without a father.'

She winced. 'He has a father.'

'Of course, of course. I mean without a father to take care of him here.'

She didn't know how to respond, and then the show's grand finale began and it was too loud to speak. Memories of Samuel, of that first circus date in Kharkiv, raced through her head as she watched the gymnasts walk the tightrope. A feeling of guilt rose in her chest. She pulled away from Maslov, leaning to the other side of the seat, her posture stiffening. Samuel, Samuel. That was so long ago, before the war, before Pasha, before all this. Samuel wouldn't be able to help her take care of Pasha for another five years. In that, Maslov was right. She glanced at her son again, at the sheer abandon of his delight. He shrieked and clapped after every stunt, and Maslov seemed just as buoyed by innocent, childish joy.

After the circus, Maslov drove them home in his government car. He talked most of the time to Pasha – about his favourite kind of warplane, about fishing in his village, about how he had hunted in the woods. Debora realised that it was the first time her son had had a conversation with a man since leaving his grandfather in Kyiv.

23

Stalingrad, March 1942

It was surprising how quickly Pasha got sick. He had seemed fine the previous night, listening intently as Rebecca read him a book of fables, and then, as usual, falling asleep next to her on the narrow bed. When the first rays of sunlight flooded the frosted panes, however, he was feverish and disorientated, shivering and then sweating so much that the sheet was soaked right through to the mattress. Debora boiled water with a drop of honey, scraping the last sticky bit from the bottom of a glass jar. But Pasha kept choking as he tried to drink. His rasping cough grew stronger during the day, and he lay in bed, listless and exhausted.

Debora herself had fainted the previous day, though it wasn't unusual given how little they all had to eat. It had been a hungry winter everywhere in the Soviet Union, and the tail end of winter was always the worst time. The rations that she picked up at the 13th Brigade headquarters had been shrinking for weeks. These days she received a quarter-loaf of coarse rye bread, some salted Volga fish, rotting potatoes, a small tin of canned meat and a packet of sugar once a week. Soldiers at the brigade ate at the canteen, and their soups and stews had become even thinner than before – both because of reduced supplies and because the quartermaster, in connivance with senior officers, was bartering some of the meat and butter for gold, jewels and clothes.

By mid March, several soldiers had developed what was widely called 'chicken blindness' – a condition caused by a severe lack of vitamins. Maslov and his colleagues at the NKVD initially thought these men were malingerers simulating an illness, but reluctantly accepted the military doctor's verdict that the condition was in fact genuine. Rebecca also worried about vitamins, especially for Pasha. More and more frequently, she went to the bazaar near the Stalingrad train station and traded a ring or a brooch with gold-toothed Azeri merchants dressed in black padded jackets and colourful headscarves for a treat of dried apricots, oranges or nuts. She was wary of buying horsemeat sausage, a local delicacy, because so much of it came from warhorses that had died of exhaustion or disease.

The brigade was finally scheduled to deploy the following month. Debora knew she wouldn't be following the troops to the front line. When the headquarters left, so would her job – and her military rations. Civilians not employed in manual labour by the defence industries were allocated significantly less food than even the meagre military rations. On the streets of Stalingrad, she saw the bloated bellies, lethargic movements and cracked skin of people being slowly killed by starvation – images familiar from a decade ago in Ukraine. There were no corpses on the streets yet, or at least she didn't spot any.

During the day, her conversations with her mother revolved around food. There were stratagems for exchanging part of her bread quota for garlic and onion, and detailed negotiations about how Rebecca could trade the scarves and gloves she was knitting for dried pumpkin and beets.

'I really can't handle this any more,' Rebecca finally erupted, the day before Pasha got sick. 'For thousands of years, humanity developed the arts, music, civilisation. You spent years studying at the university, reading book after book, learning how to appreciate the finest achievements of the human mind. And now look at us. Look at what the world has come down to. We're like animals, like cattle. An entire people, cattle. All we think about, talk about, is feed. What will the masters give us to eat? What can we forage? We are just the appendages of our stomachs.'

'I know, Mama, I know. But we'll get through this, and things will improve, and we will be able to think about art and books and all the other things again, as it was before. But first we must survive. He,' Debora pointed at a sleeping Pasha, 'he must survive.'

The doctor who visited Debora's home on the first evening of Pasha's illness fussed with his thermometer, listened to the boy's lungs, and then took off Pasha's shirt and examined the handful of tiny bite marks on his pale skin. 'Make sure to boil all your clothes and sheets,' he said, trying not to lean against anything. 'Looks like the boy has picked up lice and contracted typhus. We've already had a couple of similar cases in the crèche, and many more among the troops.'

Rebecca clasped her hands and prayed silently. She remembered the typhus epidemics of the 1920s and was terrified of the disease. Debora, forcing herself to ignore the panic that swelled in her chest, focused on practical matters. 'Doctor, what should we do? How can you help us? How can we make him get well?'

There wasn't really much to do, the doctor knew. He had read about the promising tests of a new drug, penicillin, which apparently worked miracles with various infections. But nothing of the kind was available in Stalingrad, where the majority of those infected with typhus wasted away and died, raving and ripping their sheets in feverish delirium, within a week or two.

'Give him a lot to drink, make sure he doesn't dehydrate,' he advised. 'But the main thing is that your boy – like everyone else I am seeing – is weakened by the lack of nutrition. He won't recover until his body gets what it needs to fight the disease. If you want to save him, do what you can to find him the right food. I wish you luck,' he added and left.

Once he was gone, Debora burrowed into her hiding place under the bed and took out the silver Sabbath cup and her Venetian necklace. 'These are the only possessions we have left,' she said. 'I will take them to the bazaar tomorrow. Nothing else that we can do.'

Rebecca ran her hand over the necklace, silently, just as she had done on her own wedding day, in a different world. 'Nothing else,' she repeated.

At the bazaar, nobody wanted the Sabbath cup, and the necklace didn't fetch much either. The heavily built woman at the counter looked at it closely, rubbing and even smelling the gold, and then handed it back to Debora. 'Who needs jewellery these days?' she said. 'I'd be doing you a favour to take it. A real favour.'

Debora's mouth was contorted in an ingratiating smile. 'My darling, please have a big heart. It is for a very sick little boy.'

'Everyone has got sick little boys these days, and everyone has got jewels,' the woman said.

'Please, have another look,' Debora implored. Reluctantly the woman spat on her hand, wiped away a speck of dirt and raised the jewel to check the quality of its rubies and emeralds against the sunlight.

'Just so you know, I do have a big heart,' she finally said, and put on the counter a jar of honey, four eggs, and a handful of dried apricots wrapped in newspaper. The headline was about the triumphs of Soviet agriculture.

'Is that it?' Debora flinched. 'This is a very expensive necklace, made by an Italian jeweller. My grandmother had it before the revolution.'

'You don't want?' The woman began removing the food.

'No, no, I will take it.' Debora rushed to accept, and hid the precious delicacies in her handbag.

She trudged home, careful not to break the eggs. Pasha was still running a high fever, and a rash had appeared on his chest. Rebecca wiped his forehead with a wet towel and then fed him a soft-boiled egg with a spoon. He managed to swallow most of it, despite the pain from his inflamed throat.

'I don't know what we will do now,' Debora told her mother as the two of them shared a thin slice of sour bread for dinner. The honey, the eggs and the apricots were hidden inside the pantry.

At night, she had a hard time falling asleep, with her stomach gurgling and then seizing up in a cramp. It was well after midnight when she finally sank into a blurry haze, her exhausted brain no longer recognising the difference between dream and reality. Olena was there, visiting them in Stalingrad. She sat at the table, holding Pasha in her arms, stroking him gently, laughing, the old good Olena she had known before the war, before the famine. Rebecca was cooking something, a stew, and the smell was wafting through the room. Then Olena was serving a stew, and placing a boiled boy's hand on Debora's plate, telling her: 'Try this, it is so tender, so juicy, your mama is a wonderful cook.' Debora bit off a morsel and chewed it, and it was indeed delicious. But then panic shot through her, and she started looking around, looking for Pasha, and he wasn't in the room any more. 'Pasha, Pasha,' she called. 'Where is Pasha?' But Olena was grinning, and winking and not saying anything, and Debora started wondering how they could have butchered the child without her noticing, and why the tablecloth remained pristinely white, and why there was no blood on the floor.

Her heart racing, she jolted awake. She got up and checked on Pasha, still breathing heavily and thrashing in his sleep. She returned to bed and tossed and turned until sunrise.

Pasha showed no sign of getting better, but at least he wasn't getting worse. Rebecca spoon-fed him honey throughout the day, and made sure he didn't waste even the smallest bits of boiled egg. That night, just after they had all gone to bed, there was a strong, hard knock on the door. Wearing a coat over her nightgown, Debora rose to open it. Maslov, a big canvas bag in his hands, was grinning outside.

'Hope it isn't too late and that I didn't knock too loudly – sorry, it's out of habit,' he said. 'But I've heard from the doctor that Pasha isn't doing well and thought I should visit.'

'Come in, come in and sit down,' Debora welcomed him. 'We can offer you some tea, except that it isn't really tea, it's just hot water – who's got tea these days? Would you still like some?'

'I'd love some, but we can do better than that,' Maslov replied.

He took off his snow-encrusted boots and his coat and walked into the room. Rebecca had never met him before, and was momentarily startled by the blue NKVD visor cap. 'This is my mother,' Debora introduced her. 'And this is Captain Maslov, he's also in the brigade headquarters. He's the one who got us tickets to see the circus.'

'Ah, yes, Pasha enjoyed that very much,' Rebecca said politely. Debora hadn't mentioned to her that Maslov was from the NKVD.

Pasha looked at the visitor from under his blanket, shivering. 'How are you doing, champion?' Maslov asked him cheerfully and extended his hand.

Gathering his remaining strength, Pasha responded with a limp handshake. 'I think I am going to die tomorrow,' he said plainly.

Debora froze.

Maslov laughed loudly. 'That's a funny joke, big man. You'll be healthy in no time, you'll see. And then we'll all be dancing at your wedding. You have a fiancée yet?' Pasha didn't react. 'Oh, you're shy talking about your ladies? It's okay, you can tell me later, when your mama is not around.'

He put his bag on the table and unfastened it. 'I've got some presents to cheer you all up. But you,' he turned back to Pasha, 'you have to promise me that you will listen to your mama and eat everything she gives you, okay?'

The boy nodded.

Like a magician, Maslov began pulling out items of food that they hadn't seen in months. It all came from the NKVD officers' supply depot, stocked with goods that had been confiscated from speculators. He lined up on the table a row of cans of concentrated sweet milk. There was a jar of butter, a jar of pickled cabbage, several sausages, a piece of American Lend-Lease chocolate, tea and sugar. Most importantly, there was also a big loaf of white bread, made with proper wheat, not the usual mixture of husks and wood chips.

'This is like a feast at Count Potocki's estate,' Rebecca exclaimed. 'I didn't think anyone was making this kind of bread any more.'

'Thank you,' Debora said, squeezing Maslov's hand. 'You have no idea how much this means to us. To Pasha. The doctor told us that good nutrition is everything for him.'

'Ah, this is nothing,' Maslov replied. 'He's going to make it, mark my words. He will be fine.'

Debora broke open the packet of tea and brewed a pot. They

all put a cube of sugar under their tongues, precious sweetness that slowly dissolved as they drank the rich, dark liquid. It felt like pre-war life. Like happiness.

'I can't stay much longer – duty calls,' Maslov said after they had finished the tea. 'But I will drop by again soon.' Pasha had fallen asleep, and Maslov gently ruffled the boy's hair before stepping out. Debora's hand lingered in his just a moment longer than usual.

After he was gone, Rebecca leaned on the table and surveyed their new treasures. 'This is like a jinni out of a bottle,' she said. 'Look at it all. Incredible. But nothing is free, especially not now. This man clearly wants you, you surely understand that.'

'Yes, Mama, I am not a child. Of course I understand.'

'He's not a simple man, he's a captain in the NKVD. The people who took your husband away. Does he know about Samuel, does he know where he is?'

'I hope not.'

'If Samuel had been here with us, you wouldn't be needing these gifts to survive,' Rebecca went on. 'He would have taken good care of you, and your child wouldn't be starving.'

Debora was upset. 'Mama, you think I don't know that? You think you're discovering America for me? The fact is that Samuel is away, *far* away. I don't know where he is, I don't even know whether he is still alive. What I do know is that Maslov certainly had nothing to do with what happened to him.' She raised her voice to an angry whisper. 'I don't know what he knows about this. I also don't know what exactly he wants from me. But if I have to do it to save Pasha, to make sure Pasha survives all this, to make sure he survives this stupid war, I will do it. I will. I will do anything he wants.'

Rebecca added hot water to their empty teacups and sat close to her daughter. 'I am not judging,' she said, conciliatory. 'You know the decisions that you have to make, and nobody who isn't in your shoes has the right to say anything.'

'That's true. Nobody.'

Debora's stomach was no longer used to abundant food. She felt sick with indigestion and anxiety all night.

24

Stalingrad, April 1942

Colonel Razin gave Debora a quick hug in his empty office. 'Wish us luck,' he said. 'We're off to liberate Ukraine. Soon you'll be able to head home.' The 13th Brigade headquarters equipment was already packed up and loaded into tented trucks, ready for a new offensive.

'Good luck to all of us,' she replied.

The offensive, which built on German defeats near Moscow, was meant to recapture Kharkiv, the first major Ukrainian city that would be freed from the Nazis after nearly a year of war. Who knew, maybe by summer they would be able to return to Kyiv. Debora imagined walking back into her apartment on Shevchenko Boulevard, opening the windows to let in fresh air, picnicking in the Botanical Garden.

'Are you leaving for the front line too?' she asked Captain Maslov later in the day.

'No, we've got plenty of work left back here, to protect the rear. With the tank plant and everything else, we must be even more vigilant now. There is no victory without Stalingrad,' he replied.

Sometimes Maslov wished to participate in the actual war.

But for now, he was secretly relieved to be staying behind, with Debora, with Pasha. Somehow he recognised himself in the little boy living in a household of women, the little boy who was thankfully healthy again.

Debora was now a civilian typist, living on tiny food rations on which they would have starved without Maslov's weekly offerings. It was warm in their home, with springtime bringing flies and mosquitoes. Faint sounds of marching bands came through the open window: the May Day holiday parade. Debora shared a pot of tea with her mother.

'Remember five years ago at this time how we were all waiting for Samuel? How he never came home?' Rebecca mused.

'I will always remember that day, Mama. You don't have to talk to me about it.'

'It's now halfway through his sentence. That's all I wanted to say,' Rebecca said.

'Mama, I know how to count to ten. Please, let's just drink our tea in peace.'

There was a knock on the door. Pasha, who had seemed to be asleep, jumped from his bed. 'Is that Uncle Dmitri?' he asked, excited, and ran to open it. He hugged Maslov, as usual. Then, after a brief glance in Debora's direction, he asked point-blank: 'Uncle Dmitri, can you be my papa? I want a papa.'

Maslov said nothing and just patted him on the head as he made his way inside.

'My other papa, I've never seen him. He's never here. I want a papa who can be with me all the time. Like you,' Pasha insisted.

Debora flushed red. Rebecca took the boy by the hand and led him away. 'Pasha, come, let's read a book together.'

'No, no,' Maslov objected. 'I've got something for him. You two can cook, but the men have business to attend to.'

He pulled out a brand-new chess set and handed it to the boy.

'Do you know how to play?'

Pasha shook his head. Maslov lined up the pieces on the board and began patiently explaining the game. Pasha nodded vigorously, but still moved his rooks diagonally as if they were queens and advanced his pawns by two squares throughout the game.

'Check – and mate!' he shrieked with delight half an hour later.

'You're a real champion,' Maslov congratulated him with a handshake.

Once Pasha fell asleep for an afternoon nap, Debora and Maslov walked outside and sat down on a bench. She had long dreaded this moment, but now she couldn't delay it any more.

'I don't know how much you know about my husband ...' she began.

'I know what I need to know. I've checked your file,' Maslov said, tilting his head and looking straight at her. 'Whatever he did shouldn't be tainting you, or Pasha. It's a closed file now.'

'What do you mean, a closed file? How can it be closed? He is still my husband. In five years, his term will be over.'

Maslov tried to take her hand, but she pulled it back.

'There is no term, my dear Debora. I am sorry,' he said. 'I don't know how to put this. I'm not even supposed to be telling you, but there just isn't a term. When you came to the brigade, we had to check everyone's relatives. Not all the files are in place, so many archives have been lost, but I did my due diligence, and a copy of your husband's sentence turned up. It was ten years without the right of correspondence, as you surely know.'

'Yes. Ten years. In 1937.'

'Debora, do you know how many people were arrested in 1937? Far too many. Everywhere. Do you think they really had room for that many prisoners?'

She felt food rising in her throat.

'Ten years without the right of correspondence – why do you

180

think they wouldn't want letters, or, more importantly, food and clothes parcels? Why do you think such a sentence was invented? Because they couldn't tell all those relatives, millions of relatives, all in just one year, that their loved ones had been shot. Trust me, I know very well what ten years without the right of correspondence means. It means that you will never see your husband again. It means that Pasha will never see his father again. And Pasha, you know this better than me, he needs a father.'

He fell silent for a moment and then added: 'I could be a good father to him. You know that.'

Debora didn't react, still thinking about Samuel. For the last five years, she had heard rumours, rumours that she had tried to dismiss as outlandish. Suspecting wasn't the same thing as actually knowing. Knowing for certain that he would never be coming back. She felt an almost irresistible urge to vomit.

'How can you be so sure? How can you know that he is dead? Do you actually know it for a fact?' she finally burst out. 'Is there proof?'

'You know what my job is, don't you?' Maslov continued patiently. 'At the time, the Organs were given plans, numbers, they had to fulfil a quota. They detained men, sentenced them, and those given this particular sentence were all shot, within twenty-four hours. Trust me, he's dead.'

He carefully used the third person, making sure an incriminating 'we' didn't creep in. That year, 1937, had been a very, very busy one for him. He didn't tell Debora how Comrade Raimonds, a burly man who had pulled the trigger with glee so many times himself, had dropped to his knees, wetting his pants, pleading for mercy and crying like a baby when his own turn to die finally arrived.

She got up. 'I want you to check. I want to know for sure,' she told him, and returned indoors.

He remained outside, smoking a cigarette, and then went home.

Rebecca was impatient to talk about Pasha's outburst. 'It's tough for the boy growing up like this, but he's got a father, and he must be proud of him,' she began as Debora stepped back into the room. 'You should talk to him more often about Samuel. What Pasha said to that NKVD man, it pulled my heart inside out. Have you thought about how he'll handle Samuel's return? What kind of son will he grow up to be?'

'Mama,' Debora interrupted, her voice quivering. 'There will be no return. That sentence, ten years, it was all a charade. They shot him. Maslov wasn't supposed to tell me, but he did.'

'He would tell you that, wouldn't he?'

'It's not something you can lie about. I believe him.'

'Are you certain?'

She nodded, then sat down and buried her face in her shaking palms. Rebecca came closer and kissed the top of her head.

'Now you're a widow, my daughter. We must pray for Samuel's soul.'

'Pray?' Debora stiffened. 'Pray? You know I have never prayed, Mama. I don't believe in all those superstitions. Why do you want me to pray?'

'You don't have to believe.' Rebecca stroked her hair. 'Just repeat after me. We don't have a synagogue here, we don't have Jewish men to pray with us, so we'll have to do it ourselves. But it's better than nothing, and I'm sure Samuel would have appreciated it. Don't you think so?'

'Maybe he would,' Debora acquiesced. Though they held no meaning for her, she mouthed the words of the Kaddish: '*Yitgadal ve yitqadash shme rabba.*'

She spent the rest of the evening looking at Samuel's

photograph in his pilot's gear, the one she had taken from Kyiv. She was surprised and ashamed at how little she felt. Five years was a long time, longer than their time living together as husband and wife. She had grown accustomed to being without him. She had survived without him so far, and more importantly, she had made sure that Pasha survived too. 'Farewell, my love,' she whispered. 'I have waited for you as long as I could. But you aren't coming back to me.'

It was only in the morning that she recalled Maslov's words about how he could replace Samuel as Pasha's father. She didn't find him attractive. But as she watched him with Pasha, she felt a mother's visceral gratitude every time he made the boy smile.

'I think he wants to marry me,' she told Rebecca. 'Dmitri.'

Rebecca flinched.

'He may be from the NKVD, but I can see that he is a good man,' Debora went on. 'Not like the rest of them.'

'How can you tell?'

'I just know.'

'You know,' Rebecca repeated, almost mockingly. 'And do you love him?'

'Does it matter? Love,' Debora scoffed. 'This is not a country for love. This is not the time for love. I will probably never love anyone again, but I will marry Maslov if he asks. For Pasha. Because Pasha must live. And for Samuel, because Pasha is his flesh and blood.'

Maslov stopped by Debora's home two weeks later. His eyes were red and his uniform, usually carefully pressed, was creased and dirty. 'Sorry I couldn't come earlier, but these are busy times,' he said. 'Unfortunate things are happening.'

'What do you mean?' Debora asked. 'I've just heard on the radio that we're achieving successes, that our troops are already on the outskirts of Kharkiv.'

'They were. But not everyone fought the way they should have. The Germans counter-attacked, and many of our men have been surrounded and cut off. I don't know how many will be able to get out.'

'Our brigade?' she asked.

'They're in the middle of it,' Maslov said. 'I've heard that Colonel Razin was killed. Others, I don't know. But it's bad. What this means is that the Germans are now heading this way. They are still far away, but they can move fast.'

'Will they get all the way here, to Stalingrad?'

'I don't think so. But this is war. Many things that we thought impossible have happened.'

He came closer and took her hand.

'My dear Debora, this is not what I wanted to speak to you about. I've never asked you how you feel about me, and I'm not usually good with words when I am around women. But I do have feelings for you. Real feelings. You've probably figured that out by now. I could be a good husband and a good father. I thought we would have more time to get to know each other better, but this is war, and there is no time left. So here I am, right now, asking you to be my wife.'

'I have to be sure about Samuel,' she said.

'I've made enquiries. I'm not aware of any cases of someone with that kind of sentence still being alive,' Maslov replied. 'But the actual execution documents won't be located until after the war, if at all. That's how it is.'

'Are you sure he is no longer with us?'

'As sure as one can be.' He let go of her hand. 'Debora, you must think about yourself now. You can't condemn yourself to loneliness. And you can't condemn Pasha to growing up without a father. I can make all the difference in his life.'

'I know, Dmitri, I know,' she said quietly, almost too quietly to be heard.

She had tried to fend off this moment, but time had run out. What else could she do?

'Yes, Dmitri.' Her lips came together in a faint, unconvincing smile. 'I will become your wife.'

Maslov leaned in and kissed her, his moist tongue pushing into her mouth. It tasted of borscht. Shutting her eyes, she reciprocated.

'There's one thing,' she added when he pulled away. 'When this war is over, I want to return home to Kyiv. I miss Ukraine. We all do.'

'You know that our fate isn't always in our own hands,' he said. 'But I promise that I will try as hard as I can to get us there.'

'You'll love it in Ukraine,' she replied.

'I know I will. And I know how much you want to go home.'

25

Stalingrad, July 1942

The wedding, like all wartime weddings, was short on ceremony. Maslov remained in uniform, while Debora wore a simple satin dress. He brought along a bouquet of wild flowers and a bottle of vodka, which he shared with his new wife and the officiating clerk, a woman in her fifties who smiled ingratiatingly at the NKVD captain.

Samuel's photograph was gone from the nightstand, tucked away in Debora's suitcase. 'Your father died like a hero fighting the Germans,' she explained to Pasha a week before the wedding. The boy didn't seem to mind or ask many questions – he preferred his new dad anyway. He and Rebecca watched the newly-weds kiss, exchange rings and sign their names with an ink pen in the big ledger. After that, the clerk fussed for half an hour with several documents, typing them up on thin paper and stamping each with a round blue seal.

Maslov knew what power these pieces of paper possessed in the Soviet Union. He was determined to reach bureaucratic perfection.

One of the documents annulled Debora's marriage to Samuel,

to make sure that she was no longer classified as the wife of an enemy of the state. The second certified Pasha's adoption, changing his surname to Maslov – and, just as importantly, replacing the word 'Jew' with 'Russian'. Soviet documents had always stated their bearers' ethnicity, an entry that seemed not to matter at first. But these days, being branded with the wrong affiliation could mean the difference between life and death. Before the war, the NKVD had rounded up and deported to Siberia or Kazakhstan those unlucky enough to be of Polish, Hungarian or German blood.

So far, being labelled a Jew wasn't that bad. But the mood was clearly shifting as Hitler's armies kept moving east. Maslov's job included reading stacks of intelligence reports on popular conversations, which was why he had relentlessly pushed Debora to make the change.

'Tens of millions of our citizens are living under the Germans, and every day they are told that Jews are the source of their troubles, that all the horrors that happen to them happen because of the Jews,' he told her before the wedding. 'Do you think they will forget this when the Germans are kicked out? Already here in Stalingrad, ordinary people are starting to speak the same way. Yid this, Yid that, I am sure you've heard.'

Debora nodded.

'And you will hear a lot more, unfortunately. Don't destroy the boy's life. Make him a Russian while you can,' he implored. 'In any case, you're a Soviet woman, you're educated, what does it even matter?'

'Is this really necessary?' Debora wavered. 'I know it's silly, but I feel like it would be a betrayal, like I am betraying Pasha's father by doing this.'

'You can't betray a dead man. He of all people doesn't care about it any more,' Maslov said. 'And neither should you.'

And so, in the end, Debora didn't object when Maslov proposed to amend her first name, clearly Jewish in Russia or Ukraine, to fit her new Slavic surname. The morning of 10 July 1942, she officially became Darya Grigoriyevna Maslova, married, Russian, mother of Pasha Maslov, as sealed and certified by the Stalingrad Oblast Department of Registration of Acts of Civil Status.

Her mother scoffed as she watched the clerk finish the typing and stamping. 'You can call yourself whatever you want, you can even call yourself Countess Potocki, but to these people you will always be a Yid,' she whispered. 'Don't forget that.'

'Maybe,' Debora said, and pointed at Pasha. 'But he won't be.'

That night, she and Maslov slept together for the first time. The lights were out, and she didn't have much of a look at his pink, barrel-like torso. He obviously didn't have a lot of experience and was nervous and sweaty as they undressed. She lay down and guided him. He came almost immediately, with a girlish high-pitched groan. 'I love you,' he whispered in her ear, and kissed her hair. Within a few minutes, he was snoring.

Debora cleaned herself up and returned to bed, snuggling up to him. She ran her fingers through his thinning hair. She didn't love him, but it felt comforting to lie next to a man's bulk. With Maslov, there was no instant, wordless understanding, no dissolving in each other's embrace. No energy of the kind that she had experienced with Samuel. But as she fell asleep, she felt secure. Warm. Protected. It was a good feeling.

If one moved west from the Volga anywhere in Stalingrad, the green jumble of detached countryside homes began only a few blocks away. It was in one of these homes that Maslov arranged for two rooms after the wedding – one where he would sleep with Debora and another for Rebecca and Pasha. The owner, a hunchbacked woman named Svetlana, lived alone: her husband and both of her sons were at the front line and she needed the income, particularly in the form of Maslov's food rations come winter.

Svetlana's whitewashed house had a garden, with a cherry tree that Pasha would climb every day, and a cellar. Raspberry and strawberry bushes grew at the far side, and she allowed the boy to graze there whenever he wanted. A week after they moved, Debora sat in the shade of fruit trees on the porch, looking at the bright-blue sky, dragonflies buzzing around her. 'I am finally happy here,' she told Rebecca. 'For the first time since we left Kyiv, I can say that I am happy. Maybe even for the first time since they took Samuel.'

Pasha ran up to them, his mouth smeared with raspberries.

'And look at him, look how happy he is.'

'It's quiet and peaceful,' Rebecca agreed. 'It reminds me of Uman when I was a child. It's as if there is no war.'

Maslov wasn't there that day. He spent less and less time with his new family after the wedding. A black NKVD car usually dropped him off after midnight and picked him up again at first light. He no longer made silly jokes. With every day, he looked more tired and more worried. They'd had sex only a few times since the wedding, always as quickly and uneventfully as on the first night.

Though the official communiqués never revealed the full scope of the disaster, Maslov knew that the Soviet attempt to retake Kharkiv in May had resulted in a catastrophe, with several Red Army divisions surrounded and destroyed. Worse, a surprisingly large number of Red Army soldiers had agreed to join new, Russian-only battalions raised by the Nazis. Now these battalions, together with Romanian and Italian troops, followed

German tank formations that were advancing across the flat steppe. They had already seized the coal-mining lands of the Ukrainian Donbas and were approaching the Don river. If they managed to cross the Don, there would be no natural obstacles to slow their movement all the way to the Volga – and Stalingrad.

The Soviet High Command hoped that the Red Army divisions it had sent to the Don would hold firm and eventually counter-attack. It didn't contemplate fighting in Stalingrad, still solidly in the rear and without a strong military presence. The scarce local NKVD units had just merged with newly arrived NKVD troops from Siberia to create a division that would defend the city should the Germans break through. Maslov was now attached to its staff.

As German troops reached Cossack villages on the Don, villages of the kind where Maslov had grown up, they were often greeted as liberators. He read in the daily intelligence reports how local women offered bread and salt on embroidered towels to welcome the advance units' commanders. His superiors feared similar sympathies inside Stalingrad, which was why he was hardly ever home. Acting on tips from informers, his department detained suspected defeatists and rumour-mongers. NKVD patrols and checkpoints along the riverbanks were also on the lookout for the ever more numerous deserters who tried to cross the Volga and escape further east. These were easily identified by their military haircuts and were usually shot dead immediately.

The one kind of operation that Maslov didn't like was neutralising the associates and families of Soviet officers who were believed to have joined the German volunteer battalions. The names came from NKVD intelligence reports that, Maslov suspected, were tainted by deliberately planted German misinformation. When he and his fellow NKVD men came knocking in the middle of the night, the officers' frightened wives usually had no idea about what had happened to their husbands since their letters stopped arriving. Some opened the door with hopeful smiles, expecting good news. Still, these families had to be bundled on cattle trains and shipped far away. They usually had just half an hour to pack. Their children, awakened by the intruders, wept hysterically. But these were the rules, and Maslov, as he told himself every day, was just doing his job, a job that was necessary and noble in the long run. He didn't recount the details to his new wife.

The NKVD campaign to suppress panic was a success. Unlike Kyiv a year earlier, Stalingrad still lived the measured life of a city lulled into believing that it wasn't in immediate danger. Hunger eased with the summer, as suburban vegetable patches produced abundant carrots, cabbages and tomatoes. Apples and peaches ripened in the nearby orchards. Kindergartens were open, with teachers escorting flocks of children to the playgrounds. The city's music theatre continued staging nineteenth-century vaudevilles. Train convoys and Volga river barges connecting Russia with the Caucasus and the Caspian Sea kept streaming through, carrying food, oil and armaments north. Nobody was evacuating factories or government offices – in fact, the NKVD, with its control of river crossings, was making sure that nobody useful abandoned the city. The Stalingrad Tractor Plant continued manufacturing tanks and shipping them to the ever-closer front line.

The Germans occasionally sent planes to bomb the tractor plant, on the northern outskirts of the city, but so far they had missed the main production line. They didn't seem interested in the civilian parts of Stalingrad. The air raid sirens that sounded almost every day usually turned out to be false alarms. They had also become so routine that few people bothered to run to the shelters or dive into the trenches that had been dug, as a precaution, along the roadsides.

Schools were supposed to reopen on 1 September, a day that Debora awaited with anticipation. Maslov had found her a slot in a middle school not far from their home. Now that she was the wife of an NKVD officer, she would be allowed to teach Russian literature. She had reconciled herself to the idea that she would never be in a classroom, and now she permitted herself to dream once again about sharing the books she loved, and about the students – not many, but surely some – who would share this love.

26

Stalingrad, August 1942

On Sunday 23 August, *Puss in Boots* was playing at noon in the Stalingrad municipal theatre. Pasha had just read an abridged version of the book, with Rebecca's help. Impressed by the boy's new fluency, Maslov procured tickets for the play, in the front row. He had been promised a few hours off work, time he was eager to spend watching the adventures of the fairy-tale cat.

Maslov tried to be respectful with Rebecca, but he could sense that she disliked him. That she thought him somehow inferior, uncouth. This used to happen to him often, and he didn't care that much. He had met enough people like her, urban sophisticates with refined accents, begging for their lives, on their knees. Then they no longer looked down on him.

His new mother-in law didn't have to be present everywhere and at all times, he decided as he bought the tickets. He got only three.

'What about Mama?' Debora asked him, surprised. 'Mama loves theatre.'

'It was all sold out,' Maslov lied. 'I was lucky to get these three.'

'Don't worry about me,' Rebecca interrupted him. 'You go,

enjoy. I'm happy to sit here on the porch and play cards with Svetlana.'

The sky was still dark when Debora heard distant thumps through her fading sleep. She thought at first it was a thunderstorm, but then realised the sound was different – and unsettlingly familiar. She shook Maslov's shoulder. 'What is that noise?' she asked. He opened his eyes and sat upright in bed. 'Hear that? Are those guns?' she asked.

He stretched his back, got out of bed and opened the window to listen more carefully. 'It does sound like artillery,' he acknowledged. The morning laziness evaporated and he began to dress, with the precise, rapid motions of someone who had practised military drills countless times.

'How can it be? Are the Germans so close that we can hear them now? Can it be just practice?'

'They really can't be this close,' Maslov replied. 'The front line is almost a hundred kilometres away.'

They heard the sound of a car engine, and then Maslov's black NKVD sedan rolled up the gravel path to their front gate. Leaving the engine humming, the driver hopped out. This was the first time that Debora had seen him wear a helmet. He knocked on the door and handed over a sealed envelope. Maslov cursed when he read it.

'I'm not supposed to tell you this,' he said quietly, 'but it looks like the Germans have managed to cross the Don. Their tanks spent the night driving through the steppe and are approaching the city. This is not good. Not good at all.' He was already putting on his cap and fastening his pistol holster. 'We're going to hit them hard and drive them away, but it will be messy for a while, especially in this part of town. It would be safer for you and Pasha to go to the other side of the river until things quieten down. I'm going to arrange for transport this afternoon.'

'Transport to where?'

He didn't answer.

Debora picked up the theatre tickets from the nightstand. 'What about these?'

'There is no reason why you shouldn't go. The Germans are well outside the city. I will join you if I can,' he added, plucking one of the tickets from her hand. 'But promise me that this morning you'll pack all your most important belongings, just the things that you can carry. Tomorrow, or even tonight, you should be ready to go across the river.'

Debora kissed him as he was walking out the door. 'But I don't want to leave,' she said.

She watched the tail lights of his car disappear down the path. Then she sat down on the porch, in the garden to which she had grown attached so quickly. The air was still chilly. Birds chirped in the trees, and the hum of artillery no longer seemed as loud. Rebecca joined her as the sun rose, illuminating the scattered clouds in hues of purple and pink, and handed her a cup of tea.

'The Germans are at the gates of Stalingrad,' Debora told her mother. 'Dmitri says we have to move out, maybe as soon as tomorrow.'

'Move out? Again?'

'Mama, promise me one thing: when Pasha wakes up, let's not tell him anything about the Germans for now. Today he should enjoy the show – who knows where we'll end up, and when he will have another opportunity. Let's not spoil his day.'

The tea didn't go down well. Debora felt queasy, as she often had in recent days, and had to run to the outhouse to throw up.

Afterwards, while Pasha was still asleep, Rebecca helped her pack a couple of bags, carefully arranging everyone's documents in a file folder. Debora picked out three changes of clothes, putting them on top of cans of concentrated milk and a box of biscuits. She lingered for a moment over her university diploma. 'We probably won't return before school starts,' she said.

Pasha sat sullenly during breakfast, refusing to eat, after Debora had told him that Maslov might not be able to come to the performance. As they prepared to leave, he objected to Debora making him wear a pressed white shirt and his only pair of leather shoes, which, she noticed, were becoming too small. His anger wore off, however, as they walked to the tram stop and then rode to the theatre.

Stalingrad's streets were as busy as usual. This was the day when supplies of sugar became available in the city, and long lines of women clutching ration cards had formed at the food shops. The theatre was full too, with children in their best outfits sprawling in the huge red velvet chairs. Like all the other children, Pasha clapped and cackled with abandon as the man playing Puss tricked the ogre into becoming a mouse, and then ate that mouse with gusto.

Afterwards, he wanted to go to a playground near the theatre. 'Look, Mama, there are all these other boys, please, please, just half an hour,' he begged as he pulled her towards the slides and the climbing wall. The weather was nice, and she almost agreed, but her sense of duty prevailed. She needed to finish her packing, and suspected that Maslov might be looking for them. 'Next time,' she promised. 'We'll come back soon.'

The tram on the way back was crowded, and she was relieved to jump out and walk with Pasha along the unpaved country lane to their home.

It was only once they were within a few steps of the house that she heard a whirring noise coming from the west. Turning her head, she looked up. Like an army of locusts, hundreds and hundreds of German warplanes, bulky two-engine Heinkel bombers and the lighter single-engine Stukas, filled the sky.

The swarm broke into several parts before the first planes cast their shadows over Debora's head, with some heading towards the city centre where she had just been and others to industrial areas along the river to the north. Only a few puffs of anti-aircraft fire greeted this armada, with no discernible effect. The warplanes slowed over their targets and began seeding them with small silver-white objects. These quickly blossomed into thousands of parachutes, shiny and beautiful in the dying afternoon sun. She stared, transfixed, as they floated unhurriedly down.

'Mama, what is it, it looks like big snowflakes!' Pasha exclaimed.

One by one, they touched the city's surface and exploded in bright flashes of intense white-blue fire. In a matter of seconds, neighbourhoods all across Stalingrad were ablaze. Oil storage tanks on the Volga riverbank detonated with a flash, visible several seconds before the deafening boom, and thick curls of black smoke shot skywards, covering the horizon to the east. As the oil leaked, the wide river too began to burn. Debora froze, unable to avert her eyes from the terrible, illicit beauty of the world combusting in front of her. Only Pasha's scream of visceral fear brought her back to herself.

Rebecca and Svetlana were in the garden. They stared at the next wave of aeroplanes coming from the west, aeroplanes that were aiming for the neighbourhoods that weren't yet burning. 'Quickly, to the cellar,' Svetlana shouted at Debora and Pasha. 'Run.'

They sprinted the few yards that separated them from the trapdoor. Debora pushed Pasha down the ladder and dashed inside the house to pick up the two bags she had packed that morning.

It was only as she was coming down the ladder herself, still in the high heels she had worn to the theatre, that she spotted a new cloud of small parachutes descending above her head. She shut the hatch and closed her eyes.

Then the earth shook, and shook again, and pieces of plaster, stone and wood started falling on them as she covered Pasha with her body. The cool cellar became unbearably hot, filling with acrid chemical smells.

She didn't know how long they spent underground, but Pasha's whimpering was strangely reassuring – at least it meant they were still alive. Rebecca prayed continuously, repeating the Hebrew incantations. Svetlana mouthed Russian Orthodox prayers asking for the same things in a different tongue. Debora wished she knew how to pray, but instead, as the initial shock wore off, she kept stroking Pasha, who had peed his pants, and saying quietly, so quietly that probably nobody except her heard it, 'It will all be all right. It will all be all right. Don't worry, it will be all right.'

Even after the bombs stopped dropping, there was no silence. The city was dying in a cacophony of collapsing roofs, exploding stoves and cracking beams, thousands of lives turning into luminescent charcoal, funeral pyres for all those people who hadn't got out in time.

It was many hours later, or at least so it seemed to Debora, that she heard someone knocking on the cellar's hatch. 'There are people here,' she yelled. 'Help us!'

With a screech, the hatch was pulled aside and fresh air rushed in. A flashlight shone down and Debora heard a voice shouting: 'They are here, they are here.' A soldier in a helmet jumped in and helped them climb out, guiding them onto a stretch of open road. It felt almost like daytime: fires illuminated the night.

Svetlana's orchard, the house and the homes nearby were all gone, crumpled into a smouldering heap. The only thing left standing was the brick fireplace and the chimney, towering like an antique ruin over the remains of the house. Svetlana took a few uncertain steps towards what used to be her home, and then stood motionless, watching the flickering coals.

Maslov, his head wrapped in a bloodied bandage, ran towards them from the NKVD car. He picked up Pasha and kissed him, then quickly embraced Debora. 'You're alive, you're alive,' he kept saying. 'Thank God you're all alive. I was afraid that you were still at the theatre, that you'd stayed behind in the city centre. There is nothing left there now, nothing.'

Pasha, embarrassed by his wet pants, tried to pull away, hiding behind Debora's back. His hands trembled.

'Are you hurt?' Maslov asked Rebecca, noticing a slight limp and offering his hand.

'No, no, I am fine,' she said, pushing him away. 'I will manage.' She kneeled and hugged Pasha, whispering in his ear and patting his head: 'It's all right, don't be afraid, you are a very brave boy. Come, come with me to the car.'

The soldier dropped Debora's two grimy bags in the boot. 'Get in, let's not waste time,' Maslov fretted. 'Do you want to come with us too?' he asked Svetlana. The woman didn't seem to hear. She swayed in front of the ruins, her soot-covered face frozen. After another attempt, Maslov gave up and shouted at the driver: 'Move it! Get us out of here!'

It took a long time for their car to reach Maslov's command bunker at the tractor plant compound. The driver had to zigzag using back roads, avoiding the city centre. Most of the main streets had disappeared, buried under the rubble of crushed buildings. The reek of burned flesh mixed with the smoke from house fires that had yet to be extinguished, their flames almost hidden by the thick mist of burning oil. Electricity was knocked out and water gushed from severed pipes. Here and there survivors tried to dig friends and relatives out from under the debris, using whatever implements they could find. Seeing Maslov's car, they waved and tried to get it to stop, to take the wounded, as though there were better places to take them to, but the driver just stared straight ahead and kept going. Others had already begun securing their own survival. Thin figures carrying buckets and bundles rushed to the bombed-out food distribution centre and storage depots, looting the sugar, wheat and rice that they believed would allow them to remain alive in the months ahead.

Even though the car's windows were shut, it was impossible to filter out Stalingrad's agony. Numb, her ears ringing, Debora barely listened as Maslov, agitated, kept up a continuous stream of talk. More than a year after the war had begun, this was his first direct engagement with the Germans. Adrenaline coursed through his body.

'They thought they could destroy us today, that there would be nobody to meet them and they could just roll into the city. But we were here. We've stopped them,' he told her. 'We didn't have much to fight with, but fight we did.' He pointed at his bandaged forehead. 'Shrapnel flew right by here, just a scratch.'

Debora's head hurt and she felt dizzy. Maslov pulled out a flask of vodka and offered it to her and Rebecca. Rebecca shook her head. Debora took a big gulp.

'We'll wipe them out,' he toasted as he drank from the flask.

They drove past several checkpoints and stopped at a small clearing. From there, Maslov led them through a labyrinth of deep trenches. Debora, in her theatre shoes, walked slowly, trying to avoid pieces of shrapnel and jagged casings. The command bunker, its entrance fortified by logs, was dug into a riverside slope around a bend. That night, it was one of the few places in Stalingrad that still had electricity.

'There is nowhere safer for you to stay for now. As soon as the oil in the river burns out, I will get you to the other side, but for now you have to wait,' Maslov said. He touched Pasha and was about to say something else, but an adjutant had already spotted him from deeper inside the bunker's bowels. He cupped his hands and yelled: 'Captain Maslov, the colonel has been looking for you. Where have you been? Right away, he needs you right away.'

Maslov snapped to attention. 'On my way,' he responded and, with a quick caress of Debora's cheek, disappeared. She noticed the streaks of blood on his uniform, the uniform that she had carefully ironed just the previous night.

They sat down on their bags in a busy corridor and tried to sleep. Minutes later, they were jolted awake by the sense of the air being sucked out of the bunker. One ear-splitting bang after another reverberated outside, the ground shook, and the lights went out for a minute. 'The Germans hit the 235th!' someone shouted. 'Medics, medics, we need the medics!' screamed someone else. When the lights came back on, Debora saw young nurses straining to carry stretchers with the wounded. Those more fortunate were swaying and cursing. Others were already listless, eyes glazing over.

'You two stay here.' She got up and followed the nurses into a room. 'I can help with bandages and cleaning,' she volunteered. 'I've done that before, in Kyiv.'

One of the nurses, a woman barely twenty, with ruddy cheeks and pigtails, her uniform stained by the various fluids that oozed from human bodies once they were perforated, looked up. 'Start with those over there.' She pointed at the partition curtain. 'All we have is alcohol and bandages, we're out of painkillers and the sulphanilamide powder. Both doctors are dead, too.'

Gathered behind the partition were female soldiers, all of them relatively lightly injured. Debora stripped the shirt off the first one, who was curled up on the floor, and started picking out the small pieces of metal and debris lodged in her back. Everything was caked in blood, and so she had to wash it off first, pouring alcohol from a glass bottle. She cut off the soldier's braid, tangled into the wounds. The lacerations didn't seem very deep, however.

'This will hurt for a bit, but you'll survive,' she told the woman. 'Tell me your name.'

'Inga.'

'Where are you from, Inga? And how old are you?'

'Twenty-two. From Kharkiv. I was a student there.'

'Me too,' Debora said as she dressed the wounds. 'Sit straight for a second.'

Inga had been silent since medics had brought her to the bunker, and now wanted to talk. 'We weren't supposed to be shooting tanks, you know. We were here to shoot at aeroplanes. I was a volunteer with the anti-aircraft batteries. We were all women, and until today there wasn't a lot to be shooting at. We thought we were in the deep rear. But then today, when the German planes came, so did their tanks. There was no artillery, so we had to turn our cannons around and shoot straight instead of into the sky, to try and hit the tanks.'

'And did you?' Debora asked.

'I don't know. But we stopped them for a bit, at least long enough for others to arrive.'

'This is something you will be telling your grandchildren when you grow old and grey-haired,' Debora said. 'This is something you will always be proud of.'

'None of us will grow old,' Inga said, shivering.

'You will,' Debora said. 'Now lie down on your stomach. I have to take care of the next soldier.'

*

Debora didn't have much strength left as time wore on, her motions becoming mechanical and her focus slipping away. She paid no attention at first to the adjutant entering the room and loudly shouting her new name, Darya Maslova. 'Isn't that you?' He finally shook her shoulder. 'Captain Maslov's wife?'

'Yes, it's me.'

'Time to go. Your boat is leaving soon.'

He led her back to the corridor. Rebecca sat on their bags, a sleeping Pasha on her lap. 'Where is my husband?' Debora asked.

'He's not here, he's busy doing his duty,' the adjutant said. He didn't have the time or desire for small talk, and although he didn't say so aloud, he didn't appreciate that Maslov's family had been given priority permits to leave Stalingrad ahead of other cases that he considered far more urgent. 'These are your permission slips, don't lose them. Someone will take you to the pier in a few minutes. We know where you will be going after this, and so your husband will be in touch. Good luck.'

He looked at her feet. 'Wait a moment,' he said, and returned a minute later with a pair of black army boots roughly her size. 'Take these. The owner doesn't need them any more.'

She gratefully put on the boots and followed the NKVD soldier who carried their bags. It was already daylight outside, even though the sky was still obscured by the smoke from the fires. Fog lingered by the riverbanks. The soldier led them down the slope to a jetty. Debora no longer paid attention to the thunder of shelling some distance away.

Patches of oil on the river were still burning, but it seemed navigable. There were coils of barbed wire, and other NKVD troops, wearing helmets and with bayonets attached to their rifles, scrutinised everyone's permits. Waiting by the river were mostly injured soldiers, including Inga, who seemed feverish now, and some women and children. The nurse with pigtails was there too.

'I'm just taking them across and coming right back,' she told Debora, as if she needed to justify her presence. 'I'm not escaping.'

'Of course not,' Debora said.

She spotted several bodies, their faces submerged, their limbs rigid and bloated, floating near the reeds.

'This was the field hospital ferry, the Germans sank it overnight,' the nurse said. 'But we should be okay now. There are no planes in the skies, and because of all this smoke, they shouldn't be able to see us anyway.'

Debora looked back at the city behind her, a city with its guts ripped open, bleeding into the Volga. Then she sat down under an old poplar tree overlooking the water.

'Your husband, I saw him leave for the front while you were away,' Rebecca told her, quietly enough so nobody could overhear. 'In a helmet, with a rifle. He seemed happy.'

'Happy?' Debora turned. 'On a day like today?'

'Today he was happy that he is finally fighting the Germans and not his own people. His eyes, they were different.'

There was a commotion, and they heard the sound of motorboat engines approaching in the fog. 'Here they are, they're coming,' someone shouted.

The boats were low, their rims barely above the water. Soldiers of all ages clustered inside, around artillery pieces, mortars and crates of ammunition. When the first boat hit the shore, the men silently jumped into the water and started unloading the cargo, pushing it uphill.

A stray German shell punched the hillside above them, sending up a geyser of dirt but doing little damage. A young man with sandy hair, a moustache just beginning to sprout on his upper lip, threw his rifle into the river and jumped off the second motorboat. 'Mama, Mama!' he screamed in panic as he hit the

204

water. Carried by the current, he tried to swim downriver, into a patch of bushes and reeds.

He managed only a few strokes before the NKVD officer in charge pulled out his pistol. The soldier who had escorted Debora didn't wait for orders. He raised his rifle and, after three missed shots, hit the deserter's skull. The man's head twisted unnaturally, and he stopped moving. The slow current carried him into the reeds, where several bodies from the sunken hospital ship were already caught up.

'Don't look, don't look.' Rebecca covered Pasha's eyes with her hands, but the boy wanted to see everything.

'You go now,' one of the NKVD officers shouted at Debora once the second motorboat was offloaded and the rest of its passengers, showing no reaction to the young soldier's killing, were slogging uphill to face the Germans.

There was no time to lose. Within moments, the boats had pulled away, heading towards the Volga's peaceful eastern shore. The protective fog had begun to melt and they could clearly see both banks. Rebecca looked westward, taking in what remained of Stalingrad one last time. 'How many more rivers are we going to cross as we flee?' she asked Debora.

'There are no more rivers left, Mama. The next one from here is in China.'

Halfway across, the wind started blowing away the smoke. German planes appeared again in the sky, but by the time they started strafing again, Debora's craft was already docked on the river's safe side.

It was depressing to go through the same evacuation procedures. Once again their papers were checked, and they were issued a loaf of rye bread each. At the small, crowded train station in the steppe east of the city, the loudspeaker blared patriotic songs. 'My country's wide and full of forests, fields and rivers,' went the familiar refrain. 'I don't know of any other country where a man would breathe as freely as he breathes here.'

Later in the day, they left for the south aboard a train that seemed like a twin of the one that had brought them from Kyiv the previous year. Everyone in the carriage was a family member of NKVD officers from Stalingrad. They stopped often, to make way for convoys hauling tanks and troops towards the city, and only arrived at their destination in Astrakhan a day later. From there, they took an old boat on the choppy Caspian Sea, spending most of the remaining journey seasick until they came ashore in the southern city of Derbent.

27

Derbent, August 1942

Debora slept in a deep, almost comatose state, until the blinding needle-like rays of the southern sun pierced the Persian-style shutters and fell across her face. She opened the window, inhaling the salty Caspian air. A sliver of the sea shone from behind an ancient sycamore tree in front of their new home.

Their spacious room was in one of the European two-storey brick buildings in the new part of Derbent. The landlady, a middle-aged Armenian woman named Arpine, prepared them breakfast: tea, a bowl of sour yoghurt, flatbread and dark-red pomegranate syrup. Her own husband and son were fighting, which was why she had a spare room.

'How was it there, in Stalingrad?' she asked Debora in heavily accented Russian. 'Very bad, was it?'

Debora stood up and listened. There was no hum of artillery, no crackle of anti-aircraft fire, no explosions. There was no stench of carbonised flesh, cordite or burning oil. All she could hear was the cries of seagulls and the forgotten silence of a city at peace.

'One day I will tell you how bad,' she replied. 'But not now.'

'I understand how you feel.' Arpine nodded. 'You know, I'm not originally from Derbent myself. I came here with my parents when I was seventeen, also fleeing a war. We spent a month on the road, from Van in Turkey. My brother died before we escaped, my aunt died on the way. But we finally got here. This is a good place, a place of peace.'

'I'd never even heard of Derbent,' Debora admitted. 'We are originally from Kyiv, in Ukraine. It's also far away.'

'I've heard of Kyiv,' Arpine said. 'Derbent is not a big city, but it is an old city. The oldest in Russia, they say. Older than Russia itself.'

They stepped onto the balcony in Arpine's room. To their right, the Caspian merged seamlessly into the sky, a flotilla of fishing boats sparkling on the horizon as if airborne. To their left rose the Caucasus ranges of Dagestan, with their thick forests where people in every cragged valley spoke a different, mutually unintelligible tongue. Derbent's thousand-year-old citadel towered on the hill just before the mountains began, and two parallel walls made of large boulders ran down to the coast, enclosing much of the city.

'They look like giant chess pieces,' Debora said, pointing to the fortifications' turrets.

'Derbent is from Persian, it means "closed gate",' Arpine explained. 'For a thousand years, this was the border where Persia ended and the nomads began. The Gate of Persia, between the civilised and the savage. But then Russia came, and nobody fought over it any more.'

'I like that, nobody fighting,' Debora said.

Debora and Rebecca spent the morning washing their soot-covered clothes and hanging them to dry in the sun. Then they and Pasha hiked up the hill into Derbent's Muslim heart. In warrens of curved medieval streets, old men bowed in whitewashed mosques, placing their heads on tiny clay tablets. The smell of grilled lamb and pungent, unfamiliar herbs wafted in the air. As they turned a corner, Rebecca spotted a six-pointed Star of David on a building. It was a synagogue, and unlike most synagogues in the Soviet Union, it seemed to be a functioning one.

'There are Jews here,' she said, pushing open the heavy door without hesitation. She hadn't been to a synagogue for many years. She yearned to pray, to see the familiar layout, the Hebrew Ten Commandments on the walls.

It was dark and mouldy inside. A stooped attendant in a black skullcap came out to greet them. '*Gut margen*,' Rebecca addressed him in Yiddish. The man didn't understand, replying in a guttural language they didn't speak. '*Mir zenen Yiden*,' she insisted. 'We are Jews.'

'We speak no Yiddish here, madam. Come back on Friday, maybe someone of your kind will be here,' the man replied in broken Russian. He shooed them away. 'We're closed now.'

'Everything is different here in the Orient,' Rebecca muttered as they walked home. 'Even the Jews are different.'

In her new status as an NKVD officer's wife, Debora easily found a teaching position in Derbent's Middle School No. 5, an unkempt building next to a deconsecrated Armenian church. While the school's tongue of instruction was Russian, her students spoke to each other in their own languages. She suspected that many things they were saying weren't very flattering. She preferred not to know, and she had no interest in learning the local speech. What was the point? Once the war ended, they would leave Derbent right away.

News of the death and destruction in Stalingrad, the city that refused to succumb to the Germans, filled the radio bulletins and newspaper front pages every day. When Debora thought about Maslov, recalling the last time she had seen him, his head bandaged, in the bunker by the Volga, she often wondered whether she was now twice widowed.

Dear Dmitri, she wrote to him, via the military mail, in late October. *We are all doing well and missing you. The room is cosy, and we have enough to eat. I hope you are keeping safe – we haven't heard anything from you for a while. Every day I check for the mail, hoping there will be a letter from you. When we finally get to see you, which I hope will be soon, there will be a big surprise for you. I am pregnant, and Pasha will soon have a brother or sister. He is convinced it's going to be a brother, and is already thinking up names. He is very excited that he will have someone to play with. He also misses you and asks all the time whether you will ever come back. I told him you will be coming back soon. With love, your wife, Darya.*

Their letters must have crossed paths, because Maslov's note, postmarked in November, didn't mention the baby. It was short, and written with an unsteady hand. *My dear wife*, it said. *This has been a very difficult time, as you know, and we fought very hard. Not everything can be said in a letter, but now I have been pulled back from the front line and am in a safer place. There is a chance I will be able to visit you in a month or two. Hold strong and kiss Pasha for me!*

'Well, at least one of our men has good news,' Rebecca told Debora after reading the note. There had been no word from Gersh, or from Yakov. Her Moscow cousin kept repeating the same hopeful platitudes in occasional correspondence.

What Maslov hadn't written in the letter to Debora was that he had been taken across the Volga on a stretcher, after a German bullet tore into his calf and bounced off his tibia. If the wind had blown a tiny bit to the left, the bullet would have severed his femoral artery and he would have bled out in minutes. But the wind didn't blow to the left and the artery was still intact.

Mathematically speaking, not dying or becoming a permanent cripple was like winning a lottery considering where he had spent these three months. By now, little remained of his 10th NKVD Division, mauled in the rancid maze of what was left of Stalingrad. Unlike many others who had come out of the battlefield alive just to succumb to gangrene and other infections, he healed quickly and by January was able to walk with a cane. He was predicted a full recovery, and, to free up space in the military hospital east of Stalingrad, was allowed to travel on convalescent leave to Derbent. He was still in the hospital when he received the letter about Debora's pregnancy. He read it twice, to make sure he understood correctly, and became so excited that he accidentally overturned his IV stand.

My dear wife, he wrote back that night. *This is the best thing you could have told me. You must also know something very important: I will always love my son Pasha the same way I will love our second child. And hopefully that child will never see war.*

Maslov himself no longer expected to see the front lines again either. By January, the battle for Stalingrad was finally won, after the German Sixth Army was encircled and destroyed by rapid Soviet offensives in the steppes west of the Volga. Within days, the Red Army began its march towards Ukraine, reporting the liberation of one city after another. For once, the defeatists had been proved wrong.

The victory at Stalingrad meant that NKVD officers like Maslov could return to more traditional work from their temporary infantry duties. His new job after the convalescent leave, he was told by a colonel visiting the hospital, would be in the newly liberated areas, overseeing operations to uncover and punish anyone who had collaborated with the German authorities in the mistaken belief that the Soviet order would never return.

The colonel also brought a present: a major's insignia for Maslov's uniform. The high casualty rate in Stalingrad meant quick battlefield promotions for those who managed to survive. 'There will be plenty of work for us, and you will be needed, Major Maslov,' he said, 'so recuperate quickly. There is a lot of cleansing to be done, along the Don and in Ukraine.'

'My wife is from Ukraine,' Maslov said. 'From Kyiv.'

'Good,' the colonel said. 'Makes it even easier.'

A week later, Maslov was sitting in a first-class car to Astrakhan, feasting on proper tea and American Lend-Lease biscuits. Landscapes untouched by war seemed unnatural to an eye grown so used to destruction that it kept seeing the shapes of tanks and artillery pieces, and traces of shrapnel and bomb craters, in pristine little towns along the way.

The train station in Astrakhan was crowded with hundreds of frostbitten German prisoners of war, herded in their flimsy coats towards remote labour camps in Kazakhstan from which most would never return. Back when the war first began, Maslov recalled, Molotov's radio address had explained at length how the Soviet Union nurtured no enmity for German workers, peasants and intellectuals, and was only fighting the Nazi plague. Such niceties hadn't survived Stalingrad. These days, the message was brutally blunt. *Papa, Kill a German!* screamed the posters at the station, showing a child, so similar to Pasha, standing by the corpse of his dead mother outside his burning home. *One Bullet, One German*, urged another.

As Maslov hobbled past the prisoners on the way to the pier, he stared into their faces and wondered which one of them might have fired the bullet that had injured him, and which ones were responsible for the deaths of his comrades. He had no pity, and neither did anyone else.

When the doorbell rang, Pasha ran to open it, assuming it was one of his new friends. He froze, uncertain about the uniformed man with a cane outside. By then, Debora too was at the door. Without a word, she rushed to embrace Maslov, squeezing him close and crying.

It took her a minute to notice his limp and his cane.

'What is this, have you been injured?' she fretted. 'Why didn't you tell me?'

'It is nothing, nothing.' He waved her off. 'I will be like new in no time.'

She realised that her hair was unkempt and that she was wearing men's trousers and a threadbare sweater. 'Why didn't you warn us that you were coming? A telegram or something,' she started, and then stopped. 'Oh, what am I going on about. You are here, in one piece. That is the only thing that matters.'

He sat down at the table and opened his bag. 'Come here, I have something for you, young man.' He beckoned to Pasha and extracted a wristwatch, a shiny round piece with Roman letters on the dial. 'This used to belong to a German officer, in Stalingrad, and now it's yours,' he said. 'Don't lose it. You know how to read time, don't you?'

Still shy, Pasha didn't move. 'Give him a moment to get used to you. Five months is a long time for a five-year-old,' Rebecca said, nudging the boy.

Pasha only spoke to Maslov before going to bed. 'I thought you were dead, like my other Papa,' he said. 'Please don't be dead again.'

'I promise I won't.'

There was no privacy in the room, and so Maslov didn't make love to Debora that night. She lay with her head on his shoulder, playing absent-mindedly with his hair. She liked how his hand cupped her breast.

'Dmitri, I've been thinking a lot. Why do you believe we deserve to be alive?' she whispered. 'So many people are dead, so many good people that I've known since I was little. My brother, my father, I don't know what happened to them. All these thousands upon thousands dying in Stalingrad. And also, all those people who died before the war. Why is it that they're dead and we're not? Why are we so lucky?'

'There is no why,' Maslov replied. 'It just is. It serves no point to ask questions. Let's just be grateful.'

But Debora was unconvinced. 'They were all good people,' she repeated. 'Good people.'

In the two weeks that Maslov spent in Derbent, he managed to fix many of the small problems in Debora's life. He repaired the broken table and chairs and arranged access to an NKVD distribution centre where she could get new clothes and better food. He paid a visit to her school for a friendly but stern conversation with the director. During his check-in with the Derbent NKVD office, he also submitted information requests about the fates of Yakov and Gersh. And on his last weekend, he took Debora and Pasha fishing.

The sea was unseasonably calm. The fishing boat's owner was on the front lines, and so it was his wife, a broad-shouldered woman, who went out to sea every morning instead. She had spare rods and taught Pasha and Maslov, who had never fished in the open sea, how to cast the line and reel back. Debora sat on the bow reading a book and admiring the snow-covered mountaintops that slowly receded from view. Hungry seagulls followed the boat, buzzing above them like German aeroplanes on a bombing run.

Pasha was the lucky one. The line became taut and the rod was nearly yanked from his hands. Maslov jumped up just in time to grasp it. 'Oh fuck,' he cursed, 'What is this monster?'

'Steady, steady, give it to me now,' the woman bellowed. 'You don't want to lose this one.'

She expertly loosened the line, just to pull it back again. Debora watched as the dark silhouette of the fish, struggling for life, became visible under the waves.

'You need to help, this one may be too big for us,' the woman hissed at Maslov. 'Just grip the rod and don't let go, I need to get a hook.' The water foamed up as the black fish thrashed around, its snout occasionally rising.

Pasha, scared by the violence of the convulsions, cowered, gripping Debora's knees.

'This sturgeon is going to snap the line, damn beast,' the fisherwoman warned. 'We're going to lose it.'

'We're not losing it,' Maslov retorted. 'Hold the rod.'

He pulled out his service pistol, crouched, aimed, and fired eight shots in rapid succession into the sturgeon's head. At least one of them didn't miss. Blood burst out into the sea, colouring the water, and after a few seconds of agonised writhing, the line went limp. The Azeri woman pierced the side of the fish with a hook at the end of a wooden pole and, with Maslov's help, pulled it aboard. Slimy in its prehistoric beauty, it occupied most of the boat's deck. The fisherwoman patted its bloated underbelly. 'That's a lot of caviar down there,' she said. 'We'd better get back, because there is no room for any other fish on this boat.'

Ashore, Maslov hired a horse cart to bring the fish home. Neither Rebecca nor Debora had ever cleaned a sturgeon before. Arpine, however, knew exactly what to do. As Maslov was

215

dispatched to procure a barrel of salt, the three women spent the rest of the day filleting the fish, removing the skin and its hard, bony plates. They cut out the sac with the roe, and sliced the meat into large cubes that would fit into glass jars. By nightfall, they had salted enough fish to last for months. It took another hour to clean up the blood, guts and muck from the kitchen floor.

Three days later, at the break of dawn, Debora and Pasha walked Maslov back to the pier, through this strange city, just as the call to prayer rang from the nearby mosque. His limp was almost imperceptible now. The ferry to Astrakhan was filling up quickly, with adolescent recruits heading for their first brush with the enemy, and veterans like Maslov returning from convalescent leave.

'Dmitri, I miss home. Once this is all over, I want to go back. To Ukraine, to Kyiv,' Debora said as they parted.

He hugged and kissed her. 'Who knows, maybe by the end of the year we could be there. We are finally winning,' he said. 'I will see you all in no time.'

But the war didn't end in 1943, and Debora didn't see her husband for another two years. He did, however, write often. And he didn't get killed.

PART FOUR

28

Kyiv, March 1945

Debora's stomach tightened as the names of familiar Ukrainian towns and villages appeared on railway station signs in the window. Pisky ... Poltava ... Myrhorod ... Lubny ...

The train didn't stop as it rolled past Olena's village because there wasn't much of it left. Just roofless, eviscerated houses, burned sunflower fields, and the twisted wreckage of rusted, destroyed tanks and trucks. The few people who'd survived the famine had died in the war. Yet another depopulated Ukrainian village that would soon be overgrown by the forest, a few apple and cherry trees in the wilderness bearing witness to what it used to be long ago. A place where people once fell in love, where people celebrated their weddings, where they taught their children how to ride horses and milk cows. Before ambitions and ideologies and hatred in faraway capitals wiped it off the map.

Debora pressed her forehead against the cold window as she recalled her last trip through here, with the toy dog. So frightening then, that experience seemed almost normal now, amid the daily horrors of the mind-numbing war.

Their train would reach the Dnipro river, and Kyiv, before sunset, she calculated. As they got closer, she held up her daughter.

'Nina, look, this is our Ukraine,' she said. 'We are going home. To Kyiv.'

Rebecca stood by the next window with Pasha. 'Do you remember Kyiv at all?' she asked.

'Of course,' he responded proudly, though in truth he recalled very little.

The war wasn't yet over, but the end was close. The Soviet armies had battled their way into Germany itself, and all of Ukraine had come back under Soviet rule. The last German soldiers, who blew up all the bridges over the Dnipro as they retreated, had been chased out of Kyiv months ago. The first of these bridges was now restored, and Debora's train made its way to the crossing, chugging doggedly along the tracks above the forested islands where Kyivites would swim once summer arrived. Then the deep-blue water opened up, the cliffs of the Dnipro's right bank reflecting in its mirror.

The bell tower of the Lavra, surging into the clear sky, had survived the war, and its golden cupola was shining again. Other passengers in the train, also glued to the windows, broke out in applause.

'I never thought this would actually happen, that I would see Kyiv again,' Rebecca said. She had prided herself on her restraint, but now tears rolled from her eyes. 'We're home,' she told Pasha. Nina, not yet two years old, was frightened by all the commotion and started crying too.

Maslov, promoted to lieutenant colonel in the NKGB, as the State Security organs were called these days, had arrived in Kyiv three weeks earlier. He was busy: in Kyiv, as in other formerly occupied territories, the NKGB was looking for anyone who had collaborated with the Germans – which, considering that the collapse of Soviet power seemed irreversible in the first year of the war, was a large population pool.

He made his way to the platform just as the train pulled into Kyiv's main station, a building still windowless and pockmarked. Most other passengers were, like Debora, the relatives of officials and military officers assigned to the Ukrainian capital. Maslov had grown overweight, she noted, with his smart uniform bulging over the belt and his neck struggling to remain contained by the collar. His leg was fully healed, only a small scar a reminder of the battlefield injury. His skin had a healthy sheen. The previous day, a local barber had given him a fancy haircut he had learned from the Germans. Though the man eventually had to be punished for his acts of collaboration, for now he was deemed too skilful to waste.

Pasha recognised Maslov immediately and leaped into his arms as soon as he was out of the train. Nina, however, broke into desperate sobs the moment Debora handed her over to her father. He didn't quite know what to do and gave back the child after a moment. 'She'll get used to you,' Debora said apologetically. 'She's still very little.'

'You look so suntanned,' he said. 'I can see you're coming from the south.'

'Sun is the one thing we didn't lack in Derbent,' she smiled.

They kissed briefly, dry lips on dry lips. He was doused in cologne. Overpowered by the smell, she sneezed and drew away.

On the way out of the station, Pasha proudly held Maslov's hand. A brand-new NKGB Studebaker, its polished chrome rims free of the smallest speck of dirt, was waiting for them outside. Pasha had never seen an American car before, and stopped to examine the foreign letters on its body. With a flourish, the uniformed driver opened the door, then started putting their suitcases in the boot.

'The bad old life is finished,' Maslov proclaimed. 'Welcome to the good new life.'

The family's old apartment was not far from the train station – just up the hill and then right, along Shevchenko Boulevard. This part of the city hadn't been damaged, and the pastel-coloured *fin de siècle* buildings stood unchanged, guarded by phalanxes of chestnut and poplar trees.

Instead of turning right, the car continued straight on.

'Aren't we going home?' Rebecca fretted. 'Does the driver know the way?'

'That apartment, unfortunately, has already been assigned to someone else, someone higher up than me,' Maslov said. 'But the one where we live is also quite good. Also very central.'

'What do you mean, someone else? What about our things? Our furniture?' Rebecca protested. 'We left everything behind, you know.' She'd spent the long journey from Derbent mentally cataloguing her pre-war possessions.

'I have asked,' Maslov said. 'But I have not received a clear answer.'

'I want to go there,' Rebecca insisted. 'It's my home.'

'You will, but not now. I will arrange it,' Maslov promised.

'We should go there now. They might know what happened to my father,' Debora pressed.

'I will take you,' Maslov repeated, irritated. 'As soon as possible. But not today. It's too late to be out on the streets. The city is still dangerous – criminal elements because of the war. Gangs have formed, robbers, killers, homeless children everywhere, and it will take some time to restore order. Best not to be out after dark.'

Racing through the largely empty streets, their car passed the St Sophia Cathedral, which Debora was relieved to see had survived the war, and then started the slow drive down the winding cobblestone curves of St Andrew's Descent. Until now,

Maslov had shared a room with another officer in a hostel for transient NKGB personnel. The arrival of his family meant that he could finally move into the three rooms he'd been assigned in a communal apartment on the third floor of a stately building just down the road from where the novelist Mikhail Bulgakov used to live.

The apartment had hosted a Nazi officer during the war. It had brand-new German wallpaper in a fleur-de-lys pattern, a modern flush toilet and a polished parquet floor. The provenance of the furniture was unclear, but some of it, Maslov was told, had been taken by the previous occupant from other Kyiv homes. Apart from procuring bed sheets, he'd hardly had to do anything to make it habitable. One of the three rooms was the former living room, with a large fireplace decorated with Dutch faience tiles and an elegant balcony with a wrought-iron railing.

He left the driver to deal with the suitcases and led the way up the curved staircase. 'I have always loved this street,' Debora said. 'Before the war, artists would sit on the pavement here and paint portraits.'

As they entered the living room, Rebecca stopped by the door frame, running her hand over two barely noticeable nail holes set diagonally to the right. 'A mezuzah. Jews used to live here,' she said. 'And now we're taking their home.'

'What does that matter?' Maslov replied, annoyed.

Rebecca couldn't sleep all night, and at the break of dawn, she went for a walk. The building stood at the bottom of St Andrew's Descent, before the street hit the riverine plain of Podil, Kyiv's lower city. Before the war, the area was always crowded, with a big bazaar in the middle. Neighbourhood toughs used to congregate on street corners, and despite the Communist Party's best efforts to promote atheism, ultra-Orthodox Jews in their black hats remained a frequent sight, just like in Uman. At this hour, life should already be pulsing, with shops opening up, schoolchildren heading to class, and trams clanging their way through cobblestoned squares. The trams were operating, but they were mostly empty.

Rebecca sat down at a tram stop, next to a woman roughly her own age. The woman kept glancing at her features, her fingers twitching, and then asked hesitantly: 'Excuse me, *zenen ir Yid*?'

'Yes, I am a Jew,' Rebecca replied in Russian.

'I knew it! I knew it! Were you here when the Germans were here? Is everyone really gone? Is that really possible?'

'I only got back to Kyiv last night. We were in the Caucasus, under evacuation,' Rebecca said. 'I don't know anything.'

'Yes, I myself returned just two days ago, and I can't find anyone,' the woman said. 'I am going from house to house, where everyone I used to know lived before the war. And nobody's there. I am now heading uptown to try another address.'

Their tram arrived and they boarded it. 'The government is just beginning to authorise the returns,' Rebecca said. 'So many people fled the Germans, I'm sure they will all now be coming. Just like you and me. We are here, aren't we?'

'I hope you are right,' the woman replied. 'Good luck, whatever you are doing.'

The tram line passed through Khreshchatyk, the city's main avenue. Much of it had been turned into a field of rubble by the time the city was retaken from the Germans. Its historic buildings had collapsed one upon another, with only burned-out skeletons, windows like empty eye sockets, still standing here and there. The debris had been cleared from the road itself, and the tram line neatly bisected this zone of destruction.

Just around the corner from Khreshchatyk was Shevchenko Boulevard. Rebecca got off the tram near her old home and, her heart punching her ribcage, sped up the stairs, breathless. There was only one doorbell this time, with the landing repainted and the previous bells removed without a trace. She pressed it, and after a minute, a uniformed housemaid opened the door.

'Who are you?' she asked after taking a moment to evaluate Rebecca's scruffy shoes and worn-out coat.

'I used to live here, before the war,' Rebecca began to explain.

By then, however, the lady of the house had appeared, a well-fed woman in a pink nightgown, with curlers in her hair.

'My name is Rebecca Rosenbaum, and before the war this used to be my home.'

'What do you mean, this was your home?' the woman said. She was annoyed. 'You know that we don't have private property here in the Soviet Union, don't you?' she went on, the long 'a' in her accent betraying a Moscow upbringing. 'This apartment belongs to the people of the Soviet Union, and even if you were allowed to live here at some point, it gives you no right to barge in and make demands.'

'I am not making any demands,' Rebecca said quietly. 'It's just that when we had to flee, we left everything behind. Our books. Our photographs. Our memories. My husband had to stay. He may have remained in Kyiv when the Germans came. I was wondering, maybe there are things of ours that are still here? Maybe you know something about our neighbours? Maybe you know what happened to my husband?'

The woman spread her arms across the door, barring the way.

'There was nothing left,' she said indignantly. 'We moved in six months ago, and there were no neighbours and no belongings. We even had to install new windows and doors, and a new toilet. It had all been looted before we arrived. So no, there is nothing I can help you with.'

'Can I at least come in and have a look inside?' Rebecca asked.

She was certain that the patch of colour at the end of the corridor, almost out of sight, was her Bukhara carpet.

'Absolutely not,' the woman hissed. She gave Rebecca a hard, cold look. 'Rebecca, that's your name, right? Rosenbaum? You have the nerve to come up here, all uppity, making demands. You should be happy that you are alive, unlike the rest of your people. And you should be thankful for the rivers of blood that were spilled by Russian soldiers for that.'

She stepped back and slammed the door shut.

Blood rushing to her face, Rebecca turned and went back down the stairs, banging the building's front door with all her strength, so much so that pieces of plaster fell to the ground. 'Bastards,' she muttered, 'bastards.'

She took the empty tram back to St Andrew's Descent and arrived in her new home just in time for breakfast. Pasha had woken up hungry and Debora was busy frying eggs, a rare delicacy for them. She was in a good mood, making faces at Nina every few minutes. Maslov had already left for the office.

'Mama, where have you been?' she asked breezily. 'What happened? Why do you look so angry?'

'I went to Shevchenko Boulevard,' Rebecca said. 'But they didn't let me in.'

'Who?'

'The new tenants. Some very senior Russians, with a housemaid. The woman looked at me like dirt, and she didn't let me in, probably because our things are still there.'

'What about Papa?' Debora asked. 'Did they know anything about Papa?'

'No, she didn't know anything. All the neighbours are gone, too. It's a whole new city. A new city for new people.'

Debora took her hand. 'We'll find out about Papa. And Yakov.'

*

226

Maslov didn't bother to disguise his fury when he returned home on his lunch break. Back in Stalingrad, and in Derbent, he had always pretended to be deferential to Rebecca. Now he skipped the niceties.

'How dare you, how dare you do that?' he yelled. 'I told you yesterday, very clearly, that I will handle this, and you went first thing in the morning to disturb those people at Shevchenko Boulevard, to tell them it was your home. Do you even know who lives there?'

'It was my home,' Rebecca said quietly.

'Yes? Did you buy it with your money, that home of yours? It was as much yours as it is theirs now,' he went on. 'And do you know who lives there now? The deputy minister, my boss's boss. Imagine how my morning went after his wife called the office, which she did as soon as you left.'

'I just want to know what happened to my husband, that's all. They can keep my things, but I want to know,' Rebecca replied, unmoved by his shouting. 'And I want to know what happened to my son.'

'Please don't scream at my mother.' Debora put her hand on Maslov's shoulder. 'Dmitri, you're a good man. Please show some understanding of what we're going through. Of what we have lost.'

'I understand.' Maslov pulled out a cigarette. The act of lighting it calmed him somewhat. 'I am doing all I can to help you, trust me. But if you keep doing such foolhardy things,' he turned back to Rebecca, 'you will make my job so much more difficult. Give me a little bit of time.'

Rebecca got up to serve lunch, not saying a word.

Maslov was in a better mood after eating.

'I have good news for you,' he told Debora. 'The school around the corner from here has reopened, and they are looking for teachers. I thought you'd be perfect.'

29

Kyiv, March 1945

When Maslov returned home for lunch two days later, a look of suppressed triumph sparkled in his eyes. 'I promised you that I'd get to the bottom of things, and I did,' he told Debora and Rebecca. 'We have located one of your neighbours, one Helga von Papen. Do you remember her?'

'Yes, of course, Pani Helga, the nice old lady,' Debora said. 'Where is she?'

'You know that she's German, don't you?'

'Well, yes, but a German from here. Her great-great-grandparents came to Ukraine all the way back under Empress Catherine,' Rebecca said.

'It doesn't matter how long ago, a German is German and will never be Russian,' Maslov said. 'They are our enemies and they aren't supposed to be living here among us, simple as that. Trust me, once the Nazis arrived, these Germans were more than ready to serve them. We keep catching them, and this neighbour of yours, Helga, she's been detained just recently. I can let you ask her everything you need to know about what happened here while her people were in charge.'

'When can we go?' Rebecca got up. 'Can we go right away?'

'You don't have to go anywhere, I will have her brought here this afternoon,' Maslov said. 'Be ready at five.'

Pani Helga looked unchanged, the same erect, proud posture, the same wax-paper-thin skin with its mountainscape of wrinkles and its deltas of light-blue capillaries. She was escorted in by two bulky men in leather jackets, with Maslov following behind.

'Oh, good afternoon, my dear.' Her eyes shone with recognition as she saw Rebecca, and then Debora and the children. 'You have two now. Congratulations.'

'Thank you, Pani Helga. Please sit down.' Rebecca motioned to the table, with a tea kettle and a plate of ginger biscuits. 'Have some tea with us.'

'I will take it from here,' Maslov told the guards. 'You two wait outside.'

They were reluctant to leave. 'Comrade Lieutenant Colonel, you need to take responsibility for the prisoner in that case. You need to sign for her,' one of them finally said.

'Give it to me.' Maslov yanked the form from the guard's hands and scribbled a swooshing signature. 'Happy? Now go.'

Helga picked up her tea but didn't touch the biscuits. 'I am glad that you have made it through,' she told Rebecca and Debora. 'So many people have not lived to see the end of this war. You were good people, and I am glad that good people have also survived. In war, people's character is no longer hidden. It opens up, like tin cans, and you can see what's inside. Sometimes I thought there were no good people left any more.'

'What happened to my father?' Debora asked. 'What happened after we left Kyiv?'

'I am sorry to tell you that your father is dead, my dear child.

He was taken, like others like him, to Babyn Yar, that terrible ravine, and shot dead. That I know.'

Up until now, there had been hope, no matter how slim, that Gersh might still be alive, somewhere, somehow. Miracles happened all the time in war. People presumed dead returned in good health to mothers and wives who had mourned them for years. Names could be confused, circumstances mistaken.

Rebecca, who had held her head high until now, crumpled in her chair. Debora leaned towards her. She recalled the last time she'd seen her father, his hand patting Pasha's hair through the fence of the Botanical Garden, thrusting in lollipops. Her eyes welled up.

'How do you know for sure?' she asked Helga.

'Nobody came back from Babyn Yar, my sweet child,' Helga replied. 'Nobody.'

Debora had heard about Babyn Yar. Just a month earlier, the Soviet government had released a lengthy report on Nazi atrocities in Kyiv, a report reprinted by all the newspapers. It stated that on 29 September 1941, many thousands of 'peaceful Soviet citizens' had been herded to the deep, long ravine on the western outskirts of the city and shot dead. The report made no particular mention of Jews.

'I don't know everything, but let me tell you what I do know,' Pani Helga went on. 'Your father stayed alone after you had left, and he sometimes drank tea with me in the kitchen. He always worried about how you would settle into the new place. He was a good man, your father. I never particularly liked Jews, to be honest, but he was a good man. It was in late August or early September that he too was given his papers for evacuation from Kyiv. He locked up the rooms and gave me the keys. He also had a lot of food, food that he couldn't take with him, so he left some for me and the rest for your other neighbours, the Boykos. They, they weren't good people.'

She took a sip of tea. 'May I?' She picked up a biscuit. 'They don't feed us much in detention.'

After a moment, she continued. 'Your father didn't get very far. By the time he managed to cross the river, the German armies had already cut off the roads further east, there was nowhere to go. And these crowds, these huge crowds of civilians, of soldiers, that were leaving the city, they were bombed from the air. His convoy was hit, and he was injured, his hand. Two of his fingers were blown off, I believe. He found his way back home to the apartment, all bloodied, just a few days before the German army entered the city. I gave him back his food cans, but the other neighbours, those Boykos, they kept theirs.

'Now, as you know, I am German, even though I was born and raised here in Kyiv, and I hope to die here. But my two sons, they wanted a better life – and I don't blame them – and so when they had a chance in the 1920s, they moved to Germany. My son Otto, he was a Wehrmacht captain, and he was with the unit that entered Kyiv, one of the first. You know, some people were actually happy, they were throwing flowers, they thought Hitler would make an independent Ukraine, would make them prosperous. Otto, he didn't think that. He said the thinking in Berlin was that the land should be emptied of the natives. *Lebensraum!* He didn't like it, he grew up here after all, and he used to have friends – Ukrainians, Russians, even Jews – but what could he do, he was just a captain.'

Maslov was itching to say something, his fists pressing into his lap. Debora noticed that and touched his elbow. 'Just let her speak,' she urged. 'Let her speak.'

'Otto came to see me, in the apartment, and the neighbours, the Boykos, they were very impressed by his uniform, by all the attention that an old lady like me was getting. And so the man, he came to Otto and whispered, pointing at your room and saying, "You know, there is a Jew in there." Otto was disgusted. "You have lived together for years, and at the first opportunity, you do this?" he said. He wanted to say hello to your father, to thank him for taking care of me. And your father, he spoke German, and he said, "Very nice to meet you, I always thought that the Germans are a civilised nation."'

'Enough, enough with this "civilised nation" bullshit.' Maslov finally couldn't hold his tongue. 'Civilised! We have seen how civilised you are! Dogs! Barbarians!'

'You are perfectly right, Comrade Lieutenant Colonel,' Helga said, straightening up. 'Germans have become real barbarians, of the kind that old people like me or' – she pointed at Rebecca – 'your late husband could never imagine.'

'I am not your comrade,' Maslov objected.

'That night, Otto went home to the German headquarters, in one of the government buildings along the Khreshchatyk,' Helga continued. 'I think it was in the Sputnik Cinema. I don't know for sure, I never went there. But as you know, the whole city centre had been booby-trapped by your comrades.' She looked at Maslov. 'And so the next day, when people lined up at the headquarters, ordinary people, to get their permits and their ration cards, it exploded, and then building after building after building – the whole city was on fire for days, blazing so much that night turned into day.'

'You know perfectly well that it was your Germans who blew up Khreshchatyk.' Maslov raised his voice. 'It says so in the report! Stop spreading this anti-Soviet filth.'

'Please excuse me,' Helga insisted. 'I am an old woman and I want to tell these women here the story of what happened to my former neighbour, their father and husband. So let me tell you how it was, not how it was supposed to have happened. The explosions were terrible – fire spread from house to house, and the water system had already been destroyed, so there was nothing to extinguish the flames with. And my son, Otto, I told you he was in the headquarters. The building collapsed on him, and he died that day. I wish he had never returned here.'

She took another sip of tea.

'A few days after that, posters appeared around the city demanding that all the Jews should present themselves for resettlement, with their belongings. I told your father, I am a German woman, they won't do anything to me, you can be safe here, don't go. And frankly, he was in no shape to go anywhere, his injuries were getting infected. He was feverish. But the other neighbours, they really wanted those rooms of yours, and they broke the lock and moved into two of them. Your father tried to protest, but Ostap just shouted at him, "Shut up, Yid. Your time lording over us has ended." Your father argued, saying, "Me? When have I lorded over anyone, over whom? Have some pity."

'"We've got rid of your son-in-law, we'll get rid of you too," Ostap went on. That's when your father stopped begging and started calling them names. "So it was you all along!" he screamed. "Snake! Scumbag! Informer! Curses be on you and your children."

'That afternoon, Ostap called the police – the same old neighbourhood Soviet policemen, just wearing the new armband now. Your father was taken away, to Babyn Yar. They kept hitting him as they dragged him off, which was completely unnecessary. And he kept screaming that someone should tell his wife and children what had happened. So here I am, telling you.'

'How do you know that they actually killed him?' Rebecca asked.

'Oh, they killed everyone who went to Babyn Yar, don't you

know that? All the Jews who remained in Kyiv, they were all killed. People would pretend to help, would squeeze money and gold from those trying to hide, and then instead of actually helping would give them up to the police. There was even a word for it. Schmaltzing, it was called. I am sorry,' Helga added. 'This is the truth. Your husband is dead. It is better for you to know.'

'And the Boykos, where are they now?' Debora asked.

'Well, I don't really know. After your father was taken away, they settled in your rooms, but that didn't last long. The Nazis, they had good accounting of the housing stock, and so they quickly reallocated those rooms to an officer, a real SS officer, not just Wehrmacht like my son. Gerhardt was his name. He actually quite liked the paintings that you had left behind.

'The Nazis really had no use for the Boykos, or for Ukrainians in general. I, as a Volksdeutsche, was receiving plenty of food – and look at me, I don't eat much. But the winter was bad in the city, and the Boykos had little left after finishing your father's tin cans. In the spring of 1942, they left for some village where they had relatives and I never saw them again.

'My second son, he was also in the army, and he came to see me that year. He wanted me to move out to Germany, but I refused – I told him I want to die here. He went east, to Stalingrad. I thought he'd been killed, because he stopped writing, but now I am told he had been taken prisoner.

'A year and a half ago, when the Soviet army began getting close, Gerhardt, the SS officer, packed up your paintings and some of the valuables and left. At that point, the bombing and the shelling was terrible, the city was burning again. Men, hungry and fearful, were roaming the streets, killing and looting. But I stayed, and when Soviet rule returned, nobody bothered me at first. I am an old woman and I rarely left my room. The

234

rest of the apartment stood empty at first, and it was only a few months ago that these new tenants arrived, from Russia. It took them a couple of days to figure out that I was German, and that was it. Now I suppose they have all the rooms to themselves.

'This is our life,' Helga finished. 'I think I have nothing else to tell you.' She picked up another biscuit and put it in her pocket.

'Thank you for being so frank,' Rebecca said.

'My dear, this is a privilege of old age,' Helga replied. 'Make the most of your lives now. I doubt I will see you again.'

Maslov shouted through the window, and the escort officers returned to take her away.

'I wish I knew how to kill. I could strangle them with my own hands,' Rebecca said quietly, looking at her palms. Her fingers were bony and thin, blood vessels visible under the parched skin.

'Who?' Debora asked.

'The Boykos. The Germans. I don't know. My Gersh never wronged anyone. My Gersh ... always too good,' she said. Debora had expected her mother to cry, but Rebecca's eyes remained dry, burning with cold hatred.

'The Boykos are scoundrels.' Debora nodded. She imagined herself hitting Ostap's round face with a meat cleaver, the fat flesh parting under the blow. It was a satisfying thought. 'They must pay for this.'

'They have been taken care of.' Maslov broke the silence.

'How?'

'Ostap was in the columns that followed the Germans west and were caught near Vinnytsia. He had written many articles praising the German New Order in 1941, and so the decision was easy. He was executed a couple of weeks later. His wife and children, we don't know, but we are looking. It's possible that they have made it all the way to Germany.'

235

'At least there is some justice,' Rebecca said, clasping her hands. 'And what will happen to Pani Helga?' she asked.

'She will be sent to Kazakhstan, though I personally doubt she will survive the trip,' Maslov said. 'It's a wonder that she managed to remain undetected for a whole year after Kyiv was liberated. Cunning woman. I wouldn't believe everything she said.'

'But why would she lie?' Debora asked. 'What does she have to gain? She knows she will be exiled anyway, doesn't she?'

'You never know with these Germans. A race of dogs, they are. Shouldn't leave any of them alive if it were up to me.' Maslov grimaced. 'One German, one bullet.'

Rebecca interrupted them. 'If my husband died at Babyn Yar, there must be a body somewhere. Are you exhuming them, looking for them?' she asked Maslov. 'What is at Babyn Yar now?'

'There are too many to exhume. We're talking tens of thousands. For now, there is no time for the dead. The government must worry about the living.'

'Is there a list of those killed? Can we know for sure? The Germans, they must have kept good accounts.'

'I don't think so. There were too many to count.'

'I want to go there. I want to see.' Rebecca got up.

'Now?' asked Maslov.

'Yes, now. I want to see my husband's grave.'

Reluctantly, he agreed. They drove in silence to the north-west. It wasn't far, just past the industrial areas and a cemetery. When they arrived, Rebecca strode ahead of everyone, oblivious of the snow, which reached above her ankles.

'Careful, there may be landmines, you never know,' Maslov shouted. She ignored him.

She stopped at the edge of the cliff, taking in the view and mouthing a prayer. A security guard spotted them and ran towards them, initially planning to send them away. His intentions changed once he noticed Maslov's uniform. 'At your service.' He saluted smartly.

Inside the ravine, dozens of people were hard at work with shovels, digging the frozen ground. Rebecca was encouraged. 'Are they preparing the burials, trying to identify the bodies?' she asked the guard. 'Compiling names?'

'Who, these guys? Burials? What burials?' The guard laughed. 'No, they are mining, they know they only have until the snow melts.'

'Mining? For what?'

'Gold. In teeth. And other things. Coins, jewellery. Those Jews brought a lot of stuff here, it would be a shame for it to go to waste.'

'What do you mean, until the snow melts. Why such hurry? Will there be a monument?' she pressed him.

'Monument?'

'A monument to all those who died here.'

'I don't know anything about that. What we've been told is that they will fill the ravine with refuse from the brick plant and build a stadium on top. That is the plan.'

'Makes sense,' Maslov chimed in. 'We have to think of the future. No point dwelling on the past.'

'You are going to build a stadium on top of my Gersh, and have celebration parades on his grave?' Rebecca shook her head, disgusted. 'And we are supposed to behave like nothing happened? Sick. Everyone is so sick.'

She kneeled, picked up a rock and threw it down into the ravine, praying loudly.

'What are you doing?' Maslov asked.

'We are supposed to put a stone on our loved ones' graves. This is our tradition,' she said.

'Ah, so you're one of the Jews,' the guard said. 'I should have

237

realised right away. Not many of your people are left any more.' His voice was neutral, and Debora wondered whether this fact made him happy, sad or indifferent.

'*I* am left.' Rebecca straightened up. 'Right here.'

Back at home, Rebecca opened the cupboard, pulled out bed sheets and began covering up the mirrors throughout the apartment.

'Now that we know Gersh is dead, we must sit *shiva*,' she proclaimed.

'What's that?' Maslov was puzzled. 'What's your mother doing?'

'It's a Jewish custom of mourning. Let her do it, please,' Debora said.

He was upset. 'You do realise my position, don't you? Remember, you are a Russian now. I can't have this Jewish non-sense going on in public. So only in here, behind closed doors.'

'She won't leave our rooms,' Debora promised.

'Why are you two arguing?' Rebecca overheard the conversation. 'Have you got no shame?' She came up to Maslov. 'You think you have the power to tell me how to mourn my husband?'

'It's not about that.'

'So what *is* it about?'

'You know very well. This Jewish stuff ... it's best not to advertise it. Think of Pasha and Nina's future. You never know how times will turn out.'

'I am what I am, like it or not,' Rebecca replied curtly, then she turned around and shut the door behind her.

Maslov raised his hands in discontent, sighed and left the apartment.

Half an hour later, Debora put on her coat. 'I am going for a walk, Mama. I need some fresh air,' she told Rebecca.

Rebecca glared at her. 'What do you think you're doing? Your father is dead, and this, sitting *shiva*, is the least we can do for him. You didn't do it for your husband, but you must show some respect to your father.'

'Mama, my father didn't believe in all this stuff. I never saw him pray. I never saw him fast for Yom Kippur. He didn't raise his children like this, and you know it. I'm not judging you, and you shouldn't be judging me.' Debora kept going.

'Yes, your father raised you the way he did because he thought that if he stopped behaving like a Jew, he would no longer be considered a Jew. See how that worked out.' Overwhelmed by the finality of the knowledge, Rebecca collapsed into a chair as Debora closed the door.

A week after arriving in Kyiv, Debora received an offer to teach Russian language and literature at the school next to their home, in the big market square of Podil. The school occupied a beautiful pale-blue pre-revolutionary building with Greek columns and carefree angels carved onto the façade. All she knew about the job was that she had to present herself to the director on Monday at 9 a.m. sharp.

The director already knew about her husband and – considering he had remained in Kyiv through the occupation – was determined to be as ingratiating as possible.

'Comrade Maslova, we are so glad to have you here,' he said as he greeted her in his office, standing by an arched window that overlooked the square. 'We can use all the help we can get.'

He adjusted his glasses and looked at her again. She had recognised him right away, despite the missing hair and the new wrinkles around his eyes. 'Debora?' he said uncertainly. 'Is that a mistake? Forgive me, but you look very much like someone I used to know.'

'Yes, Roman, we last talked when my son was born. Almost

eight years ago – a long time, isn't it? He will soon be a student here too,' Debora replied. 'We've made it through, and now I can teach again. And I am glad that you've made it through, too.'

Roman stood up to hug her. 'Who would have thought, who would have thought ...' He remained puzzled, however. 'But what about the name? It says here you are not Debora any more, but Darya. And your other husband, Samuel, what happened to him?'

'Samuel died, unfortunately. I have remarried and changed my name. It's as easy as that. Now I am Darya Grigoriyevna Maslova, and I can teach. There is nothing to hide any more. A new life. But all this is also something that neither I nor you should be talking about again, I think. You understand, don't you?'

'I understand, I understand,' Roman hastened to agree. 'Anyway, this is not the kind of school that you used to know. Hardly anyone studied during the war, and we had to start from scratch last autumn. The kids in the classes – they've seen everything, and they are, how shall I put it, not afraid. Not afraid of the teachers, that is. And some are really old. Your son – he's what, turning eight now? Will he be going to second grade?'

'Yes, second grade.'

'Well, some other kids with him will be as old as twelve, maybe even thirteen. Imagine how tough they are.' His face creased with concern. 'Your parents? What happened to them?'

'My mother is fine, we were evacuated together. My father, as far as I know, ended up in Babyn Yar. My brother, we still don't know for sure,' she said.

'I am sorry.' Roman touched her shoulder. 'I was here when those posters went up on the walls and the Jews were told to go to Babyn Yar. They all went, almost happily, all in one day, thousands through the city. There was arguing over who was ahead in line. So many of them really believed the Germans, believed that they would be resettled in a better place.'

'Yes, we have all been taught to believe what we're told, haven't we.' Debora nodded.

He looked at her alarmed, wondering whether she was trying to provoke him into saying something incriminating.

The elementary, middle and high schools all occupied the same building. As Roman had warned Debora, some of her sixth-graders were much older than others. Moustaches and embryonic beards sprouted from the bad skin of their prematurely hardened faces. After the school bell rang, she strode briskly into the room and, as the students ignored her, throwing paper balls at each other, loudly dropped a stack of books on the table. The bang made everyone go silent.

'My name is Darya Grigoriyevna, and the old times are over,' she announced. 'Now, everyone, listen hard. You will do what I tell you, you will study, and you will pass your exams. And those who plan on defying me, don't. Trust me, I will know how to deal with you.'

'Where are you from?' asked a boy with bright-red pimples.

'From here, from Kyiv, just like you. So don't you try playing any games with me. Understood?'

It took a few days for the students to learn that the new teacher was the wife of an NKGB lieutenant colonel. For that, she wouldn't be loved. But she would be feared, and that was enough as far as Debora was concerned.

Teaching was not easy. Many students still struggled with reading basic sentences, let alone the turgid Soviet prose that praised the achievements of collectivisation and industrial development. Once again the curriculum featured Pavlik Morozov, the young student who had been killed by relatives for reporting his father's counter-revolutionary activities. Pavlik, in Russian, was just another way of saying Pasha, it dawned on Debora as she pored through students' essays.

She realised after the first few weeks that she no longer really enjoyed teaching. All she was doing was implanting more lies in children's minds. About Stalin, the best friend of every Soviet child. About how free their country was. About how jealous the rest of the world was of their privileged fate.

My hammer
　　　　and sickled
　　　　　　　　Soviet passport...
I pull out of
　　　　my wide trousers
　　　　　　　　　a duplicate of my precious cargo
Read,
　　　envy me,
　　　　　　I am a Soviet citizen...

Everyone had to memorise Mayakovsky's fiery lines. Debora wasn't allowed, however, to tell students that life in the Soviet paradise had made Mayakovsky shoot himself two days after the Organs denied him this hammer-and-sickled passport for foreign travel.

Over the course of April, more Jews who had fled Ukraine in 1941 arrived in Kyiv. Children with names like Isaac, Rebecca and Abraham started appearing in classes. Many of their families weren't originally from the city but from small shtetls in the Ukrainian countryside, once bustling with Jews but now completely empty and inhospitable. Stepping into the courtyard during a break, Debora spotted a gaggle of second-graders

242

running after one such newcomer. 'Yid, stop, Yid, stop, we need to make some soap!' they screamed.

She stepped in, shielding with her body the frightened curly-haired boy, tears running from his eyes. As she was about to punish the ringleaders, she realised that Pasha was one of the bullies, his eyes wide and excited. She felt her stomach churn and raised her hand weakly. The boys, unhappy that their hunt had been disrupted but encouraged by the absence of punishment, turned around and dispersed, laughing.

Later, at home, over family dinner, Debora scolded Pasha in front of Maslov. 'What were you thinking, hounding that poor boy, shouting these terrible words? Aren't you ashamed?' she said.

'We just said he's a Yid,' Pasha replied, sullen. 'It's the truth.'

'And what about you?' Rebecca blew up. 'You are just as much of a Yid as that boy. Shame, shame.'

'No,' Pasha pouted. 'You are a liar. I am not a Yid, I am a Soviet man.'

Maslov leaned to pat him. 'Of course you are not a Yid. Your silly old grandmother is getting confused.' He turned to Debora. 'Don't give the boy such a hard time. It was just innocent horseplay. Boys will be boys. And do you want him to stand out? That's the last thing he should do. You won't get far by standing out.'

'They told the boy they would make soap out of him,' Debora said, enunciating every syllable. 'Soap.'

'They didn't quite say that,' Maslov disagreed. 'Don't blow these things out of proportion.' He looked at Rebecca. 'And don't you ever call my children Yids.'

Rebecca slammed down her cup, got up and stormed out of the room.

'That's just not the way to do it,' Debora told him.

He tried to have sex with her that night. For the first time, she turned away as he started touching her.

'I'm not feeling too well,' she said. 'Another time.'

He was disappointed, but didn't insist.

30

Kyiv, May 1945

The war with Germany finally ended on 9 May. For weeks the radio had been full of talk about the Soviet troops fighting their way through Berlin, and so everybody expected victory to be declared at any moment. Still, when the announcement came, early in the morning, Debora felt a surge of relief. They can't lie to us about something this big, she thought. If they say it's over, it must be over.

'If your brother is in Germany, as a prisoner of war, maybe now he will come back,' Rebecca said that morning. 'Maybe God will have pity on us.'

'Maybe.' Debora nodded. She suppressed the memory of her father's Swiss flask, wishing it away for all these years. After learning about Gersh's death, Rebecca still clung to the hope that one day she would see her son again. Debora wasn't going to snuff it out. It would be too cruel. Pointless. She kept silent about the flask. Who knew, maybe Rebecca was right, maybe Yakov *was* still alive.

Later in the day, columns of American-made Willys jeeps carrying Soviet troops, followed by tanks and self-propelled howitzers, drove through central Kyiv, past the ruins of Khreshchatyk and uphill to St Sophia. Unlike the festivities the same day in Moscow, this was a relatively small parade. The war, after all, hadn't ended in Ukraine. Western Ukrainian areas that the Soviet Union had seized from Poland in 1939 had been spared the famine and purges that had bled the rest of Soviet Ukraine into submission. Villagers there, well fed and used to their freedoms, hadn't yet absorbed the lesson that resisting Soviet power was pointless. Nearly two years of executions and deportations by the NKVD before June 1941 were enough to instil near-universal hatred of Moscow but, unlike in eastern and central Ukraine, insufficient to extinguish the desire to resist.

And so, as Soviet troops moved westwards and on to Berlin, an insurgency broke out in their rear. Soviet newspapers referred to it as 'Banderite-German bandits', even though the Ukrainian nationalists' leader, Stepan Bandera, had spent most of the war in a German concentration camp. These dispatches, however, were rare. As a result, Debora didn't worry too much when Maslov received a telegram the day after Victory Day ordering him to travel to the western city of Drohobych on forty-eight-hour notice, and to prepare to be gone for at least a month.

'It's just to help re-establish order, the way we have done over here,' he told her. 'A walk in the park. We've learned how to do it by now.'

On his last night in Kyiv, he took her to watch a new movie, *Ivan the Terrible*, in the city's officers' club. The great tsars and generals who expanded the Russian Empire used to be despised as reactionary tyrants before the war. But now they had joined the official pantheon. Stalin himself had approved the script, it was known. The audience clapped and cheered every time the fearsome tsar strengthened Mother Russia by eliminating heresies and beheading his subjects for offences real or imagined.

Debora felt repelled by Tsar Ivan, with his mad eyes and dishevelled beard, and rooted instead for the treacherous Prince Kurbsky, much more appealing in his doomed love for the tsar's wife. The handsome actor reminded her of her first husband. So did the very experience of going to the movies.

'That Kurbsky, he fled here, to Ukraine,' Maslov told her after the film ended. 'There has always been a traitorous strain in this place.'

In the morning, Debora helped Maslov pack his suitcase and watched as he polished his sidearm and slotted bullets into the magazine. Pasha was there too, transfixed. 'Can I touch it?' he asked.

'Absolutely not,' Debora replied.

But Maslov took out the magazine and let Pasha hold the heavy, cold weapon for a second. 'Just don't ever point it at someone you don't want to shoot, soldier,' he said.

The NKGB Studebaker arrived to collect him. 'If you need anything while I am gone, call my office,' he told Debora. 'My adjutant will come once in a while to check up and make sure that everything is okay.'

'Don't get shot. Would be silly now that the war is over,' she said, and kissed him goodbye.

Over the years, Debora had become used to separation. Still, she was surprised that she felt a sense of relief once Maslov was gone. He called her once every few days, always brief conversations over a crackling line, conversations that she was eager to end.

It was only with her husband away that she realised how much tension there was in their home. The hostility between him and Rebecca lingered, like the stink that seeped from broken sewage pipes, even on the happiest days. The dismissive, almost angry way he spoke about Jews – how many times had she told

247

him to watch his words? The sense of unbridled power that he brought home from work, the new habit of being obeyed that he now expected to extend to his family. In the last two years, he had climbed into the upper crust of the Organs, a change in circumstances that had transformed his personality. He was harder, colder, she thought. Or had he always been like that and in the past she'd just chosen not to notice?

Debora's circumstances had changed, too. She felt for the first time that she was part of the truly privileged class. While most Kyivites went chronically hungry that year, she shopped at a special store, hidden in a basement without a sign. Prices there were so low as to be virtually free within the generous monthly quotas set for a lieutenant colonel's family. For any other luxuries – like fresh fruit and vegetables – Maslov gave her enough cash to splash out in the farmers' market that had reopened in Podil.

She needed to buy a new set of dresses to match her transformed social standing. Good fabric was hard to find, but NKGB officers' families had access to a special tailor's shop, also serving the Kyiv military headquarters. It had just received a shipment of fine satin, silk and gauze, taken as a war trophy from Breslau. Between fitting sessions, Debora got to drink tea and socialise with other officers' wives. Unlike her, many of them seemed well used to luxury. Most were from Russia, and gently mocked the Ukrainians for their funny accents, their strange culinary tastes and their make-believe language. They also quietly resented the fact that they'd ended up in ruined Kyiv instead of the conquered European capitals like Berlin, Vienna or Prague, where fancy jewellery, watches and furs could be taken from the locals as rightful reparation.

The wives were all very nice to Debora, but she decided not to make friends in that circle once her dresses were finished. The outfits she'd picked were somewhat risqué. Why not? she thought. The summer was coming and everyone else was exposing their flesh.

At school, Roman never failed to address Debora by her new name, Darya Grigoriyevna, and behaved as if they hadn't known each other in their previous lives. He spoke in long, formal sentences and his droopy face never seemed to betray emotion. So on the Monday when three sixth-graders defaced the corridor with stolen red paint and set the chemistry lab on fire, he remained surprisingly calm. As the culprits were brought in front of him, his lips merely twisted into a mask of resigned annoyance. 'Aren't you ashamed?' he asked the teenagers, and then turned and slowly walked away. They weren't ashamed. He didn't issue any punishment.

Once he was out of their earshot, the three boys broke out laughing, a scornful snicker that young males of several mammal species emit after finding their opponent unexpectedly weak. Debora, who'd witnessed the scene, found that this sound sent a stream of blood coursing furiously to her head. It reminded her of Pasha and his friends hounding the curly-haired Jewish boy, who, she had noticed, had stopped coming to school.

'If I ever see you doing that again, I will personally make sure someone cuts off your shrivelled little testicles,' she said loudly and clearly, squeezing one of the boys' elbows until it hurt. 'And you should know I have the ability. Tomorrow, make sure your parents come to see me. Understand?'

This was not the kind of language that usually came out of a teacher's mouth, and the boys – all taller and bulkier than Debora – went pale. Once they'd scattered away, Debora remained standing, her fists clenched and her heart racing. Valentyna, the maths teacher, came up and offered her hand. 'Good on you to do this,' she said. 'Bravo.'

'Everything has been upside down the past few years, and everyone is confused,' Debora replied, her face still flushed. 'These kids, they have seen everything but they don't know what is wrong and what is right. We have to make sure they do.'

'True,' Valentyna agreed. 'Too bad our director is so soft on these hooligans. Poor soul, he's a broken man. Such an unlucky life.'

'Unlucky? How?' Roman had never spoken about his life to Debora.

'He had two sons. Both went into the army and both are missing. His wife also died, in 1943, when our troops started shelling Kyiv. Cut down by our own artillery. So he's been living all alone, just school and home, home and school. I've never seen him smile.'

'Everyone's lost someone,' Debora said.

'That is true. Everyone has their own cross to bear,' Valentyna agreed.

At home, Debora told Rebecca about the confrontation. 'You actually threatened to cut off their little thingies?' Rebecca laughed. Then she turned serious. 'You're not just angry about these stupid boys,' she said. 'You're angry that your own son is becoming one of them.'

'What do you mean?' Debora asked.

'You know what I mean. You've sacrificed everything, and he is becoming one of them. Pasha, our little sweet Pasha.'

'You're saying stupid things now, Mother.'

Rebecca put her hands on Debora's shoulders and looked her in the eye. 'It breaks my heart to be saying this, but he is becoming just like your Maslov. I love Pasha with all my heart, but sometimes I can't tell them apart any more.'

'I don't know what you are trying to say, Mama.' Debora got up to check on her son.

'You do, you just don't want to admit it,' Rebecca sighed.

The boy was in his room, drawing in a big album that Maslov had bought him. She looked at the drawing. Big men in green uniforms were firing their guns into ugly creatures with beards and funny hats. 'What is it?' she asked.

'It's our people, killing the traitors,' he said with a sweet smile. 'Look, this one is Papa.' He pointed to the biggest man, who had precisely marked lieutenant colonel's insignia, two stripes and two stars, on his athletic shoulders.

'It doesn't look like your father,' Debora said, her voice suddenly harsh.

'Yes it does,' Pasha whined. 'Don't say that, it does.'

The next morning, after a firm conversation with the mothers of the misbehaving teenagers, all of them simple women more intimidated by a well-dressed teacher than their children ever would be, Debora walked over to Roman's office.

'The school year is ending, and I think we should celebrate. The war is over, summer is here. We should have a party for the staff,' she said. 'It would be great for morale.'

Roman didn't like parties, but he didn't object. The gathering was set for early June, two days before Maslov was scheduled to return from western Ukraine. Everyone contributed what they could – Roman found vodka and wine, Debora brought sausages and cakes, and Valentyna hauled in a gramophone with several dance-music records. Women outnumbered men on the teaching staff four to one, and so Debora, in a silver silk dress that bared most of her back, ended up dancing with Valentyna, who proved expert at the tango and the cha-cha-cha. Roman found himself subjected to unexpected attention from the German-language teacher, Alina, who didn't let go of him all evening. It was the first time in a long time, everyone agreed, that he had been spotted with a smile on his face.

*

Maslov returned from his trip late at night. Pasha and Nina shrieked in delight as he woke them up and tickled them at breakfast. But once the children had left for school and he was alone with Debora, she noticed his unusually long stare. He had fixed his eyes on the wall and wasn't moving.

'How was it out there?' she asked.

He didn't reply, and instead got up and poured himself a half-glass of vodka. It was very early in the day to start drinking, but she didn't object.

'They hate us, they really hate us,' he finally said. 'Everyone – the men, the children, the women, the old grandpas and grandmas. Their fucking dogs and cats. They would all kill us if they could.'

'I am sure not all of them,' Debora tried to reason. But she saw that Maslov was different, as if some inner certainty had collapsed. 'Tell me what happened out there. I mean, tell me what you can, of course,' she went on.

Maslov didn't usually discuss work at home, and not just because violating secrecy rules was illegal. Debora, he knew, understood his job in general terms – the Organs were the Organs, after all. But general terms were one thing and the actual details another. The less she knew, the easier it would be for him to come back every night to what he had desired all his life – a quiet family hearth, just as it was supposed to be. Just as he had always imagined it. At home, he didn't want to be reminded of the blood slicks on the concrete floor of the basement, of the involuntary emissions of dying men.

Throughout his career, except for the several weeks of fighting the Nazis in Stalingrad, he'd had to deal with people already cowed, people who usually sought to delay the inevitable by claiming that there had been a terrible mistake and professing an undying loyalty to the Party. Before this trip to western Ukraine, he hadn't seen regular people, villagers of the kind he himself used to be, staring at him with open contempt. Villagers who he knew would gladly ambush and kill him, as they had killed the two members of his team who had got lost on a country road near Drohobych two weeks earlier. Even the Red Army's top commander in Ukraine, General Vatutin, had died in such an insurgent ambush the previous year.

So today he needed to talk.

'Everyone who works there with us – a village cop, a teacher we sent out from here or Russia, a doctor – they all live in fear. Any time during the night, there can be a knock on the door and a bullet to the head,' he told Debora.

'Is it that bad? Are there so many Nazis still left?' she asked. 'Why are the Germans fighting now that even Hitler is dead?'

'Nazis? Germans? I wish it were so simple, my dear. These are not Nazis. There are no Germans. Only Ukrainians. But those people over there, they aren't really like us, the Soviet people, they have a different mind. That place used to be part of Austria just thirty years ago, and Poland only six years ago, you know. Six years is nothing. They still remember. It's in their blood. UPA, they call themselves. The Ukrainian Insurgent Army, the Banderite bandits. They hope that America will go to war against us this year or next, that's why they keep on fighting. And maybe America will, who knows.'

'Tell me what happened out there.' Debora sat down next to Maslov and took his hand.

'Last Thursday. It was just before dawn, in the forest, with mist rising from the moss. There had been an ambush, and the dogs led us to a hideout. Just a heap of branches on the edge of a clearing, I wouldn't have given it a second thought myself. But the dogs went crazy. We removed the branches, and indeed, below it there was the hatch of a *kryivka*. You know what a *kryivka* is?'

253

She shook her head.

'They dig these hideouts, like bunkers, under homes, in the woods, everywhere. They spend their days down there and come out to fight us at night. You'd be surprised how big they can be. At this *kryivka* that we found in the forest, there was not a peep, not a breath from inside. I thought at first it was empty. But the dogs wouldn't let go. So we prised open the hatch and, just to be sure, threw hand grenades inside. Turns out there were three men in there. All three died right away. They never even had a chance to shoot at us.

'We dragged them out and tied them to the hoods of our Willys and drove like that to the nearest village. They were mangled, and blood and guts were dripping on the sides of the jeeps, but what else was there to do? We dumped the bodies in front of the church and set an observation point nearby, just inside the treeline.' He mimicked looking into binoculars and poured himself another shot, swaying in the chair.

'Why? What did you have to observe?' Debora didn't understand.

'Ha. Well, the bandits didn't have any documents on them, so we didn't know who we had killed. We had to wait for someone to claim them, for identification and investigation. The church had been boarded up and the priest had been taken care of by another unit. They have their own imperialist church out there, follows the Pope, not Russian Orthodox like ours. As the sun rose, villagers began to come out one by one. News spread to nearby villages, and by noon three horse carts had arrived to take the dead to their families. So much wailing! At that point, all we had to do was follow the carts. We showed up with our trucks at their family homes an hour later. They had an hour to pack – they could take one suitcase each.'

'Pack to go where?'

'To faraway places, what do you think? We can't just allow Banderite families and their accomplices to remain. There is plenty of room for them in Magadan, Vorkuta and Karaganda,' he laughed.

He stopped talking then, realising that he couldn't tell Debora everything. Memories became so vivid that he felt he was in the village again. In the garden, under the apple tree, a dead rebel's son – about the same age as Pasha and with a near-identical haircut – crouched next to his mother. Wiping her tears, the woman got up, her eyes level with Maslov's.

'A curse be upon you, and your children, and their children down to the seventh generation,' she said slowly. 'A curse. A terrible curse for what you have done to our Ukraine. God is watching, God is above us, and God knows everything.' She spat in his face.

He hadn't expected such defiance, and instead of hitting her, he just wiped the spit from his cheek. Then he moved to his car and sat there, deflated, watching through the dirty windshield as troopers herded the insurgent's relatives into a tented truck. He wasn't going to admit that humiliation to Debora.

She pulled his hand, trying to get him up. 'You're still very tired, Dmitri. You should probably go back to bed, get some rest,' she said. He complied grudgingly. She was distraught at his tale, at how casually he spoke of killing people just like the men and the women in the city around them. Not Germans, Ukrainians. But she didn't say anything.

'Those people out there, they probably hate us as much as we hate the Germans,' he muttered as she helped him to the bedroom. 'But that's fine. No problem. We're patient. We'll teach them to love us.'

31

Yalta, August 1945

'Do you know how to swim?' Maslov asked Pasha as he took off his jacket, sitting down for dinner. It was hot, and sweat stained his shirt.

The boy nodded. 'Yes, we learned in Derbent!'

'And you?' He turned to Nina. The girl laughed, embarrassed. 'Well, it's time for you to learn too, sweetie,' he announced, and pulled vacation vouchers out of his pocket, waving the sheets of stamped paper dramatically. 'Because we're going to the sea!'

'Annual leave is allowed again now that the war is over,' he told Debora. 'And we definitely deserve it. After that assignment in Drohobych, for sure. The directorate have allocated us a stay in one of the best sanatoriums. A special one, for the cadres of the NKGB.'

'Where is it?' she asked.

'Yalta. Crimea.'

'Just the four of us, or is Mama coming?'

'I am most certainly not going to Crimea,' Rebecca interjected. 'I hate the sun. I would also love to have some peace and quiet and time for myself.'

Maslov hadn't planned for Rebecca to join them, and exhaled, relieved. When Debora tried to convince her to change her mind, he adopted his most reasonable tone. 'My dear, why are you arguing with your mother? Show her some respect.' She gave him a withering stare.

The next day, he took her to do their holiday shopping: white trousers, panama hats, swimsuits for the whole family. The trip required a night's train ride, in a compartment with linen on the bunk beds, just for the four of them, and then a drive across the mountains. The road snaked through cypress groves rimmed by rocky escarpments, and past Tatar villages of crumbling stone homes, with an occasional abandoned minaret.

'What are these?' Pasha asked.

'Bad people used to live here. And now they're gone. Only good people are left,' Maslov replied.

'Gone where?' the boy pressed.

'Gone to where they belong.'

'Just look at the beautiful countryside.' Debora tried to distract him.

As soon as their car crossed the mountain pass, the shimmering Black Sea, dark blue, with clouds like cotton candy floating above it, opened up in front of them.

'The sea!' Debora said. 'Look, you see it?'

'Why is it not black?' Pasha was puzzled. 'It is the wrong colour.'

The NKGB sanatorium occupied a clifftop villa that had once belonged to a St Petersburg count. It was built in a fake Moorish style, with spiral turrets and Levantine arched windows, and was surrounded by a tropical garden. Unlike most of the rest of Yalta, the building bore no traces of the war. Women with deferential smiles, gliding swiftly and silently through the corridors, kept the premises spotlessly clean.

The Maslovs' room overlooked the beach, accessible by a steep staircase carved into the cliff. They went down the steps right after dropping their bags, treading carefully on the shiny grey pebbles and then dipping their toes into the cold, transparent water. Debora climbed onto a big boulder on the edge of the beach, spread her towel on its warm surface and lay down with her book, the way she had seen vacationers depicted in magazines. Once every few minutes, she raised her head to watch Maslov, in his oversize trunks, splashing in the water with the children. The air smelled of unfamiliar plants.

At dinner, they were served fresh fish, little sandwiches with butter and salmon roe, and a bottle of Soviet champagne. They were all sunburned by then, but not nearly as badly as their fellow guests. Everywhere she looked, the pasty faces of NKGB officers and their wives were blistered, and they sat stiffly, wincing with pain every time their backs touched their chairs.

Once the children had fallen asleep, Maslov and Debora sat down for a nightcap on the balcony. 'Thank you for this,' she said, holding his hand.

They looked silently at the stars, and then he raised a topic that he had wanted to discuss for days. 'I've been making some enquiries. The director of your school, Roman, he has come up on our radar. Not a reliable type, really. He stayed in Kyiv under the Germans, and now we have found out that both of his sons surrendered to the enemy during the war. Not someone to whom the education of our children should be entrusted.'

'His sons are alive?' Debora asked. 'He hasn't heard from them for years. He'll be so happy to see them.'

'Yes, they have both survived, though I doubt he'll get to see them soon. They are being returned to us by the British from their part of Germany, and like all these POWs, they will be resettled in special areas, far away. They failed to follow Stalin's orders.'

'Failed how? By not dying?' She pulled her hand back sharply.

'That's not the best way to put it, but yes, the orders were to fight to the last, not to give up. Many did give up, many were cowards. And who knows what they were up to in Germany. We can't just let them come back as if nothing happened. Too risky.'

'What if my brother is still alive?' Debora turned sharply. 'Will you send him to Siberia too, if you find him in the POW camps?'

'I have looked for your brother, and I haven't found him,' Maslov said in a measured tone. 'That's also something I've been meaning to tell you. To be honest, judging by where and when he was last deployed, it's unlikely we ever will. So no, I don't think he is going to Siberia.'

'Will we ever know with certainty?'

'Probably not. In war, anything can happen.'

Debora decided to tell Maslov about the silver flask from Switzerland. He paused to consider it.

'It doesn't change anything,' he said finally. 'All we know is that your brother is missing in action. And that is probably all you will ever know for sure.'

'It's hard to be in this limbo, to think that maybe one day he will turn up alive, to still have that hope.'

'Of course it's not easy,' he agreed. 'Millions of people are in the same boat. They will never be certain.'

He coughed and steered the conversation back to Roman.

'You have to think about what happens at the school once he's gone.'

'Roman is a decent man,' Debora said. 'I want you to know that. He's been through a lot.'

'It's not even my decision,' Maslov replied. 'But I am quite sure he won't be the school's director come September. Some colleagues suggested you might be suitable for the job. They have heard good things about you.'

'From whom?'

'You know we hear everything. Apparently you are popular with the rest of the teachers. Strong-willed, they say.'

Debora was irritated. 'Well, let's allow the Education Department to make their decision. I don't want this to come from you, I want them to decide on their own.'

Maslov nodded. 'Of course, of course. I won't interfere. Promise. They'll make their own call.'

He knew that the Education Department never decided such things on their own.

In the morning, the mood in the breakfast hall was tense. Guests in their panama hats were absorbed in the day's newspapers, paying little attention to the pies, eggs and sausages spread atop the starched tablecloth. The headlines were big and bold, across the entire front page.

'There's war again,' the waitress told them as she handed over a paper. 'We just finished one, and now there is another.'

Overnight, the Soviet Union had declared war on Japan. The newspapers announced that Soviet troops, meeting heavy resistance, had advanced fifteen kilometres into Manchuria, and described extensive bombing raids launched by the Soviet air force.

'What does this mean? Will they be drafting our men again? You?' Debora asked.

'I don't know,' Maslov replied. 'Japan is a big, strong country. This could take a while.'

He leafed through the newspaper, a local daily, with an experienced eye. He knew that the most important announcements were often buried deep inside, almost invisible to a novice.

'Take this.' Another guest handed him a copy of Moscow's *Pravda*. He put his finger next to a small wire item on page 4 that recounted in a few paragraphs a speech by President Truman. A bomb equivalent to twenty thousand tons of TNT had been dropped on the Japanese city of Hiroshima, heralding 'a new, revolutionary increase in destruction'. It used an atomic principle, 'harnessing the basic power of the universe', the article added.

The item was easy to miss, surrounded by reports of heroic advances by Soviet land forces. It would be the only official mention of nuclear weapons for months.

'The Japanese won't resist long after this. It will be a short war,' the fellow guest, a Muscovite judging by his accent, told them. 'I know a thing or two about atomic bombs. Go enjoy the beach, comrade.'

Nobody at the resort was recalled to duty that day. The vacationing families returned to the waterfront, and by the evening, Debora was as painfully sunburned as everyone else. The resort had a resident photographer, and so on their last day in Yalta, all four of them wore their holiday best and posed for an official family portrait in the sanatorium's gilded ballroom, a sense of sated contentment radiating from their tanned faces.

A week after they returned to Kyiv, Debora was summoned to the district's Education Department and told that she'd been promoted to become the school's new director. A bouquet of roses awaited her at home.

PART FIVE

32

Kyiv, December 1947

When Debora woke up alone in their king-sized bed in its gilded alcove, the first thought that passed through her mind was that it would be two more weeks before Maslov's return. She stretched with a lazy, satisfied yawn. She had grown to prize the weeks and months when he was away, when she didn't have to watch him get drunk and slump into a stupor, something that had never happened before these assignments in western Ukraine began. His body's smell had also changed, she noticed, and on the day he left, she'd have all the bed sheets washed and aired, to eliminate his presence from her sleep.

She decided to linger in bed this morning, letting Rebecca get the children ready. She was usually the first to arrive at school in the mornings, sternly greeting the students at the door and making sure their fingernails had been properly cut, their haircuts were in accordance with regulations and their belt buckles had been polished with acid. She no longer taught literature, and rarely had time to read. It had been months since she last bought a book.

Today she had a doctor's appointment at 11 a.m., to check up on her frequent back pain, and she used it as an excuse to skip the morning routine. The day would be long – in the evening, she was supposed to go to the Kyiv Opera to see *Romeo and Juliet*. Maslov had procured the tickets, but he was in western Ukraine, on a trip that was unscheduled and of indeterminate duration, as usual. Before his departure, he'd insisted that she should go anyway. A young junior lieutenant named Yevhen Rybak would escort her.

Rybak had appeared a few months earlier, a personal aide assigned to make Maslov's life easier. He usually remained behind when Maslov was travelling, helping Debora shop and fixing whatever broke down in the apartment. The young man, with his blond fringe and earnest eyes, was always courteous and polite, and above all glad to be spared the potentially deadly missions out west.

By now, years of daily drinking had manifested themselves in the burst capillaries of Maslov's meaty face. New acquaintances began to assume that Debora was at least a decade younger than her husband, even though the two were only a couple of years apart. Sometimes she let go of her mask as a fear-inspiring school director, the object of many of her students' nightmares, and flirted with handsome men who didn't know her, just to prove to herself that she remained attractive. But she'd never had an actual affair, and wasn't intending to have one. So as there was nothing to hide, she didn't mind Rybak's presence, and she could certainly use household help. She sometimes showed her annoyance by being needlessly harsh with the young lieutenant. She decided she would be kind to him tonight.

At about 9 a.m., after Rebecca had walked the children to school, Debora took a long bath. She dried her hair with a towel and, putting on her dark-blue teacher's dress, headed to the kitchen, feeling suddenly hungry. Though the Maslovs occupied more than half of the rooms in the apartment, there were other residents too. Yana, a former actress who worked as a secretary for the district electricity board, was busy at the stove. The other neighbours, a childless couple of mid-level bureaucrats in the Ministry of Machine-Building, had already gone to work, their dishes and food padlocked in a separate cupboard.

An old lady downstairs had whispered into Debora's ear that Yana had spent the wartime years whoring for the Germans. Apparently this was the reason why she couldn't return to acting. Debora didn't know how true the rumour was, but it was sufficient to solidify her instinctive dislike of her neighbour.

Clad in a skimpy bathrobe that she liked to wear even when Maslov was around, perhaps particularly when Maslov was around, Yana cracked an egg and poured its contents into a frying pan. 'They said on the radio it may snow later today,' she said as the smell of burning sunflower oil hit Debora's nostrils. 'Winter is going to be harsh this year.'

Debora paid no attention, and when Yana was done, she started boiling coffee and making her own breakfast, oatmeal porridge that she was going to top with dried fruit and nuts. As Yana wandered off with her plate, someone knocked on the front door, three strong, insistent taps. This was unusual: when visitors came, they usually rang one of the three doorbells, emblazoned with the three resident families' surnames, each ringing with a different chime.

After half a minute, there were three more taps, louder and more impatient than before. 'I'll get it,' Yana shouted from across the corridor. She unlocked the door with the chain still on and spoke to the visitor through the gap.

'Who is it?' Debora asked lazily. 'Is it for you?'

'It must be a mistake, Darya Grigoriyevna,' Yana shouted.

'Some man is asking for a Debora. I told him we have no Deboras here, but he won't leave.'

Debora put down her plate. 'Let me talk to him,' she replied, feeling a knot rising in her chest and moving up her throat, constricting her breath. Blood drained from her face, and she felt so dizzy in the ten seconds it took her to reach the front door that she had to hold on to the wall to regain her balance. She ran through her mind a list of people from her previous life who might have wanted to track her down. Could it be her brother, returned from captivity?

Yana was already halfway back to her room when Debora took off the chain and opened the door. She turned around when she heard Debora's gasp, and her eyes widened as she saw her neighbour slowly, hesitantly reach out to the man's face, running her fingers over the stubble on his chin as if to make sure he was real.

'You?' she heard her say. 'Is that you?'

Debora touched the man's scarred cheek, his moustache, his hair. It was cold on the landing, and his breath appeared as puffs of vapour. His skin was cold, too. In his ill-fitting, stained clothes, he was still as tall as before, much taller than Maslov. His eyes no longer burned with self-confidence, but he didn't have the dull, glazed stare of a broken man either.

'Samuel?'

He had imagined this moment for ten years, and had rehearsed it in front of a mirror last night. Still, the words that he had prepared evaporated from his mind, and it took him a second to wipe away a tear and start speaking, haltingly.

'I told you,' he began. 'I told you I would be back.'

'You are alive?' It wasn't really a question, but she kept asking. 'Alive? I was told you died, a long time ago. How ... That's why ...'

'Well, they lied. And I didn't.' Samuel took in Debora's new look. Ten years older, of course, but still beautiful, well groomed, shining with health. Just like he had imagined her all those ten years, the years he had spent digging the permafrost of the Dalstroy labour camps.

He reached out to touch her, to run his hand over her face, to examine the topography that he had tried to recall every night. Debora, without meaning to, without thinking why, moved away. Sensing that they were being watched, she turned around, catching Yana's stare.

'It's a mistake,' she shouted across the corridor, then, regaining her composure, instructed Samuel in an urgent whisper: 'Wait for me downstairs.' She slammed the door in his face. Yana looked at her incredulously and returned to her room.

Ten minutes later, Debora put on her fur coat, a recent gift from Maslov, and ran down the stairs. Yana watched through the window and jotted down in quick, unintelligible handwriting how Lieutenant Colonel Maslov's wife and an unknown male, moustache, dark hair, addressed as Samuel, referring to her by the name Debora, left the building together and headed up the street, engaged in an animated conversation. She looked at her watch, a German man's gift, and noted the exact time. Then she got dressed and walked out to deliver her report. A few more such reports, and maybe they would let her on stage again, she thought.

Debora led Samuel into a nearby cafeteria, still largely empty in this pre-lunch hour. They sat down in a corner where they couldn't be overheard. She moved without fully comprehending what had just happened, but she knew that it must be kept totally secret, at least for now.

'That wasn't the kind of welcome I expected,' Samuel said savagely. 'A mistake?'

'I'm sorry, I am. But we're not children. If you found me here, you also know that I am married, and you know what my husband does for a living.' She paused. 'You do know what he does for a living, don't you?'

'Your husband is sitting in front of you. Right here.' He stabbed his chest with his index finger, which she noticed was missing the tip where the fingernail used to be. 'I did what I promised to do. You haven't.' He caught her glance. 'Frostbite.'

'Please, please don't be angry with me,' she implored. 'I was told – I was *assured* – that you were executed all the way back in 1937. And now you're alive, and I am so happy that you are back from the dead. You know, ten years without the right of correspondence, that was what it usually meant. Execution. Firing squad. Trust me, I cried my eyes out for you, I mourned you. It broke my heart. But I had Pasha, our son, *your* son. I had to live, for him. He is alive now because I did what I had to do. I know you've gone through a hard time. But it was a hard time for all of us.' She wiped away a tear.

He leaned back in his chair, squinting as he looked at her fur coat, at the wholesome sheen of her cheeks. 'You don't really look like you have been through a hard time.'

'Don't you dare.' She cut him off. 'That's unfair. Don't you dare talk about things you know nothing about.'

He stared at the wall, past her, avoiding her eyes.

They remained silent for a minute, then another. Debora felt her strength drain as the adrenaline rush began to dissipate. It had taken her such an effort to forget Samuel, to extinguish him from her existence, to stop thinking about him, to accept his death, to accept that she would never see him again. And now here he was, upset, accusing, angry. Alive.

'How long have you been in Kyiv?' She broke the silence that was pulling them further and further apart with every awkward second.

'Three months. And all this time, every day, I have been looking for you. Every time I saw someone who looked like you on the street, I would run after them, sometimes tapping them on the shoulder like an idiot, just to look into their face. I went to our old apartment, of course, on Shevchenko Boulevard, but everybody I used to know there was gone, and the new residents wouldn't even open the door to talk to me. This city is full of newcomers, and nobody knows about the past.'

'So how did you manage to find me?'

'A bit of luck at the dentist's office.' He smiled, finally. 'I had to get false teeth – you know, dental care is not the best in Dalstroy – and in the waiting room I bumped into a man who looked familiar. Roman, your former boss at the school.'

'Ah,' Debora said. 'Roman. Of course.'

'He gasped when he saw me, like meeting a ghost. It was clear that he knew more than he let on. His appointment was after mine, so I waited until he was done and offered to buy him a drink. He resisted at first, but you know me, I can convince people. The camps. I gave him hope, that was it. That was why he talked to me. Both of his sons are out there now, and I guess me being in Kyiv, drinking vodka with him, was proof that they too can come back.

'We drank until late in the evening, and I was telling him about how life is out there, what his sons are probably doing right now, how they work, how they eat ... I mean, I didn't tell him everything, I spared the worst details. And in the end, he let it slip that you were back in Kyiv, and he told me where you lived. He only knew the building, not the apartment. So this morning I came and knocked on every door, floor after floor.'

'What else did he tell you about me?'

'He said you have two children now. One must be Pasha, and the other belongs to that man. What is his name?'

'Maslov. Lieutenant Colonel Dmitri Maslov.'

'You've traded a captain for a colonel. Well done!' Samuel whistled sarcastically.

'Don't be cruel to me. I don't deserve it,' Debora said. 'I did it for Pasha.'

'Pasha ... Do you have a picture of him? How is he? What does he look like?'

Hesitantly she opened her purse and pulled out a family photo that she carried in her wallet. It was the one taken in Yalta, the black-and-white photograph reflecting a transient instant of happiness of which she was now ashamed.

Samuel's mouth twisted in revulsion as he held it with two fingers at a distance, as if it were a poisonous plant or a dangerous insect. 'Pasha is a very handsome boy,' he said finally. 'He doesn't look the way I imagined.'

He handed back the photograph. 'Yalta, huh,' he said bitterly, noticing the resort's stamp on the image.

'Yes, Yalta,' Debora said. 'What was I supposed to do?'

'I don't know. I really don't know.'

'Ten years, it's a very long time,' she said. 'A very long time. What happened to you in all those years?'

'Well, for one, they failed to kill me. And that is a victory on its own.' Samuel perked up. He cocked his head and sat back in the chair, looking once again like the confident pilot he used to be. 'Turns out I was a strong man, stronger than most. Many, once they got there, to the end of the world, they just wanted to die. But I wanted to live, for you, for Pasha. If you hadn't come that day to the train station, maybe I wouldn't have had the courage to go on. But you did, and you told me you'd wait, and I didn't want to fail you.'

'I waited,' she said. 'I waited and waited, and then I mourned you.'

He touched her hand. 'I didn't mean to reproach you again.'

'And now? What do you want to do?' she asked, crossing her arms in front of her, as if bracing for a blow.

He was surprised by the question. 'What do you mean? I just want to reclaim what is mine. My son, my wife. Obvious, isn't it? I am a free man now, and I have some money. Not as much as that lieutenant colonel of yours, but some. This is a big, big country. We can leave, go to, I don't know, Riga, or Dushanbe, or Vladivostok. There are so many places. You and me and Pasha.'

'What about Nina?' Debora poked a crack in Samuel's dream.

'Nina? Is that her name?'

'Yes, that is my daughter's name. And Pasha, it's complicated. Pasha is his son now. He has taken his surname.' She deliberately avoided saying 'Maslov'.

'Why did you allow him to do that? To our son?'

'I was just doing what was best. You can't understand. You weren't there. We were this close to starving, all of us.' She brought her thumb and index finger together. 'There was a war.'

'I understand, I understand.' Samuel cupped Debora's hand. 'Debora, my dear, let's leave here. I will take in your daughter as if she's mine. The war is finished, I am out of the camps, we can start afresh. You're not that man's property. We can remake our lives.'

The cafeteria began filling up with people, and two uniformed officers sat down at the table next to theirs. She spotted some of her students who had sneaked out to buy ice cream during a break. They noted her too, with surprise, and scampered away. She pulled back her hand, as if scalded.

'I have to go now, my students are here.' She got up, her eyes turning cold and distant.

273

Samuel took out a notebook and scribbled his address. 'This is where I live. It's not far.'

She picked up the note and put it in her purse, without looking. 'Wait for me tonight. I will come when I can.'

33

Kyiv, December 1947

Debora didn't tell her mother or anyone else about Samuel's return. Instead of keeping the doctor's appointment, she headed to school, trying to lose herself in the comfort of routine. But as she moved through the day, hosting staff meetings and inspecting classes, everyone noticed that she seemed unusually absent-minded.

'Is everything all right? You don't seem yourself today,' said Valentyna.

'You're just imagining things,' Debora rebuffed her. 'I'm fine.'

'Is your back acting up again?' Valentyna asked sympathetically. 'You don't have to hide these things. We are all human, we understand. We all have weaknesses.'

Debora locked the door of her office behind her and curled up in a ball on the sofa. The encounter with Samuel had submerged her under an avalanche of feelings she thought she was too old to have. 'What is this, you're not a silly teenager any more,' she berated herself aloud. 'You know it can't be. It just can't be. I have no right to this.'

Most people's lives were a constant struggle outside her gilded cocoon. A cocoon provided by Maslov. She knew how the world worked. An ex-convict like Samuel didn't have many options. He was lucky to be even allowed to resettle in Kyiv, instead of remaining permanently exiled.

How would they eat? If she were to leave Maslov, she would almost certainly lose her job. She could happily relinquish her sequinned dresses, smoked salmon and Crimean vacations. But dumb hunger, the deadening cramps in a stomach that yearned for food, food that was nowhere to be found – a feeling that, once experienced, could never be really forgotten – that terrified her. In the evenings, she liked watching Pasha and Nina eat, the baby fat of their cheeks, the quiet sleep after a filling meal. Subjecting them to hunger again, that she couldn't do.

And how would they leave? Maslov was Nina's father, and – after the adoption – Pasha's too. He would never let them go, and he probably wouldn't let her go either. Samuel's idea of escaping, like in the movies, was mad, she knew. The NKGB – or MGB, as State Security Organs had recently been rebranded once again – could easily track them down anywhere in the Soviet Union, unless they moved around using fake names and fake documents, which would be impossible with children.

She closed her eyes and felt guilt burning through her chest like acid. It was as if she wished he were dead, the husband she hadn't waited for, the husband she hadn't loved enough. I was weak, she thought. He is strong. He is right to be angry.

The bell rang, marking the end of classes. She freshened up and strode to the corridor, keeping her head high and maintaining her usual expression of stern detachment.

On her way home in the afternoon, she considered skipping the Opera, but decided against changing her plans. There was no need to make anyone needlessly suspicious. She put on a white dress embroidered with roses and braided her hair, and by the time Lieutenant Rybak arrived to pick her up in the MGB-issued Studebaker, she seemed to be her usual self.

'Come on, get up, time to go, you can daydream on your own time.' Debora shoved Rybak at the end of a long, sleep-inducing performance. At least this time it was ballet, not an opera, and he could enjoy the sight of pretty ballerinas fluttering around the stage.

Debora wore her fur coat – Rybak did not know what animal it was from, but suspected a rare and pricey species. Complementing a pearl necklace were pearl-white shoes on tall, thin heels. Not the best kind of footwear in the snow and sludge of a December Kyiv. Especially not after drinking flute after flute of Crimean champagne at the Opera buffet, where Kyiv's elite – mostly senior officers and their wives in trophy German or Austrian jewellery – chattered over canapés of Caspian caviar smudged onto thin slices of lemon. Debora had eaten so much caviar and salted sturgeon during the war in Derbent that just the sight of it made her gag.

After the performance, she insisted on walking for a little while. 'Fresh air would do me good, wouldn't it, my young lieutenant,' she laughed, almost flirtatiously, and pinched Rybak's cheek. 'Come on, don't be a bore. It's such a beautiful city, and the full moon is out!'

His cheek burned, but it was also a pleasant sensation. The lieutenant colonel's wife seemed like a woman out of the magazines, surrounded by a cloud of imported perfume. Except that this sweet aroma was now overpowered by the alcohol on her breath. If she wants to walk, we will walk, he thought. It was highly unlikely that she would get far, though. He signalled to the driver to quietly follow them. How on earth did she get so drunk so quickly?

'So what did you like most about the ballet?' she questioned him, trying to balance on his arm.

He hadn't quite understood what it was about, but he nodded vigorously. 'A very high-level, cultural performance. The best.'

'Yes, it is. Romeo and Juliet. How romantic . . . They die for love, you know. Would *you* die for love?' She turned towards him.

Rybak had seen people die, some when he'd fired a bullet into the back of their head. As far as he could tell, none of them died for love. For hatred, yes; because of fear sometimes; for no reason at all most often. But love? He didn't know how to answer, and so chose the safest course.

'Of course, I would gladly give my life for the love of our socialist Motherland, for Comrade Stalin,' he answered, his voice reflexively acquiring an institutional tone. 'Wouldn't you, Darya Grigoriyevna? I'm sure you would.'

She stared at him and began laughing, tears welling up in her eyes, just about long enough for it to become an unforgivable act of subversion, an act upon which he would have to file a written report. But then, her attention distracted, she slipped on an icy cobblestone and fell into a mound of dirty snow, her heel snapping off with a crack. Her bag fell out of her hands, too, and ejected its contents.

And with this, her laughter, uncontrollable now, suddenly also became innocuous – a laugh about her fall into the snow, the laugh of a drunken, unhappy, soon-to-be-middle-aged woman's self-pity.

'What, are you just going to stand there without helping a lady?' she mocked him as she extended her hand. He pulled her up, and then, crouching, swept her belongings back into the bag. Lipstick, house keys, spare change, a piece of paper with an address.

'Maybe we should continue by vehicle, Darya Grigoriyevna,' he proposed. 'It's safer that way.'

She climbed into the Studebaker without protest. 'So about love, my dear young lieutenant,' she went on. 'It is so romantic, isn't it, to die for love. Like Juliet, or Romeo. But Juliet, she was a young girl, without responsibilities, with only herself to think of. A selfish girl at the end of the day. In a different country, too. Love … Such a selfish, irresponsible thing …' She cuddled up to him and burst out in sudden, desperate sobs.

Rybak sat straight as a ramrod. He was confused. Her full breasts pressed against his elbow, and even through the fur coat, he couldn't help imagining her nipples, her soft, warm skin.

'Everything will be all right, Darya Grigoriyevna.' He patted her on the back. 'Everything will be all right.'

But she had already passed out.

Debora dreamed of Samuel, of sitting at the circus together, of holding his hand. Then the lions and elephants and bears all jumped from the stage and raced towards them, mauling them, tearing their flesh with greedy grunts. She sat up, jolted awake, and turned on the bedside lamp. The clock showed 1 a.m. Suddenly sober, she dressed, brushed her teeth, applied make-up and slipped into a pair of comfortable shoes. Then she picked out the note with Samuel's address and, trying to make no noise, tiptoed out of the apartment. Yana didn't miss the sound of the closing front door. She pulled back the curtains, watched Debora shuffling down the road and made a note in her logbook.

Samuel lived a fifteen-minute walk away, in Podil. Once outside, Debora felt like running, and had to contain herself. He was sleepless, too, chain-smoking in the communal kitchen. When she knocked on the apartment's front door, he opened it with a cigarette dangling from his lip. Silently he looked at her, stubbed out the cigarette and threw it onto the landing.

'I've come,' she said simply, and stepped inside. 'I've come to you.'

He led her down the dark corridor and into a small room with faded wallpaper. A flickering light bulb shone over a creaky single bed and two scratched old suitcases that held all his possessions. She noticed a small model aeroplane on his desk.

'I remember you flying one of these,' she said, her index finger touching the wing. 'I watched you fly, and I was so impressed, seeing you doing all those pirouettes in the sky.'

'I remember too,' he said, motioning her to sit on the bed. 'As if it were yesterday.'

She looked into his eyes. They were still so hungry for life, even after all this.

The room was so small that it had no space for a chair. He sat down next to her and put his calloused, frostbitten hand on her thigh. It was so different from Maslov's soft, fat-swollen fingers. They remained like this, in silence, motionless, for several minutes. It was a different silence from the heavy emptiness between them in the cafeteria that morning. It was a silence that sucked them into a whirlpool of shared memories, a silence that brought them together instead of pulling them apart. Finally, without a word, she put her own hand atop his.

He turned, pulled her close and kissed her mouth. She shut her eyes. Her body remembered his touch the way one remembered how to ride a bicycle. She ran her hand over his shoulder, his chest. He quickly undid her dress, then, covering her body with kisses, gently pushed her down and switched off the light. In darkness, they both imagined themselves the way they had been before it all: before the war, before the arrests, before the camps. Before Maslov. He couldn't see her wrinkles and stretch marks, she ignored his scars. He came very quickly, but then, unlike Maslov, was ready again in a few minutes.

Their sweat soaked the sheets. Neither of them tried to keep quiet. Tonight, they couldn't care less about the neighbours, neighbours awakened by noisy lovemaking through flimsy partition walls.

Once they were done, Samuel dressed and brought in two zinc cups of tea from the kitchen. Debora sat up on the bed, her back against the wall, and stirred in a sugar cube. 'You know, I have never cheated on my husband,' she said. 'Not you, not Maslov. So this is the first time. I'm scared I won't be able to hide it.'

'You don't have to hide anything. Come with me,' Samuel said.

'You don't know what you're talking about. It's easy for you, you're only responsible for yourself. Did you think about the children? What will they do? Do you think it is so simple to abandon an MGB lieutenant colonel?' The after-sex glow had dissipated unexpectedly fast, and now she felt dirty and guilty, with a headache creeping up.

'You can't live all your life in fear like this. We'll find a way, we won't starve,' he retorted.

But she didn't want to talk about the future, and so she asked him questions about the past.

'How did you survive? I want to know everything that happened to you. All these years,' she said. 'Every little detail.'

'In a way, I was lucky to be arrested when I was, just before Yakir and all the top military commanders were rounded up,' he began. 'Their prosecution was swift, and everyone who had fallen into that trap was executed in a month or two. My case was not a priority, and so by the time it came to trial, they were more interested in manpower for the Far East. They needed gold, and they needed men to dig it out. If you were strong enough from the beginning and fulfilled your quota, they would feed you well enough to keep you working. If you didn't fulfil it, your ration would be cut. You wouldn't be strong enough to work, and you'd end up dead. I was strong enough in the beginning, and so I was fed, and I lived.

'Time is slow and dull out there, and you don't want to think about what is around you. The lucky ones, like me, could think about the past. Every night I would relive, minute by minute, a day I'd spent with you, remember the movies we'd seen, the strawberries and sour cherries we'd eaten, the smell of the forest where we looked for mushrooms. Ukrainian forests don't smell the same way as the Siberian ones. Your brain dies in the camps, and so I would practise staying alive by reconstructing every single detail, recalling what seat we were sitting in, the kind of cloud formation that was in the sky at the time. Ten years. That's much longer than the time we spent together as free people, so I had to rerun our time together in my head again and again, on repeat.'

Debora felt intense shame. She hadn't thought about Samuel nearly as much. In recent years, she'd hardly thought about him at all.

'And then there was Pasha,' he went on. 'It was maybe ten seconds, not more than that, the time you brought him to me at the train station. A blur. I tried to remember how he looked, every night, my son. Was he more like me? Or like you? I would think about whether he enjoyed reading, or whether he played soccer, whether he liked to fish. And the war — we heard that Kyiv had fallen, we found out about what had happened to the Jews. There was no way for me to know whether you and Pasha were even alive. But I never lost faith, never.'

These words hit her like a whip.

'Then, in 1945, I got lucky. They started getting ready for the war with Japan. They expected a long war, months if not years, and they needed men. Those mobilised in the war against Germany were coming home, and they needed new men. They made an offer to those of us who used to be soldiers and officers: join the *shtrafbat*, the penal battalion, and if you survive the war, you'll go home free.'

Debora had heard of the *shtrafbats*. The odds of surviving them weren't high – in the war against Germany, commanders used to send the *shtrafbats'* disposable soldiers to near-certain death along the most difficult stretches of the front line. Enforcement units in the rear shot any soldiers attempting to retreat without an order.

'Why would you do that if you were just two years short of completing your sentence?'

Samuel laughed. 'You really don't know how it works, do you? When they need slaves, it doesn't matter how long the sentence is. Nobody leaves when their sentence is up. I knew that, and I knew that taking a risk with the *shtrafbat* was my only option. So I signed up, and they transferred me to the unit in Mongolia in the summer of 1945. The boat that had taken me down the coast, it brought up the German POWs who were replacing me in the gold mine. We crossed over with them on the pier. They didn't look like they would last long out there. All skinny, all coughing. Not made for that weather.

'The *shtrafbat* training was tough, but it was so much better than the camp. They fed us, and I had so missed the heat. It is really hot in Mongolia in the summer. When the orders came down to cross the border into China and take on the Japanese, they sent our unit to go first, through the minefields. We were expecting a lot of resistance – frankly, I was expecting to die. Many of our men did, in the first days, and I got a slight injury. But then, all of a sudden, the Japanese just stopped fighting and gave up. We didn't know why at first. It took us weeks to find out.'

He paused and broke out in a smile, the giddy grin of someone who had won a lottery. 'Every morning when I wake up, I thank President Truman,' he said. 'President Truman and his atomic bomb.'

Debora smiled too. 'Well, I guess, thank you, President Truman.'

Samuel raised an imaginary glass of champagne: 'To Comrade Truman!'

He looked at his model plane. 'That's the only thing I've bought since coming to Kyiv. At a flea market. God, I miss flying. They even told me at first that they would let me fly against the Japanese. But in the end they didn't trust me enough to do that. They thought I'd fly away and never come back if I had a chance.'

'Would you have?'

'No, where would I go? I wanted to find you and Pasha.' He took her hand again. 'And now that I've found you, things are different. You've heard the Jews are creating a state in Palestine. Maybe we could go there, maybe Stalin will allow it.'

'You're still such a dreamer. They would never let us,' Debora retorted. 'Nobody is permitted to leave this country, you know that. We should make the best of what we have here.'

'I don't believe in fate,' he went on. 'And you shouldn't either.'

He picked up her empty teacup and put it on the desk. Mentally he was back in Siberia again. She noted the frown, the distant look.

'It's funny, but over there I ran across a lot of people I used to know in real life, in civilian life here. It's an entire second country at Dalstroy. Cities, railways, factories, ports, newspapers and theatres. I even saw Sasha. In 1945, not long before I left.'

'Oh.'

Debora's mind wandered off. The salty taste of Sasha's sperm in her mouth, that night in the back of his car before the war, so long ago, when she would have given anything for this moment, for being with Samuel again. It all came back, as vivid as if it had happened just hours ago. Her headache became too strong to ignore. She wondered if Samuel knew, if Sasha had bragged about it.

'What was he doing there? One of the bosses?' she asked.

'Bosses? No, a prisoner just like the rest of us. He had been a coward in the war, apparently, and had surrendered to the Germans. But then they call everyone who was a POW a coward, so who knows what really happened with him. One thing is clear: he wasn't in very good shape, going from a German camp straight to the Soviet one.'

'What happened to him?'

'At Dalstroy, if you were skinny and weak like him, you weren't going to live long unless someone chose to share food with you. That happened sometimes, but not to the disgraced men from the Organs. Nobody would share with them.'

'Not even you?'

'If you shared with an untouchable, you became one of them yourself and you didn't live long. I had to live because I had to come back to you.'

'So the two of you never talked in prison?' Her heart raced as she thought about all the things Sasha could have told Samuel.

'Never. I couldn't be seen talking to a rooster.'

'A rooster?'

'You know. They made him do things for the criminal bosses. For the real criminals.'

'What things?'

'Bad things. In the ass. They fucked him every night.'

'Oh God.' Debora winced. 'Poor Sasha. Is he dead now?'

Samuel nodded distractedly. 'Most likely. Who knows. Roosters don't live long, unless they're really young and handsome, and he wasn't. You know what? I'm not sorry for him, not after what happened to his wife.'

285

Debora got up and started putting on her clothes. 'I have to go back,' she said, rubbing her eyebrows and praying for the headache to go away. Once she was fully dressed, she kneeled, patting Samuel's hair and kissing him on the forehead.

'I will see you soon,' she said. 'Promise me you won't do anything stupid.'

'Of course not,' he replied, yawning.

34

Kyiv, December 1947

Rebecca was waiting in the living room, with the door to the corridor open, when Debora returned home just before dawn. She put down her book and stared at her daughter. 'What is this? Where have you been? Do you know what time it is?'

'Of course I do, Mama. Why are you not sleeping?'

Rebecca frowned as she scrutinised Debora's flushed face, her ruffled hair, the leftovers of her make-up.

'The phone was ringing. Your husband was looking for you.'

'In the middle of the night?'

'Yes, in the middle of the night. I told him you were sleeping, but he kept insisting. I had to lie and say that you had taken a sleeping pill. What is going on? This isn't some game.'

Debora stepped into the room, locked the door and sat on an ottoman next to her mother. She spoke in a low voice, almost whispering. Too low for Yana to overhear.

'Samuel. He is alive. He came here. Today.'

'Oh God.' Rebecca clasped her daughter's hands. 'Samuel? Alive? How did that happen?'

'It doesn't really matter. What is important is that he is here, and he wants me back.'

'If Samuel has returned from the dead, maybe our Yakov will also come back.' Rebecca exhaled. 'God is all-powerful.'

'I hope so, Mama. I really do.'

Rebecca shook off her thoughts and straightened her back.

'What exactly did he ask you?'

'He wants me to leave with him, to leave Maslov, to leave all of this. To go back to the way we were. But that place he wants to return to, it doesn't exist any more, does it? I don't know what to do . . .'

'Impossible,' Rebecca said. 'He's asking you to do the impossible. There is no going back.' She stared into Debora's eyes, like an interrogator, until Debora looked away. 'But you can't resist him, sweetheart, can you? Is that where you were all night? With him?'

Debora nodded. Rebecca frowned.

'Did you think of what would happen to Pasha? To Nina? You have sacrificed so much for them,' she said. 'I know you have feelings, but feelings are a luxury. For someone like you, with responsibilities, feelings are an unaffordable luxury.'

'I can't.' Debora started to cry. 'Every time Maslov touches me, it's like an insect crawling over my skin. I feel like I want to throw up. In these ten years, I had forgotten what a man is supposed to be like.'

'I never liked Maslov. And he has changed for the worse,' Rebecca said. 'But it's not about him.'

'We all have changed, Mama.'

Rebecca embraced her daughter, stroking her hair as if she were still a small child. 'There are no good choices in our lives any more, sweetheart,' she said. 'You must choose between bad and bad.'

*

288

Later, the phone rang again and Debora picked up the receiver. 'Hello, my dearest, what happened to you last night?' Maslov asked cheerfully.

'I think I had too much to drink at the Opera, and then didn't feel well.'

'Yes, Lieutenant Rybak has already informed me. Nothing that a good night's sleep won't heal, right?'

'Of course,' Debora said with a suppressed yawn. 'I'm feeling much better now. Going to work soon. How are you?'

'Surviving, surviving. I may be coming home sooner than planned. You know, new orders.'

'When?'

'Soon. A surprise.' He laughed. 'Kiss the kids for me, will you?'

It was a busy day at work, and for a minute here and there, Debora managed to stop thinking about Samuel. She had to catch up on paperwork, and was in her office when the door was flung open and Pasha ran in.

'Why are you so upset?' she asked him as she noticed his angry glare. He seemed ready to cry, and yet determined not to.

'Mama, a man just came up to me when I left school to go home. He asked me whether my name was Pasha and then he said he had something important to tell me.'

Debora closed the door and put her hands on his shoulders. 'Calm down now, Pasha, speak properly. What did he tell you?'

'He told me that he was my father. I said he was lying, that my father died in the war fighting the Germans, but he kept saying that he was my papa. But he is a liar, right? It can't be true, can it?'

Debora pressed him to her chest. 'Pasha, my little Pasha.'

The boy struggled to break free of her embrace, not yet realising that she was not denying anything. 'I think he must be a spy,' he went on, with determination in his voice. 'It's like I've read in the books. He is a spy who is pretending to be my old papa so he can get closer to my new papa. Even the way he spoke, it sounded funny, like he was a foreigner. We must let Papa know right away, we must call him.'

'That wouldn't be a great idea right now,' Debora said gently. 'And in any case, there is no way to reach him. You know how it is when he is on assignment.'

She was furious with Samuel, rehearsing the tongue-lashing she would give him later in the day.

'That man wanted to touch me, to hug me, but I just ran away and came here. If we call the police, they may still be able to catch him.'

Debora grasped his hand. 'But what if he's telling the truth? What if he *is* your first father, what if he didn't die?'

Pasha yanked his hand away and stared at her. 'You're a liar, a liar. This can't be!' he screamed. Then, stomping his foot, he turned around and ran out of the room.

Debora tried to stop him, using her firmest tone, but he didn't obey. He raced down the staircase and out of the building. She followed him outside, but he was already gone. Samuel was nowhere in sight either.

Half an hour later, Debora arrived home. 'Is Pasha here?' she blurted out as Rebecca opened the door.

'No, why should he be? Isn't he in school?'

'Samuel found him and told him he is his father. At school. The idiot. Pasha was very upset and ran off somewhere. I am so worried.'

'What did you expect? Your son loves Maslov. Sometimes I look at the two of them and think they're of the same blood.'

'Don't say that!'

They strode into the living room, closing the door.

'Samuel! What an idiotic thing to do!' Debora said. 'What was he thinking?'

'One thing is clear to me,' Rebecca replied. 'You don't have much time to make up your mind. You can't hide it any longer.'

The doorbell rang, a long, determined buzz. It was Pasha. Sullen-faced, the boy headed straight to his room without a word, pushing Debora aside.

'I will talk to him,' Rebecca told her daughter gently. 'You go now.'

'I have destroyed myself for him. Everything, Maslov, the marriage, all this for Pasha's sake. And this is what I am getting back.' Debora bit her lip. She tried hard not to cry.

'You don't make children because you expect them to be grateful,' Rebecca retorted. 'I've been lucky with you, but it's not about gratitude with children. Whatever you give, you can't expect anything in return. Go now.'

Debora walked down the stairs and wandered through the streets of Podil, lost in her thoughts. She didn't mean to go to Samuel's apartment, but that was where she found herself half an hour later. She walked in without hesitation, past a black Studebaker parked outside.

Nobody was home, and after a few minutes of knocking on the door, she left. It was only as she stepped outside that she spotted him. He was walking slowly on the other side of the road, observing the life of the city with the intense attention of someone who hadn't seen the bustle of busy streets for a decade.

She ran towards him and his face lit up with joy. He tried to embrace her and kiss her, right there. She pushed him away.

'You are such a fool. What on earth, approaching a child on the street, scaring him like that? Do you have any idea what Pasha is thinking now? Why didn't you warn me?'

'Because you probably wouldn't have let me,' Samuel said,

turning rigid. 'Because I saw you were hesitant, you were afraid to act. You have learned all too well to live with fear, to adapt, to follow the rules. We can't keep postponing things. You must decide. Do you want to live your life with me, or with that colonel of yours?'

'I don't know. I just don't know.' Debora burst into tears, tears that she could no longer suppress and that she tried to wipe away with her sleeve, tears that she felt made everyone on the street stare at her. 'Now, with you, I feel like I am young again, like I am alive. But I can't just think about myself. That isn't fair.'

'You're looking for excuses,' Samuel said as he hugged her. 'Yes, it may be tough at first, but you don't know that in the long run Pasha will be worse off with me.'

'You keep forgetting Nina,' Debora said.

He took her by the elbow and gently nudged her towards his building. She went along with him, into the doorway, up the stairs. 'My husband called this morning,' she said. 'He may be coming back sooner than planned.'

They didn't speak from the moment they entered the apartment. Once they crossed the threshold, Debora felt her anger fall away, like an old skin shed by a snake. It was the anger of Darya Maslova, not the feelings of the woman who was here with Samuel in this cramped room with its ridiculous model aeroplane.

Samuel sat down on the bed, pulled her onto his lap and started taking off her blouse. She plunged her fingers into his hair as she watched his tongue run up and down her breasts, circling her nipples, his hand caressing the small of her back. Then they made quick, furious love, inhaling each other's smells, leaving small bruises on each other's forearms.

Afterward, she cuddled up to the warmth of his body, fitting into the forgotten crevices that she once knew so well. 'I want to be with you,' she whispered. 'I feel myself again with you.'

They remained in bed until it became dark outside and the neighbours started returning home from work.

'I have friends in Odessa we can stay with at first,' Samuel said. 'People I met in the camps, some would call them gangsters. They're Jews, too. They owe me a thing or two, and they could arrange for new documents, for everything. I've been thinking about it. It's the best option. Odessa is very pretty, it's got sunshine, it's got the sea. We could be happy.'

Debora allowed herself to imagine that new life, her and Samuel and Pasha and Nina making sandcastles on the beach, the sun's reflection flickering in the gentle waves of the Black Sea.

'But we can't wait. We must go before your colonel returns,' he went on. He never used the word 'husband' to refer to Maslov. 'I can get us train tickets for tomorrow afternoon. Tell the children that you are going on a surprise holiday to Odessa and come here with them before two o'clock.'

'That would be a lot easier if you hadn't spooked Pasha this morning.'

'He's still a child. You should be able to explain it to him, to persuade him,' Samuel said.

'Yeah? And what do you know about speaking to a child? What did you expect, that he would run towards you and love you for ever and ever, a man he doesn't even remember?'

'I don't know, I'd never thought of that, never imagined that he wouldn't want me,' Samuel admitted. 'I thought, us being the same blood, the same flesh, it would be natural. When I imagined this moment, in the camp, I never for a minute considered that he would reject me.'

'You're such an idiot,' Debora said, but now it sounded like a term of endearment. 'Always thinking you know best, always so arrogant. Don't make even more of a mess between now and tomorrow.'

Samuel, still lying in bed, watched as she snapped on her bra and pulled up her stockings, then, still half naked, tried to restore her make-up and brush her hair.

'So, two o'clock tomorrow?' he asked when she was fully dressed and ready to leave.

She nodded. As she was about to open the door, she turned back, leaned down and gave him a long, hungry kiss.

35

Kyiv, December 1947

Pasha greeted Debora with a glower that could have made a plant wilt. He was already at the dining table, next to his obliviously cheerful sister. Rebecca was serving boiled potatoes and fried chicken from an earthenware bowl decorated with Ukrainian folk paintings of peacocks and sunflowers. 'Come, sit down, you're just in time for dinner,' she said.

Debora summoned her dourest voice, looking into Pasha's eyes. 'Young man, what you did today was unacceptable. Running away, not listening to me. Promise me that you will never do that again.'

'You can't tell me what to do. Papa is the head of this family,' the boy shot back, unrepentant. His knuckles were white, his body stiff. He didn't know, of course, where Debora had spent the previous two hours, but he sensed something personally threatening and unsettlingly unusual in how she carried herself.

'Pasha, stop it right now. Speak respectfully to your mother.' Rebecca raised her voice.

'I'm not hungry.' The boy got up, pushing back his chair, and stormed away.

'Can I have his piece?' Nina reached into his plate and scooped up the chicken thigh, without waiting for an answer. 'I want his potatoes, too.'

'He's very confused.' Rebecca shook her head. 'I've spent a long time talking to him. Confused and angry.'

With quick steps, Debora followed Pasha into his room. He was curled up on the bed, staring into the wall. She sat down and touched him. 'This man you spoke to today, what if he really is your father? You know, in wars they make mistakes. Someone they say is dead sometimes turns up alive, it happens. Shouldn't we try to meet him and talk to him? Don't we want to know what is going on?'

'He's ugly and scary, like a rat,' Pasha scoffed, still turned towards the wall. 'I don't want to talk to him. I don't need another papa. I already have one. And my papa is a real hero, not like that man.'

'Your first father was a hero too. He flew planes.' She tried to hug the boy.

Pasha pushed her away, so hard that it hurt. 'Go away, leave me alone.' He was enraged now, with foamy spittle at the corner of his mouth. 'I have my papa. I want my papa. I want him to come home now!' He seemed poised to hit her, raising his hand.

Debora recoiled and grabbed his wrist, squeezing it. 'Don't you dare talk to me like this,' she hissed. 'Never ever.'

'You're hurting me,' the boy cried, and she realised that she was leaving a bruise on his skin. She let go of his hand, turned around and left. 'I hate you,' he muttered, loudly enough for her to hear.

At the dining table, Nina had already polished off Pasha's chicken thigh. 'Why is there so much shouting?' she asked, burping happily. 'Is Pasha mean to you? He's been mean to me too, all day.'

'It will be all right, sweetie,' Debora replied. 'Go brush your teeth now, please.'

'Yes, Mama,' Nina complied, jumping off her chair.

Once they were alone, Debora closed the door and whispered to Rebecca, 'I don't know what to do. Samuel wants us to leave tomorrow, all of us, and go to Odessa. He says he has friends who will help us escape, who will make documents.'

'There is no way Pasha is going to accept that. And even if he goes along, there is no way this is going to work. They will catch you all,' Rebecca replied. 'Be reasonable.' She looked at Debora, crumpled in her chair, her face in her palms. 'You know as well as I do that it is a pipe dream, this madness,' she went on. 'The only way it's going to work, the only way Maslov could possibly let it happen, is if you leave the children behind. They will be okay. I can stay and help raise them. For you, and for them, I can even put up with that man. But are you ready to do that? Do you love Samuel strongly enough for that? Do you? Only you know the answer.'

'I don't know, I just don't know anything any more.' Debora's eyes welled up again. 'It's only been two days since he came back.'

Washed and dressed in her new pink nightgown, Nina flung open the living room door. 'Mama, stop crying,' she said, hugging Debora. She smelled of toothpaste and lavender soap. 'It was not nice of Pasha to be so mean to you. *I* will never be mean to you.'

Debora wiped her tears. 'Come here, sweetie, come hug Mama,' she said as Nina cuddled up on her lap. 'Mama will always love you.'

It was an hour before the appointed time when Debora rang Samuel's doorbell. She waited on the dank, unlit landing that smelled of urine and fermented cabbage, the habitual aroma of a

Soviet housing block. Through the flimsy front door, she heard the floorboards rasp under strong, determined steps. The man who opened it was backlit by the sun.

Debora was standing in front of her husband.

Her pulse quickened. She felt so dizzy that she needed to hold on to the door frame to steady herself.

'You? What are you doing here?' she asked, still hoping for a coincidence, a coincidence that she knew was impossible. 'Why are you here?'

'Come on in. Do you need help with your bags?' Maslov's voice was frightening in its cold politeness.

'What bags? I don't have any bags.'

'Good.' He stood aside, opening the way, and then led her to Samuel's room. She followed, too stunned to protest.

The room was bare, she noticed right away. Samuel's suitcases were gone, and so were his books, his model aeroplane and his clothes. Dressed in a neatly creased uniform, Maslov sat down on the unmade bed, on the sheets still soaked with her and Samuel's sweat.

He caught her eye. 'Not what you were expecting, is it?' Cold, suppressed rage coursed through every syllable.

She was standing in front of him like a prisoner under interrogation.

'So, my dear Darya, what is this?' He waved four railway tickets. 'Is my dear wife thinking of going somewhere? A vacation? With children? *My* children?'

She remained silent.

'For fuck's sake, say something. Don't play these mute games with me.' Springing up, he raised his hand to slap her across the cheek. His veins bulged, and a blood vessel in his left eye had burst, creating a bright-red blotch.

Closing her eyes, she braced herself, but Maslov diverted the blow at the last moment and hit the wall instead. Reopening her eyes, she stared at him, all her attention suddenly focused on the sweaty, shiny patch of his forehead and the hairs sprouting from his nose. Hatred, caustic hatred, was all that she felt for him now. She was no longer dizzy.

'Do you really think I am this stupid? That I am an idiot? That I am blind? That you can fool me?' He spat rapid words at her.

'No, Dmitri,' she replied, surprised by the calm, steady strength of her voice, by the fact that she wasn't afraid. She floated in that intoxicatingly liberating space that lay beyond fear, beyond the instinct for self-preservation. She didn't care any more. 'I think I was the one who was stupid, Dmitri. Stupid to trust your lies. Stupid to respect you. Stupid to be with you. What have you done with Samuel? Where did you take him?'

Maslov was taken aback by her glare of pure revulsion. 'Oh, your Samuel, you really don't have to worry about him. It's not like he worried much about you, in any case. He's on his way to Kharkiv, or Minsk, or Odessa. Or maybe some other city, I don't really know. It was rather easy to convince him that he shouldn't be meddling in our life any more.'

'You are lying.' Debora enunciated every syllable, as if she were talking to a child. 'Like you lied to me in Stalingrad when you said Samuel was dead. It is your job to lie. Your damn job.'

'Oh, you've got it all wrong, my dearest wife. I wish I had known he was alive at the time. I really assumed he wasn't, which, agreed, was silly of me. Should never assume things. Believe me, had I known he was alive, all this unpleasantness wouldn't have happened. I would have found a way to make sure he stayed out there for ever. I certainly wouldn't have allowed him to come to Kyiv and terrorise my son. There, he really did cross the line.'

'Please tell me the truth, Dmitri,' she insisted. 'What have you done to him?'

'I honestly didn't have to do anything. I feel nothing for him except pity. There is no fight left in him, no spark. I don't blame him, after all he's been through. He agreed pretty quickly that the best course of action was for him to start a new life in a place of his choosing, and to forget that all this craziness ever happened. He even asked me for some financial assistance, which is fair enough. He sold you out, the love of your life! For a few roubles. And now you're here, huffing and puffing about him. You think this is some Hollywood movie, love for ever and all? That is really hilarious.' He emitted a guttural laugh.

'He told me how he'd tried to talk to Pasha. And I said, "Didn't this teach you anything? Can't you see that Pasha is not your son any more, that he doesn't even want to speak with you? Why are you insisting, trying the impossible?" And he's not dumb, he thought about it and he agreed with me. It's much easier when a man understands quickly what is possible and what is not. When a man is reasonable.'

Silence enveloped the room for several minutes. 'So, no suit-cases, no children.' Maslov assessed the situation. 'You were never going to leave with him, were you? I suppose you too understand what is possible.'

She didn't reply.

'Answer me!' he demanded.

'You are right. I wasn't going anywhere. I came to tell him that. I came to tell him that the children come first,' she said softly.

'Well, that was a smart decision.' Maslov lowered his voice. 'You are reasonable too. And yes, children do come first. *Our* children.'

'Yes, *our* children,' she said compliantly.

They remained silent, both thinking, not looking at each other, as if they weren't in the same room.

After a few minutes, she cleared her throat. 'What now?'

'Nothing, my dear, nothing. Relax. Lieutenant Rybak will take you to do some grocery shopping and then you will head home and cook a nice roast. And in the evening, I will return home from my mission in western Ukraine and we will have a family dinner. I will check Pasha's homework, and at New Year we will go on holiday. I will be generous and forgive you, and everything will go on like before. Except that now you know that I am not stupid, and that there is nothing I do not know.'

'You'll forgive me? Forgive me for what? For seeing my legitimate husband, the one you told me was dead?'

'You know, Dasha, I can make sure he actually dies if I want to. Don't push me.'

Debora spoke slowly and deliberately. 'You have to swear to me that he will not be harmed.'

'Why would I harm him? I don't need to. He's on his way to his new life.'

'Stop it. You have to promise me. Samuel is Pasha's father. He has suffered enough. You have to swear to me that he will be fine, because if he's not, and if I ever find that out, I swear on the heads of our children that you will pay for it. Swear that he will be allowed to live freely. That's the only way you can have me back.'

Maslov shrugged. 'I don't care about that man,' he said. 'And the reason I don't care about him is because he doesn't really care about you. Truth be told, I was expecting him to resist. It was just too easy. Disappointing.'

He got up and opened the window, beckoning Rybak to come upstairs.

'Please be kind enough to accompany my wife,' he instructed the lieutenant, and without looking at Debora again, he stepped out of the room.

Rybak was taken aback by the scene but didn't ask any questions. 'Darya Grigoriyevna, I am sorry for all of this,' he said gently as he helped her down the staircase. 'I'm not sure what's going on, and it is none of my business, but I am sorry.'

'It's all fine. It's not *Romeo and Juliet*, nobody is going to die, my dear Zhenya,' she replied, squeezing his shoulder as she addressed him for the first time by the diminutive of his first name. 'Forget everything. Let's go shopping.'

Rebecca was in the kitchen when Debora came home with the groceries. 'He knows,' she whispered in her mother's ear. 'He knows everything.'

Yana looked at the two of them with alarm from the other side of the kitchen. Debora felt rage surging up her chest. There was only one explanation for how Maslov knew.

'Have you no shame? First you whore with the Germans, and now you spy on me in my own home.'

Yana buttoned up her bathrobe and rose from the chair. Her stare was unflinching, her pupils narrowing. Her breathing was regular. 'What, you think you are better than me, Madam Maslova?' she began. 'That I am a whore and you are not? What is the difference between you and me? I fucked German officers for a loaf of bread. True, I did. And you fucked your MGB officer for a loaf of bread, except that it was a loaf of bread with caviar on top. How are we different? How, my precious Darya, or whatever your real name is, are we different? Don't you try to pull your morality bullshit on me, because I can see right through you. I do what I have to, and you do what you have to. And we all get fucked. Tough.'

Debora wanted to hit her to make her shut up. Rebecca pulled Debora away by the elbow. 'Daughter, come with me, come now, don't you listen to her.'

'Listen or not listen, you're no better than me,' Yana proclaimed triumphantly. 'We are all made of the same shit. All of us.'

'At least the kids are playing outside and didn't have to see all this horror,' Rebecca said, more to herself than anyone else.

'I don't care,' Debora replied, her voice drained of feeling. 'I don't care about anything any more. Dmitri will be coming home soon. I'm not feeling well, and I will stay in bed tonight.'

She shut the bedroom door and drew the curtains. This is how it's all meant to be, she thought as she covered herself with a blanket, curling into the foetal position. This is a choice I had already made by myself, not to leave with Samuel tonight. Maslov's intervention had robbed her of a chance to say her goodbyes, to explain herself to Samuel, she reflected. But it had also spared her a confrontation that might have caused her to change her mind. Might have caused her to make a rash decision that she would forever regret. 'I am exactly where I belong. This, here, is my real life,' she whispered to herself.

But when she closed her eyes, drifting in and out of sleep, all she saw was herself and Samuel, a younger Samuel, together by an open window in a train taking them south, towards the waves, the sun, the cries of seagulls. She was happy on that train, happier than she had ever been, their hair waving with the wind. Somehow it was summer outside, fields emerald green, golden domes of village churches shining in the sun.

The dream ended suddenly. Debora jolted awake, hearing Pasha and Nina greet Maslov with shrieks of joy. He had brought them gifts, pilfered from a wealthy deportee's home in Lviv. Pasha got a big fire truck inscribed with another boy's initials and Nina an almost new Polish doll.

Pasha was so excited that at first he forgot to tell Maslov about the nasty man who'd talked to him at school. But when he did, Maslov remained unperturbed. He grinned and scooped the boy up, putting him on his lap. 'It's very good of you to tell me,' he said. 'But your mama and I, we have already talked about this.

Don't think she didn't tell me right away about this, she did. We have investigated this man, and like you said, he turned out to be lying, making up stories. We've taken care of him, do not worry, he will never come back.' He kissed Pasha on the cheek. 'You have only one papa, and he will always love you very much.'

Pasha hugged him tightly.

'Now, tomorrow we are all going to the movies. What would you like to see?' Maslov asked.

PART SIX

36

Kyiv, October 1952

Debora examined herself in the mirror and tried to paint over the latest bruise on her face with make-up. It was small this time, a smudge on the edge of her cheek. Easy to conceal.

She wore a lot of make-up of late.

Sometimes, during the day, she caught herself feeling as if she were watching her own life unfold from the outside, like a movie about someone else. And to outsiders, it seemed like a perfect life, a life that others – fellow teachers and the few acquaintances that she entertained outside work – openly envied. A comfortable home, a doting husband, two adorable children. Now, also, a live-in maid who'd taken up residence in Yana's former room. Getting rid of Yana was a demand that Maslov couldn't refuse. It also helped him fulfil the MGB quota on identifying former German collaborators. The entire apartment belonged to them now that the other neighbours had also moved out.

Twice a year, Debora holidayed by the sea or in the mountains, sometimes just with the children and her mother, without Maslov. Those vacations without her husband were the only ones she enjoyed. Maslov never mentioned Samuel again, and neither did Debora. But neither of them forgot or forgave. The knowledge, and the humiliation of it, remained within him like herpes, flaring up with blistering pain as visions of Debora in Samuel's arms, naked in that bed of twisted sheets, raced through his mind. It was incurable.

The first time he hit her was about six months after Samuel's disappearance. He was drunk, taking off the edge after another blood-soaked assignment in western Ukraine. In the morning, when he saw her cracked lip, he didn't even remember how and why he had given her that hard, stinging slap. He apologised, of course, but it happened again and again. She learned the telltale signs predicting a new outburst: a pall would descend over his eyes, his nostrils would flare, his fingers would start tapping an ominous rhythm on the table. She searched anxiously for these signs every time he got drunk, which now was almost every night.

The previous night, things had escalated without much of an immediate cause. It was a Saturday dinner, the maid serving salads, buckwheat kasha and pork steak, and Maslov downing small glasses of chilled vodka. Nina was fussy and whiny, fighting with her brother and breaking into tears after Pasha shoved her with his elbow. Maslov didn't appreciate the distraction. The tapping rhythm accelerated.

'You two, stop it and shut up.'

Nina, her child's sense of offended righteousness surging, pushed away her plate and got up. Maslov sprang up too, unbuckling his belt.

'Sit down right now,' he bellowed. 'You're not done here.'

Unbuckling the belt meant a whipping. That had happened before, and Nina didn't want it to happen again.

'Come right back, or you'll be sorry,' Maslov roared as Nina ran out of the room. 'You little rat, come back.'

Pasha sat motionless, afraid of attracting attention. Maslov's hand was already gripping the thick leather. He was ready to charge after Nina.

Rebecca barred his way.

'Sit down, Dmitri, leave the child alone. She's only nine. You've had too much to drink. What kind of example are you showing your children? Aren't you ashamed?'

Maslov had never hurt Rebecca before, but this time he pushed her aside irritably, just a little shove, or so he thought. She fell to the floor, screaming, more from the shock of sudden humiliation than physical pain.

'Shut your trap! Who are you to tell me what I can and can't do in my own home?' he howled. The effort strained him, and he had to lean on the table to remain upright. His breath was laboured. 'You people always tell us what we should do in our own country, always so superior. But don't worry, the end is coming soon, don't you worry about that.'

Rebecca scrambled back up. Debora's eyes were unfocused, looking into the distance. She gripped the edge of the table so hard that her knuckles turned white. Cold sweat dripped from her forehead as her foot nervously tapped on the floor.

'Shame on you.' Rebecca stepped up to Maslov's face. 'Shame on you, a grown man, raising your hand against an old woman. Is this what your mother taught you?'

'My mother?' Maslov broke out in a laugh. 'The fuck you know about my mother? Did you ever have to pick up manure with your precious little hands like my mother did? You people have always had it easy.'

Pasha, sensing an opportunity, tried to leave the room. After all, nobody knew where this eruption of anger would turn next. But Maslov noticed the movement from the corner of his eye and banged his fist on the table. 'Sit, I said, sit!' Pasha complied.

'Are you one of them too? A snake like them?' He looked at the boy. 'Are you mine, or are you one of them?'

Pasha didn't understand the question and stared blankly, too frightened to say anything. Maslov sighed. All of a sudden he felt tired, too tired to chase after Nina. He crumpled into the chair, poured himself another shot of vodka and emptied it into his mouth. 'Ah, this is good stuff,' he groaned. His posture softened and he struggled to keep his eyes open. 'To the family. Family is everything.' He raised another glass. 'Drink with me,' he demanded, looking at Debora. 'Drink to our family.'

'You are too drunk,' she replied, motionless and looking away.

'Drink. To the family.' He grabbed her by the cheek, pulling her towards him. 'Drink.'

'I will, I will, just stop, you're hurting me.' She obediently downed the vodka. 'Happy?' Imprints of Maslov's fingers remained on her skin.

He burped, satisfied, and closed his eyes, his belly sticking out. A minute later, the belt fell from his hand, landing softly on the carpeted floor. He was asleep. Debora touched him. He didn't react. Quietly she got up and went to look for Nina.

Quiet sobs emanated from the closet in the master bedroom. 'Is that you, sweetie?' she asked, opening the door. 'Come on out. Don't be afraid. He is asleep, he won't hurt you.'

'No!' Nina cowered in the dark recess behind the coats and dresses. 'Go away.'

'You can't stay there, sweetheart. It's late. I promise he won't hurt you.'

But she refused to come out for another half an hour. When she did, Debora understood why. Nina had peed herself, and was standing barefoot in a small puddle that had soaked Debora's shoes.

'Don't cry.' Debora hugged the child, leading her to take a bath.

The next day, Debora sat next to her mother once the children had gone off to play outside and stroked her hand. Rebecca had long, aristocratic fingers, and still took great care of her nails. But her skin was wrinkled and dry, with the blue lines of blood vessels bulging underneath.

'Mama, I can't go on like this,' Debora said. 'I have no more strength.'

'No, you can't. This man is evil. You must divorce him before something bad happens.'

'You know very well he will never agree to a divorce. He won't let me go. Certainly not with the children. There is no way out!'

'There is always a way out.' Rebecca put her hand atop Debora's.

'I just hope he drinks himself to death quickly,' Debora sighed. 'That one day he passes out and never comes back.'

'That won't happen,' Rebecca replied. 'Only the good ones die early.'

37

Kyiv, November 1952

After changing at home and putting on a new shirt, Rybak headed straight to Debora's apartment, hefting two sacks full of food up the building's staircase: cheeses, sausages, hams, dried fruit and Lviv chocolate. As he entered the corridor, so did a fog of bad aftershave that he had applied liberally to his face. While still working for Maslov, Rybak was no longer just his personal aide. Promoted to captain, he had his own files to follow, his own enemies of the state to uncover. Ever since the promotion, he no longer accompanied Debora on shopping trips or visited frequently. Today was just a favour for the boss. They had all travelled on a mission to Lviv for a secret new operation against the insurgents. The mission was over, a resounding success, but Maslov had had to stay back to help with interrogations.

'This is for you from Comrade Lieutenant Colonel,' Rybak said after ringing the doorbell. 'Delicacies from out west. He's going to be back in a few days and asked me to pass this along.'

'Come in, come in, Zhenechka, don't be shy. Let me make you a nice cup of tea. Would you like some of my cherry pie?'

Rebecca ushered him in, addressing him with a tender diminutive more appropriate for a small boy.

He obligingly handed off Maslov's food parcels and sat down in the living room. 'Major celebrations in Lviv. I can't say much, but we've had quite a lucky break. A very big fish has gone down, and so everybody involved got a bit of a reward.'

Debora, who had been showering, strode into the room and sat down to join them. She was wearing a fluffy white robe, her hair still wet. He tried hard not to look in the direction of her breasts, where a triangle of exposed flesh tantalised his eyes.

'And how are you doing, Zhenechka? I haven't seen you in a while. Still unmarried, a handsome young man like you?' Rebecca pressed him.

'Too busy.' He smiled sheepishly. 'No time for anything other than work.'

'What a shame, what a shame.' Rebecca clicked her tongue. 'Isn't it?' she asked Debora. 'Such a catch he would be for a lucky maiden.'

'Oh, I am sure all the girls are lining up for a date with him. Aren't they?' Debora teased Rybak.

'You shouldn't be joking like this,' he said meekly.

'I'm sorry,' Debora giggled, getting up to fetch Rebecca's cherry pie from the kitchen. As she passed Rybak, her hips swaying, she brushed against his shoulder and her bathrobe pulled back just a little, revealing the pale smoothness of her leg.

Rybak's face broke into a blush.

He ate an entire plateful of Rebecca's pie. It was delicious, but even if it weren't, he would not have wanted to upset the old lady.

As he was leaving, Debora caught up with him in the corridor. She held his hand for a fleeting moment, and gently kissed his cheek. 'Come back soon, don't forget us,' she whispered into his ear. Her lips were warm and she smelled of rosehip. She smelled like no other woman, in Rybak's experience. He felt blood coursing to his groin and was afraid she would notice the arousal.

'Of course, Darya Grigoriyevna,' he said, sticking to the respectful patronymic.

'I am not your schoolmistress. You can just call me Dasha,' she laughed. 'Promise? Don't forget us.'

After the door closed, Debora returned to the living room.

'So what was that? What game are you playing exactly?' Rebecca asked sternly.

'What do you mean, Mama?'

'He looked at you like a horny puppy, that boy. And you egging him on, parading half naked in that bathrobe? What has come over you?'

'He's not a boy, Mama. He is a nice young man and I am just being kind to him, that's all.'

Rebecca squinted and clicked her tongue. 'I hope you know what you're doing. That's all I am going to say.'

38

Kyiv, December 1952

The next time Rybak came to Debora's apartment, she was lying on the floor with blood gushing from her forehead. He wasn't supposed to be there, but Maslov hadn't answered his phone, and a message for him from headquarters was too urgent to be left until the morning. It was already so late that the streets were empty of people as the captain raced up the stairs of the building on St Andrew's Descent. He was going to press the doorbell, but noticing that the door was already half open, he announced himself and stepped inside.

'Oh, what a miracle that you are here,' the maid greeted him. 'Come, come quickly to the kitchen.'

Maslov, his stare immobile, sat hunched at the dinner table, his shirt half unbuttoned to reveal a hairy chest stained with borscht. Broken plates were strewn on the floor, in the starburst pattern created when a tablecloth is yanked in a fit of fury. Rebecca, on her knees, was putting chunks of ice wrapped in a towel to her daughter's forehead, muttering silently. As Rybak crouched to help, he didn't realise right away that the red liquid oozing from Debora's forehead wasn't beetroot soup.

'What happened? Do we need a doctor?'

Debora opened her eyes and smiled at him faintly, stretching out her hand. 'Zhenechka,' she whispered. He clasped her fingers, noticing at the same time that her other arm was twisted at an unnatural angle. She whimpered in pain.

'We definitely need to take her to a hospital. Do you have a car? Help me to get her up,' Rebecca instructed him. She was now in charge.

Maslov awoke for a moment, shaking his head vigorously, and banged his fist on the table. 'Leave the bitch alone.' That outburst consumed all his energy, and he fell back into his drunken stupor.

'He won't be satisfied until she is dead. Pig,' Rebecca cursed.

Rybak was too overwhelmed to think. Helped by Rebecca and the maid, he lifted Debora and they carefully navigated the stairs. Once outside, he laid her on the back seat. With Rebecca in the front, he drove to the emergency ward of the nearest hospital, flashing his MGB identity card to secure immediate service.

When the nurse, a sheaf of paperwork in her hands, asked what had happened, Debora squeezed Rybak's wrist, a signal for him to remain silent. 'I tripped and fell in the kitchen. An accident, a domestic accident,' she said.

The nurse shook her head sceptically.

'Are you sure?' she asked. 'An accident, huh?'

'Very sure.'

'Well, let's get your broken arm, your accidentally broken arm, fixed then.'

Rebecca and Rybak remained alone once Debora was wheeled away for the surgery.

'This was no accident. What happened?' he whispered urgently. 'Why did he hit her?'

Rybak was used to violence, even to killing, but it was always

316

in an organised framework, for the noble, greater cause. That kind of violence didn't bother him. But senseless drunken violence in the kitchen, beating up a woman so badly that she ended up in hospital, that disturbed his sense of appropriate order. He felt blind anger building up against Maslov, against the fat, booze-drenched colonel who failed to appreciate just how lucky he was.

'What happened? Nothing that hasn't happened before, my dear Zhenechka,' Rebecca replied. 'Nothing.'

'Why don't you tell the truth to the nurse?' he asked.

He already knew why, of course, and Rebecca didn't bother replying.

'I'm scared, I'm very scared. I don't know how this is all going to end,' she said. 'It can't end well.'

Once the surgery was over and Debora was assigned a room of her own in the ward – another MGB perk – Rybak persuaded Rebecca to return home. Then he settled in a chair next to Debora's bed and watched her breathe, finally at peace under sedation. Her arm in its fresh white cast rested on her chest, moving up and down almost imperceptibly.

Debora was the first to wake as the sun broke through the curtains. Rybak was slumped on the chair, snoring and twitching sporadically. His was the shallow sleep of a man who was always alert, always watching out for danger. The rustling of Debora's sheets as she sat up in the bed jarred him awake.

'I am sorry. I am so sorry.' He opened his eyes, springing to his feet and wiping the sweat from his forehead with the back of his hand.

'Zhenechka, I am so happy to see you here. I don't know what I would have done without you. You are my saviour. A real prince.'

She raised her unbroken arm, and as if drawn by a magnet,

he stepped forward and touched her fingers. The touch lasted a moment, a moment that seemed infinite, until she clasped his hand and pulled him down. Almost losing his balance, he kneeled by the bedside, his hand landing on her thigh. It was cool and smooth. 'Dasha, Dasha,' he whispered.

She looked into his eyes and caressed his hair. Then she drew his face towards hers. He could pick out her perfume even through the sharp tang of disinfectant and medicine, the hospital smell that he had managed to tune out.

He closed his eyes just as the wet warmth of her lips touched his mouth.

As Rybak was leaving the hospital, his heart racing and his thoughts confused, he noticed Maslov at the far end of the corridor. He held in his hands a bouquet of wilted roses he had bought along the way, and wasn't paying much attention to his surroundings. Rybak managed to duck out of sight just in time.

Debora heard Maslov's heavy officer's boots hitting the marble floor well before he entered the room. She pulled the blanket over herself, closed her eyes and pretended to be asleep. He called her name in a low, apologetic voice and then stood there silently, not knowing what to do. Finally he whispered into her ear, 'I will come back later,' left the flowers on the chair where Rybak had spent the night, and stepped out, gently closing the door behind him.

Debora opened her eyes, looked at the roses and finally let herself go, dissolving into slow, gut-wrenching sobs. She only stopped crying when the nurse came back to check up on her.

'It will be all right. Trust me,' the nurse assured her, even though she knew from experience that it probably wouldn't. 'It will all be all right.'

39

Kyiv, January 1953

'So, that boy? Do you love him?' Rebecca asked her daughter the day after the cast on Debora's arm was removed. Rybak was always around these days, taking Debora to the hospital and back, bringing food, and exhibiting all the care and attention that her husband didn't provide.

The day after the surgery, Maslov apologised to Debora, standing in her hospital room and breathing heavily, like a dog that had misbehaved. She said she had forgiven him even as she stared through him with unadulterated contempt. That stare made anger bubble up again in his chest, made him think about Samuel, about the betrayal. A couple of weeks later, he was lost in a drunken fury again, angry at Debora for making him feel guilty and cursing himself for having fallen for an arrogant snake who would never accept him and would never respect him.

'Do I love him? Rybak?' Debora chuckled, the bitter laugh of someone who could detect the all-too-familiar traces of poison in the sweetest dishes they tasted. 'Mama, you know what kind of life we are living. I am dead inside and incapable of love. And why would I love someone like him?'

'But you are sleeping with him.'

'Yes, I am fucking him. So? Does that make me a bad woman?'

Rebecca looked on disapprovingly. She hadn't been brought up that way. She always felt an involuntary shrinking inside when Debora cursed, and Debora cursed much more frequently these days.

'I am not here to judge you, daughter.'

'Thank God, Mama, thank God.'

'But what will happen when your husband discovers this? You know he will one day.'

'Mama, I am a bad woman,' Debora said. 'And I know what I am doing. Remember what you told me the other day.'

'What?'

'That it's only the good ones who die early. I am not yet ready to die. I won't be good any more.'

Rybak and Debora had worked out a secret routine. Once every week or two, on her lunch break or after work, she would sneak into his apartment, a few blocks away from school. She decided when and how, and he always feared this would be the last time she'd allow him to pull down her dress, to cup her breasts with his hands and to kiss her long neck.

He was an inexperienced lover and had no idea how to make her come. But she faked it well, moaning and gripping his forearms, and complimented him generously on his skills every time. 'I've never felt so good, Zhenechka, never. Thank you for making me feel this way,' she murmured, licking his ear lobe, as he lit up a post-sex cigarette.

They didn't have much time tonight: Maslov would expect her to be home for dinner.

'Zhenechka, I am so afraid,' she said as she began to dress. 'I am afraid that he will find out. You know he will kill me, squash me like a fly, without pity. And he will probably kill you too. He must never find out.'

'No, never. He won't,' Rybak assured her.

But he knew they couldn't fool an MGB lieutenant colonel for ever.

How had he ended up in this situation? He knew he was being stupid; he knew he shouldn't be doing any of this. But alone at night, he couldn't stop thinking about Debora's body, about how her cheeks flushed and her mouth half opened, revealing glistening white teeth, that sweet moment when he'd just penetrated her. He was hungry for her, more and more so with every passing week. Every woman he had slept with before had just opened her legs and let him do his thing quickly, clearly an unpleasant mechanical chore. With Debora, it was as if he had melted into her. He wasn't ready to let that go.

'This is it, no more travel out to Lviv. I will be far too busy here in Kyiv from now on,' Maslov announced at dinner. Debora didn't say anything, and he furrowed his brow. 'I bet that doesn't make you too happy, does it?'

'I am happy, Papa,' Pasha hurried to say. 'Maybe you can teach me how to shoot?'

'We are all very happy, Dmitri,' Debora said, serving him potatoes and spicy boar sausages.

'It's important that you learn how to shoot well. The son of a Chekist must know how to handle a gun.' Maslov patted Pasha's head. He was in an unusually good mood tonight.

'What is it that you will be so busy with?' Rebecca asked.

'Wouldn't you like to know?'

He didn't say anything else, stuffing his mouth with sausage. There was no vodka on the table this time, just chilled fruit soup and Borjomi mineral water from Georgia.

In the morning, like every morning, Debora presided over a short 'political information' session at school, during which the day's newspaper headlines were read out to the student assembly. She hadn't seen the papers yet, and so listened absent-mindedly as a tenth-grader began the recital.

"'Our noble State Security Organs and the Party have uncovered a terrifying new plot, murderers in doctors' white overalls",' the student, a pimpled young man in a brown uniform, read with gusto. "'These so-called doctors, in reality animals in human shape, have infiltrated the Kremlin clinic and other hospitals, and have poisoned some of our leaders. They falsely diagnosed and murdered Zhdanov. And if they hadn't been stopped, they would have wreaked total havoc. Vovsi. Kogan. Feldman. Greenstein. Edelman.'" He rattled off the names and then raised his gaze and beamed a smile. "'Recruited to their murderous cause by the Zionist criminals of the Joint Distribution Committee.'"

'Jews again,' someone shouted.

Debora felt suddenly alert.

'I'm not surprised,' exhaled the physical education teacher, a stocky former army officer. 'I always knew you couldn't trust them. Those fucking Jews have tricked us again, Darya Grigoriyevna.' Like everyone else at the school, the man assumed that the MGB lieutenant colonel's spouse was a Gentile.

Later in the day, Valentyna stopped by Debora's office. 'We've received a notification from the district party committee that we must hold a rally to condemn the Zionist criminals,' she said. 'Tomorrow at five. This is a very sensitive matter, considering where we are. You know, here in Podil, there are many people of, well, Hebraic nationality. Many students of ours. So all eyes are on us.'

'Of course,' Debora said. 'Let's make sure we are ready.'

It had been a while since the school had been required to hold a rally condemning the latest batch of the enemies of the people, something so frequent back in the 1930s. Already at the first break, a scuffle among fifth-graders ended with a boy who happened to be called Kogan losing a tooth. 'His dad is a poisoner, kick him, kick him,' his classmates howled in the courtyard.

Debora broke up the fight, and at the end of break, she pulled Pasha aside. 'Don't you dare pick on Jewish boys again, you hear me?' she said.

'If I don't, the others will think I'm one of them. And I won't be one of them. I have no choice,' he replied. He pushed her away and ran off.

When Debora came home from work, Rebecca was sitting at the dinner table, busy reading the newspapers that blanketed its surface.

'Have you heard the news?' Debora asked. 'Do you think it's all starting again? Like before the war?'

'Of course I've heard the news,' Rebecca replied. 'I've been doing nothing except reading the papers all day. Starting again? It never stopped. We've been lucky not to be touched by it. Remember in 1949, when they shot all those Yiddish writers and poets? Once Israel was created, once we Jews got a land of our own, everything changed for us. They will never trust our loyalty, just as they will never trust the Poles, the Germans, the Turks, the Hungarians, none of the minorities that have their own country.'

'Land of our own? What have I got to do with Israel? I am from here, this is my country,' Debora protested. 'We are from Ukraine. We are from Uman, not from Israel.'

'It doesn't matter what you think. It matters what *they* think.'

Rebecca passed her a copy of the evening newspaper, *Vechirni Kyiv*, that had just been delivered by the postman. The drawing on page 3 depicted a bald, fat, long-nosed Jew in a bathrobe and slippers, lounging on a chair made of money and holding a plate with more cash dropping on it. The article was ostensibly about the director of a local children's clothes factory, one Isaac Glazmann, and how he'd mismanaged the production and filled the main jobs with corrupt 'kith and kin'. Just to make sure it was clear who these kin were, the article listed the names: 'Goldstein, Zeitlin, Shapiro, Salzmann, Steinberg'.

'This looks like those leaflets the Nazis used to drop on Kyiv in 1941,' she said. 'And I can bet that there will be a similar article, also just with Jewish names, day after day from now on. Maybe this means that our time has come. I don't know.'

'Don't say that,' Debora said. 'Don't compare our Soviet government to the Nazis. Stalin would never do something like that. The only reason we are alive is because he defeated the Nazis. You know that.'

'Stalin didn't do it for us.' Rebecca waved her hand dismissively. 'And you know as well as I do what he inflicts on people he doesn't like. The Chechens, the Kalmyks, the Crimean Tatars – all gone in one night. You think he can't do the same to us, to the Jews? Because we're so special? People will applaud him on the streets if he ships us all to Birobidzhan tomorrow.'

'He would never do that,' Debora said. 'Birobidzhan? In Siberia? You're just imagining things. This was only about those stupid doctors, and who knows, maybe they really were poisoning their patients. And this newspaper article, it was a coincidence.' She very much wanted to believe her own words.

'Did you see how long his nose is in the drawing?' Rebecca tapped the cartoon with her index finger. 'Nobody draws a nose this long by coincidence.'

'It is a very long nose,' Debora reluctantly agreed.

*

324

The following day, several other newspapers ran similar stories. Debora was aghast when she saw students in the school's art class preparing posters for the rally. The teacher had given them the caricatures from the newspapers to copy, and the students assiduously drew long-nosed Jews with grubby hands.

She bit back the words that rose to her lips. Safer to stay quiet these days. Especially if you had secrets.

The rally went off without a hitch, and the Jewish students – like everyone else – chanted at the top of their lungs about the need to crush Zionist intrigues and root out Zionist agents lurking amidst Soviet society. In fact, the Jewish kids tried just a bit harder than the others, aware that their enthusiasm was under particular scrutiny today. A reporter from *Vechirni Kyiv* was there to take a picture of the rally, which ran on the front page.

Lyudmyla, a peroxide-blonde teacher of history, anxiously took Debora aside after the event.

'You know, my son has been sick, losing a lot of weight, getting fevers all the time, so I pulled some strings and took him to the best doctor in Podil, Dr Rubinstein, who gave us pills. But things have only got worse since then, and now I am very worried. I'm wondering, what if that Rubinstein is one of them? What if he's poisoning my Slavik deliberately?'

'I'm sure he's not,' Debora said. 'Why would he?'

Lyudmyla looked at her with suspicion. 'You never know with these people. They hide in plain sight.'

'Maybe you should take him to a different doctor, for a second opinion,' Debora suggested.

'Yes, one of ours,' Lyudmyla agreed. 'Maybe someone in the MGB clinic can see him.'

'I will ask my husband,' Debora promised.

'Oh, Darya Grigoriyevna, you are the best. I always knew I could rely on you!'

Maslov came home exhausted and late, and attacked his food with the absent-minded greediness that came from a combination of hunger and stress. 'The doctors' plot, is this why you are so busy?' Debora asked him. 'Are you planning to deport the Jews?'

In Podil, this was now the question on everyone's minds. A bomb had gone off in the Soviet embassy in Tel Aviv, and Stalin had responded by severing diplomatic relations with the new Jewish state. Already some of the Jewish students had stopped coming to school, their parents packing suitcases for what they expected to be an imminent deportation.

'Jews, Jews, what do you care? As long as you stick by me, Darya not Debora, you have nothing to be afraid of,' Maslov replied. 'You're not one of them any more. We took care of that problem ten years ago, remember?'

'But what about my mother?'

'Worried all of a sudden?' Maslov said mockingly. He slurped another mouthful of fish soup, then lifted his eyes and looked across the table at Rebecca. She sat immobile, staring back at him. 'You should be worried. Your time is coming,' he said slowly, with a satisfied smirk. He enjoyed being cruel to Rebecca.

The phone rang. Debora picked up the receiver and heard Rybak's voice on the line. 'Tell Comrade Maslov that he is wanted in the Ukraine-wide headquarters uptown. We have another urgent phone conference with Moscow. I will be coming with the car in five minutes.'

Maslov reluctantly left the dinner table, pushing his chair aside. He fastened his uniform belt, straining on the last notch, pulled on his boots and headed towards the door. 'Save some of that roast for me for when I return later tonight,' he instructed the maid. The car, as usual, would wait for him at the bottom of the street, a few hundred yards away. It was impractical to drive to the building's entrance on the one-way St Andrew's Descent. Maslov always walked that short cobblestoned stretch.

Once the maid had left the dining room, Rebecca moved to sit across the table from Debora, leaning towards her. 'We have to do something,' she said. 'Maybe we should poison him, like those doctors everyone is talking about.'

'Mama!' Debora put a hand to her mother's lips. 'Stop it. Stop all this nonsense. The walls have ears.'

40

Kyiv, February 1953

It had been two weeks since Debora had last come to Rybak's apartment. He ached for her body, for the smell of her skin, for the light, caressing way her fingers ran over his back. He thought of her every night, the nights he spent alone in his cold bed. But she didn't pick up the phone, and he was afraid to call too often. By now, he was beginning to feel mild resentment. Why is she avoiding me? he thought.

So as he walked home through Podil, he was taken aback to see Debora waiting for him in the entrance to a building near his apartment.

'Come in, quickly.' She pulled him into the doorway. 'We must talk.' She stepped into the darkness behind the staircase.

'Why are you here? Come with me to my place,' he said. He began to feel the usual anticipatory tingling in his belly, thoughts of her body cramming his head.

'Zhenechka, I am afraid. I am so afraid.' She broke down in tears. 'My husband suspects. He definitely knows something. What have we done ... what have we done?'

He tried to hug her. 'Dasha, Dasha, why do you think this? Did he say something?'

'It's the way he looks at me now, a cold, satisfied, furious way. I am certain he knows. He mentioned your name the other day, and I'm sure he was trying to see how I would react. He said something bad about you, and it was as if he wanted me to defend you.'

'What bad thing?' Rybak stiffened.

'Oh, nothing in particular.' Debora thought furiously. 'Just that he believed you were lazy, untrustworthy.'

'Lazy? Untrustworthy?'

'Yes, that. Unreliable, that was what he said, unreliable. Couldn't trust you. Have you noticed anything strange in how he's treating you, Zhenechka? Anything out of the ordinary? Any detail? Think!'

Rybak reflected for a moment. Yes, there was a new, harder edge, a new energy in Maslov's moves. Was it because he realised he had been cuckolded? Or because of the big operation they were all busy setting up? He shuddered involuntarily. His memory raced to those days in the forests of western Ukraine. He recalled how Maslov had looked with a gun in his hand, ready to pull the trigger with the same ease with which one drank a glass of water. His desire vanished, his penis shrivelling in his pants. His hands turned sweaty.

'I don't know, Zhenechka, maybe I'm imagining it, but I feel like I'm being followed,' Debora said softly. 'I was careful on the way here, but I don't think I should go to your place for now.'

'You must be imagining it,' he tried to reassure her, but he wasn't so sure himself.

'You know he will kill you if he finds out what we have been up to. He will not hesitate,' she whispered. 'You need to do something.' She leaned towards him, hugged him and kissed his neck. A shiver ran down his spine.

'I know.'

'I love you.' She kissed him again, this time on the lips, probing his mouth with the tip of her tongue. 'Promise me you won't let him harm us. Promise me you will do everything you can. Please.'

'I promise. I'll do anything. On my honour.'

'I am so afraid.' She shed a tear that smudged his jacket lapel.

When they separated, she walked home with a determined, bouncy step, past the building where she'd last seen Samuel, sucking on a caramel candy to remove the taste of Rybak from her mouth. She was proud of herself, of her new strength. Enough of being a victim, she thought. Enough of trying to be good.

The next morning at the MGB headquarters for Podil, Rybak spotted Maslov speaking to his driver and a junior lieutenant, a recent arrival, in a corner of the courtyard. They were discussing something in low voices, and became suspiciously quiet when he approached them. 'Good morning, comrades,' he greeted them cheerfully – maybe a touch too cheerfully.

'Morning.' Maslov waved him away. 'Tell everyone to be ready for the staff meeting at ten.'

Rybak was rattled by Maslov's coldness. It could be nothing. Or it could be everything. Podil wasn't that big, and Maslov's wife, with her beauty and her expensive foreign clothes, definitely attracted attention. Could it be that her visits to Rybak's apartment had been reported? The new young lieutenant – what was his name? Ivanov? Was that a sneer in his eyes? It was foolish to have allowed her to come to his place. Worse than foolish, unprofessional.

He told himself to calm down, but as the day progressed, his fears only grew. Maslov snapped with open contempt when he made a remark during the meeting: 'Nobody asked your opinion, Captain. Sit down and listen, maybe you will learn something.'

Rybak wasn't the only one Maslov was rude to, however. He knew he would soon be leaving Podil, promoted to full colonel. Though long anticipated, the promotion had finally come through that morning. Once the current operation was completed, he would be transferred uptown, to the MGB's main headquarters for the Ukrainian SSR. His hard work had paid off, his achievements had been noticed by his superiors. Who knew, in the new job he might even be able to protect his mother-in-law, the mother-in-law whom he despised wholeheartedly but to whom his children were unfortunately so attached.

At the end of the meeting, the Podil party secretary burst into the room. He was aware of Maslov's promotion and, suddenly obsequious, rushed to offer his congratulations. 'Comrade Colonel, may I?' He enveloped Maslov in a bear hug, then turned towards the assembled officers. 'The party leadership has great appreciation for the work you have all done, under Colonel Maslov's wise guidance. Please, a round of applause for the colonel.' Everyone clapped. 'Tonight, a proper send-off,' he bellowed. 'We are starting at eight. No excuses for absences!'

After the meeting was over, Maslov beckoned Rybak. 'Captain, you and I have some things to discuss. Tomorrow morning, nine o'clock sharp,' he said with new steel in his voice. Rybak had been a good aide. Trustworthy. It might be wise to take him along to the new office uptown, he thought. He didn't pay attention to the blood draining from the captain's face.

'Of course, Comrade Colonel.' Rybak saluted. 'At your orders.'

Maslov's smile seemed full of ominous threat. He patted Rybak on the shoulder. 'Good, we certainly do have plenty to talk about.'

Rybak burst into a bout of coughing. 'I am sorry, I think I've picked something up. The flu,' he added apologetically. But Maslov wasn't listening. Waving his hand dismissively, he turned and strode into a meeting with the junior lieutenant, locking the door behind him. He never used to do that, Rybak thought.

Rybak went home early, two hours before the party began. The coughing was fake, but the paleness, the irregular heartbeat, the sweats – all that was real.

The decision had been made for him, he thought. He looked around as he entered the building: there appeared to be no surveillance. Should he warn his lover? No! That would only endanger the plan. She must be kept out of it.

Ripping a sheet from a brand-new school notebook he'd purchased on the way, he drew the trident symbol of the Ukrainian Insurgent Army and started composing a note in large block letters. He had often examined similar notes pinned to the bodies of executed government officials in western Ukrainian villages. Ukrainian was his mother tongue, and he remembered the words well enough to manufacture a credible replica.

The resistance has a long arm and the Ukrainian Insurgent Army is everywhere, he wrote. *The Muscovite-communist occupiers and their accomplices will find no peace anywhere in Ukraine. Glory to Ukraine. To heroes, glory. To enemies, death. To the MGB dog, eternal damnation.*

Satisfied with the calligraphy, he looked under the blankets at the bottom of his cupboard and pulled out a Walther PPK wrapped in a towel. The pistol, picked up during a raid near Lviv, was beautifully made. It was unregistered, and it had a silencer.

He spent a few moments examining the weapon, transfixed by the reflection of the light bulb in its smooth surface. Then he disassembled it, carefully cleaning every part. He couldn't afford it to jam tonight, and he also couldn't afford fingerprints. He used the towel to wipe every round before he slotted all nine of them into the magazine. In case of emergency, there was also his official MGB sidearm. Then he packed everything in his briefcase and left it inside the cupboard. No point taking the Walther, with its bulky silencer, to Maslov's promotion party. There would be enough time to come home before the party was over. He knew Maslov's habits as well as his own. As usual, the colonel would be dropped at the mouth of St Andrew's Descent once the party ended, to walk home up the hill. He would almost certainly be too drunk to offer any resistance. All Rybak needed to do was wait, patiently. That, he knew how to do.

41

Kyiv, March 1953

The assassination of an MGB colonel in the middle of Kyiv was a shocking event. It would never be reported in newspapers or on the radio, of course. But it caused the government's machinery to launch into a frenzy of investigative work, with MGB agents checking up on informers, searching for witnesses and rounding up random undesirables. The municipal clean-up crew had found Maslov's frozen body under the pre-dawn snow on St Andrew's Descent. The corpse had been removed quietly and quickly: nobody wanted a show of vulnerability that could provoke copycats. The bloodstained note from the Ukrainian Insurgent Army had been filed away in an evidence bag, its very existence now a closely guarded state secret.

It was only natural that a trusted aide like Rybak would be one of the two officers given the job of informing Colonel Maslov's unsuspecting widow of the terrible crime. He arrived, appropriately sombre, with Major Sidorov, the new acting head of the MGB in Podil, at 9 a.m. Debora opened the door. It was clear from her face that she hadn't slept all night.

'Why are you here? Where is my husband?' she demanded. 'Why isn't he home yet?'

'We regret to inform you that Colonel Maslov fell in combat last night,' the major said, stepping closer to offer a hug. 'You must be strong.'

'What combat? Combat here in Kyiv? What are you talking about?' Debora pushed the major away. She breathed rapidly, the blood draining from her face. Was she faking it, or did she really have no idea what had happened last night? Rybak wondered. He felt feverish, his vision blurry.

'Where is my husband?' she screamed. 'I need to speak to my husband.'

The children, the maid and Rebecca were all in the corridor now. The apartment started to fill with a cacophony of shouts, sobs and groans. 'I am so sorry,' Major Sidorov kept repeating. 'Colonel Maslov died a heroic death. We are here to be of any help, Darya Grigoriyevna. Captain Rybak can stay with you if you need any assistance.'

Rybak's muscles tightened. Yes, he wanted a few minutes alone with Debora. He itched to tell her what he had done, what he had done for her. He tried to touch her arm, but she swatted his hand away.

'Go. All of you, go now,' she shrieked. 'Leave me alone.'

Rybak tried to say something, but the major cut him off. 'Show some respect,' he hissed, before returning to his previous tone of forced bonhomie. 'Darya Grigoriyevna, I understand completely. We will come back in the afternoon. You need some rest now. All I can promise you is that we will find the culprits and punish them in the severest possible manner.' He bowed humbly.

'The severest possible,' Rybak echoed, his words interrupted by a bout of coughing.

Debora stared into his eyes. He didn't like what he saw.

'In the meantime, please do not discuss the circumstances of what has happened with anyone,' the major went on. 'We don't want idle gossip, speculation, anything that undermines order. We don't want our enemies to gain any advantage. We will be back soon.'

Once the officers had left, Debora turned and shut herself in the bedroom. Rebecca consoled the wailing, frightened children as best as she could. There wasn't much she could say apart from 'It will all be all right, it will all be all right.' They wouldn't be going to school today.

'Who killed my papa?' Pasha demanded to know. 'Was it that other man, the man who claimed to be my father? Did he kill my papa?'

'Don't be silly.' Rebecca tried to embrace him. 'Why would you say such a silly thing?'

'I don't believe you!' The boy pushed her away.

Major Sidorov didn't return to Debora's apartment that afternoon, and neither did Rybak. By the time Maslov's body was consigned to the morgue and the initial forensic examination was concluded, strange rumours had started swirling through the MGB building in Podil. There was something very unusual going on in Moscow. Something that would demand everyone's attention.

'Is there something you're not telling me?' Rebecca asked her daughter once they finally had a moment alone, the children having cried themselves to sleep. 'I don't believe in coincidences, you know.'

'What do you mean?'

'Someone randomly gunned him down, the night he was being promoted, outside his own home? Here, in Kyiv? It just doesn't add up.'

336

'Mama, I have no idea what you're talking about.'

Rebecca took her daughter's hand. 'No matter. It's all for the better, my dear. All for the better. I just hope you've been careful about it.'

She looked Debora in the eye, trying to spot silent confirmation. But Debora averted her gaze.

'Of course it's a sin, a cardinal sin,' Rebecca went on. 'I don't know if God will ever forgive you. But I, I see no blame. To survive, we have to do what we have to do.'

'Mama, what God?' Debora replied in a dull, exhausted voice. 'You and your God . . . If there is a God, he can go fuck himself for what he has done to us all. And to this whole country.'

'You don't know what you're saying, my love,' Rebecca said. 'It's been a very hard day.'

'I know exactly what I am saying.'

Before going to bed, Debora made the maid change the sheets, hoping to eliminate Maslov's presence. Still, his clothes in the closet, his shoes, his toothbrush – all of it, like a radioactive rock, emitted particles of his essence. She couldn't sleep, changing position in the king-sized bed that would now be permanently empty on one side. Getting up before dawn, she made herself a cup of coffee. As always, she switched on the wired-in radio set to listen to the news. The morning broadcast seemed unremarkable: reports of enthusiastic wheat-sowing campaigns followed up by reports of enthusiastic voting for the local councils in Latvia and Kazakhstan. There was no mention of the assassination of an MGB colonel in Kyiv, of course.

But, strangely, there was no daily calisthenics show that Maslov liked so much either. Instead, the radio played non-stop classical music. The children joined her at the table after nine. Pasha kept rubbing his red eyes. Nina had calmed down and was playing with her doll while the maid cooked blinis.

'I want to become like Papa. I want to shoot all the enemies,' Pasha said coldly. 'I need to learn how to shoot well.' He looked at his mother. 'I don't want to go to my violin class any more. I want to learn about guns. I want to be in the Organs, just like him.'

'Pasha, you can learn the violin and how to shoot at the same time,' Rebecca said gently.

Pasha's hair had turned dark, his face looking more chiselled as the first traces of a moustache sprouted under his nose. He's a man now, Debora thought. A man who's starting to look so much like his father, his real father. And yet inside he's become a pure Maslov. It was hard to love the boy. She felt the venom of disappointment, disappointment with him and disappointment with herself, building up in her chest.

She got up and went to the phone, to call Major Sidorov and Rybak at MGB headquarters. They weren't available to take her call. In fact, to her frustration, nobody was available.

'What is this strange sad music on the radio all the time?' Rebecca finally noticed.

'I don't know, Mama.' Debora was distracted. 'I should probably go to the school, take care of unfinished business. We need to organise the funeral. So many things . . .'

As she was dressing, the music on the radio stopped and the deep baritone of the newscaster came on. He sounded sombre, the kind of voice that announced a war. Comrade Stalin, he informed them, was gravely ill and had temporarily yielded his position at the helm of the state and the Party. Comrade Stalin had suffered from a partial paralysis. The worst was yet to come: Comrade Stalin, the newscaster confided, had also developed Cheyne–Stokes breathing.

Debora had never heard of Cheyne–Stokes, and neither had Rebecca.

'Cheyne–Stokes? Cheyne–Stokes?' she repeated. The very name sounded like an evil imperialist plot. An entire country was puzzled about it at that very moment. She strode into the living room and queried the pages of the appropriate tome of the blue Great Soviet Encyclopedia set that occupied an entire bookshelf.

'What is it, Mama?' Debora asked impatiently.

Rebecca's face lit up with a grin that seemed almost mad. She put down the tome, opened the cabinet and pulled out the silver cup for Sabbath wine. Filling it with aged Ararat brandy, a bottle that Maslov had reserved for special occasions, she held it out to Debora.

'Drink, daughter, drink. It's deliverance,' she said. 'Passover has come early this year. You say there is no God, but you see, sometimes prayers are answered. Cheyne–Stokes means he's as good as dead.' Her eyes burned like candles. 'Soon it will be all over.'

'Mama, have you lost your mind? If he dies, it's only going to get worse from now on.' Debora spoke quickly but quietly. Stalin was everything. Nobody dared to think, let alone speak, about the likelihood of him disappearing. She could envision a life without Maslov. Life without Stalin, that was simply impossible to imagine. 'Maybe they will blame the Jewish doctors for this. Maybe there will be war again, and famine, and pogroms. How will we live without him? What will happen to us?'

Rebecca pushed the cup into Debora's hands. 'It will not get any worse. It can't get any worse than this. Drink.'

Reluctantly Debora sipped the brandy. 'I hope you're right,' she said. 'But in this country of ours, it can always get worse.'

At the MGB headquarters in Podil, a new guard didn't recognise Debora and she wasn't allowed access. The building seemed like a beehive today, with cars driving in and out and everyone rushing around in a state of combined determination and panic. She left a note at the checkpoint for Major Sidorov and Rybak.

In the late afternoon, Rybak came to the apartment. This time, he arrived by himself. He had an official reason to be there: a message that Maslov's funeral would have to be postponed until the current circumstances around Comrade Stalin's health were resolved. The colonel's body, for now, would remain in the MGB morgue. Just like his remains, the investigation into the assassination was also frozen, for now. The MGB had more important things to worry about.

Rybak was aching to be alone with Debora, to hold her, to tell her what he had done. He imagined her grateful tears, her soft kisses, her warm embrace. It was unbearable to keep it all inside, to have no one to confide in. He needed to tell her in the smallest detail how he'd shot Maslov and why he'd been pushed to that final step. How he'd felt afterwards, the heady cocktail of relief, fear and pride, pride that he'd managed to rescue them both. Save their lives. He was also proud of his ruse of sending investigators to pursue non-existent insurgents.

Debora wasn't alone. Her mother was also in the room, no longer attentive to Rybak, no longer offering cake. The radio was transmitting the latest details of Stalin's deterioration.

Rybak smiled hesitantly, but there was no complicity in Debora's eyes, only a veiled irritation. She asked him about funeral logistics, about her pension, about when she could see the body. He answered what he could, mechanically.

Finally he couldn't hold it in any longer. 'Darya Grigoriyevna, could we talk privately?' he asked.

With a puzzled look, Debora shrugged and motioned Rebecca to leave the room.

Closing the door, Rybak sat down next to her. He felt like taking her hand, but restrained himself.

'Dasha, my love, I've done it. I did it for you, just as you wanted,' he whispered. 'You were right. He knew. It was now or never.'

'You've done what?' She looked at him with uncomprehending eyes. 'What are you talking about?'

'Dasha, let's not play games. You know what I'm talking about. You asked me to do it.'

She got up, crossing her arms. 'I don't understand any of this, Zhenechka. What did I ask you to do? What is this? What are you talking about? I haven't asked you to do anything at all.'

'Dasha, we are not children. I did this for you.'

'For me?' Her eyes turned to fiery slits and she spoke in an even, surgical voice. Every word was like a cut with a sharp scalpel, painless at first but definitive in severing the tissue. 'I must have misheard,' she said. 'Are you confessing to my husband's murder? And trying to implicate me somehow?'

'No, no, not at all,' he protested, not knowing what else to say. 'You misunderstood me.'

She got closer to him and delivered her verdict. 'Good. Excuse me, please, I am not myself. I must have definitely misheard.'

He remained silent.

'From now on, please stay away from us. Far away. For our safety and for yours.'

She flung open the living room door and ushered him out.

'Thank you for coming, Comrade Captain,' she said in her normal voice. 'I appreciate you finding a moment. We won't keep you from your busy schedule any longer.'

Rybak, feeling dizzy, picked up his blue-rimmed MGB cap and shuffled out. He felt anger building in his chest, anger that had nowhere to go. He tried to find a charitable explanation for what had happened, but there was none. He felt deceived and deflated. At least he didn't have to disguise his turmoil. The entire Soviet Union was in turmoil now.

Once around the corner, he leaned against a tree and started banging his fist on it in hopeless anger, animal sounds escaping from his throat. An old peasant woman in a home-knitted headscarf patted him gently on the shoulder. 'Don't cry, my son, don't cry. Comrade Stalin will make it, he will come out of this, you'll see,' she said. 'Comrade Stalin is strong.'

'Thank you. Of course he will,' Rybak replied, straightening up.

At 6 a.m. the following day, the radio confirmed what everyone by now expected, either with horror or with the most carefully disguised joy. Stalin was dead. There was no Stalin any more. How could it be?

By the time Debora arrived at school for the morning meeting, it felt as if war had broken out again. People avoided each other's eyes, not knowing what was safe to say and what wasn't. The school's loudspeakers, as per instructions phoned in by the district party committee, blared classical music through the halls. Classes were suspended.

By 11 a.m., the orders had arrived. Debora had to deliver a speech to the school assembly. Years of absorbing official verbosity, the flowery language of propaganda broadcasts, had given her confident fluency in this special tongue. Words rolled off naturally, at just the right pitch.

'The sun has stopped shining over our heads today, the dear father who has given us all so much happiness and sustenance over the decades has disappeared,' she began. 'The mourning of the Soviet people knows no bounds, so hard is this blow. Everything we have, every hour of joy in our lives, every smile on the faces of our children, we owe to the unparalleled genius of Comrade Stalin.'

The children, especially the little ones, broke down sobbing as she spoke. Debora herself had to wipe a tear from the corner of her eye. After the speeches, the school was dismissed.

342

The official mourning for Stalin meant that mourning for Debora's husband was an afterthought. People broke into hysterical wailing in the middle of the street. Eclipsed by the cosmic event of Stalin's disappearance, Maslov's death turned into a small tributary of the river of tears that coursed through the entire Soviet Union, one sixth of the planet's land mass.

When Maslov's state funeral finally happened, two weeks later, in the official section of Kyiv's Baykove Cemetery, it was a hurried affair. True, the military band was there. The district party chief, the deputy mayor and a general from the MGB's Ukrainian SSR headquarters all delivered eulogies, praising the heroic colonel but skirting the cause of his death. Yet everyone's minds were elsewhere. The MGB had just been merged with the MVD, the Ministry of the Interior, in one of the new regime's first decisions. The new boss of this internal-security giant – the freshly appointed interior minister of the Ukrainian SSR – had just arrived in Kyiv. His first orders were shocking in their boldness.

The day was sunny, that first hint of spring that came after a long, hard winter. Debora had to squint as she watched Maslov's coffin slowly lowered into the grave. Nina wailed, clinging to her skirt. Pasha stood with his arms crossed, unapproachable.

Major Sidorov had positioned himself next to Debora. Rybak was there too, but she studiously ignored him. He didn't dare say anything beyond the same standard condolences that were mouthed by everyone else. Once the funeral ended, the big shots didn't linger. There was no time to lose when the country's fate – and their own – was being decided. Only a handful of Maslov's former colleagues – not nearly as many as Debora had expected – piled in their cars to drive to her apartment for snacks and vodka. The table was crowded with far too much food.

'Darya Grigoriyevna, you will always remain like family to us. Come any time, for anything you need,' Major Sidorov said after the first round of drinks, patting Nina's head. 'We really appreciate that you've kept your silence about this. Panic is not what we need in these trying times.'

Debora drank with him, enjoying the burst of warmth as the vodka burned its way down her throat.

'Thank you, Comrade Major. But how is the investigation going? Have you found the killers?'

'We will, we will, but times are changing. It's not so easy these days. Not easy at all,' Sidorov sighed. He was visibly perplexed as the certainties around him started to crumble. He wasn't supposed to be talking so much, but he couldn't keep quiet.

'What do you mean?' Debora asked him.

'For one, those doctors, they're being freed. It's all been a mistake. A very bad mistake. It will be announced in the morning,' he said.

'I thought the party didn't make mistakes.'

'We all used to think that, didn't we?' Sidorov nodded. 'And yet it turns out we don't know everything. And it's just the beginning. An amnesty has been signed in Moscow. Hundreds of thousands, maybe millions of people will be let out, to flood the streets of our cities. Of Kyiv. Of Podil. What do you think they will do?'

Debora listened intently.

'Meanwhile, our hands are tied. There is a new order from Moscow: you can't even touch a prisoner any more. I don't know how we will investigate anything.' Waving away the thought, he poured himself another shot, swallowed it and got up. 'But enough about us. We should be going. Thank you for being so hospitable in such a dark hour.'

She hugged him. 'It means a lot to me.'

As Sidorov put on his coat, the rest of the officers followed suit. Rybak thought of trying to linger behind, but the major pushed him along. 'Come on, Captain, don't be so slow. We are all leaving. The poor widow needs to rest.'

On the staircase, Rybak asked the major about the amnesty. 'If they're freeing so many of them, do you think they will need so many of us?'

'They will always need us, Captain,' Sidorov replied. 'Those new things can't last.'

42

Kyiv, May 1953

The 9 May celebratory concert at the Kyiv Opera was an annual event where the city's big men – and their wives – came together. Debora wasn't sure whether she would be invited this year, or whether she would go if she did receive an invitation. The false bonhomie of these gatherings, a bonhomie that concealed every-body's cold fear of inadvertently making a lethal gaffe, usually made her queasy. In previous years, when Maslov was alive, she'd occasionally faked an illness to stay home. But she knew she couldn't resort to such excuses too often. People noticed these absences. People noticed everything.

Though Maslov was dead, the concert's organisers decided they shouldn't strike the fallen colonel's widow off the guest list, at least not this year. The postman brought the invitation on a sunny morning. The city was in full bloom, and as Debora opened the envelope, she felt the urge to look pretty again. For the first time since the funeral, she spent an hour at the hair-dresser's, getting ready for the concert. She slipped into a black silk dress and pinned a diamond brooch in the shape of a snake above her left breast. It wasn't nearly as nice as her grandmother's

Venetian necklace, but it had been manufactured in Prague in a similar style. The dress was sober enough to fit her new role as a widow, and yet snug enough to highlight her curves.

On the way to the Opera, she took in the changes around her. Stalin's huge portraits had started to disappear from the buildings – not altogether, but enough to make people talk. The Jewish doctors had been freed, their accusers arrested. The new regime in Moscow had also begun to empty out the parallel country of the Gulag camps, shutting down slave-labour projects. Just before the May holidays, trains disgorged thousands and thousands of former inmates, still astounded by their unexpected freedom, into Kyiv and other Ukrainian cities. They roamed the streets, basking in the forgotten heat.

The square around the Opera was festooned with red flags and posters celebrating the defeat of the Nazis. As soon as Debora strode into the theatre's hallway, she spotted Major Sidorov. He was clad in his parade uniform, his chest covered with glittering decorations. His wife, a lady with an elaborate hairdo of unnatural colour, planted a thick kiss full of pity on Debora's cheek, imprinting a smudge of crimson lipstick.

'So good to see you, my dear Dasha, how are you holding up?' she asked.

'Not easy, not easy,' Debora replied. She had found this to be the most convenient answer.

'Not easy for anyone,' Sidorov sighed. He couldn't disguise his sombre mood as he chewed on the caviar canapés, picking them one by one from a pile that filled his plate. He offered one to Debora, but she politely declined.

'Nobody is afraid any more.' Sidorov's wife channelled his thoughts. 'People are asking, how can you free these doctors after you've said they were traitors? How can we believe anything after that?'

Sidorov nodded. He felt apprehensive. Everything seemed the same in some respects, and yet at the same time completely different. People were just a little bit less respectful, just a little bit less intimidated. He looked away from Debora's eyes, hoping she would not ask him about the investigation into Maslov's death.

The major's wife picked up a second flute of the fizzy wine, gulping it down as if it were water. 'And this amnesty! It's a terrible, terrible thing. These criminals, all of them with nothing to do and no fear left in them, flooding our cities. It's dangerous to walk the streets at night again. You never know what's going to happen.'

'Oh come on, don't exaggerate now.' Sidorov cut her off. 'We've got the situation under full control. Kyiv is completely safe.'

'Of course, of course,' she hurried to agree, recognising the irritation that had leaped into his voice. 'Completely safe.'

There was a commotion in the hall, with doors banging and a shuffle of heavy steps. A uniformed man with a ruddy square face topped by a shock of thick hair walked in, followed by a retinue of officers. All the other officers in the theatre, including Sidorov, coalesced around him, moving like metal shards pulled by a magnet. Spouses – and Debora – formed the outer ring. 'It's Meshyk, the new minister,' Sidorov's wife whispered into her ear.

The minister had the ease of someone who knew he possessed undisputed authority. He cleared his throat and started to speak, loudly and clearly as a radio broadcaster. 'Dear comrades, I congratulate you on the anniversary of our great victory. The Soviet Ukrainian people are proud of our country's achievements, under the leadership of the great Communist Party, and the Party is united with the people like never before. As one of our great poets has written, "Love Ukraine like the sun, love Ukraine like the wind."'

Debora recognised the verse by Volodymyr Sosiura, celebrated immediately after the war and then forbidden and struck off the school curriculum.

Dispensing with Russian, Meshyk went on in fluent Ukrainian – a language that many of the assembled officers, including Sidorov, didn't quite understand. Debora saw strained eyes, mouths contorted in irritation. Looking around, she noticed that the propaganda posters all over the hallway had been replaced with new versions in Ukrainian – and omitting Stalin's name.

In the corner of her eye, she caught sight of Captain Rybak. Standing next to Meshyk, he started to clap, and within seconds thunderous applause enveloped the new minister. Even Sidorov applauded, standing ramrod straight, his eyes burning with fury.

Once the applause eased, Debora sensed Rybak's stare on her skin. He remained transfixed, unable to stop looking at her even as the minister and the rest of the entourage moved into the concert hall, squeezing their broad frames into the narrow seats of the VIP opera box. The orchestra's musicians were already adjusting their instruments, filling the air with disjointed notes that pierced the hum of the guests' conversations and laughter. Following the general movement of the crowd, Debora headed inside the hall. Stepping forward, Rybak blocked her way.

'You look gorgeous, Dasha,' he said. She saw sweat forming above his eyebrows, his nostrils widened by heavy breathing.

She ignored him.

'We have to speak.'

'Stand aside. Now is not the time,' she replied in a near-whisper.

'No, now is not the time. I am sorry,' he agreed. 'Tonight, after the concert, I will meet you near your home, on St Andrew's Descent.'

Not wanting to make a scene, she didn't reply.

The final bell before the show rang, and the usher shooed her inside, making Rybak yield the way.

The performance was mediocre, not that Debora was paying much attention. She hadn't expected to encounter Rybak at the Opera. All these weeks, she'd attempted not to think about the captain, hoping that somehow all this would go away. But Rybak clearly didn't have any intention of going away. Seeing him in his parade uniform, with his slicked-back hair and all those clattering medals, made her stomach turn. He was just like Maslov, a younger Maslov. And like Maslov, he wanted to control her, to possess her. The intoxicating power conferred by their jobs made all these officers the same, she thought.

During the intermission, she slipped away, taking the tram home. She wanted to reach her apartment before Rybak showed up.

He was already there, waiting for her on the very same spot where he had killed her husband. Instead of a gun, he held an oversize bouquet of red carnations.

'What do you want?' she confronted him. 'Why are you here?'

'Come, walk with me.' He grabbed her by the arm. It was a strong grip, an MGB officer's grip. Professional. He tried to give her the flowers with his free hand, but she pushed them away. His muscles flexed. She felt pain in her arm, but didn't say anything.

They turned the corner. He was leading her up the winding side street, into a dark, overgrown park atop the hill where local alcoholics froze to death during the winter.

'Where are we going?'

'Somewhere nobody will hear us. We need to clear up a few things, my dear Dasha.'

'Aren't you afraid?' she asked. 'Aren't you afraid that they will investigate the killing and find you guilty? Don't you think that the best thing for you is to forget about me and not arouse suspicion?'

'Investigate? Suspicion?' He laughed. It was a dark laugh, and it stopped abruptly as he bowed to her hair, loudly inhaling her smell and then kissing the nape of her neck. She tried to pull away, but he wouldn't let go.

'Sit,' he ordered, pointing to a bench under a blossoming chestnut tree and dropping the flowers.

She complied.

'There is no investigation any more, dear Dasha. You saw what the new minister said, and how he said it. Time to put Ukrainians in charge in Ukraine again. The Party is admitting mistakes and rectifying them. And this means it's time to turn the page and make peace. Hell, we're even bringing Bandera's sisters from Siberia for negotiations. Nobody is going to waste energy on what happened in the old times.'

'Old times? It was barely two months ago.'

'It was another age. Now that Comrade Beria is in charge in Moscow, everything will be turned upside down. And I'm very much on my way up.'

He lit a cigarette. Debora heard rustling in the bushes behind her. Must be a cat or a dog, she thought distractedly.

'I work with Minister Meshyk now. He needs real Ukrainian cadres, and he's replacing ministry officials on every level. That fool Sidorov will be gone soon. I may even get his place! The future is bright these days.'

'And what do you want from me?' Debora asked. 'I'm an old woman who needs to raise her children. Plenty of young girls must be running after you now.'

Rybak sat next to her, stubbed out the cigarette and wrapped his arm around her waist.

'First of all, my dear Dasha, I want you to say thank you,' he said quietly. 'To say thank you for what I have done for you. Don't pretend you didn't want it. Don't play those silly games with me ever again. You and I, we are now bound by this for ever. It's like a blood bond, do you understand?'

She stiffened.

'Say thank you.' He raised his voice.

She bit her lip.

He put his hand on her elbow, squeezing the flesh until it hurt. She remained silent.

'I can wait. I know you will thank me sooner or later. You belong to me now, Dasha,' he went on. 'All mine. Don't try to escape, don't try to ignore me. Above all, don't try to threaten me. It will not end well for you, or for your children.'

She yanked his hand away with a strength he didn't expect and sprang up. 'Don't you dare speak about my children again, you ...'

She was not scared. All she felt was contempt.

'I am not yours,' she enunciated her syllables. 'No matter what happens, I am not yours and I will never be yours. I am not afraid.'

Rybak leaned back and erupted in good-natured laughter, the kind of jolliness usually reserved for the cute pronouncements of toddlers. 'Not afraid? Oh, you would be surprised.'

The leaves parted and a man in a faded striped T-shirt, with prison tattoos on his bulky forearms, emerged. He wore a black kepi, reeked of booze and lacked several teeth.

'What do we have here, lovebirds having a spat? How lovely!' He stared at Rybak's uniform, and at the medal ribbon bar on his chest. His face twisted into a scowl. 'Ah, we have a comrade captain from the Organs,' he pronounced. 'Happy Victory Day, Comrade Captain!'

'Happy Victory Day,' Rybak replied warily. He got up from the bench, his hand on his pistol holster.

The man stepped forward, pulling a bottle of moonshine from his trouser pocket. 'Drink with me to victory, Comrade Captain,' he said. 'How was it for you, our glorious victory? For me, it was not so good. For me, it was going from a camp in Germany to a camp in Russia. And you know who sent me there? NKVD bitches like you. NKVD bitches who never set foot anywhere near a German bullet but who didn't think twice about making me rot.'

'Stop.' Rybak raised his voice. 'Don't come any closer.'

'Don't come any closer!' The man mockingly repeated the words, and then whistled loudly as he slowly inched forward. Rybak fumbled, trying to open his holster.

The blow to his head was unexpected. Leaping from behind a tree, another man, skinny and dark-haired, wedged the sharp end of a rock into the captain's skull. Rybak, his eyes suddenly blank, crumpled onto the grass, his body contorted in an unnatural position. With another blow of the rock, the man crushed his nose, turning his face into a bloody mess. Wasting no time, he picked up Rybak's gun and started ripping off his decorations.

Debora remained frozen. From the corner of her eye, she saw a woman enter the clearing.

'Well done, Gypsy Boy,' the woman laughed. 'Well done. We're in luck with this pig. Now check out how much money he's got in his wallet.'

Her hair was covered by a dark scarf. Her thick frame was squeezed into a colourful dress that hadn't been washed for weeks, and she wore black leather jackboots of standard infantry issue. She coughed as she spoke, spitting out mucus and blood. There was something oddly familiar in her voice.

'Give me that.' The man in the kepi took the gun, checking the rounds in the chamber and then sliding the weapon into the small of his back.

Gypsy Boy noticed the diamond brooch on Debora's chest, and with a swift pull, he yanked it off, ripping her dress. He whistled appreciatively as he examined the pale skin of her exposed breast. 'What have we got here,' he said, greedily touching her. 'Always wanted to know what a Chekist's bitch tastes like.'

She didn't recoil. It was as if she wasn't even there.

'Sorry about your lover boy, Comrade Madam.' The man in the kepi grinned. 'He may be out of commission now. Such sad times. The whole country is mourning, you know. Terrible loss.'

'He is not my lover boy,' Debora replied. She was surprised at how dull and detached her voice sounded.

'What do you think?' The man in the kepi turned to the woman in jackboots. 'What shall we do to this bird?'

The woman squinted as she looked at Debora.

She took a cautious step forward.

They recognised each other at the same moment.

After two decades in the camps, Olena looked haggard and old, old enough to be Debora's mother. Her crooked front teeth had fallen out. But it was still Olena. She had an air of brutal authority about her, her eyes no longer clouded by madness. In a split second, the defiant joy in her expression had yielded to heart-rending sadness, the sadness of a woman who remembered the distant past when she could still love, when she could still hope. The past that was so long ago that it might never have really existed.

'Oh God,' Debora gasped, taking a step back. She was overwhelmed and repulsed at the same time, her eyes locked with Olena's. She felt a knot in her stomach, that tugging feeling of missing something precious. Missing the innocence that they had both lost. Their youth. Their future.

With a menacing laugh, the dark-haired man tugged at Debora's bra. She put her hand on her chest, trying to resist. The bra snapped loudly.

'Drop it, Gypsy Boy,' Olena ordered him in her raspy voice, taking another step towards them.

He didn't listen.

'I mean it, don't touch her.' Another step.

He didn't listen.

Whoosh. Olena smacked the side of his head with a precise blow, knocking him off his feet. He bounced back quickly, his fists clenched, his eyes narrowing.

'She said don't touch her, didn't she?' The man in the kepi moved in between them, his right hand behind his back, cradling the gun. 'So don't touch her.'

Gypsy Boy shook the dirt off his trousers and unleashed a sequence of expletives. 'Have you all gone mad? Why are you protecting this whore?'

'None of your business,' Olena shot back. 'We're done here.'

'Done? I'm not done,' he protested. 'I'm not at all done with her.'

'If she says we're done, we're done,' said the man in the kepi. 'Let's get going.'

Unhappily, Gypsy Boy complied.

As the two men started walking away, Olena ran her eye over Debora, noting her high heels, her hairdo, her skin that had been softened by expensive creams. Then she glanced at her own boots, thick, hard leather coated with splatters of mud.

'You're the lucky one, Debora. You always have been, like an alien from another planet, all evil bouncing off you like water off a goose,' she said quietly. 'Don't waste that luck.'

'Thank you,' Debora whispered.

Olena started to walk away, but then stopped and turned.

'That was a very nice dog, by the way. I thought of it often. Pink. Fluffy. Must have been so soft. Just the kind my little Taras would have loved. Too bad he didn't get to play with it.'

'I am so sorry,' was the only reply that Debora could muster. 'So sorry about everything.'

'Sorry? That's all between me and God now,' Olena replied. 'I'm bearing my own cross, every day and every night. I don't ask for anyone else's understanding or pity.'

'I know. But we're not all that different, Olena. I have done some terrible things too,' Debora said.

'Bullshit.' Olena spat on the ground. 'You don't know what you're saying. You and I, we couldn't be more different.' Then she turned and shuffled off unsteadily into the darkness.

Once Olena and the two men were gone, Debora heard the whimpering. Rybak was lying on his back, choking on his own blood, blood that foamed at the edges of his mouth. 'Save me, save me, call someone,' he implored, his eyes widening in panicked helplessness. He gripped her hand.

'Of course, Zhenechka,' she said. And she took a few steps, intending to do just that. But after a moment she stopped, picked up Rybak's MGB felt cap and placed it on his face. She kneeled, transferring the whole weight of her body to her palms, and pressed on the cap, hard, ruthlessly, until the wriggling and the moaning and the breathing finally stopped. 'I do not belong to you,' she said slowly as she lifted the cap and looked into Rybak's face, contorted in a final surprise.

Then she took her bouquet from the ground and went home.

Epilogue

Truskavets, July 1954

The mineral water had to be drunk from special cups with ceramic beaks that supposedly protected teeth from corrosion. Its source lay in the middle of Adamowka, an English-style park dotted with statues of Polish heroes and poets shaded by giant pine trees. After lining up to fill her cup in the pavilion, Debora spat out the first sip. The water was warm, with a swirl of natural oil, and tasted foul. A nurse gave her a withering look. 'This is a precious substance, madam, which will heal you inside.'

Apologising, Debora refilled her cup and, pretending to take occasional sips, went for an afternoon stroll in the park, greeting other vacationers with a nod. They all took this 'taking the waters' stuff far too seriously, she thought. She couldn't help chuckling at the sight of grown men in panama hats and shorts striding with a sense of purpose, the cups' ceramic beaks in their mouths, frowns of determined concentration stamped on their foreheads.

It was cool and pleasant in the Carpathian foothills, and this year, for the first time since the war ended, it was finally safe to vacation in Truskavets. The western Ukrainian insurgency had dissipated, with rebels burying their guns until another day that would never come. Once an elegant spa town of the Habsburg Empire, Truskavets was packed with crowds of tourists from Kyiv, Moscow and beyond. All, just like Debora, arrived with vouchers from their employers, a reward for their dedication to the Soviet cause. Between the two wars, this had been Poland. Bankers and politicians from Warsaw and Cracow used to come here to cure their ailments during the day and to party at night. Debora's sanatorium, built in the 1930s to emulate a Swiss mountain chalet, used to be among the most fashionable ones. Now, it showed the effects of more than a decade of neglect. Still, the staff, in their tattered but starched and ironed white coats, remained much more solicitous than anyone she had encountered in Kyiv, their habits of pre-Soviet service not yet completely gone. 'Madam', they addressed her, not the usual 'comrade' or plain 'woman'.

As Debora crossed Adamowka on her way to the chalet, she paid no attention when someone shouted her name.

Her real name.

Everyone nowadays called her Darya or used the diminutive Dasha, the Russian name that she'd kept along with the Maslov surname. Only stubborn Rebecca insisted on addressing her daughter with the unequivocally Jewish Debora, though she didn't do it in public.

'Debora? Debora? Is it you?' The man, now close, tapped her shoulder.

She turned around, squinting in the sun.

'Debora!'

His face broadened into a grin, but not an entirely happy one. 'Debora!'

It was him. But he had become a different man. Like the other vacationers, he wore a panama hat and a short-sleeved khaki shirt that accentuated his bulging waist. His eyes, once fiery and hungry, were dulled by sated contentment. His hands had grown puffy, and Debora noticed that he wore a wedding ring.

She felt dizzy. Her eyes widened. 'Samuel?'

'Debora! What a coincidence! What brings you here? You look fantastic.'

'You too, you look like life has been good to you.' After a brief moment, she added: 'I am glad you're not dead. I thought you might be dead.'

'Well, that's good to hear,' he chuckled.

They sat down on a shaded bench. 'How have you been?' she asked.

'Can't really complain. I live in Odessa now, a new life. I help run the city circus, of all things. You know how much I loved the circus, remember?'

'Of course I remember.' Images of the past flashed before her eyes.

'Finally things are settling a little in this country. It's good not to be afraid all the time any more,' he went on. 'To wake up in the morning without having to wonder: is it today that they will come for me? To be able to make plans.'

'Yes, after *he* died, everything changed,' she agreed. It was self-evident that she was referring to Stalin.

'Have things changed for you? Are you still married?' Samuel asked. 'To that colonel? Must be a general by now.'

'No,' she said simply. 'I am not married any more. That is over.'

'Oh.'

She pointed at his wedding ring. 'But it looks like you are.'

He seemed mildly embarrassed. 'Yes, what can I say? I have a wife now, Rachel. A good woman.'

'Children?'

'One little boy. David.'

'Congratulations . . .'

They sat in silence for a moment. So much had happened. So many questions to ask. A moment about which she had dreamed for years. After Maslov's death, she had made enquiries, as much as she could, but nobody knew what had happened to Samuel Groysman. And now that they were here, on the same bench, almost touching each other, she didn't know what to say.

'How is Pasha?' Samuel asked.

'Difficult. You know, teenagers . . .'

There was so much more she could tell him, about how Pasha was never the same after Maslov died, about how he never wanted to speak to her, as if his suspicions over Maslov's death had poisoned their relationship. How he had just left home to join the KGB academy, blessed with the recommendations of Maslov's former colleagues in the Organs, eager to become a State Security investigator. A true Soviet man. And as of late, a fond raconteur of anti-Semitic jokes.

'He's handsome, very clever, very energetic,' she said. She was too proud to let Samuel poke the incurable wound of a rejected mother. 'But you know, they never grow up to be the way one imagines they will.'

'Is he here?' There was a mixture of apprehension and hope in Samuel's eyes.

'No, I'm by myself. Solo traveller. The children are in Kyiv, with their grandma.'

She looked intently at his face. He seemed relieved. She disliked that.

'Ah,' he replied. 'And how is Rebecca? Still cooking up her feasts?'

'She's fine. She's taken to gardening, says it passes the time. And she still hopes that my brother will turn up alive one day.'

'Maybe he will,' Samuel offered.

'Maybe.'

Debora was beginning to get frustrated with the superficial conversation.

'Samuel, I must ask you a question. What happened in Kyiv? What did they do to you?'

He straightened his back. It was a lazy summer day and he was not in the mood for quarrels, but the question irritated him.

'What did you think would happen once you sent your colonel there?'

'What do you mean? I didn't send anyone.'

'You didn't confess to Maslov and tell him where I was?'

'No!' Debora flung her hands wide. 'What are you talking about? Of course not. He found out through that woman who opened the door to you at the apartment, the neighbour who spied on me. It was his job to find out, of course. He was from the Organs.'

'So it wasn't you?' Samuel's mouth remained open. 'All this time, I was blaming . . .'

'You really thought I would do something like that, betray you that way?'

'What else could I think?' Samuel grew defensive. 'Maslov was persuasive. When the doorbell rang in the morning, I thought it was you. I was afraid it would be you coming to tell me that you'd decided to stay put. But instead, it was your colonel. I recognised him right away, from that photograph.

'He was very polite. It was a simple conversation. He said you had told him that morning about our encounter, about our plan to escape, and that you had realised how foolish it would be to abandon your children, to abandon everything, for someone like me, who could never provide for you. Under the law, as a former detainee, I wasn't even allowed to live in Kyiv or Moscow or Leningrad, he reminded me. "I am not a vengeful man," he told me. "I will offer you clemency as long as you get out of town immediately. Be reasonable. It's that or back to the camps." Not much of a choice really.'

'No, not much of a choice.'

'Were you going to leave with me?' Samuel asked. 'If Maslov hadn't found out, would you have come that afternoon? Would we have taken that train to Odessa together?'

'The train to Odessa … No, I wasn't going to do that,' Debora admitted. 'I wanted to, I wanted so much to leave with you, more than anything … Well, almost anything. But Pasha would never have gone with us and Maslov would never have let him or Nina go. I came to the apartment that day to look you in the eye and tell you the truth, the truth that I just couldn't abandon my children. That my happiness, and your happiness, had to come second. But then instead of you, it was Maslov who opened the door.'

'What happened then?'

'Samuel, we don't have to speak or think about him any more,' she said. 'That marriage is finished, he's out of my life. But you … Where were *you*? I've been looking for you, but I didn't know where to find you. I've asked myself often, why didn't *you* look for me? I thought he might have had you killed. After all, you always knew where to find me. We still live in the same apartment. St Andrew's Descent. Never moved.'

'So much time, so much water under the bridge,' Samuel sighed. 'I was certain that you didn't want me to look. That you didn't want me to bother Pasha.'

'So much time …' she repeated. *Were you too afraid to look for me?* she wanted to ask, but bit her tongue and kept silent.

He looked at his watch and stood up. 'Shall we go for a walk?'

'Do you have to be somewhere?'

'I do, but I want to see you. It's such a miracle that we are both here. We must celebrate.' He pulled her close and hugged her. 'We have so much to talk about, to catch up on. Shall we have dinner tonight? At the Sovietski restaurant at eight?'

'What about your wife?' Debora asked. 'Does she even know about me, about Pasha?'

'Don't worry about my wife,' he said. 'Sovietski at eight.'

'Sovietski at eight,' she agreed.

The Sovietski restaurant, with its starched tablecloths, crystal chandeliers and waiters in bow ties, clearly pre-dated its new Soviet name. These days it was the place where vacationing colonels, district party chiefs and other minor members of the establishment dined to break up the monotony of their sanatoriums' canteens. Samuel had booked a table by the window, and they watched vacationers pass by, often looking covetously at their meal. The summer days were long, and it was only when dessert – a chocolate soufflé – arrived from the kitchen that it became dark enough to light the candles on their table.

In a smart jacket and without his panama hat, Samuel looked more like his old self. With every glass of wine, Debora felt the forgotten circuits of their relationship, the connections that she had presumed extinct, reviving again. Sometimes their hands brushed against each other, and that sense of touch felt oddly comforting.

Samuel didn't speak about the past, or about his wife and child. Instead, he regaled her with tales of circus life, tales that might or might not have been true.

'Last month, we had a trained elephant come down from Moscow, a very famous one. He would deliver flowers to the spectators with his trunk, amazing stuff. Except that he didn't really take all that well to the Odessa diet.'

'What do you mean?'

363

'Well, let's say he had a little accident on stage. Actually, a very big accident. It took the cleaners an hour to remove all his crap.'

She laughed loudly. 'What did the spectators do in the meantime?'

'Ah, everyone up front just fled, as you can imagine. But you know what the worst thing is, we have the orchestra just by the stage. And these poor guys, they had to keep playing and playing, as if everything was normal. Luckily we are all prepared for nuclear war. I remembered that we had a stockpile of gas masks for the staff in the basement. I had them distributed – imagine the sight, the orchestra playing their violins and pianos all wearing gas masks. Only the guys on the trombones were screwed.'

Unlike Samuel, Debora didn't feel like talking about her job. It had become a dreary, mind-numbing chore. Staff meetings, inspections, promotions. Making sure that the red banners with the latest slogans sent down from the ideological department were painted on time and didn't contain any dangerous mistakes. She found it a strain to read books. After work, she usually settled with a cup of tea in front of her recently acquired KVN-49 television set.

They talked until the restaurant closed. When it did, Samuel offered Debora a nightcap in his room. She didn't hesitate, and they walked hand in hand through the park.

'I feel like it's fate, like we are actually meant to be together,' he said, and at the time, it even seemed true.

In the room, they drank Armenian brandy, and when Samuel awkwardly moved to kiss her, she didn't resist. They made love slowly, as if trying to remember each other's bodies. Move after move, Debora realised that she felt nothing. It was like a ritual, a re-enactment, rather than the real thing. A cruel joke.

Once Samuel finally came with a moan, she turned away and

pretended to fall asleep. He didn't have to pretend, and for hours she listened to him snore.

Early in the morning, she showered, noting a child's toy, a floating duck, in the corner and a woman's hairpin by the wash-basin. When she left the bathroom, Samuel was already awake, sitting on the bed in his underwear.

'Were your wife and son here?' she asked.

'Yes, they left yesterday. I had to spin quite a lie about why I had to stay behind. Invented a telegram from the Odessa mayor!'

'You really shouldn't have done that.'

He raised his eyebrows. 'I was serious about what I said yesterday. About how we're meant to be together.'

'I don't know about that.'

The connections that had seemed so real the previous evening had vanished, gone like morning mist. She trembled slightly, not enough for him to notice.

'We are so lucky that we have this opportunity,' he went on, his tone as self-assured as always, not really taking into consideration the possibility that she might refuse. 'The whole country has gone through a meat-grinder, everyone's lives have been upturned and torn to bits. Think of it – Ukraine in the last two decades was probably the deadliest place on the whole planet, even more so for us Jews. No place for love. But we, Samuel and Debora, we have beaten the odds and survived, and can start again.'

The room was faded and messy in the harsh morning light. She looked at Samuel's protruding belly, at his balding head and sagging cheeks. She also caught a reflection of herself in the mirror, dishevelled hair showing grey streaks, and wrinkles all too evident without make-up. Little of what they used to be had remained undamaged, uncorroded. All she wanted now was to leave.

'We have survived,' Samuel repeated triumphantly. 'Survived!'
She avoided looking at him as she buttoned up her blouse, getting ready to walk out into the sun and never see him again. 'Have we?' she asked quietly. 'Have we really?'

Acknowledgements

The idea to write this novel came to me in 2014, as Russia seized Crimea and sparked the war in eastern Ukraine. I was stuck in Kabul, where I served as the *Wall Street Journal*'s Afghanistan and Pakistan bureau chief, and tried to explain the tragic and complex history of the country where I was born, and the reason why it yearned so much to finally get rid of the Soviet legacy.

It took a while. I finished the book shortly before Russia launched a full-fledged war in 2022. Weeks later, as my hometown came under fire, the book's imagined descriptions of wartime Kyiv materialised in real life. It was too similar.

I can't thank enough my agent Elias Altman, who had faith in this project since the beginning and who found it a great home after offering superb editorial advice. Clare Smith at Abacus was a dream editor, thoughtful, sharp and attentive. My thanks also go to Zoe Gullen at Abacus and to my British agent, Caspian Dennis.

To all my friends who read the early drafts and provided vital suggestions, thank you again!

Born in Kyiv, Yaroslav Trofimov is the chief foreign affairs correspondent of the *Wall Street Journal*. He covered the Taliban takeover of Afghanistan in 2021 and was based in Ukraine from January 2022. He joined the *Journal* in 1999 and previously served as Rome, Middle East and Singapore-based Asia correspondent, as bureau chief in Afghanistan and Pakistan, and as Dubai-based columnist on the greater Middle East. He is the author of two works of non-fiction, *Faith at War* (2005) and *Siege of Mecca* (2007).